GOOD COP, BAD COP

Roland Graeme

**MENAGE AND MORE
MANLOVE**

Siren Publishing, Inc.
www.SirenPublishing.com

A SIREN PUBLISHING BOOK
IMPRINT: Ménage and More ManLove

GOOD COP, BAD COP
Copyright © 2011 by Roland Graeme

ISBN-10: 1-61034-665-3
ISBN-13: 978-1-61034-665-8

First Printing: May 2011

Cover design by Jinger Heaston
All cover art and logo copyright © 2011 by Siren Publishing, Inc.

ALL RIGHTS RESERVED: This literary work may not be reproduced or transmitted in any form or by any means, including electronic or photographic reproduction, in whole or in part, without express written permission.

All characters and events in this book are fictitious. Any resemblance to actual persons living or dead is strictly coincidental.

Printed in the U.S.A.

PUBLISHER
Siren Publishing, Inc.
www.SirenPublishing.com

DEDICATION

For Paul B.

GOOD COP, BAD COP

ROLAND GRAEME
Copyright © 2011

Chapter One: A Sunday Morning Special

"Are you a good cocksucker, boy?" the Dom demanded. "I expect all of my boys to be expert cocksuckers."

"Yes, sir," the sub gasped, staring at the hefty erection the Dom was offering for his inspection. He was on his knees, and he leaned forward, mouth open, ready to capture the head of that prick between his lips and draw it inside his mouth.

The Dom slapped him on his cheek, roughly. "I didn't say you could have it yet, did I, boy?"

"No, sir."

"Damn right, I didn't. Don't you dare try to get ahead of yourself with me, you little bitch. I want total submission from you, and if I don't get it, there'll be hell to pay."

"Yes, sir."

"Mealy-mouthed little bitch. God damn whiny punk. You want that cock so bad, let's hear you beg for it."

"Please, sir. Please let me have your cock. Please put that big hard thing in my mouth and let me suck on it. Please let me suck your cock, sir."

"Aw, shut the fuck up! Your damn whining makes me sick. As long as you're down there, let's see if that mouth of yours can do anything besides piss and moan. Open up!"

Before the sub could react and part his lips, the Dom had taken his cock in his hand and jabbed its head against the kneeling sub's mouth. The sub opened wide and let the turgid manhood force its way deep inside his mouth. With a moan, he closed his lips around the shaft and began to suck. His head bobbed back and forth at the Dom's groin. The Dom, evidently not entirely pleased by the rhythm his cocksucker had set, corrected it. He grabbed a handful of the long, thick blond hair at the base of the sub's neck and, maintaining a tight grip on it, he held the sub's head steady while he fucked his bearded face.

"You're doing just fine," the Dom said, his voice like a caress. But then he tightened his grip on the back of the sub's neck and forced his mouth all the way down on the bloated shaft of his prick. The sub gagged on its bulk. "But you can do a hell of a lot better, you lousy punk slave!" the Dom growled. "And you'd better start doing better right now, if you know what's good for you! Now, you get all of that meat in your mouth and down your throat! All the way down on it, bitch, and stay down on it. Choke on it!"

The sub had no choice but to acquiesce in the rape of his mouth and throat. Desperately, he forced his mouth to surrender to the penile onslaught, to accept the hardness he was being force-fed. He gagged repeatedly as the thick, blunt tip of the phallus jabbed against the back of his mouth and down into his throat, threatening to cut off his air supply.

"That's more like it, boy," the Dom jeered. "You're getting the hang of it now. You're here to be used. That's all you're good for. Don't just suck my dick. Worship it! Nothing else had better be on your mind, boy, except my cock and what that mouth of yours can do for it. You'd better make that cock of mine feel good, or I swear to God, I'll hurt you. I'll hurt you real bad if I feel you slacking off."

The sub sucked and gagged and sucked in a regular pattern of frantic oral activity. Finally, though, his tormentor released his grip on his head and pulled his saliva-dripping prick free of the gasping mouth.

"Get on the bed!" the Dom ordered. "On your belly! Spread your legs and open your ass! You're going to get fucked."

The sub, still trying to get his breath back after the prolonged blow job, obeyed. He lay face down with the Dom on top of him. He felt the other man's cockhead press into the deep cleft between his buttocks, searching blindly for his hole. It found the aperture and began to push its way inside. Pain seared the sub's body as his sphincter began to be stretched by the invading bulk. No condom, no lubricant. The Dom was going to fuck him bareback!

"No," Trent gasped. "God, no!" He tried to rear up, tried to throw the Dom's weight off his back, tried with one hand groping behind him to push the other man away and protect his already half-penetrated ass. The Dom slid one brawny arm around the sub's neck in a choke hold, squeezing it hard, then used his weight to press Trent back down flat on his belly on the bed, and with his other hand, he grabbed the wrist of the sub's groping hand and used it to twist his arm behind his back, between their bodies.

The sub let out a muffled cry of protest and pain as his face was shoved into the pillow under his head.

"Stop resisting!" the Dom shouted. "Don't you dare try to fight me, boy! Your ass is mine!"

"Yes, sir," the sub gasped.

"I don't hear your safe word coming out of your mouth, punk," the Dom jeered.

"No, sir."

"You ready to get fucked? You ready to get fucked, any damn way I choose to take that ass of yours?"

"Yes, sir. Any way you want, sir. Fuck me, sir. Please fuck me!"

"You hot-assed little bitch. I can already feel that hole of yours, squirming against the head of my dick. You want it real bad, don't you, boy? Well, you're going to get it. Right now! Whether you're ready for it, or not!"

And then, as though to demonstrate his point, he completed his possession of that ass in one fierce thrust, which drove his cock deep into the sub's cringing guts.

"Yeah!" the Dom gloated, as the sub began to squirm beneath him, and his cock started its rough back-and-forth rhythm inside the sub's ass. "That's the way, boy! That's the way to take a man's cock! When I'm done with you, you'll know how to submit to another man, how to satisfy him. You've got the makings of a first-class little cock whore, boy. All you need is a little more training." The Dom humped harder and tightened his choke hold on Trent's neck. "And I'm just the man to give it to you, you hot-assed little bitch!"

Trent Carothers awoke with a start. He was naked in his bed, and, fortunately, he was alone. He wasn't really being fucked bareback. It had only been a dream—a sex dream, exciting and somewhat disturbing, like so many of the sex dreams he'd been having recently.

He had a hard-on, as he so often did when he woke up in the morning. He was tempted to start playing with himself, to masturbate himself to orgasm, but a glance at his bedside alarm clock told him that he'd better haul his horny ass out of the bed and start getting ready. After all, he had a date, of sorts. With a sigh, he threw the sheet off his body and climbed out of bed, then stumbled into the bathroom.

Still stark naked, Trent leaned over the sink to watch himself in the mirror as he scraped gingerly at his lathered face with a new razor blade, trimming the areas around his mustache and beard. Trent grinned at his own reflection with insolent familiarity, feeling his usual surge of narcissistic pleasure as he examined his face in the mirror, then looked down at his powerful body. He was a good-looking young stud, and he was only too aware of the fact. He could recite his vital statistics from memory as promptly as any professional bodybuilder might have done. His height was six two, his weight was two hundred and so forth. His big frame was packed with solid muscle, the product of his regular workouts with heavy weights down at his gym.

It was a hot body—not that the face was anything to be ashamed of, Trent thought gratefully, studying his features as he splashed a double handful of water over his face to rinse off what was left of the shaving cream. It was a good face, its owner decided, strong, but still youthful, with a square jaw and straight nose and flat, jutting cheekbones. His eyes were a cool blue, so light that they appeared almost colorless. His thick, dark blond hair, streaked paler in places from exposure to the sun, almost touched his broad, tanned shoulders. No wonder, in all of his most lurid, secret fantasies, the Doms wanted to fuck him!

Trent dried his face with a towel then mopped his chest with the damp terrycloth to wipe off the sweat that was already breaking out all over his torso. It was a hot summer in this Gulf Coast city, and he always sunned himself in the nude if possible so that his sleekly muscled body was brown all over, except for where he'd tucked a cloth over his genitals to protect them from the sun.

Trent spread his legs wider, shifting his bare feet on the cool, tiled bathroom floor, and his hand stole lower down over his body, over the silky blond tangle of his pubic bush, and cupped his balls in his sweaty palm. They were big, and they got bigger when they reacted to his touch, swelling up inside their blond-furred pouch and gradually drawing up closer to his crotch muscle. His cock, too, stirred in response to his manipulation of himself. Trent licked his lips as his limp cock began to twitch and sway, standing out slightly from his groin as the spongy erectile tissues became turgid with warm, tingling blood. Trent was getting hot. He gave his balls a final, affectionate squeeze, grunting pleasurably at the sensation, and moved his hand up to the base of his now-erect dick.

It was big, too, a good match for his balls, and it felt even bigger once he'd wrapped his fingers around the lengthening, thickening shaft and began to stroke himself into full erection. The velvety skin that covered his cock felt moist to Trent's touch as he worked his calloused fingers around the thick column of hard flesh. He wasn't cut, and the smooth knob at the end of his hard-on had already pushed its way free of its close-fitting sheath of foreskin.

A low, deep-pitched chuckle erupted deep in Trent's throat as he continued to play with himself, coaxing his cock into its maximum degree of arousal, feeling the snug foreskin sliding back and forth over the solid core of the blood-engorged penis. His moist palm slapped noisily against his cock as he beat off, the heel of his hand smacking against his come-charged balls from time to time. Trent grunted, his mouth set in a grim line of concentration, as he became aware of his increased heartbeat, of the way the swollen vein that ran along his dick pulsed against his palm, of his general feeling of intense and accelerating horniness.

He knew that if he didn't cut it out soon, he'd pop his nuts all over the bathroom sink, and so, reluctantly, he slowed his pumping fist. Trent had no inhibitions about jacking off, but he had an appointment on this Sunday morning. Laughing breathlessly, he took his hand away from his aching hard-on and let his body calm down a bit. He remained rock-hard, and, looking in the mirror again, he was excited by the hot, aroused expression in his eyes and on his flushed, reddening face. He was beginning to sweat again in the intense heat, but it felt good—sexy. Wiping his damp forehead with the back of his hand, Trent caught a whiff of his own musky crotch odor on the hand he'd been jacking off with. That was sexy, too. Shaking his head, he stumbled into the bedroom and got dressed in casual clothes, since the man he was meeting wasn't particularly fashion conscious, at least not on his day off from work.

He'd agreed to meet Xerxes Kostopoulos at an unpretentious little coffee shop downtown, a place they'd patronized before.

When they'd first met and started working together, Kostopoulos had tested Trent, ribbing him about any number of things, trying to get a rise out of him to see whether Trent could take it. He'd even mocked Trent's name.

"Trent Carothers," he said. "It sounds like some kind of a

goddamn yuppie. It makes you sound like a spoiled little rich boy."

Trent refused to rise to the bait. "Well, sounds can be deceiving, I guess, just like looks can. My family are perfectly ordinary, working-class people."

"So are mine. We're a typical Greek-American family, descended from immigrants."

"Xerxes Kostopoulos is quite a mouthful. And I've never met anybody named Xerxes. Is that a common Greek name?"

The other man laughed. He explained that "Xerxes," pronounced "Zerk-zees," was a traditional name for the men in his family. One of his ancestors had gotten his history confused, and had assumed that Xerxes, the Persian king, instead of trying to invade and conquer the ancient Greeks, had been their ally. "But nobody except my grandmother actually calls me Xerxes," Kostopoulos said. "Everybody calls me 'Zerk.' And don't bother to say anything like, 'Oh, it rhymes with jerk?' or make any 'Zerk the jerk-off' jokes. That was all real funny—the first hundred times I heard it. After the second hundred times or so, it started to become a pain in the ass to listen to."

"I kind of like the sound of 'Zerk,'" Trent remarked. "It suits you." He didn't specify why. Had he been pressed on the point, he might have said something like, "It suits you because it's blunt and butch, like you."

And so he and Zerk, after a certain initial wariness, had begun to bond. Soon, they'd been spending so much time together on the job that it only seemed natural when Zerk called Trent on Saturday evening and suggested they meet the following morning for brunch.

"We'll do something afterward, if you want," Zerk had said vaguely. Trent wondered exactly what the other man might have in mind.

Zerk, looking rumpled and sleepy, was already at the coffee shop when Trent arrived. They shared the Sunday newspaper while guzzling coffee and stuffing their faces with the shop's breakfast sandwiches—eggs and ham, inserted between English muffins.

"So," Zerk mumbled around a mouthful of his sandwich, "what'd you do after I talked to you on the phone last night?"

"I watched some TV, and then I went to bed."

"Alone?"

"Of course."

"A young stud like you? You didn't go out on the town, pick up somebody, and get laid? I can't believe it. What a waste."

"All these strange hours we've been working, Zerk—working late at night, including Friday and Saturday nights—sometimes it's not exactly conducive to dating, you know. Doesn't do much for a guy's sex life," Trent pointed out. *Except that all the pent-up frustration seems to make me dream about sex a lot!* He smiled at his partner. "What about you? I suppose you went out and got laid last night, as late as it was."

"No," Zerk sighed. "I just went to bed—and dreamed about you, good-looking."

"Don't make me laugh."

"You think I'm kidding?"

"I know you are, Zerk. I've known you long enough by now to know better than to take anything you say too seriously. Anything that's not job-related, that is. Anyway, what—" Trent suddenly interrupted himself and lowered his voice. "Take a look at the guy who just walked in."

The instinct for potential trouble, which Trent had developed ever since he'd started working with Zerk, told him to pay close attention when a crummy-looking young punk in a dirty leather jacket and torn jeans, his eyes bleary and red-rimmed—from drugs, Trent was sure—staggered into the coffee shop and up to the counter.

"Yeah, I see him," Zerk replied, also in an undertone. "Are you packing?"

"Yes."

"So am I. Maybe it's a false alarm."

"I doubt it."

And indeed, Trent wasn't the least bit surprised when the punk pulled a gun—a snub-nosed Saturday night special, or perhaps more accurately, given the circumstances, a Sunday morning special—on the flustered kid behind the counter and mumbled, "Gimme the money—all of it!" Trent didn't have to kick Zerk's shin under the table to get his attention as the guy behind the counter nervously opened the cash register and started pulling out the money with shaking hands. Zerk, who'd always been the more streetwise of the two of them, had already noticed what was coming down.

They waited patiently until the junkie, clutching a paper bag with the coffee shop's logo on it—a paper bag now full of cash—began to stumble toward the door. When Trent and Zerk were sure that the kid behind the counter and the few other customers were out of the line of fire, they pulled their own guns out and jumped up.

"Freeze, fucker!" Trent bellowed, kicking over a chair that was in his way and leveling his Glock at the thief. Zerk, also covering him, hurried over to him, shoved him against the wall, and took his gun away before starting to frisk him.

"Spread 'em!" Zerk roared, using his foot to push apart the perp's feet. "Spread 'em wide! And don't you move!"

A woman having breakfast at another table started screaming her head off. Trent wished she'd shut up. It was bad enough that they'd had to handle this crap on their day off, but he had a slight headache, and the woman's shrill outbursts weren't helping it any.

"Oh, my God, oh, my God," she kept repeating, when her companion finally succeeded in calming her down a bit. "Shouldn't somebody call the police?"

"That won't be necessary, ma'am," Zerk said politely as he handcuffed the punk. "We *are* the police."

Chapter Two: The Rookie

Trent was probably among the tallest and best built of the succession of nervous rookies who had reported, one after another, for work at his new precinct assignment, mid-town vice. He was by no means the most ambitious, although, at twenty-four, he had scored decently on the police department's entrance exam and had done well at the academy, distinguishing himself especially in marksmanship. Unlike some of his fellow graduates, he didn't think there was anything particularly unpleasant or degrading in having been assigned to vice. It was just another job, Trent thought, like being a cop in the first place. And it had the advantage that he didn't have to wear one of his crisp new uniforms, for the time being. They hung, carefully ironed but otherwise neglected, in his closet.

The moment he walked into the precinct he'd been assigned to, Trent knew he'd found a home. The headquarters looked exactly like a vice squad set from a B movie of the forties. There were dirty, glass-enclosed cubicles for the supervisors in the rear, and the center of the room was filled with battered wooden desks where the men and women officers who worked on the gambling, prostitution, and porno squads sat, guzzling coffee and talking on ancient-looking desk telephones. The computers on some of the desks looked like anachronisms. Only one man took any notice of Trent when he first walked in.

"Can I help you, kid?" he asked, in a tone of voice that implied his fervent wish that the answer would be *no*. He eyeballed the big blond youth suspiciously, as though already stripping him, in his imagination, to search for concealed weapons, drugs, or other contraband.

"I'm Carothers," Trent explained, flashing his shield and ID. "I think the captain is expecting me."

"Shit! No kidding? So you're going to be the new undercover, huh? Hell, they make 'em younger and better-looking every time," the other cop said, nodding.

Trent was pleased that he hadn't been "made" right off the bat as an obvious cop. He'd been instructed to report for duty in plainclothes, street attire, and with his shoulder-length hair, beard, tight faded jeans and motorcycle boots, he looked as though he belonged on the street—either standing on the sidewalk outside a gay bar, giving it away for free—or on the prowl in a meat rack, selling himself to the kind of johns who liked their hustlers super-butch.

Trent had a good talk with his captain on that first day. The man was gruff, but Trent sensed that he was amiable enough behind that tough, no-nonsense exterior. But Trent was mildly surprised when his assigned partner, Xerxes Kostopoulos, showed up and was introduced to him. Not at all small, wiry, or even particularly ethnic-looking, as Trent had pictured him when he'd first been told the name, Kostopoulos was a big man, broad-shouldered, with light brown hair that was bleached almost dark blond here and there from exposure to the sun, and a thick mustache. He was wearing a get-up right out of an old movie about a biker gang—a soiled, cracked black leather jacket, a studded leather belt, torn skintight jeans, and a ragged work shirt open to the waist, exposing a very hairy chest and an abdomen with an impressive six-pack and a pierced navel. Two surgical steel spheres were screwed onto either end of the little barbell that was inserted vertically through his navel. They looked like the two dots of a colon, punctuating his belly.

Kostopoulos saw Trent staring at his exposed torso. "Like the jewelry, do you?"

"Yes. You're in great shape, obviously," Trent said.

"You think so? Feel this fucking arm," Kostopoulos invited. Trent did so. The bicep was incredibly solid, throbbing with contained power. Kostopoulos grinned. "I used to play football, too, believe it or not. Oh, don't look so surprised. I read up on your background. I know all about you." Surely not *all* about me, Trent thought, a bit anxiously. "You can call me Zerk, everybody else does. We're going to make some hot team, aren't we? The gay guys are going to go crazy over us. They're going to think we're lovers, and they'll keep asking us if we'd be interested in a threesome."

Trent found Zerk's blunt manner and peculiar sense of humor rather disconcerting, but the guy seemed to know his stuff.

Zerk introduced Trent to some of his coworkers, three men and a woman. One of the men, a husky Puerto Rican named Alejandro De Soto, looked Trent up and down in a way that made the rookie feel distinctively nervous. Then De Soto emphatically shook his head.

"I'm sorry, kid," he told Trent. "Nothing personal, but you just won't do."

"What do you mean?" Trent asked, more than a little defensively.

"You'll never make it working vice. You're so white bread you ought to be wearing peanut butter and jelly smeared all over you. You'll be made as a cop right away."

"Aw, come on, De Soto, give the kid a chance," Zerk urged.

"He's just too damn straight-looking," De Soto insisted. "You do realize, Carothers, that you're going to have to do things on this job like go to gay bars and pass for gay, don't you?"

"Sure. I can do that," Trent declared.

De Soto snickered. "No one is ever going to believe that you're gay."

"I can act gay," Trent said, with a sense of growing desperation. "If I have to."

De Soto laughed. "Prove it."

"Aw, let him alone," Zerk said.

Trent was grateful to Zerk, for standing up for him, but he was determined to show that he could fit in. "Prove it? How?" he asked.

"Go ahead. Act gay. I know," De Soto said, as though struck by a sudden inspiration. "Go up to Kostopoulos, over there, as if he was some dude you're cruising in a gay bar. Go over to him, sit in his lap, and give him a kiss. If you've got the balls to do it, which I doubt."

Zerk, at the moment, was sitting in a chair, drinking coffee. "Don't let De Soto talk you into doing anything you don't want to do, Carothers. He's an asshole."

"No, I'll do it, if you'll let me."

"I'll let you do it, sure, just to make De Soto eat his words," Zerk said. "Come on, kid. Sit on my lap and tell Santa what you want for Christmas. We'll show him."

"It's got to be a real kiss, guys, on the mouth—and not just a peck," De Soto warned. "No faking it."

"What are you, all of a sudden an expert on how to kiss another guy?" Zerk retorted. That, Trent noticed, shut De Soto up, if only for a moment.

The others were watching this byplay with great interest and amusement.

Trent tried to look and act casual as he walked over to Zerk and swung himself down into his lap. "I'm a little heavy," he warned.

"That's okay. I think I can handle it," Zerk responded. He smiled up at Trent as Trent gingerly lowered his weight onto him, putting his hands on Zerk's shoulders to steady himself. "Yeah, you *are* a big boy, aren't you? Go on, kid, plant a big wet one right on me," Zerk urged. "Don't be embarrassed. Pretend you're a whore, and you want to talk me into going home with you. Show 'em what you got!"

Trent leaned forward and let his bearded lips touch Zerk's. He was a bit surprised when Zerk reached up, placed a hand on the back of his neck, and exerted a slight pressure, forcing their mouths more tightly together. Trent was even more startled when Zerk's tongue parted his lips and pushed its way into his mouth. Well, it was supposed to be a gay kiss, after all, and a real one, with no faking, so he allowed Zerk's tongue to probe the interior of his mouth, and used his own tongue to duel with it. Zerk's other hand suddenly slid down Trent's broad back, cupped one of his buttocks, and gave it an impassioned squeeze through his pants.

Trent heard the other cops laughing and applauding as he broke the kiss. Zerk was still smiling at him, a bit smugly.

"All right," Zerk announced triumphantly. "Each of you owes me five bucks! Pay up, suckers!"

De Soto groaned. "I didn't really think he'd fall for it, Zerk. He looked a little smarter than the last rookie you pulled that routine on!"

It belatedly dawned on Trent that he had been had. He turned his head and saw that De Soto and the other cops were all holding out their cell phones toward him and Zerk, taking their picture. "You sons of bitches!" he exclaimed, as he jumped off Zerk's lap. "You set me up!"

"He's not a bad little kisser," Zerk reported gleefully. "And he's got a really nice ass!"

"Wait'll you see the shot I got, of you with your tongue in the kid's mouth," one of the cops chortled. "Don't worry, Carothers, I can get some nice prints made for you, as many as you want."

"We'll want a big one, of course, to put up on the bulletin board," De Soto said.

"Don't forget the police union newsletter," Zerk said. "This ought to be front page stuff."

"Yeah," De Soto retorted, "front page, because Kostopoulos finally got some action!"

"Sons of bitches," a red-faced Trent repeated, fuming.

Zerk was collecting his five dollars, from each of his colleagues. "Yeah, I'm a son of a bitch, all right, but I'm a son of a bitch who's twenty dollars richer than I was a minute ago. Thanks, Carothers. Any time you want to make out again, just let me know! Maybe we can get to second base next time."

Trent was furious at being so easily duped, although he tried his best to hide it, because he knew that if he wanted to be accepted by the other cops, he was going to have to prove that he could take it. And later, at least, De Soto had the grace to come up to him and say a few words to him in private.

"Don't sweat it, Carothers. We give all the rookies and the new transfers a hard time the first day. At least you're a good sport. And Kostopoulos likes you, I can tell. If he didn't, he'd have made it a lot worse for you."

"What you do mean?" In his current mood, Trent didn't see how it could possibly have been worse.

"Well, the last rookie we had was a stuck-up little hotshot who walked in here with a real attitude. He rubbed Zerk the wrong way, right off the bat. So Zerk got even. We pulled the same 'I bet you can't act gay' thing on him, only Zerk pulled such a head trip on him that the kid ended up bending over the edge of a desk with his pants and his boxers pulled down and his bare ass sticking out for everybody to see, yelling 'Fuck me, fuck me!' That's how desperate *he* was to prove he could act gay. We got some *really* good pictures that time. Okay, so that horny bastard Kostopoulos sucked your face and copped a feel—shit, that's nothing!"

After everyone in the precinct had enjoyed a good laugh at the rookie's expense, Zerk finally got around to talking to Trent, one on one.

He explained that their current assignment was to gather information about the local bars, including gay bars and strip clubs, and who was really running them. The unit suspected that several of these businesses had been taken over by organized crime and that some owners who'd resisted had been beaten up, or had their joints trashed and, in one case, even firebombed. It was a joint investigation with the IRS into bar and after-hours club owners who skimmed cash without paying taxes.

"It's boring shit work, in other words," Zerk said bluntly. "We've got a list of places, all of them real dumps, and we're supposed to just hang out there, blend in, get friendly with the bartenders and the regular customers, and pump 'em for information—see who picks up the money from the tills and estimate the actual income from the number of empty liquor bottles. Crap like that.

"All kidding aside, Carothers, you look okay. Pretty hot, as a matter of fact. Your pants are certainly tight enough. But lose the belt, okay? No self-respecting gay man would wear that kind of a skinny belt with that kind of a plain buckle. It's too damn preppy-looking. And open the top and bottom buttons of your fly."

"Why?" Trent was naïve enough to ask.

"So you look like the kind of sleazebag who's always whipping his dick out and is careless about buttoning up his fly afterward." Zerk produced a piece of sandpaper from a desk drawer. "Put your hand in your pocket," he instructed. "All the way down, so you can grab hold of your dick through the pocket. Do you hang it left or right?"

"Ah, right, usually."

"Okay, shove it down your right pants leg, the way you usually tuck it in, hold it there, and let me use this sandpaper on you—the denim over your crotch has got to look the way mine does, as though you've spent hours rubbing your cock through your jeans with your hand to keep it hard and pricktease the other guys you see on the streets and in bars. Hey, does that T-shirt you're wearing got any sentimental value, as far as you're concerned?" he demanded suddenly as he matter-of-factly rubbed the sandpaper back and forth across the bulge Trent's cock made in his jeans, taking off the top layer of denim and quick-ageing the cloth.

"No, it's kind of old, and getting worn out," Trent replied, struggling to keep his mind off sex, to disregard the pressure Zerk's hand was exerting against his crotch—against his twitching, thickening prick. He'd thought kissing Zerk was bad enough, but this was worse. What if the other cop noticed he was springing a hard-on?

"Mind if I rip it?" Zerk asked.

"No, but what the fuck for?"

"To make you look hotter, asshole, what else? More like a gay slut on the make. We want the guys in the bars to come up to us, talk to us, and try to get us to go home with them. Hold still." Zerk examined the T-shirt closely, fingering its seams, until he found one that was beginning to loosen as a result of the repeated launderings. He carefully inserted a fingertip to start the hole then ripped a gap in the shirt from Trent's hairy armpit across his solid pectoral muscle, to expose one large brown nipple.

"All right!" Zerk exclaimed, pleased by the effect of his handiwork. "Nice tits to go with the nice ass, I see. Now you look so fucking hot that those cocksuckers are going to have their tongues hanging out of their mouths, drooling spit, over you. Let's go. Might as well get started, now that you're dressed for the part."

They drove to the first club on the list in Zerk's car—a vehicle that was nondescript and even somewhat the worse for wear on the outside, suitable for undercover work. The engine and the other mechanical parts, Trent suspected, were, by contrast, exceptionally well maintained.

They found the place in a warehouse wedged between two meat-packing plants, appropriately enough. It was only one of several gay joints in the neighborhood. As they parked, they saw men coming and going, and sometimes loitering on the sidewalk. Judging by the clientele, this particular bar catered to the rough trade crowd—muscle boys, tough guys dressed all in black leather, often embossed with metal studs. They strutted about in their tight jeans and leather pants, which grossly accentuated the bulges at their groins. Trent realized that he and Zerk were actually outfitted rather conservatively, by comparison.

"Half of these guys have an extra handkerchief stuffed in their crotches—besides the color-coded ones in their hip pockets." Zerk snickered as he and Trent walked toward the bar.

One leather freak whistled at Zerk and called out, "Hey there, big man! You like to fuck? You sure look like you got the equipment for it!"

Zerk smiled and waved at the guy. "Maybe later," he replied.

"How about your good-looking friend?" the man asked, staring at Trent.

"Oh, I've got *big* plans for him, later, too," Zerk said, with a laugh.

Trent forced himself to smile and act casual as the burly vice cop put his arm around him, gave him a hug, and whispered in his ear, "That fucker likes you. And why not? You're fresh meat. You'd better hold my hand when we get inside, to make it look good," he added maliciously, grabbing Trent's sweaty palm and squeezing it tightly, possessively, as they went inside and got into a freight elevator that lifted them to the club level of the building.

"Is this another bet?" Trent asked.

"Aw, you're not going to hold that against me, are you?"

Trent didn't bother to answer because the hard rock music blasting from speakers inside the bar, and spilling out into the entranceway, was deafening. A huge-muscled bouncer with tattooed arms and multiple piercings collected the five dollar cover charge from each of them and waved them toward the dimly-lit barroom.

The stale air and cigarette smoke hit them like a wall. For the first few minutes, they had trouble seeing clearly.

Zerk, though, was completely in his element. During the next hour, he danced with half a dozen other patrons, struck up conversations with both bartenders and the bouncer, cruised, and got cruised shamelessly. Trent felt like a wallflower by comparison as he stood stiffly, nursing his beer. One thing he'd already discovered was that wearing leather, even partial leather in the form of body harnesses or open vests over bare torsos, was no joke in this warm climate. Everybody inside the bar was sweating, despite the air conditioning, which seemed none too efficient. Trent studied the crowd. Two men next to him, oblivious to all else, noisily sucked on each other's tongues. Trent finally edged closer to Zerk and asked him in an undertone whether he didn't think the whole scene was repulsive.

"Don't make me laugh," the other cop snickered. "This is pure vanilla. You want to see what really goes on in a place like this? Come with me. We can't stay away from the bar area too long, though, because I've already seen where they're stashing the surplus cash. See the guy behind the counter slipping money into that little zipper bag every now and then? Sooner or later, somebody's going to come to pick it up, so watch for him."

"Maybe they're just going to take the money to deposit in the bank," Trent theorized.

"God, you *are* naïve!"

Zerk led Trent through the crowd, toward a doorway at one end of the room.

Beyond the door, they found themselves in a room about thirty feet square, lit by dim red lights. Bare mattresses, much the worse for wear, were thrown on the floor. Men were necking and groping each other as they stood against the walls. In the center of the room, several guys were standing in a circle, watching a young number kneeling before another man whose jeans and jockstrap were pulled down around his knees. The guy who was standing upright groaned, threw his head back, and twisted his hands around his partner's neck. The kneeling youth's head was moving back and forth rapidly against the other guy's pelvis. Saliva was dripping from the kneeling cocksucker's mouth as he fed on a thick, solid, throbbing piece of meat. Some of the other men in the circle had their pricks out and were either humping air or tugging frantically on their cocks.

Zerk, Trent noticed, was watching the action impassively, and Trent did his best to imitate his partner's casual attitude. In a corner, Trent saw a stark-naked man stretched out on the floor facedown with his arms folded under his head, forming a pillow. A second man knelt over him, spread his ass cheeks wide apart, and licked hungrily at the first man's anus. Several men in the orgy room were passing joints around. A few others were cracking open capsules of amyl nitrite and sniffing at them. The acrid aroma drifted through the air and reached Trent's nostrils.

"How do those guys get that real amyl without a prescription?" Trent whispered in Zerk's ear, under the pretense of kissing him on the cheek.

"They probably do have prescriptions," Zerk replied. "They find a gay doctor who'll write it out for them for a few bucks or in exchange for sex."

"We'd better go back and check out the bar again. We don't want to miss the pickup."

"What's the matter, kid, can't you take it?" Zerk teased him as they left the back room. "Shit, this is nothing! Nobody was even being fisted, which is unusual. Of course, it *is* kind of early. Things'll get a lot raunchier later on, tonight."

They got back to the main room just in time to see a young number, dark and deeply tanned, about twenty-five, with a solid, rather chunky weekend athlete's physique and a tough, virile face, heavy with dark beard stubble, leaning over the bar and talking quietly with one of the bartenders who casually handed him the little zipper bag stuffed with paper money.

"Catch you later, Marco," the bartender said as the guy turned to go.

"Bingo," Zerk said quietly, with satisfaction.

"Do we bust him?" Trent asked.

"Of course not. We just follow him to see where he makes the drop. Come on, and try not to look too obvious. Act like all you're interested in is me, and you don't even notice the guy we're tailing."

Outside, on the street, the dark-haired number dug into the pocket of his jeans and splurged on a cab ride. Trent and Zerk followed him cautiously in the car. The cab pulled over to the curb in front of one of the city's several steam baths. The courier paid the cab driver and vanished through the door after ringing a buzzer to have the door unlocked from within.

"Now what?" Trent asked.

His partner shrugged. "Follow him, I guess. He could just be killing time, trying to get laid, or he could be handing the money off to somebody inside. I'll wait here, and you go in. It'll look less suspicious if only one of us goes in at a time. If you don't come out soon, I'll follow you."

"Why am I the one who has to go in there and get naked?" Trent complained.

"Because you take your orders from me, because you need the experience, and because you look more like a fag."

"Thank you and fuck you, Kostopoulos."

"Hurry up before you lose him. And whatever you do, don't lose your cherry in there, kid. Save it for me."

Trent got out of the car and hurried across the street. Inside, the entrance to the bath was a large wall mirror in which departing patrons could check their appearance before they hit the streets again. Trent paused to take a look at himself, thinking about his partner's crack. Well, he certainly didn't look like a *cop*, in any event.

"Hey, man. You want a room or a locker?" the bored-looking attendant asked.

"Uh—a locker," Trent mumbled as he paid. He fought back a smile at the thought that he could've flashed his badge and gotten inside for free, but that would've caused a mass stampede toward the exit once word got around that the heat was taking the steam, so to speak.

The attendant handed Trent a towel and a key on a flexible plastic band which could be fastened around one's wrist or ankle. Trent passed through another door into the locker area. There, Marco was standing naked, closing and securing the door of the locker he'd been assigned. He had his own towel slung over his shoulder, and his erection was being flaunted for all the world to see and covet. The bag with the money was presumably now inside the locker.

"Hi," the black-haired stud greeted Trent, with such unmistakable intent that the cop was tempted to bust him on the spot, before he reminded himself that they were after bigger game than a cheap solicitation rap.

"Hi."

"I haven't seen you in here before."

"No, I'm new in town. Is this a good place?"

"It's a dump, but *you* won't have any trouble getting laid."

"Well, that's what we're here for, isn't it?" Trent replied, feeling stupid as he said it, but his display of gaucheness seemed to fit the situation.

Marco merely smiled in response and stood there, watching, while Trent stripped to the waist in front of his own locker. Embarrassed by being cruised by the guy he was tailing, Trent had no choice but to go all the way—to unzip his jeans and push them down—but, to his relief, his tail didn't wait around to inspect the rest of the merchandise. Apparently satisfied by the preview of coming attractions, Marco grinned even wider, turned on his heel, and, with a twitch of his hips and muscular, hairy ass, he marched down the ill-lit corridor toward the steam rooms.

"Catch you later," he called.

"Sure." Blushing, Trent finished stripping, wrapped the too-small towel around his waist, and set off in pursuit.

Customers had the option of wearing their towels in the steam room, or leaving them on a row of hooks provided for the purpose on the wall just outside the wooden door. With a shrug—anything for the department—Trent added his towel to the collection, baring all, before he pushed open the swinging door and stepped into a hot, moist cloud of billowing gray steam.

It was hot inside the large tiled room, the kind of wet, muggy heat Trent associated with a smoggy August afternoon before a thunderstorm blew up to relieve the oppressive atmosphere. He couldn't see a thing at first, but he groped his way across the damp tiled floor to the tiered wooden seating platforms that lined the walls.

At last he distinguished Marco. The humpy young stud was sitting on the second tier with his legs spread, supporting himself on one elbow while he pulled at the rope that controlled the steam input with his other arm. He was filling the room with hot, stifling steam, but Trent could now see why. He was trying to drive out the other two customers in the room, both of whom were overweight, balding businessman types who were giving Marco and Trent the eagle eye through the fog.

A hand brushed over Trent's ass cheek and thigh, and he nonchalantly brushed it away.

"I just want to work up a sweat," Trent told the man, apologetically.

Marco was more direct about rejecting the other man's pass. "Get lost," he announced with boredom when a wet hand began to caress his calf muscle, working its eager way up toward his bent knee.

Discouraged, the two older men simply sat down and waited. Feeling very conspicuous, Trent decided to stretch out on the wooden boards, about a yard from Marco's shapely bare feet. He couldn't help noticing that the guy was in good physical shape, and hung like the proverbial horse. Marco began to play with his impressive sexual endowment in a blatant come-on, spreading his muscular legs even wider to give the young cop a good view. He'd stopped tugging on the rope, and about time, Trent thought. He was already drenched in sweat and panting for breath. Beside him, Marco's nude body looked red and shiny from the intense heat.

They all waited—for something to happen.

"Let's do it, man," Marco's clear, virile voice cut through the humid air.

Trent was startled by the guy's openness. "Do what?" he asked.

"Each other. What's the matter, big guy, don't I turn you on?" was Marco's mocking response.

"I don't like doing it in front of an audience," the young cop blurted out, as the first excuse that came to mind. "Maybe I should've got a room, instead of just a locker."

"Don't be silly. You're getting all uptight about nothing. I *do* like an audience. It turns me on to suck cock in front of other guys."

Marco immediately set out to prove that he wasn't exaggerating. He got onto his knees and, leaning over, took the head of Trent's moist cock in his mouth. The heat and humidity had conspired to give the rookie half a hard-on, and the first electrifying touch of Marco's lips did the rest. His cock snapped to attention inside the other young man's mouth as Marco began to apply skillful, steady suction around the thickening shaft, running his wet tongue all over the velvety-smooth head of Trent's by-no-means negligible meat.

After the initial shock, the young cop decided that he'd only make Marco suspicious if he tried to push him away. *Better to just grin and bear it. Time to take one for the team.* Hell, this assignment was turning out to be fun, after all!

"Suck it, man," Trent gasped.

He spread his legs to give Marco unhampered access to his crotch and buried his hands in the guy's sweaty black mop of hair. The two spectators decided to initiate a little audience participation. Trent felt a hand pat his ass, another stroke his chest, pinching the nipple—he was tempted to tell the men to fuck off, but then he decided, *What the hell?* It felt pretty damn good.

Not nearly as good, though, as the incredible blow job Marco was giving him. The guy had his palms spread over Trent's thighs, holding him down as he milked the entire length of the cop's shaft with his warm, sucking, saliva-lubricated lips.

"Oh, yeah," one of the two men who were watching moaned. Marco, oblivious to their presence, continued to cop the cop's joint with all of his considerable oral expertise. He would use his warm lips to push the dark-colored sheath of Trent's foreskin down so that the smooth-fleshed bulb of his penis was exposed to the slightly rough surface of his caressing tongue. Then Marco would tease that throbbing, hyper-responsive cockhead, until the young police officer's pre-cum—pungent, heady, and stickily viscous on the tongue—was oozing from the pouting lips of his piss slit in a steady trickle.

Trent gasped for breath in the stifling, muggy room as he pushed Marco's head up and down on his cock and tried to generate enough friction to bring himself off. The other guy sensed that his steady mouth and throat action was bringing Trent close. He pulled away despite the cop's efforts to stop him.

"Don't come yet. Don't waste it, man. Put it in me," Marco panted. "Fuck my ass!"

"I don't bareback. Not ever." *Except in my fantasies and my sex dreams.*

"We don't have to. I've got a rubber right here, in my towel." Marco reached for his discarded towel, which lay on the platform nearby, and, like a magician pulling a rabbit out of a hat, he retrieved a condom from its folds.

It was so hot in the steam room that, for a moment, Trent speculated about what the melting point of latex might be. But Marco seemed to know what he was doing. Trent doubted this was the first time the guy had gloved his dick under these hot, humid circumstances. Trent was too horny by now to let anything stand in the way of getting his rocks off, but he made the purely formal further protest, "We don't have any lube, unless you brought that in here with you, too."

"I can take it dry," Marco boasted. "It's better that way, in fact. I like to feel a little friction when a guy pushes his prick inside me. I like to really know I'm getting reamed out by a big stud cock!" He was already on his hands and knees on the wet wooden platform, thrusting a tantalizingly butch-looking ass into Trent's direction. "Shove it in me, stud!"

The two older men were busily fondling the younger pair, but neither Marco nor Trent protested. They hardly took notice of the roaming hands and mouths as they prepared to join their bodies in the most intimate way possible.

Trent was soaked with sweat, and his hard-on felt wet and slick when he rolled the rubber down over it then guided it between Marco's buttocks. He slipped it inside the delivery man's asshole with surprising, breathless ease. His cock touched home against Marco's prostate, buried deep in that tight, hot, writhing anus, and he began to fuck the sexy young stud dog-fashion, kneeling behind the kneeling Marco with his groin jammed into that beautiful, tanned butt, his arms wrapped around Marco's waist to hug him close, his chest pressed to the small of the guy's wide, hard-muscled back.

They fucked, Marco groaning and moving his hot ass in a way that made Trent's implanted dick leap and twitch with an intolerable exciting arousal. He thought he'd faint from the combination of the steam, the constant pressure on his ass-embedded cock, and the sheer thrill of fucking another young guy with such animal abandon.

Their audience got into the act. One chubby executive type, looking for all the world like a pale, beached walrus, squirmed with unexpected agility beneath Marco's body and began to blow him. The second man knelt behind Trent and buried his face between the cop's ass cheeks. Trent repressed a shout of pure, bestial lust as a wet tongue poked its way inside his asshole and the man began to rim him as though he'd been starving for a taste of man-ass.

"Yeah, eat it, you bastard!" Trent hissed. He fucked Marco even harder, the nastiness in his voice only spurring his rimmer on to yet more violent feats of tonguing. "God damn it, yeah! Like that! Just like that! Suck my ass, you son of a bitch! Lick it!"

Trent was dizzy with sexual excitement. He couldn't believe how hot and responsive his anus was, as it welcomed the tongue working around inside it in rapid, swabbing circles, cleaning him out. At the same time, Marco was tightening and relaxing his sphincter muscle and grinding his hips lewdly, to give his fucker the ride of his life. And, all the while, the other fat man devoured Marco's monster prick with greedy, noisy slurps and gulps and sucking, drooling sounds that only got Trent hotter as he listened to them.

He came inside the stud's ass, his sperm rushing from his palpitating cock on rapid, gunfire-like spurts, only to be trapped and contained by the condom. The flexing, involuntary spasms of the muscles in Trent's pumping butt only seemed to excite the man who was eating out his ass that much more. His tongue stabbed into the handsome young cop's hole as far as he could drive it, and it stayed there, multiplying the force of Trent's orgasm until he thought he'd never stop shooting his molten lava into the steamy depths of Marco's anal canal.

"Hell, yes!" Marco grunted. "Fuck, yes!"

Trent knew that Marco was coming in his cocksucker's mouth. Their twin climax seemed to go on for minutes on end, until they finally slumped, exhausted, on top of the poor bastard who swallowed Marco's cum, practically smashing the man flat beneath their combined muscular weight. The second businessman type went right on rimming Trent's writhing ass, and the burly young cop felt his dick regaining its rock-like rigidity inside Marco's clutching anus. His ears rang, he felt weak and giddy as he clung to the naked, sweaty body he was fucking, and, to his disbelief, he came *again*, firing a few more wads of come into the condom that he'd just flooded with one load of his thick, livid semen!

Groaning as his exhausted body was drained completely by this unexpected second coming, Trent went limp as a rag doll soaked in water on top of Marco. For a moment, he almost passed out.

He was revived by the unceremonious but effective means of a handful of room temperature water, from a wall tap nearby, splashed over his face and throat and chest. Trent stirred, opened his eyes, and sat up slowly. Marco, grinning, was kneeling beside him. The other two men had vanished.

"You okay, stud?"

Trent rubbed his pounding forehead then felt his limp cock to make sure it was all still there. "I guess so." He looked around. "What happened to our friends?"

"They couldn't take the heat, I guess. That was one wild fuck, man, but a guy could have a heart attack or a stroke, fucking in the steam room like that, if he's not in good shape. Sorry I was too much for you to take," Marco apologized impishly. He gave Trent a long, lascivious kiss on the mouth, plunging his tongue deep inside, and patted his ass. "See you around, stud."

Marco left the steam room, but Trent remained for a couple of minutes to rest and collect himself. Then he went to the showers. He was still wearing the condom. He peeled it off and tossed it into a trash receptacle before he went to stand under the showerhead. More customers had begun to trickle into the bath house, but Trent ignored the passes that were thrown in his direction. In the locker area, Marco was already dressed. His locker was open, but the bag was gone.

So he's already handed it off, either to somebody who works here or to another customer. Now what?

All right, remember what they taught you in those training sessions. You're working undercover—that means you're not being yourself, you're playing a part. In this case, you're a whorey young gay guy who jumps into bed with other guys and thinks nothing of it. You're a total slut. So—what would you do, how would you behave, right now? With a guy you've just had sex with?

"Hey, do you want to give me your phone number?" Trent asked. "I'd love to get together with you again, sometime. I sure could use another trip up that sweet ass of yours. In bed, next time, where we'll be a lot more comfortable."

Marco hesitated, then shrugged, and told Trent the number, which Trent entered into his cell phone. Marco smiled knowingly at Trent, said, "So long," and left.

Trent threw on his clothes and followed. In the vestibule, he was relieved to spot the bag, sitting on top of a small safe, which the attendant was opening. The man quickly unzipped the bag, put the money in the safe, and closed and secured the door again. Then, casually, he handed the empty bag back to Marco, as the latter turned in his locker key and used towel at the desk. Trent hung back in the hallway so that the two men wouldn't realize they were being observed.

He left the bath house and joined Zerk in the car.

"Our boy just started walking down the street," Zerk reported. "What the fuck took you so long in there? I was just about to go in after you. Hey, you're all wet."

"Of course I am. It's from being in the steam room. I'm still sweating, even though I just showered," Trent explained cheerfully. "Don't bother to follow him, Zerk."

Zerk started the engine. "Why not?"

"The bag's empty. He passed the money to the desk clerk, who put it in the safe."

"That's interesting. So what, exactly, went down in there?"

Trent suppressed a smirk at his partner's use of the slang expression, "went down." If only Zerk knew! "Nothing," he lied. "The guy just took a nice, long steam bath. So I had to go in there, too, since I wanted to keep an eye on him."

"You're kidding! *Nobody* goes in a place like that just to take the steam!" Zerk scoffed.

"I just did," Trent reminded him, still lying as naturally as breathing. "Of course, a couple of guys put the make on me, but I brushed them off. Obviously, the management of the bath is in on it—should we stick around to see if anybody comes along to pick up the cash from the safe?"

"No, it'd probably be a waste of time," Zerk said. "They probably leave it in the safe overnight. Not bad for a rookie. You did good work, Trent."

Trent flushed with pleasure at his partner's compliment. "Oh, I just got lucky. And I forgot—I got that guy, Marco, to give me his phone number."

Zerk laughed. "Oh, aren't you the sly one! You *did* do good work! We can run that through to get his last name and his address. But how the hell did you get him to give you his number if nothing went on in there?"

Trent shrugged. "The guy liked my looks. He cruised me, so I cruised him right back. He talked to me in the locker room while we were getting dressed. He suggested we might get together for coffee or a beer sometime."

"That might not be such a bad idea, Trent. Wait a day or two, then call him. You could string the guy along, work him a little, pump him for information."

"What if he wants to go to bed with me?"

"Tell him you like him, but you have a jealous boyfriend or something. Maybe he's the romantic type who likes to take it slow and date the other guy a few times before he tricks with him. Hell, if you're not bullshitting me, Trent, then you two were the only guys in that place who were using your mouths to *talk* to each other, instead of using them *on* each other," Zerk quipped.

Trent was beginning to feel a little guilty about lying to his partner. "Yeah? And speaking purely hypothetically, what if I am bullshitting you, Zerk?" he asked, trying to sound as casual as possible. "What if I let that guy suck my cock in the steam room just so he wouldn't get suspicious?"

Now it was Zerk's turn to look and act blasé. "It wouldn't be a big deal. Not as far as I'm concerned. All in the line of duty, as they say. Sometimes, on this job, you have to do things you ordinarily might not do."

"Take one for the team, so to speak."

"Exactly, kid. You catch on fast."

Chapter Three: Undercover Work

Trent made sure that the man lying on his bed was fast asleep. Then he slipped out of the bed himself and, naked, went into the living room of his apartment. He retrieved his cell phone from the pocket of his discarded pants, and, keeping his eye on the bedroom door, which he'd closed behind him, he went to the far end of the room. He punched in Zerk's number.

"Zerk," Trent whispered, when his partner answered. "It's me, Trent. Can you talk?"

"Yeah. What's coming down, kid?"

"I've got that guy Marco here in my apartment with me."

"He's there with you right now? Are you sure he can't hear you?"

"I'm sure."

"Good work. You get anything out of him?"

"I sure have. Once you get him talking, it's hard to shut him up. He started boasting about how much money he makes working for the mob, and I pretended to be really interested and envious. When I asked him how you get started in that kind of work, he offered to introduce me to a couple of people who might be able to use me. Do you think I should go ahead and tell him to set it up?"

"Absolutely. But you don't actually meet up with anybody, unless I'm there, tailing you, to watch your back." Zerk snickered. "It sounds like you and this Marco character are starting to get real close."

Trent hesitated. "Zerk, what if he wants to get *really* close to me, and I can't get out of it without making him suspicious?"

"Go ahead and have sex with him, if you have to," Zerk said bluntly. "Let him suck you off. He's probably real good at it."

"Jesus, Zerk. That's easy enough for you to say. What if, after we bust him, he files some kind of a complaint, tells everybody we tricked together?"

"He won't. Not when we're done with him. You leave that to me. And who's going to believe him, anyway? It'd be your word against his. That's the oldest trick in the book—accuse the cop who took you down of doing this to you, and doing that to you, to try to wiggle your way out of the charge. Don't worry about it, kid."

"But how would *you* feel about it, Zerk, if I went ahead and did something like that?"

"I'd feel fine. But I'm not the one you'd have to worry about. The only thing that matters is, are *you* okay with it?"

"That's what I'm not so sure of," Trent admitted.

"It's like I keep telling you. On this job, sometimes you have to do what you have to do."

"I guess so. Listen, Zerk, I probably shouldn't risk staying on the phone any longer. Can we talk about this tomorrow, when I see you face-to-face?"

"Of course."

"Thanks, man."

Trent hung up and put the phone back in his pants.

He felt better, even though he'd told Zerk a half-truth, at best. What was the expression—locking the barn door *after* the horse had been stolen? He'd probably sounded like some sort of a coy virgin on the phone, worried about protecting his honor. Knowing Zerk, it was quite possible that the more experienced cop suspected the truth—that his new partner had already gone all the way with Marco.

Trent returned to his bedroom.

The windows were open, the curtains flapping as the hot wind swept into the darkened room. The breeze had blown the top sheet half off Marco, who was sleeping naked on the bed, one arm flung over the half of the mattress where Trent's body had left a still-visible impression. Smiling, the tall blond cop examined Marco's sleeping form for a moment.

His trick was shorter and stockier than Trent, less symmetrical, almost muscle-bound—an amateur athlete's physique. Trent's eyes narrowed with lust as they swept over Marco's broad, ruddy, copper-tanned torso, the heavy shoulders flattening the pillow, the solid pectoral muscles crowned by two brown nipples. The white, sweat-spotted sheet had blown down over Marco's heavy thighs, and his crotch was exposed. His balls and limp cock nestled in a thick jungle of crotch hair, the same glossy black as the hair on his head. Marco had a nice face, relaxed now in sleep, the guileless sleep of post-sex weariness.

Trent bit his lip, feeling a sudden flurry of both guilt and excitement as he centered his gaze on his trick's groin. He was using this guy, who was, after all, one of the bad guys. Trent was getting close to him, pumping him for information, in order to make a bust. Having sex with a suspect was, of course, crossing a line. Zerk could rationalize it all he wanted, but it was surely unethical to say the least! But Marco was a hot fuck.

Marco's cock was circumcised, the rosy head fully exposed as it lay in the crease between his belly and thigh. It was fatter than Trent's cock appeared in its soft state, but Trent now knew from experience that, when they were both hard, he and Marco were about equal in the length department. Trent's mouth watered for another taste of that cock!

He sat on the bed and leaned over to kiss Marco lightly on the lips. Marco groaned faintly and stirred, his long legs kicking at the sheet, but Trent had already turned his head aside. His long blond hair rustled over Marco's throat as he pressed his mouth to his trick's left tit. Trent sucked as much of that firm, juicy pec into his mouth as he could. He could taste the slight saltiness of Marco's skin on his tongue as he licked the nipple, teasing it into immediate stiffness.

Still only half-awake, Marco grunted, moved on the bed, and flung one arm around Trent's waist, his hand groping uncertainly for the back of the blond's neck. Marco's fingers buried themselves in Trent's thick hair, and he pressed Trent's face against his heaving chest. A long moan of pleasure escaped from Marco's lips as Trent's mouth and tongue worked on his sensitive tit flesh. Encouraged by the other guy's response, Trent lapped away even more urgently. Trent slid his wet tongue across the broad brown expanse of Marco's chest, leaving a glistening trail of saliva behind, and then he started in on the right nipple. He kissed and licked and sucked it until he had Marco fully awake and grinding his hips in restless agitation.

"You fucker, ah, Jesus!" Marco muttered happily. Despite his protests, he seemed delighted by his trick's unorthodox way of waking him up. Just as Trent had anticipated, Marco was surrendering his body completely to the sensations produced by that expert tongue action on his tits.

Trent had already found out that Marco was especially sensitive there. Marco seemed to be the kind of young man who had no qualms about being taken advantage of, not sexually, at any rate. He was developing one hell of an impressive new hard-on as Trent pressed their naked bodies together and went on sucking his pecs. Marco caressed the big blond's hair with both hands, as though to urge him on. Not that Trent needed any such urging, as he savored the taste of the other man's flesh on his tongue.

"Suck on my tits, man," Marco begged unnecessarily. "Suck on 'em, bite 'em, really get me *hot!*"

They'd sucked and fucked for what had felt like most of the night before falling asleep together, but now Trent felt as horny as though he'd gone without sex for a week. He suspected that he had a similar effect on Marco. Trent knew what it was like to feel enslaved to another muscular young man's body and cock and not seem able to get enough of them. He was determined to work on Marco until the other guy was just as besotted. It was no longer just a question of keeping Marco's guard down, so he wouldn't suspect Trent's true motives. No, Trent was genuinely aroused and enjoying every minute of what had begun as a calculated seduction.

Trent was still sprawled on top of Marco's body, sucking his tits. He thrust one hand between the dark-haired guy's thighs and massaged Marco's hard-on roughly, his fist tugging the stiff rod into still-firmer erection. Trent's fingers separated Marco's balls within their hairy sac and rolled them around in his palm. He ran his hand back up the length of Marco's cock to where a drop of glistening semen was oozing out of the pouting lips of his piss slit. Trent caught the drop on his hand and rubbed it all over the head of his trick's hard dick, getting Marco hot.

"Suck my whang," Marco pleaded, spreading his legs wide and kicking the crumpled sheet to the foot of the bed so that Trent could get at his groin without impediment. "C'mon, man, suck on it!'

Trent laughed, teasing him, then, giving Marco's broad left nipple a final kiss, he slid his tongue down the other husky stud's ribcage with slow, licking strokes, each of which made Marco grunt and squirm with impatience. He shoved his fingers into Trent's hair and tried to push the blond's head down to his lap, but Trent resisted, giving Marco's balls a squeeze in playful retaliation. Trent noted with smug satisfaction that, apparently resigned to the delay, Marco lay back on the bed, panting, while his sex partner proceeded down his torso at his own speed. Trent's tireless tongue flicked over Marco's belly. Stiffening his tongue, he drilled it into the deep pit of the navel for a long, tantalizing moment. Then he moved his big hands to Marco's hips to hold his body in place as he ran that wet, limber piece of flesh down the other man's lower belly and began to kiss and lap at his thighs.

"Shit, it's hot in here," Marco complained. "I'm all sweaty. Why don't you have air conditioning, for Christ's sake?"

"I told you I'm trying to save money," Trent replied. Which was, in fact, true. He had been making a conscientious effort to bank part of his salary each time he got paid and to keep his living expenses low, avoiding unnecessary spending. What he'd told Marco, though, as part of his cover story, was that he did construction work but had been laid off by the company he'd worked for and was collecting unemployment insurance benefits, which would soon run out. Trent had told Marco this was why he was willing to do just about anything for money, even bend, or break, the law. By coincidence, Trent's modest living arrangements made his cover story seem plausible.

"Anyway, I thought you *liked* it hot and sweaty and dirty," Trent teased the other guy. "You know, like this?" He resumed his tongue work on Marco's body.

"C'mon, fucker, you're driving me crazy!" Marco protested. "Quit prickteasing me! Stop playing around and *do* it!"

"Who's playing around? This is serious business! You want me to do what—*this*, maybe?" Trent retorted. He paused to wet his lips. And then, quick as a flash, his tousled blond head sank into Marco's crotch and his warm, wet lips closed not around Marco's cock, as the other man had surely expected and hoped, but around one of his cum-swollen, hairy nuts.

"Ah! Jesus, man! Yeah! Suck on 'em!" Marco moaned, twisting his hips on the bed. "Work on those fucking balls!" Marco buried his hands in the bearded blond cop's hair and shoved his head down between his own spread thighs. Trent used his tongue to pull the bloated testicle all the way inside his mouth. Then he opened his mouth wider and crammed Marco's other ball inside. He closed his lips firmly around the loose flesh that joined the scrotum to the root of the cock and tongued the two spheres he had trapped in his mouth, rolling them around, washing them with his spit, which seemed to drive Marco wild with lust.

Marco pulled his legs up, bending them at the knees, and thrust his pelvis down against Trent's face as the blond sucked on his nuts. He tried to grab his own aching dick and jack off, but Trent promptly slapped his hand away. He wasn't about to let Marco off that easily. He wanted the stud to be completely in his power, unable to resist his erotic wiles.

When he felt that he had teased Marco enough, Trent released his balls, one at a time, letting the spit-soaked nuts bounce back into place between the stocky guy's thighs. He was panting for breath as he seized Marco's hard-on firmly around its thick base and bent the shaft of solid flesh back toward his lips. Trent planted a quick kiss on the tip and tasted another drop of leaked seminal fluid. He worked his tongue around the head of Marco's cut meat, teasing the especially sensitive, responsive area just below the flared crown. He ran the tip of his tongue along a throbbing blue vein until he reached the root of the phallus, then went back up, until, finally, taking a deep breath, he opened his mouth wide and went down on all that solid, male salami.

His lips closed around the shaft about halfway down its remarkable length, and his mouth was stuffed with Marco's hard cock as he struggled to relax to clear his throat and allow the huge, mushroom-like head of that prick to slide right down into it.

Marco sat up on the bed, which only drove his cock in deeper, and Trent was sure he was looking down and watching as Trent began to deep-throat him. The realization that he was being observed as he performed the act only made Trent suck harder. Marco's cock jerked violently between Trent's lips, as though he was about to pop his load right then and there, but Trent wanted to prolong the blow job for as long as possible before Marco exploded and gave his cocksucker the jism Trent so eagerly wanted to swallow.

* * * *

Trent's face was set in a grim look of intense concentration. He labored to take Marco's massive iron in his throat without choking on it. His face was beet-red under its bronzed tan. His hair, matted with sweat, was plastered to his forehead and cheeks. Some loose strands of it brushed sensuously against the hot skin of Marco's thighs and tickled his balls.

Trent was making guttural noises deep in his throat as he worked the muscles there to milk Marco's sweet-tasting cock. Marco, looking down, could see how his stiff ramrod was distending the other guy's throat, making it look thicker than usual. He saw Trent's lumpy Adam's apple bobbing rapidly up and down as the blond kept clearing his throat to make room for Marco's cockhead and snatching quick breaths whenever he could.

Marco ran trembling hands over Trent's shoulders, over his puffed-out cheeks. He felt the way his cock throbbed and twitched through the skin of Trent's throat.

"Lay down so I can blow you while you do me," he suggested.

Trent grunted a muffled, "Uh-huh." He didn't miss a stroke as he let most of Marco's prick slip from between his lips, keeping only the thick head in his mouth. Clumsily, the two naked men rearranged their sweating, muscular bodies into a tight sixty-nine position. Marco gasped at the sensation when, twisting his lower body around, he felt his cock turning within Trent's mouth and being scraped by the edges of his teeth for a second. But then they had their heads thrust between each other's thighs, and Trent was going all the way down on Marco's meat again, giving him incredible head, and Marco was staring at the uncircumcised head of Trent's own trembling fuck tool waving only inches from his hungry lips. He wet his lips quickly and shoved his face at that enticing bulk. His mouth engulfed the head and he sucked most of the thick shaft into his mouth in a single, eager gulp.

Trent grunted, and his hips jerked in involuntary reaction. Marco spread his hands over the lush, tanned mounds of his trick's butch ass cheeks and, digging his fingers into the firm buttock flesh, he pulled Trent against his face until the head of that delicious hard-on struck the back of his mouth and jabbed into his throat, and Marco's gaping, cock-filled lips touched Trent's balls and brushed against his tawny cock hair.

Anything you can do, I can do better, cocksucker! He began to deep-throat the other man with the same lusty enthusiasm that Trent was exerting at his own groin.

* * * *

The two naked men fed greedily at one another's crotches. Their heads bobbed up and down, and their big, hard dicks slid wetly in and out of their throats and were caressed by their warm, sucking lips. Trent felt the bristly hairs of Marco's coarse beard stubble chafing his thighs as they rubbed against Marco's cheeks. In mock retaliation, Trent rubbed his own bearded chin back and forth over Marco's skin, massaging it with his silky facial hair.

Suck it, you bastard—really suck that thing! Trent wanted to shout, but all that emerged from his cock-crammed throat was a muffled, sexy series of gurgling and chortling noises. *Suck on my dick, you bastard! Suck the jism right out of me!*

Marco was getting as good as he gave. The two men coaxed and teased each other's hard tools steadily toward a double explosion. They were lying on their sides with their arms thrown around each other's hips and thighs, each man pulling the other's prick into his throat as he sucked. Marco worked one hand between Trent's buttocks. The heel of his hand brushed over the thick blond fur that lined the deep cleft, and his fingertips touched the tender pink flesh that guarded the entrance to Trent's manhole. With the tip of his long middle finger, Marco pressed the tensed ring of muscle that surrounded the actual opening. He teased it until it yielded, and the first joint of his finger slipped inside that hot, tight anus to the knuckle. Trent grunted again and ate Marco's cock even faster when he felt that insistent digit working around inside his butt.

Marco pushed the second joint of his finger up Trent's ass and really began to finger-fuck the big, sweating stud whose uncontrollable shudders and gasps clearly betrayed his excitement at this invasion of his asshole. Marco tongued the thick cock he had trapped deep in his throat and forced the rest of his middle finger through Trent's sphincter. His fingertip rubbed into the hyper-responsive nub of Trent's anus, and the blond man jerked his powerful hips as he started to come in Marco's mouth almost at once. That blunt finger up his ass plus the expert blow job was just too much! He started to blast his nuts down Marco's throat as the dark-haired guy gripped his ass cheeks to hold his cock steady in his mouth.

* * * *

Marco thrilled to the salty tang of Trent's cum on his tongue when the first wad of jism was spat into his mouth. He held his breath and kept right on sucking that big dick as it shuddered and quaked in his mouth and fired volley upon volley of high-velocity sperm down his throat. His mouth was filled with the sticky stuff, and he had to swallow fast and repeatedly to keep from choking on Trent's seemingly inexhaustible load, which the big, blond stud emptied into his mouth.

* * * *

Trent wasn't a selfish lover. Although his whole body was shivering in the throes of orgasm, he didn't take his mouth off Marco's cock or stop sucking for a second, even as he poured his hot cream out into his trick's throat and belly. Quite to the contrary, he jammed all of Marco's meat down his own throat in a frenzy of lust, and, his face turning purple from the exertion and the lack of oxygen, he applied a fierce, nonstop suction to the head of Marco's rod in a desperate effort to bring the other stud off before his own climax subsided.

He succeeded. Marco almost gagged on the last few spurts of Trent's jism as his own orgasm obviously took him by surprise and upset his breath control. His dick leaped and thrashed about like a live eel inside Trent's throat, and then a veritable torrent of semen gushed out of his prick and flooded Trent's esophagus and guts. The blond cop gulped it all down like a man dying of thirst in the desert who'd just made it to a water hole before collapsing. Marco shot again and again. His orgasm seemed to go on forever, spasm after spasm convulsing his sturdy frame. His arms and legs thrashed, entangled with Trent's. Finally, as his cock spat out its last angry spurts, Marco let Trent's dick pop out of his mouth. Trent heard him gasp for breath. Out of breath himself, Trent flared his nostrils and desperately inhaled through them, to fill his overheated lungs with fresh air before he passed out from the sheer intensity of the experience.

Trent's cock slapped against Marco's cheek and left a smear of cum across Marco's face and mouth as the blond's last drops dribbled from the gaping piss slit of his spent organ. Marco fell back on the bed and let Trent finish sucking him off, greedily swallowing the rest of his foamy load. He threw one arm over his forehead to wipe the sweat away before it ran down into his eyes and blinded him. Smiling, he ran his dry tongue around his lips to lick up Trent's cum.

Christ! What a come!

"What a come!" he repeated aloud. "God damn it, I thought I was never going to stop shooting in your mouth! What a great fucking come!"

Trent took his mouth off Marco's drained prick long enough to reply, "I never wanted you to stop, fucker." Then he began to lap up all the cum that had dribbled from Marco's sagging, deflating erection. He used his tongue to swab the fat penis from its base to its tip, then back again, licking it clean. The salty tang of Marco's semen stung his tongue. As both young men relaxed and recovered from their violent climaxes. Trent licked up every drop of semen he could find, taking his time, determined that none of the cum would escape him. He reluctantly kissed Marco's cock and balls good-bye for the time being before throwing his big body on top of Marco's and seeking the other man's mouth.

They kissed passionately, breathlessly, their tongues thrust into each other's mouths, until Trent could no longer distinguish the taste of his own cum on his partner's tongue from the residue of the other guy's sticky load left in his own mouth. Trent reached down to fondle Marco's now-limp prick as they kissed and hugged each other in a bath of sweat and cum, their wet bodies sliding freely against each other.

If this is what police work is going to be like, I may have to volunteer to work overtime!

Chapter Four: Suppressed Desires

Zerk had a high sex drive and was susceptible to male beauty. And Trent Carothers, damn him, wasn't just beautiful, he was a stunner. The slightly unkempt look he affected, for the purposes of their undercover work, only added to his appeal. Zerk preferred them butch. He might not have fallen so hard for a young guy who was merely pretty. There was a rough edge to Trent's good looks that was especially provocative.

And so Zerk endured some nights in which he found it difficult to fall asleep. His bed became a fertile ground for erotic fantasies, all of them inspired by his sexy new partner.

In his heated, overactive imagination, he and Trent were already fuck buddies, and they'd established a nighttime routine. First, Zerk would get his golden-haired, tawny-bodied young stud lover's massive fuck tool fully erect and well-lubricated with his spit by sucking on it for minutes on end, maybe as long as a quarter of an hour or so, nonstop. Then he'd wriggle his butt against Trent's crotch to turn the big guy on even more, begging him, "Fuck me, stud, shove it up my ass and fuck me, hard!" Trent was a fast learner, Zerk had already discovered, and so at last Zerk's butch ass, which he didn't surrender to just anybody, would end up being screwed like never before. They'd fuck like hot, horny animals until they both spurted their hot jism helplessly, coming and coming together.

His impassioned nocturnal fantasies always made Zerk's cock swell into erection immediately, as the thick, rounded head slid out from within its sheath of dark-colored foreskin and glistened with moisture and oozing cum. Zerk couldn't help himself. Jerking off alone was kid stuff, in his opinion. But he gave in every time and abandoned himself to his sensuous thoughts. He would spit into his palm to wet it, take hold of his pleading prick, and stroke that super-sensitive, throbbing flesh as it grew thicker and longer, harder and stiffer, pulsating with pent-up lust. And, in Zerk's imagination, Trent would materialize as though by magic next to him on the bed, in the stifling, sweat-inducing heat of the bedroom, as horny for Zerk as Zerk was for him, as eager for the two of them to unite their bodies in sex in every way possible.

The phantom Trent would urge Zerk on in his sexy, throaty voice. "Yeah, partner, please fuck me. Fuck my ass. Stick your big, hard cock up my asshole all the way to the hilt—I really want to get fucked! I've been saving it for you, so do it now. Ram it up into me, up my hot ass. Fuck me!"

And Zerk, panting with lust, would lie back on his bed and try to imagine what it would be like to oblige the other cop.

On other nights, Trent's voice would be soft, a half-ashamed whisper as he licked his bearded lips to wet them and then moaned, "Let me suck it! Your big, hard dick is so beautiful, Zerk, that I want to suck on it forever. I want to be your sex slave. I want to please you. I want to satisfy you with my mouth. Oh, don't come for a long, long time. Please, let me have it, sir, let me take it in my mouth and down into my throat. Choke me with it, if you want to, I don't care. Just let me suck it! Let me get my hot tongue down around it. Let me deep-throat you. Oh, you stud cop, you! I want to blow you so bad—I want to taste your jism!"

Masturbating himself into an erotic frenzy as the sweat ran from his powerful, naked body, Zerk would spread his legs, grit his teeth, and gasp out breathless encouragements to his phantom lover. "Yeah, Trent, suck it, suck my hot dick, you sexy little motherfucker! You hung son-of-a-bitching stud! Take it, since you want it so bad. Suck it, oh yeah, just like that, only do it harder! Take it all, the rest of it, go all the way down on it. Get all of it down your throat and suck it good. Make me come. I'm almost ready to come in your mouth. When I do, take it all, swallow my hot load, you fucker. Use that tongue of yours to lick the cum right out of my cock—oh, shit!"

Finally, he would blast, all over himself, imagining the whole while that it was Trent's mouth and throat receiving his cum, drinking it down, or that he was pumping his semen up into the depths of that muscular stud ass of Trent's. Zerk would get himself hard again and beat off frantically for a second, even a third time, pushing his body to its limits of endurance before, exhausted, he would at last sink into a deep, contented sleep, filled with sensually colored dreams.

In his calmer moments, Zerk admitted to himself that he had no evidence whatsoever that Trent Carothers was gay. The kid might even still be a virgin, to judge by his general air of genial naiveté about most matters sexual. Planning to seduce him seemed hopeless, an exercise in frustration for sure. Not that Zerk ever stopped thinking about the possibility!

The question, as far as he was concerned, was not *whether* to try to seduce Trent, it was how to go about it. How to play the cards he'd been dealt without taking the chance of scaring the big, dumb rookie off!

At work, Zerk had a reputation for being tough, and good at his job. He had few secrets from his colleagues, and his sexual orientation was not one of them.

Zerk had to snicker at the thought that Trent was probably the only cop in his precinct who wasn't one hundred percent sure that he was gay. It was common knowledge around headquarters that the big, tough-talking Zerk swung both ways, but with a definite preference for male sex partners, and that he liked it rough. Zerk knew for a fact that some of the guys had even been known to joke about it among themselves, warning each other, for example, to watch out whenever Zerk pulled out a pair of handcuffs. The careless police officer, rather than some perp in custody, might end up being the one who got cuffed!

That might not be such a bad idea, so far as Zerk was concerned. He could think of two or three of his fellow cops whom he wouldn't mind having at his sexual disposal!

The police commissioner himself had discovered Zerk's not-so-well-kept secret one day when he'd strolled into the locker room with the intention of congratulating Zerk for a job well done during a recent bust. Zerk had been changing his clothes in front of his open locker, and he got a little flustered when the other man made his sudden, unannounced appearance at his side. The commissioner had caught a glimpse of the pin-up that Zerk was trying to conceal on the back of the locker door and had laughingly swung the door wide open to get a look at the "hot piece of ass you've been jerking off over, Zerk." The photo had turned out to be a centerfold of two guys fucking, nude and in glowing color, torn out of a gay porno magazine. The image had caught Zerk's fancy, and he definitely got off on looking at it. When the commissioner had recovered somewhat from his attack of near-apoplexy, he'd simply told Zerk to "carry on," and then, as an afterthought, had suggested he report to his office later for "a little man-to-man chat."

Zerk had his resignation letter from the force already composed in his head when he showed up. He never told anybody just what went on in the commissioner's office. Afterward, he knew, a wild rumor went around the precinct to the effect that the commissioner had admitted that he, too, was gay, and that he and Zerk got it on together right there in the office, imitating what the two models in the sex photo were doing on top of the desk!

Zerk wished he'd been that lucky. But, in fact, the commissioner was decent about the whole thing, and he and Zerk reached an understanding. The upshot was that Zerk went right on about his business as though nothing had happened. Since the department had a no-discrimination policy, and was, in fact, trying to recruit more gay men and women as cops, and since Zerk was well liked by his fellow officers, it was really no big deal in the long run.

* * * *

Meanwhile, Trent was experiencing some erotic turmoil of his own. Eager to make good and to prove himself on the job, he was rather neglecting his sex life, and was suffering considerable frustration as a result. He found himself resorting to nightly masturbation before he went to sleep.

His consolation was that he seemed to be accepted by the other cops as a member of the team. And, because Trent was so obviously butch-looking and -acting, nobody suspected that he, too, was gay or bothered to confirm his increasing suspicions about his new partner and mentor. With one exception.

One afternoon, Trent was changing his clothes, in the locker room, when Alejandro De Soto happened to pass by. De Soto paused and gave Trent the once-over without making any effort to conceal the fact. It made Trent a little uncomfortable. The other cop was friendly enough, but Trent couldn't say that they'd exactly gotten to know each other very well.

"Is something on your mind, De Soto?" Trent finally asked.

"Yeah. I was just curious about whether Kostopoulos has made his move yet."

"What do mean, 'made his move'?"

"Jesus, you *are* dumb, aren't you? Whether he's put the make on you."

Trent could feel his face reddening. "Aw, knock it off, De Soto."

"You think I'm kidding?"

"I know you are," Trent bluffed, trying to project a confidence in the matter he was, in fact, far from feeling.

"You wait. You'd better watch your back, kid. The minute you turn it on that horny Greek bastard, he's likely to shove his cock up your ass and pop your cherry. Don't say I didn't warn you."

"Thanks for the warning," Trent said sarcastically. "I'll keep it in mind. I assume you're speaking from personal experience?"

De Soto scowled at him. "Watch your mouth, rookie."

"Sorry. I don't want to fight."

"You may end up having to fight or fuck, like they say in prison," De Soto taunted him. "You know what they call one guy fucking another one up the ass in Greece?"

"I can't imagine."

"Birth control." De Soto snorted with raucous laughter at his own politically incorrect joke as he moved away from Trent's locker. "Like I said, you better watch your ass, rookie," was his parting shot.

Trent was rather disturbed by the incident. He wanted to get along with all of his fellow policemen and -women, and he certainly didn't want to make an enemy of De Soto. He noticed that De Soto and Zerk kidded each other, sexually, all the time. Both men had a penchant for gay jokes and teasing, the more explicit and outrageous, the better. Trent was tempted to tell Zerk about the encounter with De Soto to get his reaction, but he thought better of it.

And Trent had plenty of other things to think about as he got used to his vice work. He still came away from the long nights spent touring the bars and baths feeling physically dirty and emotionally drained by what he saw. One early morning, he stumbled across an orgy room in a leather club, where several leather-jacketed muscle men were abusing two writhing, naked slaves, using their gloved hands to slap them around as they "forced" them to kneel on the dirty floor and lick their boots.

"Come on, big guy, join in the fun," one of the glowering top men invited Trent. "These pieces of shit will do anything you want!"

"Ah, no thanks," Trent replied. "I just want to watch."

"Don't just watch," the second top man invited him. "Whip it out and beat it off. Let's see what you've got."

Trent had demurred, pleading fatigue. Shrugging, the two sadists lost interest in him and went on abusing their willing victims.

Trent reported to Zerk, later, how disgusted he had been.

Predictably, Zerk was less than sympathetic.

"You should've at least pulled your dick out, like the dude invited you to, and let the two bottoms blow you," he advised. "Just watching the action and not joining in, it could look suspicious. Haven't you ever gotten into *any* S and M?"

It was the first time that Zerk had ever asked him anything directly about his own sex life, and Trent was so startled by the blunt question that he'd simply blurted out, after a moment's guilty hesitation, "No, not really," by way of considerable understatement. "Just a little fooling around with it, maybe, here and there."

Zerk, to Trent's relief, or his disappointment, didn't pursue the subject. Afterward, when he had time to think about it, Trent wasn't sure which response he really felt. Maybe he ought to just come out and admit to Zerk that he was gay.

And Trent had to admit to himself that there was perhaps more than a little hypocrisy in the revulsion he claimed to have felt. It might've been more accurate for him to say that he felt he *ought* to be disgusted. On a deeper level, he was aroused by what he'd seen. All of this exposure to the more sordid side of the local gay scene, with its unrelenting emphasis upon sex, was beginning to get to him. It was tapping some need deep within him—a need which he'd denied himself, ever since he'd joined the police force.

Chapter Five: Experimentation

Trent had been a practicing homosexual long before he became a college football star, let alone a policeman.

He had had two gay affairs when he was eighteen. His first time was within the protecting walls of a house under construction in the quiet, suburban neighborhood where he'd grown up. A buddy lured him down there with the promise of marijuana. After they'd smoked the pot, he urged Trent to pull down his jeans and his briefs and show him his dick, and then he did the same. They compared cock sizes, with Trent's stoner friend making the predictable, crude jokes, and then they held and rubbed each other's potent, young pricks until all of a sudden it happened—they ejaculated, virtually at the same moment, shooting their high-pressured young sperm all over the place. This was *much* better than jerking off alone, Trent decided. The feeling of gratitude that Trent felt toward his buddy for having shown him the ropes amounted to a kind of first, innocent love.

They got together frequently after that, always getting high first before they engaged in mutual masturbation. When his friend's family moved out of town a few months later, Trent thought that his sex life was effectively over before it had really begun. But he was wrong.

At the time, Trent was already starting to grow into the impressive size he would attain as a man. He was over six feet, gangling and awkward, but muscular, and the girls always went for him at the kind of parties where liquor flowed and inevitably led to pairings-off for necking and petting. Trent couldn't understand why the other guys were so excited by all this, since embracing a girl just made him uneasy, and the contact of their cold, wet lips against his was repulsive to him. But he did his best to go along with the gang, pushing his mouth down hard against the girls' during these make-out sessions, and even sliding his hands down inside their bras to fondle their breasts.

Afterward, when the guys compared notes, smirking and exaggerating, Trent listened politely, but he still thought it was all a stupid waste of time and energy. When he had erotic daydreams, they were always about his horny, well-hung, sexually precocious jerk-off buddy, who had taken care of his needs so well before he'd moved away.

Trent was somewhat disconcerted to realize that he often caught himself speculating about his current circle of male friends—trying to decide which of them he found the most attractive, and which of them might be persuaded, under the right circumstances, to engage in a little guy-to-guy sex play.

Am I gay? Trent thought. *No, I'm just lonely, and horny. Maybe I'm bisexual. I'm curious, that's all. I want to try a variety of things.*

Within a year, though, he had formed a new homosexual attachment. This liaison was with a husky, sunburned, big-biceped youth who pumped gas at a neighborhood service station, and who pumped iron at a neighborhood gym in his spare time. Trent struck up an acquaintance with the guy, who got him interested in working out with weights. He was older than Trent, nineteen, but not very bright. Most of the other guys made fun of him, although they envied his solid physique.

Trent, who was wiser now and knew more about what was possible, picked up on the bodybuilder's signals. One night after working out together, he went to his apartment with him, penetrated him from behind at his invitation, and fucked him to orgasm. His new buddy was intelligent enough to insist that Trent use a condom, and he took it like a man, moaning and declaring over and over again that Trent's cock was the biggest one he'd ever had up his ass—which added to the intense pleasure Trent found in the act.

He cornholed the guy regularly after that, but once again, the affair came to a premature end when his fuck buddy went away to a vocational school in another town to study automotive repair.

In college, the pickings were better for Trent. There had been enough time for other young men his age to decide what their sexual preferences were. They were away from home and direct parental control, and, of course, there were also a few eager, though discreet, professors and instructors, who made good use of the pool of horny young males who were so readily available to them.

Trent had a couple of physically soothing but emotionally unsatisfying contacts with his classmates before he was approached by the handsome assistant football coach, whose name was Dominic and who said he wanted to recruit Trent for the team.

As the coach was leaving his dormitory room after their little man-to-man pep talk, Trent did what he had rarely dared to do up until then—he took the initiative. He gave the older man a lewd, inviting smile, and asked in a desire-husky growl, "Is that *all* you wanted to recruit me for?"

To his delight, Dominic turned around at once, seized him, and pushed him down on the unmade bed, his hands already tearing all of Trent's clothes off his sturdy body while his tongue plunged deep into his open, panting, willing mouth.

"You'd better lock the door," Dominic gasped. He was no fool. He wanted Trent, but he wasn't going to risk getting caught, and losing his job, over him. "And what about your roommate?"

"He's got a class," Trent replied. "And even if he were to come back early, we've got a signal. If one of us puts this sign on the door, it means he's in here either jerking off or getting laid." The sign was a "Do Not Disturb" one, swiped from a motel. "This'll be the first chance I've had to use it for anything other than jerking off, myself," Trent admitted. "I'm not very experienced, I'm afraid."

"That's okay. Put the sign out, lock the door, and then I'll start teaching you everything you need to know!"

When Trent came back to the bed, they kissed passionately, their hands groping for each other's crotches and toying with what they discovered there. Trent had Dominic's big cock in his fist, and he thrilled to the feel of it, to the heavy weight of the coach's hard-muscled, bronzed body pressed sweatily against his. He was excited, too, by the way the husky stud explored Trent's body as familiarly as though they were old lovers, who'd shared their bodies often, intimately, and with relish. Trent threw himself into their rough-and-tumble foreplay as they rolled about on the mattress. He pushed Dominic off him and began to use his tongue and his hands on as much of the older guy's superbly muscled physique as he could reach.

He quickly worked his way down to Dominic's crotch and sucked his penis into his mouth, deep-throating him in the way he'd learned in the course of his brief but intense sexual education to date. Dominic grunted and began to jerk off Trent's impressive nine inches with both of his calloused fists. Then he took one hand away and used the other to feed the head of Trent's hard dick into his mouth, and the two naked men were soon sixty-nining as though there'd be no tomorrow.

They had sucked on each other's cocks for long, delightful minutes when Dominic abruptly broke away from Trent and began kissing him on the thighs and belly.

Then Dominic paused, looked Trent in the eyes, and with a strange, intense look on his face, he asked a question that would have far-reaching consequences for Trent. "Are you into any B and D at all?"

"I don't know," Trent said. "What's B and D?"

"Bondage and discipline. You know, when you tie up the other guy and force him to do things. Treat him like a sex slave."

Trent was more than a little shocked that Dominic was into such things, but he tried not to show it. He didn't want the coach to think he was just some dumb kid who didn't know anything.

"I don't think I want to be tied up," he said, warily.

"That's all right. Have you ever fucked a guy?"

"Sure, lots of times," Trent boasted. "They all said they liked it."

"I'll bet they did, once they had that big dick of yours in them," Dominic said salaciously. "Okay, you can tie me up and fuck me. You can pretend you're raping my ass. It'll turn us both on, I promise you. You got anything here to grease that horse cock of yours up with before you shove it in me?"

Trent fumbled in the drawer where he kept his supply of condoms, and a tube of lubricant, and tossed both items onto the bed.

"Good!" Dominic had retrieved one of his own training shoes, which he'd kicked off when they'd both stripped, and he was busying himself yanking the lace out of the eyelets. "You can use this to restrain me, stud," he urged, his voice tight with desire. "Now, sit up and let me put the rubber on you and grease up your cock."

Trent obeyed. His nine-inch fuck tool throbbed almost painfully between his tanned thighs as he anticipated taking this hot Italian-American number up the ass. Dominic wasn't a callow boy. He was a mature man, obviously very experienced sexually, and Trent was eager to learn from him.

Dominic put the condom on Trent, carefully rolling it all the way down to the base of his shaft. The rubber had a tiny semen reservoir tip, so that it almost made Trent's erection resemble an inflated balloon. Dominic next squeezed a dab of the lubricant onto his palm, rubbed his hands together, and then massaged them all over the latex covering of Trent's cock, slicking it up with the lube until the long, thick bludgeon gleamed from the sticky moisture.

"Yeah, that ought to do it," Dominic said. "I'm going to need some of that stuff myself, if I'm going to take you!"

He put a second dab of the lube on his fingertips, reached behind himself, and massaged the lubricant thoroughly into his ass. Grunting with satisfaction, he put the cap back on the tube, set it aside, and wiped his hands on his own muscular thighs. He took both pillows from the head of the bed and plumped them down on top of each other in the middle of the mattress. Dominic rolled over onto his belly and positioned his hands together, wrists crossed, in the small of his back, like a criminal waiting for a cop to slap a pair of handcuffs on him.

"Tie my hands together!" he gasped, his excitement audible.

Trent took the shoelace, wound it around Dominic's wrists, and began to tie a knot.

"Tighter," Dominic told him. "Pull it really tight. Don't leave any play in it. I want to be your prisoner, man! I want to be helpless, so you can do anything you damn well want to do, to me!"

"Man, you're really a freak, aren't you?"

"Yeah," Dominic gasped. "I'm a total fucking freak!"

Trent found the situation oddly, inexplicably arousing. When he was restrained, his wrists bound tightly together behind his back, Dominic rolled over, onto his back. He stared lustfully at Trent, who watched him as he squirmed to position his butt on top of the piled-up pillows, lifting his ass into an ideal position to receive Trent's cock.

"Are you going to rape my dago ass?" Dominic asked, crudely.

"I sure as hell am." As he made the threat, Trent was already moving into position, on his knees on the bed.

"Wait! You got a dirty jockstrap?" Dominic asked.

"Sure. Why?"

"Is it *really* dirty?" the assistant coach pressed.

"It's filthy. I wore it when I worked out in the gym, this morning. It's right over there, in the laundry bag."

"Get it! Put it down here beside me, on the bed."

"I thought *you* were supposed to be the sex slave, and *I* was supposed to be the guy giving the orders," Trent grumbled, good-humoredly. But he found the funky athletic supporter and deposited it on the mattress, beside them.

"Oh, fuck! I'm getting so turned on, I can't stand it," Dominic moaned. "I'm getting turned on, just from imagining you working out and wearing that jock. Your hot fucking body, all wet with sweat—

your big dick inside the pouch of that jock—! Jesus, my asshole is tingling already, because it wants you in there so bad! Okay, now you kneel on the bed between my fucking legs and shove your cock right between my buns! Get that big dick of yours in my ass and fuck me with it!"

Trent, feeling excited yet nervous, got into the position Dominic wanted, and guided his dick into the deep, hairy crack that separated the older man's smooth, white ass cheeks.

"Shove it in me hard!" Dominic gritted when Trent felt the tip of his slippery hard-on rub against his coach's anal rim, and hesitated before beginning to push. "Just ram it right up into my shithole, fucker! Take me! Rape my ass!"

Trent groaned as he did what the other guy wanted. He was astonished by how violently Dominic was responding to what Trent was doing to him. The guy was a fucking freak!

* * * *

Dominic was ecstatic. Not only had he connected, sexually, with this hot freshman, he'd already managed to talk Trent into topping him, at least to a limited extent. The kid had real potential!

As for Dominic, he liked it either way, but at the moment he was making the most of being the bottom. He always liked to feel a hard cock ramming deep into his guts, and, if the initial thrust usually cost him some pain, he prided himself on being man enough to take it without complaint. And he was taking it this time, all right. All nine inches of it, he thought with grim, hot satisfaction as Trent shoved forward blindly and Dominic felt the boy's blunt cock slam right through his carefully relaxed sphincter muscle and penetrate his anal opening. It hurt, all right, but not as much as he'd anticipated, and so, groaning more with lust that discomfort, he squirmed his butt to literally push Trent's cock into his hole.

* * * *

"Oh, yeah, man!" Dominic shouted. "Really give it to me, now! Shove the rest in, all of it. I can take it. I want it! Oh, fucking Christ! Give me the rest of your big dick! Fuck me with it! Shove the rest of it right up my ass and fuck me with it!"

Wild with lust now, Trent jabbed his cock into that beautiful, butch ass. He encountered a momentary resistance as, despite Dominic's extraordinary anal control, his powerful anal muscles knotted up in reaction to the invading prick. But then, with incredible, breathtaking ease, that tight, hot male hole just opened up, and his cock slid right up into the hot sheath of ass flesh until it was buried to the hilt inside Dominic's steamy tunnel, and those same strong anal muscles clamped down on Trent's hard tool and began to squeeze and caress and tug at it.

Trent gasped and fell forward, grabbing both of Dominic's ankles and using them to hold his legs up and apart as he drove himself in and out of his ass. His mouth found Dominic's and kissed him frantically, his tongue stabbing into Dominic's open mouth as violently, and in the same rhythm, as his cock was thrusting up into his asshole.

With an agility unusual for a guy of his massive build, Dominic flung his legs up and threw them over Trent's shoulders, so that the two men were locked tightly together in humping position. Trent's cock was jammed deep in Dominic's body, and their chests were crushed together, with Dominic's own pulsating hard-on trapped between their taut bellies. Trent's probing tongue restlessly explored the interior of Dominic's mouth as they drooled their spittle onto each other's faces in their uncontrollable excitement.

Dominic's big arm muscles bulged and rippled as he yanked uselessly at the shoelace that was tied around his wrists, behind his back.

"Fuck me! I can't do anything to stop you, can I?" Dominic

moaned between kisses, losing himself in his fantasy of being an unwilling victim, who was being taken by force.

"No, you can't," Trent gasped. "Your ass belongs to me, bitch!"

He quickly found his pace and began to screw the hell out of the assistant coach's ass, loving every wild, hot, sweaty second of their uninhibited coupling. He nearly came on the spot when Dominic, abruptly tearing his mouth away from Trent's, ducked down and, pressing his open mouth to Trent's left pec, began to suck and bite and chew on his tit.

"Bitch," Trent panted. "Horny, fucking bitch!"

In not altogether playful retaliation, he shoved his right hand between their jammed-together bodies, took Dominic's huge, throbbing hard-on in his fist, and began to squeeze and jerk it with the kind of ruthlessness he knew would turn the big man on.

"Ah! Not so rough, fucker!" Dominic pleaded. "Don't jerk it so hard!"

"What're you going to do about it?" Trent taunted him. "Your hands are tied behind your back—go ahead and stop me, if you can!"

"Fucker! Oh, you dirty fucker! You animal!"

"Shut the fuck up."

"Make me!" Dominic dared him.

Trent gave Dominic a light, tentative slap on the face with the open palm of his other hand. "Shut up," he repeated.

"No, not like that!" Dominic's voice sounded hoarse with excitement. "Use the jockstrap! Shove it against my face! Gag me with it!"

Trent continued to work on Dominic's cock with his right hand, massaging it roughly. With his left hand, he grabbed the jock, wadded it up in his hand, and pressed it against Dominic's face, covering his mouth and nose with the pouch.

"All right," he jeered. "You like fantasizing about me wearing this so much—well, here's your chance! Go for it! Knock yourself out, you fucking freak!"

Dominic inhaled deeply, then emitted a deep groan of pure lust. He made a half-hearted, token effort to turn his head to one side and break the contact with the athletic supporter.

"Oh, no, you don't." Trent pressed the jock more forcefully against the lower part of Dominic's face, holding it in place. "You're the one who wanted this. You asked for it, so now you're going to get it. I think I will gag you with it. That ought to shut you up!" He forced part of the wadded pouch between Dominic's lips. Dominic tried to yell something that sounded like "fucker," but the outburst was effectively muffled by the jockstrap gag.

Trent's humiliation of his partner had a dramatic effect. The athletic, purely masculine associations inspired by the jock seemed to push Dominic over the edge. The combined effect of Trent's fist on his cock and the unrelenting pressure of the young stud's dick against his prostate triggered an explosive climax, deep in his pelvis. Dominic came. He bit down on the jockstrap wedged between his teeth, and ejaculated. All over the sheets, all over his own sweating, writhing torso, all over Trent's belly and chest and masturbating hand, as their bodies ground together in the tight, gritty intimacy of sexual release.

"Whore!" Trent cried. "You dirty, perverted whore! Fuck! You're doing it to me! I'm coming, too!"

It was true. The look on Dominic's face as he chewed on the jockstrap, combined with the friction of Dominic's rapidly-flexing ass on his cock, had pushed Trent over the precipice of his own orgasm. His prick, barely contained by the condom, burst inside that tight, butch asshole. In his ejaculatory abandon, Trent drove himself in and out of the seething anal tunnel, until Dominic, still gagged by the jock, was grunting and sobbing with pleasure under him.

Trent had never before experienced so intense and so prolonged a climax. It seemed to go on for minutes on end, with his seemingly depleted cock drawing on new, unsuspected reserves of semen stored deep in his body. At last, though, Trent, too, was spent. He slumped down on top of Dominic's body. Dominic's throat and chest and stomach were wet not only with sweat, but streaked by rivulets of his own semen, and Trent, too, was drenched in the slimy fluid as he lay panting on Dominic's chest, with his arms wrapped tightly around him.

When he got his breath back, Trent withdrew from Dominic, rolled off him, and got rid of the rubber. Then he turned Dominic onto his side and undid the knot in the shoelace, freeing his wrists. Dominic sat up and rubbed his wrists.

"God damn. That left marks on your wrists," Trent noticed. "I'm sorry."

"Don't apologize. That was fantastic. These'll go away in a day or so. I'll rub some vitamin E oil on them when I get home."

"But what if somebody notices in the meantime?"

Dominic grinned at him. "So what if they do? Who's going to have the balls to say anything? Don't worry about it. I loved every minute of that scene, Trent. That was an incredible turn-on for me. Thank you."

Dominic gave him a kiss.

That was the first time they had sex, but it was hardly the last. They were insatiable for each other's bodies, and even after a hard day's training, it took very little to persuade them to start fooling around with each other. They indulged in prickteasing foreplay that inevitably led to many other torrid sex sessions. These took place in the shower after practice when the other guys on the team were gone, or in the assistant coach's office behind a carefully locked door, or in Trent's dormitory room, with the Do Not Disturb sign posted on the door. Most often, though, they indulged themselves in the secure privacy of Dominic's off-campus apartment.

Trent discovered just how much Dominic liked to be restrained during sex, especially while he was being fucked. He and Trent experimented with a variety of wrist restraints, including rope, rawhide cord, handcuffs, and the kind of padded leather wrist cuffs linked by a short length of chain that were sold in sex shops especially for bondage and discipline scenes.

The big double bed in the bedroom of Dominic's apartment had been selected by him on the basis of its sturdy steel frame. The four metal bedposts were massive, and each one was topped by a large, spherical finial. Dominic liked to lie flat on his back on the bed with his arms tied to the two bedposts on either side of the headboard. On special occasions, when he was exceptionally horny, he would turn over onto his belly, spread his arms and legs wide, and allow Trent to bind his wrists and ankles to all four bedposts. Then he would let Trent fuck him, not only with his cock, but with his extensive collection of butt plugs and dildos.

Meanwhile, Trent found, in football, the sport he had been looking for, just as he found his first real gay lover in Dominic. It was hard to separate the two in his mind. Nothing in other sports had prepared him for the bruising delight of real body contact with other males or the shameless camaraderie of the locker room. Nearly all of the other players on the team were straight, as far as Trent could tell without actually cruising them, but Trent immensely enjoyed just being around all that husky male nudity, swapping sex stories that were purely fictional ones, on his part. He even pretended to be interested in the young female sluts on campus.

As a result of their discretion, no one except Dominic's other tricks ever suspected that he and his star player were balling their brains out together every chance they got. Trent discovered that tying Dominic up then verbally abusing him while shoving his cock down Dominic's throat or up his ass and humping away madly until he lost all his sperm, was an even better high than winning a game.

Dominic didn't demand monogamy, and Trent cheated on him every now and then. These flings were usually with fellow students, football groupies who admired Trent's athletic prowess, and whose hero-worship of him easily spilled over into lust. After a game, whether the team won or lost, the players would quickly shower and change clothes, then head out to a favorite local bar to celebrate or just to unwind and blow off steam. The bar would be crawling with fans, many of whom happened to be willing coeds or town girls. The manager of the bar would always make sure that the players were plied with free food and drink. It was good for business to have the popular football players patronizing the establishment in such close proximity to the regular paying customers. And, of course, any of the women who wanted to literally rub shoulders, or other body parts, with a couple of the young college studs knew that the bar was where they could find them.

And so did the occasional college boy, or local man, who was bold enough to try his luck. By the end of the evening's drunken revelry, there would always be several girls and older women clustered around the players' table for them to choose from, if they were so inclined. Trent usually had no difficulty identifying the guys who were interested in *him*. They tended to be less aggressive, even shy, making their availability apparent to him without doing anything to draw general attention to themselves. It was a subtle game and one that Trent enjoyed playing. His strategy was to strike up a conversation with the guy he liked, and, eventually—usually under the pretense that he'd had enough to drink—leave the bar with him, just the two of them, ostensibly to go get some coffee, so Trent could sober up. They usually skipped the coffee and headed directly for the nearest bed.

Trent was under no illusions. He never deluded himself that these guys were interested in him because he was such a brilliant conversationalist or because of his academic record. No, they wanted to go home with him because he was a football hero with an attractive face and a hot body. He was a sex object, fulfilling a fantasy.

What was strange was that Trent increasingly found himself vaguely dissatisfied with "vanilla sex," as he now thought of it. He preferred the slight kinkiness of what he and Dominic did together. The dynamics of their sex, in which the two men indulged in role-playing, never got boring.

Their relationship continued throughout Trent's four years at college.

Since he was no scholar, Trent gave some serious thought to trying to pursue a career in professional football. But he doubted that he was really good enough. And, speaking of sex objects and fantasies, he had always been interested in police work. Men in uniform, in general, and cops in particular, turned him on.

He took the police department's entrance exam almost as a lark, accompanying a fellow graduate who was serious about getting into law enforcement, to give him moral support. Trent was surprised when he scored so well and the academy accepted him. Police work now seemed like a definite, viable alternative.

The physical fitness training, which some recruits found grueling, was almost a joke for a young athlete in Trent's superb condition, but he found the firearms training more challenging, and he worked hard to master it. He was still so naïve about the police force in general that he didn't know, at first, that cops had to buy their own uniforms and guns. His father paid for his first service weapon, a Glock 22 40-caliber semi-automatic pistol, a strange gift for a man to give his son on his twenty-fourth birthday.

A few days later, Trent reported to his first assignment, as a fledging vice cop.

Chapter Six: A Surprise Encounter

Unlike some police officers, Trent had little difficulty adjusting to the irregular schedule required by undercover work. He lived alone, after all, and he was unattached. There was no one in his life to complain about the late nights he kept.

When Trent finally did have a day off, he almost didn't know what to do with himself. In the evening, especially, he found himself getting bored and restless.

He found himself, alone in his apartment that night, retrieving a magazine that he'd picked up in one of the bars, which he'd rolled up and shoved into his jacket pocket for future reference. It was the kind of inexpensively printed periodical that was distributed, free, in the gay community's bars, baths, and bookstores. The pages contained a few articles but were mostly filled with advertisements—not just for the kind of bars, baths, and bookstores in question, but for porno DVDs, sex tours, gay tourist attractions, phone and Internet chat lines, and male prostitutes, who, of course, invariably described themselves as escorts or masseurs, or both.

Trent found the advertisements for the escorts especially intriguing. For one thing, he couldn't imagine what it would be like to have sex indiscriminately with any guy who happened to agree to a set fee. For another, some of these whores looked in their photos, and sounded in the accompanying ad copy, extremely hot. He told himself, as he scrutinized the ads, that he was taking no more than an appropriate professional interest in them. As a vice cop, after all, prostitution came under his bailiwick.

"I'm an easy-going guy, with an open and friendly personality,

Good Cop, Bad Cop

and a good sense of humor," one sullen-looking young number named Eric somewhat improbably boasted. "I like to make things happen, and I would like to make something special happen for you right now. Versatile. In/out/overnight."

"Slut," Trent muttered out loud. "Dirty little slut!"

Another advertiser, Darren, claimed to be a "nineteen-year-old college student, specialist in sensual erotic naked and Swedish massage. Candles, oils, hugs, body contact."

Trent couldn't help wondering whether it was possible to give a massage *without* body contact. He also assumed that "hugs" was this dude's indirect way of warning potential customers that there'd be no kissing. And were "sensual erotic naked and Swedish" four distinct alternatives on the menu, or was this just one way of describing a single massage experience? Trent sighed. He was still pretty green when it came to some of this stuff, he realized. He'd have to ask Zerk for enlightenment provided he was willing to put up with the older and more experienced cop's ribbing. Knowing Zerk, he'd tease Trent unmercifully for once again betraying the fact that he was still such a dumb, naïve rookie.

One ad in particular caught Trent's eye. This escort called himself Royce, and in his postage-stamp-sized photo of himself, he was posing naked with his back turned to the camera and his arms extended slightly out to either side. He was flexing his impressively broad and deep back muscles, and the pose concealed the lower part of his face, which was turned away from the camera and tucked down behind his bulging shoulder muscle. You could still tell he was handsome, though. He had thick black hair, and the face-obscuring pose didn't quite hide the fact that he was sporting an equally thick black mustache. The facial hair was in strong contrast to his smooth-shaven body. When the copy claimed, "Muscular, sexy, masculine guy," it wasn't exaggerating a bit. "Gym 6 times per week, excellent massage. Any fantasies you have, ask me! I'm very open-minded as long as it's safe. In/out/overnight."

"Shit!" Trent exclaimed. It sounded almost too good to be true—a guy who looked like *that*, who'd be willing to try just about anything, for the right price!

He almost threw the magazine into the trash, but then he thought better of it and secreted it in the drawer of his nightstand. It might provide good jack-off fodder some night, inspiring masturbation fantasies and maybe even another good, hot sex dream. He wouldn't mind dreaming about this stud Royce. The only question was which would be hotter, imagining him as the top, or the bottom?

He decided, on impulse, to go out, and, specifically, to go to one of the city's leather bars. It might be amusing to check out the action there purely for fun, rather than as a part of his work. And, thanks to Zerk's tutelage, Trent now knew how to dress the part of a young, hungry leather-enthusiast on the prowl. He chose what Zerk called, "a basic butch look," jeans, laced work boots, a black leather belt, a plain T-shirt—live drab, to lend the ensemble a hint of a quasi-militaristic quality—and the obligatory black leather motorcycle jacket.

In the dimly lit bar, Trent soon felt rather at home and began to enjoy himself, especially when more than one hopeful number approached him to introduce himself, chat Trent up, and make his sexual interest in him obvious. Trent hadn't come here with any conscious intention of serious cruising, but now he found himself entertaining the possibility of inviting some guy to go home with him.

He was alone for a moment, standing by himself, when he happened to glance across the barroom and see a guy in an outfit similar to his own, only topped by a baseball cap, getting a fresh beer from one of the bartenders. Something about the dark eyes under the brim of the cap was strangely familiar. When the man looked up after paying for his beer, Trent got a better look at his face. It was none other than his fellow police officer, Alejandro De Soto.

No sooner had Trent recognized De Soto than the other cop saw *him* and a flicker of recognition passed quickly over his face.

Trent had enough sense not to openly acknowledge the other

Good Cop, Bad Cop

cop's presence with a careless look or gesture, let alone go over and greet him. For all Trent knew, his colleague was on duty, working undercover. So, having made the brief eye contact with De Soto, Trent casually wandered over to another area of the bar, observing the other patrons, cruising and being cruised. Then, slowly, he made his way toward the men's room, not looking back to see whether De Soto was watching him. He was confident the other cop was doing just that, but furtively.

A young guy, by no means unattractive, but definitely wasted, was in the men's room. He wore jeans, boots, and a flannel shirt pulled out of the waistband of his jeans and unbuttoned all the way down the front so that it flapped about his torso and exposed his bare chest. Over the shirt, he had on an unzipped black leather motorcycle jacket, scuffed, dirty, and in generally ruinous conditions, its seams split open in several places.

"Christ, I'm drunk!" The guy giggled, sounding absurdly pleased with himself as he staggered over to one of the urinals, unzipped his fly, extracted his cock, and, swaying on the heels of his boots, began to relieve himself, with none too sure an aim. De Soto came in, glanced around the john, and went over to one of the sinks, lifting his cap and pretending to inspect his hair. Then, as the drunken bar patron seemed inclined to linger, De Soto took a great deal of time washing and drying his hands, stalling for time.

All this while, Trent simply stood there, leaning against one of the walls and staring idly into space. No one who might come into the men's room and observe him would be likely to find his behavior unusual, let alone suspicious. It was a gay bar, after all, and there was nothing odd about a customer loitering in the john.

Finally, the grinning drunkard stumbled out of the room after stuffing his dick back inside his jeans, which he had some difficulty zipping up.

The two police offers were alone. De Soto approached Trent.

"This never happened, Carothers," he said, in a low, urgent voice.

"You never saw me tonight, because neither of us was ever here."

"I got it."

"I mean it, kid. I'm not fucking around. You'd better develop instant amnesia."

"I'm not stupid. I got it, man. Are you working?"

De Soto hesitated. "I guess I could just lie and say yes, but no, I'm not."

"Oh." Trent couldn't quite conceal his surprise at this unexpected revelation.

"I'm married, Carothers. I have kids. My wife doesn't know that I come to places like this sometimes. She thinks I'm out on a case tonight."

"You don't have to draw me a diagram. I understand."

"What about you? Are you here with Kostopoulos? Are you guys working?"

Trent decided to imitate De Soto's own candor. "No, I'm here all by myself. I'm off duty. I just came here for a drink and to see what's going on. Maybe have a little harmless fun."

"Jesus Christ. I wouldn't have ever pegged you for gay. Not really. I mean, I know we've joked about it, down at the precinct, but—!"

"I'm not ashamed of it, but I'm not exactly out," Trent admitted. "So that instant amnesia thing you were talking about works both ways."

"It stinks in here," De Soto said, wrinkling his nose. "Let's go get a drink."

They went back to the bar and ordered beers. De Soto insisted on paying.

"Let's find a quiet place where we can talk," he suggested.

They found a table and got comfortable. Leaning toward each other over the table, drinking their beers, they looked like any two bar hoppers flirting with each other.

De Soto now seemed more relaxed and relieved, at having the

opportunity to talk frankly with somebody.

"Tell me something," he asked. "Have you always known you were gay?"

"Not always, no, but I was still kind of young when I began to realize I had a definite preference."

"You're lucky. I didn't know until a few years ago. And don't get me wrong, I'd never give up my wife and kids, for anything. But every once in a while I just have to have a dick, to put it crudely. To get it out of my system, for a while."

"That doesn't make you gay," Trent argued. "It makes you bi, or straight but curious. Adaptable. That's all."

"Maybe. You're an incredibly good-looking guy, by the way. I can't believe you don't have a lover."

"I haven't met the right guy yet, I guess. Hell, with this work schedule lately, I haven't met hardly anybody. Anybody decent, I mean, as opposed to all the sleazebags. Right about now, I'd settle for a good fuck buddy."

"Or for a one-night stand?"

"Sure. Why not?"

"It must be nice to be young and good-looking and unattached."

"Yeah, well, 'unattached' means coming home to an empty apartment every night, remember. It's got its disadvantages. And you're not exactly old or ugly, man."

De Soto laughed. "Thanks. It's been a while since a man has paid me that kind of a compliment."

"In fact, I was thinking…"

"What?"

"You came here tonight looking for some action, didn't you?"

"Maybe," De Soto replied, cautiously. "I might not turn it down if it happened to come my way."

"Maybe it already has," Trent said.

He ended up inviting De Soto to his place. They left the bar, went to their cars, and De Soto followed Trent home.

"You want a drink?" Trent asked as he led his guest inside his apartment. "I've got beer."

"I don't want to get home too late," De Soto said. "Or get home too wasted."

"Okay." Trent correctly interpreted the other cop's statement as shorthand for, *Let's not waste any time—can we go right to bed?*

"I feel a little grungy. Do you mind if I jump in your shower?"

"No, go right ahead. Help yourself to a fresh towel. There's a stack of them in there."

De Soto began to strip off his shirt as he went into the bathroom. Trent went into his bedroom, took off his own clothes, and turned down the bed. He heard the shower running. He created a suitably intimate, seductive mood by lighting a candle on his dresser, leaving the room otherwise in near-darkness.

De Soto emerged from the bathroom, nude except for a towel wrapped around his waist, looking refreshed and desirable. Trent hadn't realized what a nice body he had. In particular, he had a well-developed and very hairy chest. And he had a tattoo, a blazing orange and red and yellow sunburst, highlighted with fine black lines, on his left shoulder.

"This is nice," De Soto said, looking about the bedroom. "I don't mean just the apartment. I mean being here with you." He concentrated his gaze on Trent's nude body. "Jesus, you're hot."

"Lose the towel," Trent suggested as he stretched out on the bed.

De Soto flung the towel away and joined him, and they lay there side by side, flat on their backs on the mattress. De Soto leaned over Trent to caress him lightly, as though he was afraid Trent might break if he touched him too forcefully.

"I'm kind of shy, the first time with a guy," he explained, in a whisper.

"It's okay, Alejandro. Take your time." The name felt odd on Trent's lips. No one down at work ever addressed De Soto, or referred to him, by anything other than his surname.

It quickly got sexual. De Soto pushed the sheets down to the foot of the bed to get them out of the way as he moved his other hand from Trent's hip to the curve of the blond's tanned belly and stroked him there. Then he was gripping Trent's thick cock in both fists, jerking him off as he rolled over to bring their warm, naked bodies into full, arousing contact. Their chests and thighs touched then rubbed restlessly, shamelessly together. Trent, moaning with arousal, threw his strong arms around De Soto's torso and pulled his fellow cop close to him. His tongue licked the inked flesh of the Puerto Rican's shoulder, lapping at the tattooed sun.

Their panting mouths sought and found each other, locking in a breathless kiss. Trent's wet tongue darted deep into the warm, moist cavity of De Soto's open mouth. He felt the other man tense against him, then gradually accept him, and he was surprised to realize that De Soto must still have some inhibitions about open-mouthed kissing between men. Trent suspected that, as a married guy in the closet, the other cop probably had mostly quick, furtive, anonymous sexual encounters, the kind in which there was probably more emphasis on no-nonsense, let's-get-off genital contact than on this sort of lingering tenderness and foreplay. Well, Trent was just the guy to show this number what he had been missing out on all this time!

He used one hand to stroke the solid prick that throbbed beneath his ministrations, and with the other, he rubbed De Soto's squirming body to reassure him. As he concentrated on making their kiss as delightfully prolonged and as tender and arousing at once as he could, De Soto stopped struggling and obviously began enjoying. Trent's big, sunburned hands gripped De Soto's head, twisting the silky brown hair, and he pressed their lips still more tightly together. De Soto's tongue slithered out of its hiding place to tease Trent's and toy with it, like a limber eel going through some intense yet lighthearted mating ritual.

Their hard-muscled bodies ground together fiercely, De Soto's hard-on rubbing along Trent's tough perineum muscle when he thrust it between the blond's parted thighs after the younger cop had rolled over on top of him. They were both panting hard for breath when they finally, reluctantly, broke the kiss, only to let their wet mouths slide restlessly over each other's cheeks and chins and throats. Each man responded to the other's soft murmuring inhalations and exhalations with near-articulate breaths of his own in a private, shared language of desire. Their hands ceaselessly explored each other's nude bodies, caressing powerful muscle and hard sinew, each man growing increasingly impatient to carry this play to its inevitable next level.

"Trent?" De Soto whispered.

"Yeah?"

"I'll suck you if you'll suck mine."

"Sure."

"Maybe we could even do it to each other at the same time?"

Trent had to chuckle at the other man's audible embarrassment. "It's called sixty-nine. It's not exactly a new invention, you know."

"My wife and I—we really don't do much except plain fucking, with the lights out. She thinks cocksucking is dirty."

"She's right," Trent joked. "That's what makes it so exciting. Come on, let's get down and dirty together."

He turned around on the bed, getting quickly and efficiently into position, pushed his head between De Soto's legs, and grabbed his cock by its shaft, guiding its tip to his mouth. He sucked it deep inside and began to work on it with his lips, keeping his fingers lightly curled around the very base of the thick tool to steady it and stroke it while he fed upon it. De Soto let out a hoarse groan of surprise and delight, and then he began to reciprocate, imitating what Trent was doing to him with an alacrity and skill that suggested he was by no means inexperienced at fellatio. No doubt the hot Hispanic cop had made the most of his opportunities to trick with guys he'd picked up in bars.

Concentrating on the pleasure he was giving and receiving, Trent lost track of time. He teased De Soto's asshole with an exploring fingertip, and the digital invasion of his pucker only made De Soto suck harder. This was promising! De Soto was about as butch as they came, but Trent knew from past sexual adventures that, often, the butcher they were, the readier they were to get fucked!

Suddenly, De Soto pulled his mouth off Trent's cock.

"I don't want to come yet," he gasped. "I'm getting close!"

"What *do* you want to do?" Trent asked.

"God, I don't care. I'm already so turned on I think I could blow my wad any minute."

"Well, try not to. You decide. This is your party. You're my guest. Let me do something to make you feel good."

"I'd like…I want you to do something my wife can't do for me," De Soto blurted out. "I want to get fucked!"

"No problem. No problem, whatsoever." Trent fought back a smirk at having had his suspicions confirmed. He would've been happy to assume either the active or the passive role, but there was an extra jolt of excitement at the thought of possessing De Soto's undeniably masculine ass.

"You're going to use a rubber, aren't you?"

"Of course I am. I always do."

"Oh, Jesus. I'm dripping cum, just thinking about you putting that big thing in me. Hurry up. Hurry up and fuck me, before I shoot."

"Get on your back," Trent instructed as he reached into the top drawer of his nightstand and availed himself of a condom and the lube. "Shove that pillow under your back to lift your ass up. Put your legs up over my shoulders. You want to get fucked so bad? Well, you're going to get it right now. You came to the right guy!"

Trent inserted himself quickly and started to fuck De Soto—hard! It took him longer than usual to get close to coming. He settled in for a long, leisurely ride. He thrust himself into the other cop's body innumerable times, until it seemed as though they'd been balling like this all night.

Trent lost track of time, of space. He forgot everything except that, after a succession of lonely nights devoted to masturbation, he was not only in bed with another man—he was fucking him! He reveled in his possession of the other cop's body, fucking his butch ass without letup.

"Oh, Trent!" De Soto moaned. "This is what I wanted, man! What I've been thinking about, ever since you walked through the door of the precinct that first day! Fuck me, rookie! Fuck me, you stud bastard!"

"You're getting fucked, all right," Trent retorted. "You're getting fucked good and hard. Take it, big man! Take that cock of mine all the way up your ass!"

Trent could feel himself getting close at long last, so he fucked harder now, with faster, deeper strokes. De Soto gasped as Trent continued to plow his ass so ruthlessly with his unrelenting tool. The muscles in De Soto's calves and thighs and lower back had probably begun to ache from the strain of remaining in this position, with his legs thrown up over Trent's shoulders and the other big man's weight coming down on him every time his fucker made a new lunge. But Trent didn't care. He was indifferent to De Soto's discomfort. He went right on fucking him!

"Fucked!" Trent chanted hoarsely, between thrusts. "Fucked! That's what you wanted, isn't it? And that's what I'm doing to you, man. I'm fucking that ass of yours as hard as I can, stud! And you like it, don't you? Oh, you like it a lot, I can tell! So take it, cop! Get fucked, cop! Get fucked!"

"Yeah!" De Soto cried. "Fuck me! Fuck my ass! Oh, fuck me hard!"

After a few more minutes of this savage fucking, Trent was already ejaculating helplessly. Groaning, straining, his hands gripping both of De Soto's upraised ankles to hold his legs in place, he pounded his way through his sudden, violent orgasm. De Soto hadn't dared to touch his own dripping cock until now, but now, in the height of passion, he seized himself in his right hand and pumped away. It took him only a few strokes to push himself over the edge. Even as Trent let out a final gasp of pleasure while he finished spurting, he saw De Soto's hot, white cum fly free from his cockhead in jets of liquid lust. The semen spattered over De Soto's belly and chest, some of it flying far enough to smack him in the face. A few stray drops rained down on Trent's own sweaty torso as he humped his way through his climax.

"Oh my God, oh my God," De Soto moaned. "I haven't been fucked like that in so long!" He pulled Trent down on top of him, kissing him wildly. Gradually, both men calmed down, and their breathless, heart-pounding excitement was replaced by a sensuous languor.

De Soto hugged Trent close to him. "Thank you, Trent," he whispered into Trent's ear.

"You're welcome, Alejandro. Any time."

De Soto treated himself to some further kissing and caressing, before he finally got out of the bed and began to put on his clothes. "I have to go," he apologized. "I have to get home."

"Sure. I understand." And Trent did understand—even though the all-too-familiar sight of one of his tricks getting dressed, eager to leave after the sex was successfully concluded, was one he found rather depressing.

"I don't want you to think I'm rushing off, like this was just some sort of a cheap pickup for me. It wasn't. This was fantastic. I'm really grateful to you."

"I'm glad you enjoyed yourself. I had a good time, too. Come on, I'll walk you to the door." Suppressing a yawn, the inevitable by-product of a strong late-night orgasm, Trent escorted De Soto to his front door, nude. De Soto embraced and kissed him again, with surprising tenderness this time.

"You won't tell Kostopoulos about this, will you?" De Soto asked.

"I hadn't planned on telling anybody about it. But why are you worried about Zerk finding out, in particular?"

"You know how Xerxes is. He'd never let me live it down."

Trent found it interesting that De Soto had referred to Zerk by his real name, rather than his nickname.

"Well, he won't hear it from me," Trent promised. "Remember that instant amnesia we talked about? I can already feel it kicking in."

"Thanks. And there's another reason. You might as well know. Xerxes and I had a thing going, for a while. It didn't last long. I guess I was too conservative for him. He wanted to do things in bed that I really couldn't get into, and he got bored."

"Oh? Such as?" Trent asked automatically, distracted by the revelation that his two fellow cops had enjoyed a fling together.

"Oh, you know. All that kinky stuff. Taking turns tying each other up and slapping each other around. Sick shit. Leather sex, like they call it."

De Soto looked and sounded embarrassed, so Trent decided to let him off the hook.

"Interesting," Trent said, with a casualness he was in fact far from feeling. "Well, I'm sorry you have to leave so soon. Good night, Alejandro."

"Good night, Trent. Can I call you sometime?"

"Sure. Here, let me give you my cell number." Trent wrote it down for De Soto.

"I'd like to get together with you again," De Soto said, wistfully. "Not too often, though. I wouldn't want to risk that. I might find myself falling in love with you."

"Don't be silly. I'm not the kind of guy men fall in love with."

"Don't sell yourself short." De Soto gave Trent a good-night kiss, and then he was gone.

Trent went back to bed alone. He could visualize De Soto driving home, sexually sated, to a house or apartment in the quiet suburbs, Trent imagined, a suitable place to bring up the kids. De Soto's wife, like most wives of police officers, was no doubt used to him keeping odd hours and being away from home late at night. She probably didn't wait up for him. She'd probably gone to bed, where her sleep was fitful at best. When De Soto got home, he'd get undressed and slip quietly into bed beside her, trying not to wake her, but she'd be awake, she'd know he was home, and she'd be relieved, however much she tried not to show it.

She surely wouldn't suspect that her husband had been out cheating on her, and with another man, at that. Trent sighed. He was in no position to judge. He'd never really been close enough to another guy to feel resentful or jealous of him and any other sex partners he might have, either openly or behind Trent's back. He'd never been in that kind of a committed relationship, one on one with some other man.

Only Dominic, back in college, had been a possible exception. Trent had really liked him. Trent was willing to admit that, now. He ought to give Dominic a call sometime, he decided, impulsively. Damn! Wouldn't Dominic be excited to learn Trent was now a cop? They might get together for a weekend—for a weekend of nonstop sex! Complete with handcuffs!

He thought about what De Soto had told him about how he and Zerk had had a brief fling. So Zerk wasn't just gay, he was the kind of promiscuous, gay man who liked to play the field and didn't even draw the line at having sex with a married fellow cop. Trent could picture the two of them, Zerk and Alejandro, together, having sex, and even though De Soto was a nice guy, Trent could understand how a guy like Zerk could have gotten "bored" with him, as De Soto had put it. Alejandro was married, after all. He wasn't in a position to give himself unreservedly to another guy. Every time, just when things were promising to get really hot, he'd have to return to reality and go home to his wife.

Trent was beginning to feel drowsy. Oddly enough, it was not Alejandro De Soto, the man he'd just had sex with, but Xerxes Kostopoulos, whom he was thinking about and speculating about as he fell asleep.

Chapter Seven: Dirty Cops

Trent and Zerk expanded their undercover operation to include the local porno bookstore and massage parlors, constantly on the lookout for signs of organized crime involvement. Trent didn't mind this change in venue, if only because the bookstores and massage parlors, however sordid they were in their own right, provided some relief from the meat rack atmosphere of the bar scenes. He was repulsed by the sweaty, forced intimacy, the groping, the haunted loneliness and desperation he saw in too many of the men's eyes as they cruised everybody in sight, and weren't too particular about who they ended up with. Trent's recent encounter with Alejandro De Soto had left him with ambivalent feelings about bar-hopping, in general, at least for the time being.

And, as chance would have it, it was in a porno bookstore on one hot night that he and Zerk finally connected with one another in a way that had eluded them up until then.

It was stifling hot, and it stank in the rear of this particular smut shop. The rancid odor of semen splattered against painted plywood made Trent nauseous, but he dutifully continued to feed tokens into the peep machine inside one of the curtained booths. He had watched the same film, a "short subject" depicting two bored-looking hustlers sucking and fucking, three times in a row. Twice since he'd entered the store, other customers had invited him to join them in one of the booths for a quickie. They weren't surprised or upset when he refused, and they quickly picked up somebody else. Over the rattle and whir of the little projector machines, Trent could hear the rustle of clothes being unfastened, and then the slurps and groans of fast, frantic oral sex. The muscle-bound young number in a tight tank top who was manning the cash register at the front counter ignored the action in the rear of the store, although he, too, had cruised Trent when this unusually attractive customer had first entered the store, also to no avail.

Trent was bored, but he had to wait because Zerk was supposed to meet him here in a few minutes. They'd split up in order to cover more ground. Trent walked back out to the front of the store, to the magazine racks. There was a section for every taste, including and emphasizing the tasteless—bondage, rubber, interracial, water sports. Trent was examining a particularly engrossing periodical called *The Quarterly Review of Fisting* when Zerk sauntered in through the turnstile at the entrance, wearing skintight black leather pants tucked into motorcycle boots and held up by the kind of wide, studded, leather belt that the guys in the magazines liked to apply across the bare buns of their cringing slaves. Zerk's own buns weren't exactly concealed by those clinging leather pants. The crotch piece was packed with what looked like a full mouthful of solid male meat, and then some. Zerk was stripped to the waist except for a leather vest, cut to guarantee maximum pectoral exposure, and a black neckerchief knotted around his throat. He noticed Trent at once and smiled then casually made his way toward him, like one stranger cruising another.

"Anything?" he asked softly as he, too, leafed through a fuck magazine.

"No," Trent replied. "It's a waste of time. I think this place is clean."

Zerk grunted. "I didn't come up with anything at the dumps I checked out tonight, either. Let's get the hell out of here and call it a night."

To cover themselves, Zerk bought two magazines and a DVD on their way out—paying cash, as a further precaution, so there'd be no record of his identity. The cashier leered at them as they left together, no doubt convinced they'd picked each other up at the magazine rack and were going home together. Trent was surprised when that was exactly what they ended up doing.

"Why don't you come to my place? We can take a look at this garbage," Zerk suggested, indicating the DVD. The title was *Dirty Cops*, which was no doubt what had attracted Zerk to this particular selection when he'd seen it on a shelf. The cover photo on the DVD box featured a muscle-bound, hairy-chested number, nude except for a police officer's uniform hat, brandishing a nightstick and smiling invitingly at the camera. "It ought to be good for a laugh, if nothing else. I've got plenty of cold beer."

"Okay, Zerk," Trent said, a little nervously.

They went to Zerk's place without talking much. Trent suspected that it was going to be pretty much a sex thing, at least at first. They'd save the chit-chat for afterward.

"Give me a kiss," Zerk commanded the minute he had the door closed and bolted behind them.

"What?"

"Stick your tongue in my mouth, kid."

"Is this *another* bet?"

"Are you *ever* going to let me live that down? Just shut up and do it."

Trent obeyed blindly, unhesitantly, thrilled by the way the other man was taking charge. Their mouths met and crushed together as Zerk embraced the younger guy's muscular body through his clothes and eagerly explored the warm interior of his mouth with his tongue, tasting the sweetness of Trent's breath.

"What was that for?" Trent asked after they'd broken the kiss.

"For the hell of it." Zerk laughed softly. "I'm glad we got that out of the way, aren't you? It's been kind of hanging out there, waiting, all this time. Like waiting for the other shoe to drop. How about that beer now, huh?"

Trent numbly allowed Zerk to serve him the beer, which he gulped nervously while Zerk loaded the DVD into his player. He had quite an elaborate home theater setup, with multiple speakers, attached to his large flat screen TV. Trent was glad that watching the porno movie relieved him of any need to make small talk. As though they hadn't just kissed, as though nothing out of the ordinary had happened, Zerk settled down beside him on the couch and sipped his own beer, while the video began playing. Zerk, who was obviously an experienced consumer of video porn, used the remote control to skip over the title and credits, so that the action began abruptly with a buffed young stud driving a sports car aimlessly through a large city's streets, while the soundtrack pulsed with a fairly decent jazz improvisation, a saxophone moaning erotically over piano and drums.

"This must be what they used to call the 'redeeming social value.'" Zerk snickered, and Trent couldn't help laughing, forcing himself to concentrate on the screen as he felt his face getting hot with lustful anticipation of the sex scenes they were about to watch and of whatever the hell he and Zerk were going to end up doing together before the night was over.

"Oh, fuck!" Zerk gasped, eloquently enough, when the camera abruptly zoomed in on an exceptionally well-packed crotch, vividly displayed in tight, faded jeans. The camera pulled back slowly, lingeringly, to reveal that the basket belonged to a humpy young hitchhiker, who smirked as he stuck out his thumb and his pelvis. What happened next was no surprise—the cruiser picked up the pedestrian and, after a very brief exchange of pleasantries, the two young men were shown entering a motel room together. After a further minute or so of heavy breathing and languishingly seductive glances, they were necking. A quick editing cut and they were on the motel's bed, naked. The soundtrack went into high gear, saxophonist panting and wailing, pianist and drummer banging away, and so did the two porno actors.

Despite the hitchhiker's repeated protests that he was a virgin who had never done anything with another guy and didn't know what to do now, he began to demonstrate the kind of sexual skill that can only come from natural inclination honed by long experience. Trent bit his lips and squirmed in his seat as the two young studs on the screen swung their muscular bodies together in the steady, undulating rhythms of a protracted and intense sixty-nine, their cocks sliding in and out of each other mouths, their cheeks puffed out with the effort of taking each other's thick schlongs all the way down into their throats. Their hands played restlessly with each other's ass cheeks, fingers searching for the holes tucked away between them. The camera glued itself to the hitchhiker's buttocks in order to capture, in lurid detail, the obscene spectacle of the guy being finger-fucked by his costar as he sucked and was sucked by him.

Another jolting cut brought about a complete change in the situation. Now the hitchhiker was spread-eagled face down on the bed, his wrists and ankles strapped to the four corners of the bed frame. The other guy had a huge wooden paddle in his hand and was using it to warm up the lush, up-thrust ass cheeks of his supposedly helpless pickup, whose shrieks and pleas and writhings, though no doubt faked, were highly stimulating, nevertheless. Trent thought about Dominic and couldn't help empathizing with the actor who was getting beaten. He wondered what it would be like to get into a really heavy S and M scene like that again. But, rather daringly, he found himself picturing himself in the role of the bottom man.

Naked! he thought, excitedly. *Tied down on the bed, so you couldn't get loose if you wanted to. Your bare ass exposed to the other guy, he could do anything he wanted to do to you, and there wouldn't be a damn thing you could do about it except lie there and beg him not to do it! And then, when he went ahead and did it to you anyway, all you could do would be lie there and take it—hot, hard cock shoved up your ass, raping you, fucking your ass, whether you liked it or not! And then, after the horny bastard came in your ass, you'd still be tied up. Your body still at his mercy, at his disposal, to do whatever he wanted to you, no matter how dirty—oh, damn!*

"Oh, damn," Zerk groaned next to him, between swallows of his beer, as though he could read Trent's thoughts. "Have you ever done anything like that to another guy, Trent? Or had it done to you?"

"Of course not!"

"You say that as though it was something to be ashamed of. As though I might think badly of you, if you told me you did."

"Wouldn't you?"

"No. It's just kink. Lots of guys are into it and into all sorts of other things. You'd be surprised."

"I guess I'm kind of conservative. And not very experienced," Trent confessed.

"You don't strike me as being all that conservative. You seem very adventurous, to me. Are you? *Are* you adventurous, partner?"

"I…I don't know, Zerk."

"I'd like you to do that to me," Zerk declared, shocking him.

"Don't be silly, Zerk."

"I'm dead serious. I'd like you to tie me up like that, and really work me over. I bet we'd both get off on it, and—oh, shit!" Zerk interrupted himself and moaned as the actual fucking began onscreen, the voyeuristic camera getting so close to the hot action on the bed that Trent expected the lens to steam up! The actors, no doubt at the director's instigation, teased the viewer by drawing out the business of the top man unrolling a condom down over his dick, and then coating it with a lubricating gel, to infuriating lengths. Zerk almost reached for the remote control to avail himself of the fast-forward button, but before he could, he squirmed and moaned again, his body hot and sweaty against Trent's on the couch as that slicked-up, latex-sheathed cock was finally thrust between the brutally parted buttocks of the bound man and buried in his ass all the way to the balls, in extreme close up! The actor's cries of exaggerated anal agony were nearly drowned out by Trent's and Zerk's increasingly heavy breathing as they watched.

Trent was mesmerized in spite of himself, fascinated by the sight of the huge dick that filled almost the entire screen as it slid in and out of the tight asshole that quivered and quaked and contracted in involuntary muscle spasms as the fuck got faster and fiercer. It was such an extreme close-up that he could trace every throbbing vein along the shaft of that titanic hard-on as it pulsed beneath the thin coating of translucent latex and glistening lubricant, and he could count every hair lining the fuckee's asshole. Trent's own heartbeat sped up considerably as he imagined himself in the fucker's place, ravaging that helpless "virgin" asshole, forcing it wide open, tearing it apart with his hard meat!

After long minutes, the stud who was doing the fucking pulled his cock out of his victim's ass and, in order to satisfy the viewers that they were getting a real orgasm for their money, peeled the rubber off his prick and shot his load all over the hitchhiker's buttocks and back. The instant the ejaculation ended, the cum shot was repeated in slow motion! The two writhing bodies seemed to move in dreamy, jerky movements as one blur of white semen after another made its slow, torturous way from the fucker's prick lips to streak in a pale trajectory across the screen and splatter all over the bound stud's heaving, sweat-soaked body. Each drop created a miniature splatter of its own before it finally came to rest. As a further refinement of sadistic titillation, the top man—still in slow motion—thrust his hand into his victim's disheveled hair and yanked his head up from the mattress. With a grunted command of, "Eat it," which was distorted into a deep growl by the slow motion, he pressed his slimy prick between the moaning, parted lips of the hitchhiker, who obediently let all of that still-stiff cock slide into his mouth and down his throat.

Trent had forgotten the video's title. After another cum shot, a facial this time, the guy who'd done the throat-fucking and the spraying untied his victim, who sat up slowly on the bed, looking dazed.

Then the fucker pulled a badge out of his discarded pants and shoved it in the hitchhiker's face. "You're under arrest," he growled.

"You're a *cop?*" the hitchhiker demanded, echoing Zerk and

Trent's own incredulity.

"Yeah."

"You can't bust me. For what?"

"For solicitation."

Zerk laughed as they watched the hitchhiker being cuffed. "I must've missed the part where he propositioned the cop or any money changed hands," Zerk commented.

"It's a setup," Trent elucidated. "That's why he's a *dirty* cop, I guess."

After another cum shot, the scene shifted abruptly from the motel room to a bedroom in which the blond hitchhiker, now alone, did a slow striptease then masturbated himself to climax on the floor, even though there was a perfectly comfortable-looking bed only a few feet away. Apparently, the director of this mini-masterpiece wanted to avoid the predictable. Seconds later, however, the guy was dressed again—in black leather, this time—and was busy soliciting johns, first outside, and then inside, a gay bar, having evidently been transformed from virginal innocent to hardened hustler in the course of that single sex session in the motel room. Either that or he had decided that, since he'd already done the time, he might as well attempt the crime.

His libido seemingly unfulfilled by his earlier jerking off, he picked up his first trick, a big brute of a man with a shaven head and tribal tattoos, who was certainly ugly enough to have to pay for sex, and, after some money exchanged hands, they retired to the grimy men's room of the bar.

It now became clear that the director wasn't going to waste much more expensive film footage on such niceties as plot or dialogue. A handsome black dude who was reading the obscene graffiti on the wall of the men's room as he pissed—in close-up, of course—joined in the frantic three-way that soon got under way in one of the doorless toilet stalls. Apparently forgetting all about charging a fee for his services, the hustler unzipped his tight leather pants and thrust them down to his knees while he straddled the toilet bowl. The black man knelt in front of him and took the blond's soft cock between his lips. It didn't stay soft for very long. The ugly, skin-headed motherfucker stripped completely, tossing his clothes on the floor and pausing only long enough to take a condom out of the pocket of his discarded pants and put it on. Then he got behind the blond hustler and began to fuck him.

There wasn't much doubt, from the rapt look on the guy's face as he stood there, giving and taking hard cock, that he was enjoying himself immensely. Things rapidly built to a climax in which some fairly professional-looking quick cutting switched back and forth between the two orgasms, to show first the blond pulling his dick out of the black's mouth and spraying his face with his cum, and then the ugly brute performing a similar service for the hustler's ass, bathing his butt cheeks in his slimy jism.

This time, both the ugly motherfucker and the black dude turned out to be undercover cops, presumably working in tandem. They pulled out badges, and the blond guy got handcuffed *again*.

"I'd say it's time that dumbass tried another line of work. He doesn't seem smart enough to make it as a prostitute, since he keeps getting busted. Enjoying yourself, kid?" Zerk teased, moving closer, so that his shoulder pressed against Trent's shoulder as they both stared at the screen and the lurid images filling it.

"Oh, sure. Very much," Trent muttered. And he *was* enjoying himself, in a perverse sort of way. He had a raging hard-on trapped in his pants, and he couldn't wait until the movie was over so that he and Zerk could do something about it. What that something was going to be, he wasn't sure, but he knew that he needed and wanted relief.

He forced himself to relax and enjoy the last few sequences of the DVD. Three powerfully built men, all wearing peculiarly tight-fitting cop uniforms, which showed off their gym-toned bodies, were seated around a table, drinking coffee and, yes, eating donuts out of a flimsy cardboard take-out box in front of them. This was apparently the director's way of injecting a little humor into the mix.

"Did you see that hot little blond bitch they brought in a minute ago?" one of the cops asked. The actor had a pronounced East European accent and spoke his line carefully, as though reading it off a teleprompter.

"Yeah. What's he in for?" Cop Number Two asked.

"Prostitution, public indecency, and anything else we can throw at him," the first cop replied.

"Where is he now?" asked Ersatz Police Officer Number Three.

"In one of the holding cells," said Number One.

"I've got an idea," Number Three declared. "If you two bastards are as horny as I am, why don't we take the punk down into the basement, into the 'special interrogation room,' and give him a good working-over?"

"Yeah," Number Two drawled salaciously. "A good working-over with our dicks!" He licked powdered sugar from his fingers and leered at the camera.

Zerk groaned. "You have *got* to be kidding!" he protested.

"Oh, I don't know, Zerk," Trent retorted. "It seems perfectly realistic to me. This sort of thing goes on down at the precinct all the time, doesn't it?"

"I *wish*," Zerk said, with a laugh.

The action plunged unexpectedly into a full-scaled S and M episode, set in a convincingly dungeon-like basement playroom.

The same three musclemen, all of them now naked except for boots and leather torso harnesses, were putting the hitchhiker/hustler through an exhaustive ordeal that progressed from whipping to forcible cocksucking to fucking to fistfucking. Trent shivered in his seat with arousal and awe as he gaped at the obscene spectacle of two of the torturers prying open the blond stud's ass cheeks with their gloved hands while the third man plunged his greased-up bare hand into the guy's asshole, right up to the elbow!

"Ahhh!" Trent's own startled cry was echoed by the ecstatic cry of the guy who was being fistfucked on the screen, reproduced with stunning clarity through the speakers of Zerk's home theater system, in multichannel sound.

"Turns you on, doesn't it?" Zerk asked.

"No! It's disgusting. Absolutely disgusting. The sort of thing you see in the back rooms of those bars you're always dragging me to."

"Disgusting, huh? That must be why it's giving you that big hard-on." Zerk laughed.

"I just don't see how such a little guy can take all that up his ass." In his preoccupation with all of the sex taking place on the screen, Trent hadn't even noticed, until now, that Zerk had reached over and deftly unzipped his bulging jeans. He hadn't noticed it, that is, until he felt his partner's hot, sweaty hand reach inside the gap, seize his aching prick, and yank it out of his open fly!

"Hey!" Trent protested frantically, trying to pull away from his buddy's insistent grip. "No groping allowed!"

"Don't fight it, kid," Zerk whispered heatedly as he began to beat off his own big cock while he pumped on Trent's with his other hand. "Just sit back and relax. I'll do you real good, I promise."

Trent turned his wide-eyed gaze back to the TV screen, just in time to catch the scene's climax. The blond stud howled as one top man's greased forearm plowed up his asshole in savage thrusts and withdrawals while the second man masturbated himself to orgasm and, in another obligatory cum shot, fired his thick white fluid all over the victim's face and hair and into his open mouth! The third sadist quickly moved to push his erection inside that defiled mouth, fucking the blond's face until he, too, came, taking care to pull out first so that he could explode onto the blond's face and force him to swallow a second load of semen.

Then, still impaled anally on the big man's fist and forearm, the blond fell to his knees on the playroom floor and pressed his cum-stained lips to the tip of one of the top men's black leather boots, licking it with his wet tongue and begging all three men for "More! More! More!"

Cop Number One stepped forward, stroking his cock.

"Read him his rights!" he growled, in his distinctive accent. "And then we can all fuck him again!"

Suddenly, the screen went blank, and then, after a moment, the words *The End* appeared, followed by the slow scroll of credits.

"Aw, what a fucking rip-off!" Zerk laughed. "It's like you said, I've seen hotter action in the back rooms of some of those sleazy bars we cruise, and so will you, if you stay on this assignment long enough." He turned to Trent. "So?" he said simply, looking his partner in the eyes.

Both of their cocks were still out, and Zerk was still grasping them, stroking them, one in each hand.

"So?" Trent retorted, still a little nervously. "So what?"

"Your cock feels good in my hand. You're really hung big, partner. You've got what it takes to satisfy another horny dude, don't you? I want to be a slave tonight, like that whore in the movie. I want to be *your* fucking slave, kid."

"Stop calling me a kid. I'm a man, damn it."

"Yeah? Then why don't you start proving it? Why don't you take charge, and...?" Zerk released their dicks and took Trent in his arms. "Think you can handle it? That fuck film give you any ideas?"

"One or two, maybe."

"I've got one or two ideas, myself," Zerk whispered. "In fact, there are quite a few fantasies of mine that I haven't gotten around to fulfilling, yet. For example...I'd really like to have two or three guys take me down, the way we cops take down a perp who's dumb enough to resist arrest. I'd like to be wrestled to the ground and cuffed...and then get roughed up and fucked!"

"Jesus, Zerk. That does sound kind of hot. Too bad I'm only one guy," Trent joked, desperately trying to cover up his lingering nervousness.

"Oh, you'll do for now, rookie. You'll do just fine, I think. Now come on. Gimme another kiss!"

They kissed. And then Trent's warm hands were caressing the hot, sticky skin of Zerk's bare chest under his leather vest, sliding down from his pecs to stroke his belly and its barbell navel ornament before plunging eagerly into the gap of his open pants. Zerk gasped, and taking the blond's head between his hands, he kissed him even more passionately than he had before, upon their arrival at the apartment, as he felt Trent's hands grasping and kneading the bulky, hard-rubber hose of his cock. Zerk was already getting hard, and he soon had a full, proud erection as a result of those expert hands working on his meat, pulling it free from his shoved-down leather pants and rubbing the head of it over Trent's own naked fuck tool.

Whimpering now from the intensity of his desire, Zerk ran his hands down over Trent's shoulders and arms and began to masturbate him again, clutching Trent's massive prick in his own sweaty fist and stroking it. They kept right on tongue-kissing, their mouths glued together as they caressed and toyed with each other's hard dicks.

Suddenly Trent released Zerk and gave him a push that nearly sent the shorter cop sprawling.

"Take off your fucking clothes," Trent hissed, his eyes hot with lustful fury. "Get out of that leather drag, if you want to be a slave so bad. I want you bare-assed naked, *slave!*"

Trent noticed that Zerk was actually shivering, just a bit, as he began to strip with trembling, clumsy hands. Trent fought to suppress a smirk of satisfaction.

His long affair with Dominic had taught him a few things. He knew that Zerk wanted the two of them to get into a Dom-and-sub scene, with clearly defined roles. Zerk was about to play the role of the masochist, of the bottom man, submissive, abject. He wanted Trent to take charge of the situation—and of him.

The thought of topping the other cop, who was his partner and his mentor, and who always seemed so utterly self-confident and in control when they were on duty, excited Trent so much that he could feel his heart pounding away almost audibly inside his chest. As for his cock, it was already rock hard and ready to take charge!

Zerk peeled his socks off his feet and flung them aside, on top of his other discarded clothes. Then he stood up, naked, to face his partner.

"Nice," Trent whispered. "Nice fucking body!" He thought for a moment. "Put your boots back on, that's all," he commanded quietly.

His hard, up-jutting cock was still thrusting its proud way out of his unzipped fly. He watched Zerk pull his boots back on, and then he picked up Zerk's discarded, studded belt and examined it. Zerk winced in anticipation and dread. Trent folded the long leather strap in half and, grasping one end, smacked his open palm lightly with the other to test it.

"This looks like it'd be useful for inflicting a little discipline," Trent remarked.

"Maybe we'd better discuss limits," Zerk suggested.

"Maybe you'd better make up your mind, right now, that you're going to satisfy me," Trent retorted. "All right, what about limits?"

"I don't have many," Zerk admitted. "But we need a code word. You know, a safe word."

"I understand. We'll use 'partner.' That would be rather appropriate, under the circumstances, don't you think? You say 'partner,' and whatever we're doing, I'll stop, right away."

"Okay."

"Let's get started. Lead the way into your bedroom, slave."

Zerk obeyed.

"Lie down on the bed, face down, and spread your arms and legs, just like that young punk did in the movie. Wider! Spread 'em wider, as wide as you can! Now grab hold of the bedposts and hold onto them while I whip that hot, butch ass of yours!" Trent gritted out.

"You can tie me down, if you want to," Zerk gasped.

"Shut the fuck up. If I want to tie you down, I'll damn well do it, and I won't need your permission. I'm not going to tie you down, not yet, anyway, because you're going to lie there and take it. Willingly.

You're not going to move. If you do, if you take your hands off those bedposts, if you try to get off that bed, I'll give your butt a beating you'll never forget."

"You don't have the balls to do that," Zerk dared to retort.

"Oh, I don't, do I?"

"You're not man enough to use that belt on me."

"We'll see about that, slave. You're just digging yourself in deeper with every word that comes out of your cocksucking mouth. You're just begging for it, aren't you? Well, you're going to get it."

Trent paused for a long moment, to drag out the suspense. Gasping and sweating, Zerk tensed, gripping the bedposts with both hands and, curling the toes of his boots over the bottom edge of the mattress at the foot of the bed, he waited.

Crack! The leather belt whistled through the air and bit into the tender flesh of Zerk's muscular, unprotected ass cheeks. He groaned and made a half-involuntary effort to sit up and reached behind himself to touch and sooth his burning ass.

"Stay down!" Trent barked. "Don't you dare move! You move, slave, you so much as twitch, and I swear to God I'll tie you down and whip you twice as hard," Zerk's partner threatened viciously. Zerk had barely complied, slumping flat on the bed again and seizing the bedposts again with both hands, when the strap smacked into his taut buttocks for a second time, harder this time.

"Yeah! That's right! You lie there and you take it! I want that butch ass of yours burning hot when I fuck it!" Trent hissed.

"You dirty bastard. You dirty, cocksucking, punk bastard!"

"Mouthy little bitch, aren't you? Well, I got the cure for that right here. That attitude of yours had better improve, slave, and fast, if you know what's good for you!"

Trent observed with sadistic satisfaction that Zerk had sunk his teeth into the pillow, no doubt to keep himself from screaming, as blow upon blow stung his butt. Trent might have been a relative novice as a top man, but he was skilled enough to take care not to hit the same area twice in succession. He took pains to aim each swing of the belt differently, so that not one square inch of Zerk's buttocks and the backs of his thighs escaped punishment.

As aroused though he was, Trent retained enough presence of mind to observe his victim closely, to make sure he wasn't going too far. Zerk, it was true, hadn't uttered the safe word they'd agreed on at the start of their session. He was obviously an experienced bottom who could take a lot of punishment. But it was still Trent's responsibility, as the top man, not to go too far.

Zerk shuddered and wept into the pillow, his sweaty palms losing their grip on the smooth, polished wood of the bedposts as the torture continued. He kept his face buried in the pillow and chewed on a mouthful of the pillowcase. His ass cheeks were already bright red from the repeated strokes Trent had laid across them. They looked as though they were burning hot, and in between blows, Zerk writhed about on the bed as though in a futile effort to relieve the pain.

"Settle down," Trent ordered, curtly. "Stop that squirming, slave! You lie there, still, and you take your punishment like a man."

Zerk froze. "Yes, sir!" he groaned.

"That's better." Trent rained further blows down upon those inflamed-looking buttocks, making the recipient suck in his breath in hoarse rasps. "You seem to be enjoying yourself, pretty little Greek boy," Trent taunted. "Is your cock hard?"

"Yes, sir. So hard…so fucking hard it hurts!"

"I bet you're dripping jism already, you horny bitch. I bet you're already wetting the bed with your goddamn cum!"

"Yes, sir. I'm going to come if you keep beating my ass like this! Oh God, I'm going to come!"

"Don't you dare come. Not until I give you permission to, slave. Don't you even think about shooting your load until I tell you to. You don't want to mess with me, slave." Trent panted. "I got a mean streak in me, and you're sure as hell bringing it out! I think it's about time you started begging, boy, begging me for forgiveness, for being such an uppity, defiant, mouthy little bitch!"

"Oh, you fucker! You fucker!"

"You better start begging, unless you want me to go on beating your ass for you like this all night!"

"I'm sorry, I'm begging you, I'm begging you to forgive me—I'm sorry I'm such a mouthy bitch!"

"I don't hear much conviction in your tone of voice," Trent grumbled. "But I guess that's a start!"

He continued to abuse Zerk's butt with the belt. At last, when he suspected Zerk could endure no more, Trent flung the belt to the floor with a curse.

"Fuck! Now get up on your goddamn hands and knees and suck my cock." The blond cop panted.

He peeled his sweat-soaked, suddenly too-tight T-shirt up over his head and off with such impatience that the seam gave way with a loud ripping noise. Stripped to the waist, his massive shoulders and pecs glistening with perspiration, the veins in his biceps and forearms standing out in high relief, Trent towered over his cringing partner as Zerk scrambled around on the bed to get into the position Trent demanded. He slipped one hand behind his back to rub and soothe his burning buttocks, and this indiscretion was promptly rewarded by a smart slap across the face.

"Take your hand off your ass and put it around my cock!" Trent thundered. He threw in a second, stinging slap, for good measure. "Lousy fucking slave!"

The blond had his hard-on in his fist, jabbing it toward Zerk's lips. Panting, the Greek-American cop licked his lips to wet them and buried his hot face in Trent's sweaty crotch.

"Get a good whiff of my crotch smell, boy," Trent instructed his sub. "Breathe it in, motherfucker! Breathe it in deep!"

Zerk obeyed, snorting loudly through flared nostrils as he inhaled deeply and repeatedly. Moaning, he flicked his tongue out from between his lips and ran it over the smooth, rounded head of that big cock. He dug the tip of his tongue beneath the rim of retracted foreskin and cleaned out Trent's smegma. Trent grunted with surprise and satisfaction. It felt good—damn good!—although he wasn't about to let Zerk know that.

But Zerk had also disobeyed him, technically speaking, by taking the initiative and attacking his master's foreskin without having been granted permission to do so. Trent knew that no self-respecting top man could let a bottom get away with something like that. He bent over and smacked Zerk hard, right on his burning ass!

"I told you to suck it, not to lick it, slave! Now eat that meat!"

"Yes, sir," was all that Zerk had time to get out before Trent slammed his pelvis forward and drove his dick right between Zerk's parted lips. The head of that rigid cock struck the back of the other man's mouth, and Zerk gagged. But he closed his lips firmly around the thick shaft and began to suck. He closed his eyes and let Zerk's every hip movement thrust that huge fuck tool of his in and out of his mouth. Zerk let the hard shaft slip from between his lips until only the blunt head of his tormentor's dick was still trapped in his mouth…then he'd curb his wet lips down the saliva-lubricated column of throbbing steel until Trent was buried in Zerk's mouth to his balls, and Zerk had to hold his breath while that gigantic, pulsing cockhead slid right down into his throat and lodged firmly there for a moment.

When he could no longer keep that dickhead in his throat without choking on it, Zerk would pull his head back and relieve the torture, grabbing a quick, deep breath. He repeated the process again and again. Once he'd established a steady rhythm, he began to put his tongue to good use to stimulate the hot meat in his mouth. He worked his throat muscles to massage that relentless hard-on that was being fed repeatedly down his gullet. He deep-throated that big hot dick passionately, his own fuck rod snapping to attention between his thighs as he knelt on the bed. He planted his hands on the backs of Trent's hairy thighs then stroked the twin muscular mounds of the stud's buttocks he blew him.

"Take all of that hard meat down into your throat, you cocksucking punk slave!" the husky blond cop ordered roughly.

Trent was panting for breath. His upper body glowed with sweat over its deep tan, and his legs quivered as the erotic tugging sensations on his cock spread through the rest of his body, and he felt his orgasm building up, gradually, from its place of origin deep in his loins. His balls ached to blast their hot, wet load into that warm mouth, down that greedy throat he was fucking!

"Oh, yeah, suck it, suck on that thing!" He gasped, stroking Zerk's disheveled hair and puffed-out cheeks with both hands. "Yeah, that's good, that's real good! You're a good little slave boy, a good, cocksucking bottom! You make a good bitch! Go on, keep doing it, you punk. Eat that meat, deep-throat it. Yeah, suck my hot dick!"

His master's praise and encouragement seemed to be all that was needed to push Zerk over the edge into unrestrained sexual excess. Obviously not caring whether Trent punished him or not, Zerk thrust one brawny arm down between his thighs and took his pleading cock in his fist. Grunting, slurping noisily, obscenely, as he worked on Trent's cock, Zerk began to beat his own twitching meat with quick, hard pumps. He sucked harder and faster, with desperate concentration.

Trent knew what his cocksucker was trying to do to him. Zerk wanted him to come! He wanted Trent to shoot in his mouth! He craved the taste of Trent's potent male seed on his licking tongue.

But Trent had other plans for the fiery load of spunk that was boiling up in his swollen balls. He didn't want to waste it down Zerk's throat. He saw that he had inflamed the dark-haired stud to the point where Zerk would deny him nothing.

"That's enough, goddamn you!" Trent exploded. He pushed Zerk back and pulled his dick from between those expertly sucking lips, just in time to avoid a premature ejaculation that would've spurted hot cum all over the other guy's hot, red, open-mouthed face. "Get on your belly!" Trent stormed, seizing a handful of Zerk's sweat-soaked hair and throwing him down violently on the bed. "Roll over and spread your legs!"

Zerk did as he was told. He lay there passively, face down, naked and vulnerable, as he had when Trent had beaten him with the belt.

Trent plunged a hand into the hip pocket of his tight jeans and pulled out a leather cock ring with blunt-pointed chrome knobs on it.

"Open your legs wider!" he barked. When Zerk struggled to do so, Trent reached between those brawny thighs and groped for his victim's cock and balls. Zerk groaned loudly when Trent fist gripped his cock and yanked it down and back until it was bent and pointing toward the foot of the bed. Trent fitted the cock ring around Zerk's cock and balls and snapped it tight shut. Zerk gasped again as his scrotum swelled up even larger, chafed by the narrow leather band, and the hard metal knobs dug into his thighs every time he moved! His prick wobbled, rock-hard, the blood in it unable to escape. It was hard, and it would stay hard until Trent decreed otherwise and removed that genital tourniquet!

"That's better, slave," Trent taunted. He was stripping, pulling off his own boots and tugging the tight jeans down his legs. When he was naked, he put the leather boots back on then took two rawhide thongs from a pocket of his discarded jeans and used them to tie Zerk's wrists to the bedposts, pulling the thongs taut enough to dig into Zerk's wrists and leave red marks that would be visible for days afterward but not quite tight enough to cut off his circulation altogether. "Now I'm going to shove my cock up your ass and fuck you," Trent announced.

"Yes, sir!" Zerk moaned.

"Jesus, you're hot for it, aren't you?" Trent taunted. He pressed his hand between Zerk's sore, whipped buttocks. The bound man groaned as a blunt fingertip touched his sphincter muscle then drilled its way right through the taut, puckered anal opening!

When Zerk tried to clench his ass cheeks and his internal anal muscles to resist, Trent only snickered and pushed harder, completing his finger-rape of Zerk's tight anus. Zerk gasped helplessly as that probing digit dug deeper into his ass, and a fierce involuntary reaction racked his writhing body.

"Yeah, you're really good and tight!" Trent gloated. He was really going to enjoy fucking that butch ass! The fact that Zerk was putting up a token fight was only making it that much more exciting!

"Please, please, sir, take it easy at first, when you first put it in me. You're hung so big, grease it up first with the stuff I got right there, beside the bed," Zerk begged. "I don't know if I can take it dry!"

"That's what they all say," Trent retorted. "And then, once they've got it in them, they all turn into whores, begging for more." Then he remembered his obligations as Zerk's temporary master. "I'm going to tell you this just once, slave, and you'd better get it right," he warned. He stabbed his finger into that twitching asshole as far as it would go, and, at the same time, he gave Zerk's bruised buttocks a stinging slap with the flat of his other hand. "I don't give a shit whether you can take it dry or not! I don't want to hear another word out of your mouth about 'please do this and please don't do that,' or you 'can't take this and you can't take that.' You're here to satisfy me, whether you like it or not! You got that? And when you talk to me, you damn well better remember to call me 'sir.' And you ask for 'permission to speak, sir,' before you open your cocksucking mouth to me again!"

He punctuated his remarks with another slap on Zerk's ass.

"Oh!" Zerk groaned in pain. "I'm sorry, sir! I won't do it again, sir! Permission to speak, sir?"

"Granted. What the fuck do you want, slave?"

"Please grease up your dick before you fuck me, sir. I can't take it without some lube, because you're so big, sir!" Zerk babbled.

"All you're going to get is a little dab of lube, slave," Trent grumbled. "I want you to really know you're getting fucked! You're going to feel it all, all of my hard meat up your hot, tight ass!"

He pulled his finger out of Zerk's ass, opened the top drawer of the nightstand, and rummaged through its contents. There was an open box of condoms and a large tube of lubricant.

"What a whore," Trent jeered. "Got everything right here, ready, don't you? Ready to take a dick up your ass. You lousy whore!"

Trent ripped open the little foil packet containing a condom and unrolled the rubber down over his agonizingly erect cock. He squeezed out a glob of the lubricating gel and massaged it thoroughly over the latex which now covered his erection.

"Can't believe a guy who looks as butch as you do is really such a goddamn horny cock whore," he taunted Zerk. He leaned forward as he spoke and used his weight to drive his stake inside that tiny opening.

"Oh! Oh, oh!" Zerk cried out wildly as the strong pressure thrust his anal aperture open and the thick head of Trent's dick, impossibly bulky and solid, forced its way through his hole and into the narrow chute that lay beyond it, inch by inexorable inch.

"Yeah, slave! That's some good, tight, hot ass you've got there! Take it! Open that ass and let me shove my cock right up in there!" As he spoke, Trent shoved harder, and he felt the resisting ass open and accept him. He encountered a momentary obstacle, a bend in Zerk's rectum. Grunting, he repositioned himself and pushed in furiously. A hoarse shout of agony burst from Zerk's lips, and he tugged at his bonds in a useless effort to free his wrists. Another brutal lunge, and Trent's dick was inside him the rest of the way. Trent's pelvis banged against the bottom curves of Zerk's butt, and his prick wedged itself securely deep inside Zerk's body.

"Fucking tight," Trent moaned as hot, firm anal muscles gripped his impaling prick. Zerk was already squirming under him, working his anal muscles in an instinctive effort to expel his cock, and the friction that resulted was fantastic!

Trent began to fuck his partner with long, steady thrusts and withdrawals, his face pressed to the back of Zerk's neck, his hands sliding under both their bodies to seize and pump on Zerk's cock-ringed prick, his hot breath brushing over Zerk's skin. Their naked bodies slapped together as their sweat mingled. Trent's piston of a prick moved in and out of the smoking-hot cylinder of Zerk's asshole like a well-oiled engine being revved up. Both men were moaning and panting desperately for breath. "Permission to speak, sir?" Zerk begged in a breathless whisper.

"Granted."

"Fuck me! Fuck me, sir! Oh, please, sir—fuck my slave ass!"

"Your ass is mine, boy!" Trent exulted.

His cock rammed in and out of that hot, squirming hole even faster than before. His excitement built to the point at which he could no longer control himself, and he would soon have to blast his wad, no matter how much discomfort he was costing his only-too-willing partner.

"Tell me how much you like it," Trent commanded heatedly. His tongue darted out to swab the interior of Zerk's ear, brushing aside the locks of brown hair. "Tell me how much you like to be fucked!"

"I like it, sir. I love it. You know I do." Zerk's body lunged up off the mattress to meet Trent's savage downward thrusts and increase the violence of the fuck. Their bodies impacted loudly together. "Oh, fuck me, sir! Come in my ass! I'm coming, sir, I can't help it, I'm there, I'm shooting!"

"Go ahead, slave. Lose that load!" Trent urged. The blond cop buried his prick in Zerk's asshole and took a tighter grip on Zerk's cock, his fingers digging into the cum-laden balls and pressing the blunt-pointed studs on the leather cock restraint into the underside of Zerk's shaft. The other cop screamed and began to come, his cock jerking so violently within Trent's fist that the rookie nearly lost his grip on it. But he held on and masturbated Zerk through the course of his ejaculation, laughing as the milky spurts spat from the tip of Zerk's penis and splattered thickly all over the bedclothes. Trent's fist pumped Zerk dry, making him shoot his full load. Cum smacked onto

Zerk's belly, dribbled down over his shivering thighs, and drenched Trent's fist.

Zerk sobbed as his climax shook him. His asshole tightened up in involuntary response when he came, and the extra pressure on Trent's cock was finally too much. He let go of Zerk's spent dick and wrapped both his solidly-muscled arms around the other guy's waist. Trent slammed his prick into that tight ass and himself burst deep inside Zerk, his climax none the less forceful for being contained by the condom. Zerk, the poor guy, was on his hands and knees beneath Trent's body, his wrists tugging at the rawhide cords that bound them to the bedposts, his booted feet hammering at the mattress, his mouth wide open in a cry of ecstasy as he wrenched his head back against Trent's shoulder and his whole body shook.

Trent crushed their hot bodies together, plunging his cock up Zerk's asshole to the hilt and keeping it there until he had pumped the last drops of his fiery fuck fluid into the rubber, which was pressing against Zerk's prostate.

Both men collapsed into a tangle of sweaty limbs on the bed, Trent's cock still planted between Zerk's buttocks. Gradually, though, Trent could feel his dick softening as the other stud's flexing sphincter continued to grip and massage it. He finally pulled out of Zerk's body and stripped the condom from his cock.

"No, give it to me." Zerk gasped when Trent stretched out his arm to deposit the used rubber on the nightstand.

"What the—?"

"I want to taste it. I want to lick your cum out of it."

"Pervert. Fucking pervert!" But Trent pushed the filled sac of the rubber under Zerk's nose.

* * * *

Zerk stuck his tongue out of his mouth, inserted it into the open end of the condom, and swabbed up the salty, slimy gel of Trent's jism. Then he buried his hot face in the crumpled pillows of the bed and let his entire body quake in the delicious throes of post-orgasmic muscular relaxation.

"Bitch," he heard Trent gasp. "Dirty, perverted little bitch!"

Zerk heard the taunt, but he didn't care. He *was* Trent's bitch, at least for tonight, and he exulted in the fact.

He fucked me! Trent fucked me! At last! And man, did he ever fuck me good! God damn, am I ever glad they gave me this big-dicked, blond bastard to be my partner!

Chapter Eight: Make Mine Vanilla

Relations between the two partners were slightly awkward the next day. Trent was having second thoughts. It was bad enough that he'd once again had sex with another cop, a guy he had to work with. That alone put him, especially as a rookie, in a vulnerable position. He didn't want to risk acquiring a reputation as the precinct's resident gay slut. And, worse, he and Zerk had gone really far together, getting into a much deeper scene than Trent had ever intended.

Up until now, Trent had been too caught up in his job to give much serious thought to his possible sexual and romantic future. He assumed that, some day, he might meet some guy he was especially attracted to, really compatible with, and they might settle down together. Having a lover, Trent imagined, would be basically like having a glorified roommate. They'd live together, sharing an apartment, and maybe they'd eventually think about buying a house. Because Trent certainly had no intention of getting involved with some irresponsible slacker, he took it for granted that there'd be two incomes coming into this purely imaginary household. Beyond that, Trent's thoughts about what domesticity with another man might be like, in the long run, were decidedly vague.

He liked Zerk, not only as a partner and a mentor, but now as a sex partner. The other cop was hot. He was obviously much more experienced than Trent. He could show Trent the ropes—literally, Trent thought, not without a flash of wry humor. But Trent couldn't picture himself falling in love with Zerk. The idea was absurd. For one thing, Zerk was all too obviously a cynical, play-the-field kind of a guy. For another, you couldn't actually *love* a guy with whom you were trading off verbal and physical abuse. Could you? What he and Zerk had done together was just an unusually intense, exciting way of getting their rocks off together. It was just a wild game guys played together to heighten the sexual experience. It didn't *mean* anything. It didn't mean that he, Trent Carothers, was really a sadist, or a masochist, or both, or whatever the hell he now feared he might be turning into!

Trent was flustered, and he was sure Zerk noticed his nervousness. Zerk waited until they were having their lunch break together at a diner. He glanced about to make sure no one in the other booths could overhear them before he took the initiative and broached the subject.

"All right, Carothers. Sooner or later, we're going to have to talk about what happened last night."

"I—well, what is there to talk about? We got our rocks off. It was just two horny guys helping each other out. You wanted to get a little kinky, so I went along with it."

"Oh, so it was all my doing, huh? You just went along for the ride?"

"You were the instigator," Trent said stubbornly.

"Don't try to pull that 'innocent little old me' act on me. That's almost as tired as 'I was really drunk, so I didn't know what I was doing.' You knew exactly what you were doing, and you got off on every minute of it. Man, I've got to hand it to you. You almost had me fooled. Here I thought, all this time, that you really weren't all that experienced. But you sure as hell didn't learn some of those moves overnight."

Trent tried to bluff it out. "I'm *not* very experienced. Not when it comes to that kind of rough sex. I was just making it up as I went along."

"Bullshit. This is another cop you're talking to, remember? I suppose you just happened to be carrying those two rawhide thongs around with you, Boy Scout? Damn! My wrists still hurt."

"I had them with me, ah, as just part of my undercover outfit. You know, my leather drag? So I'd blend in, in the bars—"

Zerk snickered. "Don't ever break the law yourself, Carothers, and get busted. You'd fold under interrogation in a minute. Now, getting back to your performance as a top man, last night—"

Trent blushed. "I don't want to talk about it anymore."

"Why not? There's nothing to be embarrassed about."

"Last night may have been a mistake, Zerk. Maybe we ought to cool it."

Zerk stared at him. "Cool it? What the hell are you saying? That I'm only good enough for a lousy one-night stand, as far as you're concerned?"

"Don't get mad, Zerk. We have to work together. Getting involved in some kind of a relationship outside of work—that would only complicate matters. That's all I meant when I said that now I think last night was a mistake."

Zerk's eyes narrowed. "Why, you stuck-up, arrogant little bitch!"

"I wish you wouldn't take it like that—"

"I'll take it any damn way I want! Jesus! I can't believe it. Played for a fool by some dumb, young punk, at my age!"

"Nobody's trying to play you for a fool, Zerk."

"Unbelievable," Zerk ranted on. "Letting my head get all fucked up by a kid like you, who's still wet behind the ears. Hell. You wouldn't last a minute on this job, if you didn't have me looking out for you, watching your back."

"Okay, I admit that," Trent said, a little coldly. "I'm new here, and you're not. You know a lot more than I do. I have a lot to learn. No argument about that. What they didn't tell me, when I signed up for this job, was that having you hit on me was part of the job description."

"There you go again. Me hitting on you. You, the complete fucking little innocent! You didn't put up much of a fight last night to protect that precious virtue of yours. You were hot for it. God damn hypocrite. Fucking prick teaser."

"If you want to tell the captain you don't want me to be your partner anymore—"

"Oh, shut the fuck up! Don't be so goddamn full of yourself. Don't make such a big drama out of it."

They both fell silent as the waitress brought their order, and they ate in a sullen, mutual silence, too.

Trent finally summoned the courage to speak as they were finishing. "Please, Zerk—" he began.

"Let's not talk about this any more right now, okay?" the other cop asked. "I might say something I'll regret. We're both pretty hot under the collar. Let's just go about our business, and give ourselves a chance to cool off...okay?"

"Okay," Trent agreed.

Trent had to give Zerk credit. For the duration of their shift, the other cop gave him neither the cold shoulder nor the silent treatment, but spoke to him amiably enough. Trent noticed, though, that Zerk did studiously avoid any discussion of personal matters.

Trent was grateful that the next day was his day off. He'd made no special plans, and, once he'd taken care of a few errands and household chores, he found himself going slightly stir-crazy. He was honest enough with himself to admit that much of this was the result of lingering anxiety about his quarrel with Zerk. Trent rehearsed, in his head, various speeches that he planned to try out in the morning to attempt to pacify his partner and restore some degree of equilibrium between them.

He had showered and changed into casual clothes, with the vague intention of possibly going out on the town for an hour or two, when his cell phone rang.

"It's me, Zerk," his partner announced unnecessarily, because his voice was unmistakable.

"Oh, hi."

"Are you still mad at me?"

"What are we, in high school? I was never *mad* at you, Zerk," Trent insisted. "We had a disagreement—that's all."

"What are you doing?"

"Nothing. Well, as a matter of fact, I thought I might go out, just for one drink."

"Why don't I meet you somewhere and we can have that drink together?"

"I don't know, Zerk. I kind of want to make an early night of it tonight. You know, get a good night's sleep for a change?"

"Then why don't you come on over to my place, or, better yet, I'll come to yours?"

"I don't think so, Zerk. Not tonight."

"Afraid I'll take advantage of you again, huh?"

"It's not that."

"No? What is it, then?"

"I don't know. Like I said, maybe we ought to cool it for a while."

"All right. I can wait."

"What do you mean, you can wait?"

"Until you come around, kid. Until you make up your mind and decide you want some more of what you had the other night. You'll come back begging for more, all right. They always do!"

"Why, you smug bastard, you!"

"Yeah, that's right, kid. Get mad. Go ahead and get good and mad. You're pretty hot when you're mad, as I recall."

"Stop talking that kind of shit. And stop calling me a kid!"

Zerk snickered. "I will, when you stop acting like one. When you man up and start acting like a grown man!"

"You son of a bitch!" Trent hung up in a rage.

He was angry, all right. And although he would never have admitted it to Zerk, suddenly, inexplicably, he *did* feel horny. His amorphous plans to possibly go out instantly solidified into a definite course of action, not unlike a flaccid penis that had suddenly stiffened as the direct result of some external stimulus.

I'll show him. I'll show him I don't need him or his weird ideas about sex. I'll go out and have myself a good time. I'll get laid, if I have anything to say about it!

He grabbed his car keys and left the apartment—a man on a mission.

He was able to think coherently enough to decide to avoid the kind of places where he might run into any of his fellow cops, let alone Zerk. And he was certainly going to avoid the sort of dives he and Zerk had been "working" lately as part of their job.

He drove to a comparatively upscale bar, which attracted a mixed crowd but was known as a gay pickup spot. This early in the evening, the place was crowded with businessmen types, some of them accompanied by female dates. Others were parts of small male groups or were alone and thus possibly on the prowl.

Trent was halfway through his first overpriced drink when he began to suspect he'd made a mistake by coming here. In order to fit in among the other patrons of this establishment, let alone hope to connect with one of them, he'd need a haircut, for starters, and would have to spend several hundred dollars on new clothes, jewelry, and cologne. He was the recipient of some looks from the other patrons that were more bemused and disapproving than inviting.

He had decided to finish his drink quickly, then go and try his luck elsewhere, when a guy came into the bar who made even the most blasé of the other customers turn their heads to check him out. He was handsome, with black hair and an unstylish thick mustache. He was a big man, and he had an incredible body. Trent had often heard the expression "built like a brick shithouse," but it didn't do justice to this guy's physique. An outhouse designed by a master architect to resemble a miniature Palladian villa might be an adequate comparison. The man had the kind of muscles that could only come from a serious, hardcore weightlifting regimen, but he was perfectly proportioned, which prevented him from looking bulky or clumsy. His jeans and orange polo shirt displayed his physique to its full advantage.

The man ordered a drink at the far end of the bar, and then, instead of taking one of the unoccupied bar stools, he carried his drink with him as he wandered into the crowd. Trent didn't want to be caught staring, so he concentrated on his own drink.

He had a nagging feeling that he'd seen this stud somewhere, once before. Well, perhaps that wasn't so surprising. Trent and Zerk had been spending a lot of time in gay bars and other hangouts lately. If this muscle man had patronized one of them on a night when Trent had also been there, of course Trent would have noticed him and remembered him now.

Maybe the dude's got an arrest record, and I recognize him from his mug shot!

He was sure that a hot number like the bodybuilder in the orange shirt was there to meet somebody, his girlfriend, for all Trent knew. Even if the guy was gay, he was no doubt so used to being admired, lusted after, and hit on that he could afford to be extremely choosy. Trent, who was beginning to feel not only unkempt but downright grubby in the midst of so many sleekly turned-out yuppie types, doubted he could ever have a chance with a guy like that.

He set his glass down and was about to push his stool back and stand up when he heard the voice, close to his ear.

"You're not leaving, are you?"

"Huh? What?"

"I said, you're not leaving, are you? You and I seem to be the only guys here who aren't wearing suits. If you go, I'll be all on my own."

It was, incredibly, the muscle man standing behind Trent and smiling down at him. God, he *was* massive. His shoulders, biceps, and chest kept the fabric of the polo shirt stretched taut across his torso, and even the fingers with which he was holding his drink looked as though they had well-developed muscles.

"Sorry," Trent said. "I wasn't paying attention."

"I'm not bothering you, am I?"

"Not at all. I was just—my mind was wandering, that's all."

"Let me buy you a drink."

"All right." Trent wasn't about to refuse an offer like this!

The big man got the bartender's attention and ordered another screwdriver for Trent and another club soda for himself.

"I'm a cheap date," he explained with a laugh. "I don't drink alcohol very often."

"Because you're in training?" Trent guessed.

"Yes. That's why I come in here, sometimes. I'm a personal trainer, you see, and some of my clients come here. It's a good place to get word-of-mouth referrals and to hand out my business cards." The bodybuilder smiled at Trent. "I'm Brandon, by the way."

"Trent." They shook hands. "I'm sorry I was a little out of it, before. You see, this guy and I had a fight."

"Boyfriend?" Brandon asked.

"No, just a guy I work with. It'll blow over. How'd you know I was gay?"

"I noticed you checking out all the other men in here and not paying attention to any of the babes."

"I wasn't necessarily looking at them as potential tricks," Trent joked. "I was wondering what it would be like to afford to dress the way they do."

"Oh, that's not difficult. All you have to do is be willing to max out a credit card. Anyway, it's too bad," Brandon said. "About you *not* having had a fight with a boyfriend, I mean. 'Rebound sex,' or 'revenge sex,' or 'getting back at the other guy sex,' whatever you want to call it—that can be some of the hottest sex there is."

"Oh? Do you speak from personal experience?"

"Sure. I think I'm an easy-going kind of a guy, but I've been known to pick a fight with the guy I was fucking around with, just for the pleasure of going out and cheating on him with somebody else, and then, of course, making up with him so we could have 'makeup sex.'"

"It sounds awfully complicated, Brandon. What kind of sex are you out looking for tonight?"

"Whatever kind I can get. And now that you bring it up, how'd you like to go back to my place and fool around for a while?"

"I'd like it just fine," Trent admitted. Then he hesitated. "You're not into anything kinky, are you?"

Brandon seemed surprised by the question. "No. Are you?"

"Yes. Sometimes. The only reason I ask is because I'm really in the mood for some just-plain-vanilla sex tonight. You know, nothing that requires a tool kit, or that's likely to turn into some sort of an acrobatic contest."

Brandon laughed. "I suppose I can be pretty boring in bed, if I try hard enough to be."

"You could never be boring in bed," Trent declared.

"Let's go, then."

Trent could already feel a stirring in his groin at the prospect of tricking with this hot number. "Yeah, let's."

Brandon, it turned out, lived close enough that he'd walked to the bar. They drove the short distance to his apartment in Trent's car. The apartment, a loft in a converted old warehouse building, was furnished with an eye for comfort, rather than ostentation. Brandon invited Trent to sit down beside him on the leather couch.

"You want something to drink?" Brandon asked.

"No, thanks." Trent hesitated. "Ah, Brandon…before we get started, I have a confession to make."

"Oh yeah? What's that?"

"I've never been with a guy with a body quite like yours. Athletic guys, in good shape, sure. I like that. But you're incredible. It's kind of intimidating."

Brandon smiled. "There aren't any muscles in the penis, you know," he joked. "Mine works just like any other guy's. But I understand what you mean. Some guys don't like bodybuilders. I've heard us referred to as 'fucks from outer space.' As in not quite human, or real."

"You look as though you've got what it takes to send me into orbit." Trent adopted his host's light-hearted tone.

"I'd like us to blast off together. Come on. Relax. Make yourself comfortable. You want to hear some music?"

"Sure."

"Put on something you like," Brandon suggested, "while I go tidy up the bedroom a little. I wasn't really planning on having company tonight."

"Don't go to any trouble on my account."

"You haven't seen the condition of the bedroom yet. I just want to make it semi-presentable." Brandon disappeared behind an open-ended brick wall that served as a partition in the large open space of the loft.

Trent stood up, went over to the shelf containing Brandon's audio equipment, and examined his collection of CDs. He chose a soft jazz disc, inserted it into the player, and turned it on. After a moment, the room was filled with sound—drums, piano, bass, a saxophone, a trumpet.

Brandon returned. "Oh, good choice," he said. "I like that one. Is there *anything* I can get you?"

"Yeah," Trent retorted boldly. "You can get naked!"

Brandon grinned at him. "All right, but you're going to have to strip, too."

They both undressed quickly, depositing their clothing on the floor.

"God, you've got a fantastic body," Trent exclaimed as he drank in the sight of Brandon's chiseled, hard-muscled nudity. "But I guess you hear that a lot."

"You're not so bad, yourself. Come here," Brandon urged.

When they were standing face-to-face, Brandon put his hand on the back of Trent's head then leaned toward him to give him a kiss.

"I believe you said something about keeping it vanilla tonight," he whispered as he nuzzled his lips over Trent's cheeks and chin before zeroing in on his mouth.

"Do you mind?" Trent whispered back.

"No, vanilla is good. Give this a taste, and tell me if you like it."

They began kissing, lips brushing together lightly at first, then pressing against each other with increasing urgency. Brandon slipped his tongue inside Trent's mouth, and Trent responded by using his own tongue-tip to push against the supple, fleshy invader.

"Come on into the bedroom," Brandon invited after he'd broken the kiss.

He led Trent behind the brick wall. The sleeping area was a large, open space, with floor-to-ceiling windows that had the drapes drawn over them at the moment. Brandon's low, king-sized platform bed, metal-framed, was set in the center of a big Oriental rug and had a small chest of drawers on either side of it. Brandon's tidying-up had evidently consisted mainly of gathering up some clothes that had probably been on the bed and on the floor and piling them onto a nearby chair. He'd also turned down the bed, plumped up the pillows, and turned on a small lamp set on one of the chests of drawers. Its shaded light cast a warm glow on that side of the bed.

The sheets and pillowcases were shocking pink. "Nice sheets," Trent couldn't help commenting.

Brandon laughed. "I do like bright colors," he admitted. "Let's see what you look like lying on them!" He gently pushed Trent down on the bed then got on top of him. His muscular body seemed to cover Trent completely and weighed him down on the mattress as he took the cop in his arms and began to kiss him again.

"Am I too heavy on you?" Brandon asked between kisses.

"God, no. You're just right."

The combination of Brandon's kisses and his weight on him was literally taking Trent's breath away. His hands roamed restlessly over every part of Brandon's body that he could reach, trying to find some area that wasn't solidly muscled, but finding none.

Trent was panting hard with raw sexual excitement when Brandon finally pulled his mouth away and began to kiss and lick and suck every part of the smaller man's body. Brandon ran his tongue over Trent's chest, lapping at his rounded pecs and pausing to suck each dark brown nipple in turn. Trent buried his hands in Brandon's thick, dark hair and groaned as the bodybuilder moved down over his belly, digging his tongue-tip into the deep pit of Trent's navel. Then Brandon licked the sleek skin of Trent's abdomen.

Trent knew that his crotch would be next, and, sure enough, with a low moan of lust, Brandon buried his face in the cop's groin. His bristly mustache rubbed against Trent's balls. He drew both spheres into his mouth at once, rolled the imprisoned nuts around with his tongue, and bathed them in his warm saliva before releasing them.

Brandon put his fist around the shaft of his trick's hot, horny cock and stuffed the head of it into his mouth, sucking passionately on it, and began to deep-throat Trent with long, excruciating yet delightful strokes that soon had Trent writhing and moaning with excitement on the bed.

* * * *

Brandon had been working so hard lately that it had in fact been some time since he'd taken any time off and allowed himself to pick up another guy for his pleasure. And it had been a long time indeed since he'd had a sex partner as attractive and as virile as Trent! He was determined to make the most of this opportunity to indulge himself.

As he blew Trent, Brandon ran his hands over as much of the other guy's nakedness as he could reach, stroking his chest, his flanks, his thighs, cupping the firm, muscular mounds of his buttocks in his palms and squeezing them possessively. He thought about how great it was going to feel to sink his inches of thick, throbbing steel between those buttocks and fuck this hot, young blond number

Good Cop, Bad Cop

shitless. But first he would have to get Trent thoroughly warmed up. The blow job ought to take care of that!

Brandon's wet lips slid up and down the shaft of the cock. He took more and more of the pulsating meat into his throat with each stroke. Down, down inched his sucking lips until he felt the massive cockhead push against the walls of his carefully cleared throat, cutting off his breath completely for a moment. He had to stop swallowing it or he'd choke!

There was still an inch or two of cockshaft outside Brandon's mouth. Trent was exceptionally well hung, rivaling Brandon's own endowment. But Brandon, try as he might, just couldn't take it all. Only an anatomical freak with an elastic esophagus could have deep-throated that whole thing and survived! It was just too fucking big!

He turned his head to get it into the best angle for comfortable deep-throating, and, holding Trent's squirming thighs firmly in his hands to keep the other man's lower body in place, he began to suck on that potent young prick, applying a fierce, uninterrupted suction from deep down in his dick-plugged gullet, milking that huge cock with every muscle he had in his neck and mouth. As Brandon had predicted and had been counting on, Trent lost all control!

"Suck it! Oh shit, yes, suck it!" Trent moaned. His hands twisted in Brandon's hair, tugged at the big man's ears, and stroked his reddening, puffed-out cheeks as the bodybuilder deep-throated him lustily. "Suck that dick, you big, muscle-bound freak!"

He sat up, which only rammed his cock deeper down Brandon's throat, and, clutching the muscular stud's hair, began to pump himself in and out of his cocksucker's mouth and throat. Brandon's mouth moved as he, too, got more excited. His lips took Trent's shaft all the way down to its thick root and then, retreating, caressed the entire throbbing length of the penile piston until only its blunt knob was still trapped between his warm lips. Brandon would inhale sharply through flared nostrils at this point to fill his straining lungs. Then he'd begin the process all over again, taking Trent's dick into his throat again and massaging it expertly with his throat muscles.

His tongue licked every square inch of the surface of the huge tool in his mouth with wanton, rapid flicks and strokes. Brandon took more and more of that cock into his throat. He could feel it throbbing and pulsing with a frantic life of its own as he sucked on it!

"Oh, God, Brandon, what a hot cocksucker you are!" Trent cried.

Brandon noted with satisfaction that his pickup was sobbing for breath and obviously wildly excited as a result of Brandon's expert fellating of him. Trent's body, wet with sweat, thrashed from side to side on the bed. Brandon's skillful tongue brought him ever closer to ejaculation.

Brandon knew what delicious torture the recipient of his oral attentions was going through. He knew what Trent must be feeling, understood why Trent jumped each time Brandon's tongue lashed up and down and coiled around his prickshaft like a cracking whip. He clamped his lips down still tighter around Trent and washed the saliva accumulated in his mouth back and forth between his cheeks to lave that hot young cock in the most erotic way imaginable. He was no longer just sucking Trent's cock. He was worshipping it with his mouth!

* * * *

Trent would have been happy to lie there and let Brandon blow him forever, but the bodybuilder was just too skilled at fellatio. He was quickly, inexorably, coaxing the hot semen right out of Trent's throbbing cock. Trent shuddered from head to foot as he felt himself starting to come.

"Oh, man, I'm coming! I'm going to shoot! I can't hold it in anymore!"

He moaned with relief when his sperm finally boiled up in his balls, rushed through the core of his dick, and blasted its way into Brandon's slurping mouth and grunting throat. The big man greedily swallowed it all, devouring spurt after spurt of the thick, hot fuck-cream Trent fed him.

"Oh, shit," Trent exclaimed when at last he had stopped firing his warm load down the other man's throat and his cock began to go soft and tender in Brandon's mouth. He laughed with nervous relief now that his orgasmic crisis was past. He took Brandon's face in his hands and pulled the husky stud against his chest so they could kiss. His tongue slid boldly into Brandon's panting mouth, and Trent tasted his own salty cum on the other man's tongue and lips. It tasted good!

Trent broke their long kiss and lay breathing hard against Brandon's huge chest, his chin resting on the other guy's shoulder. Brandon played with Trent's firm, smooth ass cheeks and silently encouraged Trent to keep toying with his immense hard-on, which had been neglected during the prolonged blow job.

"You didn't come," Trent pointed out.

"No, not yet. You want to suck mine?" Brandon whispered.

Trent hesitated for no more than a second. "You're hung so big, I don't know if I can take it all. Oh, what the hell?"

He was already slithering down Brandon's husky body, working his tongue over the muscleman's pecs and tits in awkward imitation of what Brandon had done to him. His haste betrayed his eagerness to get down to Brandon's aroused and enticingly musky-smelling crotch.

Keeping his hand wrapped firmly around the base of Brandon's cock, Trent buried his face in his pickup's groin and began to kiss and lick the head of the huge, throbbing penis while he masturbated it lightly.

Brandon gasped and put his hand on the back of Trent's neck, pushing down gently but insistently to urge the cop to go down on him all the way. With a moan, Trent opened his mouth as wide as he could and let the big cockhead slip between his lips. He began to suck, his jaws straining to accommodate all of that solid, masculine meat. He took more and more of the shaft into his mouth.

* * * *

"You give great head!" Brandon said. He leaned back and enjoyed the ride, working his hips slowly to ease himself back and forth inside the tight, wet oval formed by Trent's sucking lips. Brandon savored the way the blond put his tongue to work around his cockhead while he sucked. He caressed the mussed, fair hair that tumbled down over Trent's neck. Trent's head bobbed steadily up and down between Brandon's spread thighs. Brandon could feel his cock pounding madly within the other guy's warm mouth. He got more and more excited as the blow job went on. He would've liked nothing better than to have fired his sperm down Trent's greedy, receptive throat, but he had other plans for the hot load he could feel building up to fever pitch deep in his seminal vesicles and his swollen balls.

"Get it good and wet, baby," Brandon murmured huskily, stroking his cocksucker's cheeks, "because it's going to go right up your ass in a minute!"

Trent, sucking away uninterruptedly, merely grunted. Brandon knew he had succeeded in getting the guy so hot for his cock that he'd take it any way Brandon cared to put it to him.

He felt a spasm of near-ejaculatory response ripple through his dick, and he quickly tugged at Trent's hair, forcing the cop to pull his mouth away and let Brandon's meat go before the big stud shot prematurely. Trent was panting, his eyes glazed. He stared at the hard-on, slick with his own saliva, that waved only inches from his lips.

"Roll over," Brandon commanded tersely. "Get on your belly. I'm going to fuck that ass of yours, and fuck it good!" Without waiting for Trent to obey, he grasped the cop's waist and flipped him over as effortlessly as a short-order cook flipping hotcakes on a griddle.

And a tempting pair of hotcakes they were that now stared Brandon in the face. Trent spread his legs wide and buried his flushed face in the pillows, thrusting his firm ass high into the air, tacitly begging Brandon to fuck him. Brandon opened the top drawer of the chest of drawers on the right side of the bed, grabbed a condom, and put it on. He applied a tiny dab of lubricant. He didn't want his dick to be too slick. He wanted a little friction. Trent would just have to take it as it was—hard and horny and throbbing almost audibly with fuck-lust as Brandon prepared to ram it right up that tight ass!

The stud bodybuilder gripped Trent's ass cheeks and parted them roughly. When the cop immediately reached behind himself with both hands to take over, holding his buttocks whorishly wide open, Brandon was free to seize his cock in his fist and press its latex-sheathed tip into the hairy groove Trent was inviting him to violate. He gradually let his considerable weight sink onto the blond's body while his cock struggled to find the tiny anal opening and enter it.

* * * *

Trent moaned faintly and shuddered all over when he felt the huge head of Brandon's cock grind against his sphincter, but he'd been fucked often enough before, and so he forced himself to go limp, to relax, and to fight his instinctive urge to clench his muscular buttocks tightly together and squeeze his asshole shut to repel the anal attack.

Brandon's weight was all on him now, crushing him, gluing their bodies together with a film of sweat. The weightlifter jabbed his dick with undisguised eagerness against the small anal ring. It began to yield, and both men grunted in surprise, delight, and horny impatience as Brandon's cockhead pressed right through and was lodged firmly inside Trent's asshole, filling the narrow channel and stretching its walls.

"You're mine, boy!" Brandon gasped.

"You're so big!" Trent replied in disbelief.

Cold sweat seeped from Trent's pores as his body tried to adjust to the sudden feeling of fullness and friction, and Brandon began to push the rest of his mighty instrument inside him. His ass tightened up despite himself, and there was a moment of searing pain. Trent nearly blacked out!

"Christ!" he howled.

"Take it! That ass of yours is mine! Don't fight it! Open up! Open your ass and take my cock!"

"Shove it in me quick." Trent moaned frantically. "The rest of it, give it to me all at once!"

He opened his mouth in a scream as Brandon took him at his word and did what he'd asked, ramming half of his shaft after the head of his cock and forcing the cylindrical anal sheath to stretch wide around the steady onslaught of inserted prick. Trent cried out again but bravely gritted his teeth and slammed his ass backward and upward until he was completely impaled on Brandon's manhood and the bodybuilder was buried in hot anal flesh up to his balls!

Moaning, Trent went limp again but instinctively began to work his hips and his anal muscles to ease the pressure deep inside him. His abandoned movements seemed to drive Brandon wild. The bigger man began to long-dick the smaller one in a frenzy of unbridled lust, bracing himself on his elbows and knees on the mattress and using his powerful thigh muscles to drive his cock back and forth inside the tight, clasping tube of hot rectal tissue that now gripped and caressed him so intimately.

But as Brandon's humping motions began to equal Trent's in their lusty violence, the blond stud's rectal muscles tightened up and began to resist the steady pumping rhythm of the bodybuilder's cock in and out of his ravaged ass.

Brandon slackened his furious pace a bit. "You okay? Am I hurting you?"

"Fuck me! I don't give a shit if it does hurt! Fuck me, big man! Oh, God, *fuck me!*"

Brandon began to fuck Trent again, more gently perhaps, but insistently, never letting up. He eased himself in and out of the tensed anus in long, slow strokes and soon had Trent moaning in a way that suggested lust had begun to overpower any pain he might still feel. Brandon slid his massive arms under the lithe young body, fondled Trent's cock, stroked his belly, and played with his tits. He pressed his face to the back of the blond's neck and began to kiss him repeatedly, reassuringly. His excitement mounted once more, and he and his partner soon reestablished that initial wild fucking rhythm, in a no-holds-barred celebration of intense male lust.

Trent was taking Brandon's cock now like a seasoned pro, and he was doing everything in his power to be the hottest fuck Brandon had ever had in his life! Brandon was all the way inside him now, his tool lodged deep inside Trent's cringing butt. And Trent was responding to his thrusts and withdrawals now with frenzied eagerness, taking the bodybuilder's cock and loving it.

"Fuck me, fuck me, Brandon!" he shouted. "Fuck my goddamn ass!"

"I'm fucking you, all right, you've got my dick all the way up your hole!"

Brandon thrust forward and seemed to sink even deeper into the anal canal that now welcomed him unreservedly. They were both dripping with sweat. They fought for breath. The mattress creaked loudly beneath their jammed-together, impacting bodies. Trent's ass was relaxed completely now, the muscles giving way to Brandon's cock, accustoming themselves to the reaming. Brandon pulled back, only to plunge forward again and again. Trent tightened his ass up, but only to increase the friction that was sending both men into a dizzying orbit of erotic excitement and mindless sensual gratification.

Big stud bodybuilder on top of me, fucking me! Hard muscles pounding away on top of me, driving that dick in and out of my ass! Fucking me! Oh, God! The only way this could be any better would be if this big muscle stud tied me up and made me into his slave!

"Fuck me!" he groaned aloud again, rearing up each time Brandon rammed into his guts. He grunted, gripped Brandon's grinding hips awkwardly with both of his hands, and then slipped his fingers between their bodies to keep his ass cheeks spread wide apart so Brandon could fuck him as deeply as possible. Pulling farther back, Brandon pushed into that insatiable ass again. He was rapidly losing all self-control. But Trent couldn't have cared less. "Fuck me, man!" he yelled. "Fuck me as hard as you can!"

* * * *

"I am fucking you," Brandon moaned. "And I can't believe the way you're taking it, man…your ass is so hot…you're the hottest fuck I've had in a long, long time!"

Brandon raised himself on his hands for a moment, as though he were performing push-ups, to look down at the beautiful young body surrendering itself totally to his brutal thrusts. Trent's butt was a double mountain of writhing, solid flesh, curving up enticingly from the valley of his trim waist and the small of his arched back. And Brandon's thick cock was jammed between those ripe buttocks, plunging in and out of the deep gorge between them, and his groin was slamming against the resilient flesh of those firm ass cheeks with bruising force, bouncing upon that hard, athletic young frame with complete abandon. Brandon's dick looked slickly oiled with lube and sweat as it disappeared inside the red, inflamed-looking sphincter muscle rubbing tightly all around its bulk.

But, as usual, when he risked taking a look down at just what he was doing, at the exciting, obscene spectacle of his prick violating another guy's butt, Brandon could feel his long-delayed orgasm coming upon him in a rush of semen, wild and uncontrollable. He grunted, pistoned his cock in and out of Trent's body in a frenzy, then collapsed on the blond man's back and prepared to pour out his liquid lust into him without mercy.

He was barely conscious of Trent's rhythmic moans, or of his fists flailing against the pillows, or of his back corded with taut muscle. Trent absorbed shock after shock upon and inside his body.

"Take it, man, here I fucking come!" was all that Brandon had time to gasp out into Trent's ear by way of warning before he came in torrents up the cop's quaking asshole. Brandon cried out in heart-stopping fury as his whole body spasmed, the way it did down at his gym during a good workout. Often, while lifting the weights, he got the kind of pump that was more painful than pleasurable because he'd forced his aching muscles to take more punishment than they could bear and he could feel the warm rush of extra blood surging desperately into his capillaries to soothe the strained tissues. He felt just that kind of a pump now, but this time the ache was concentrated in his penis!

He exploded again and again inside Trent's tight ass, his cum filling the condom.

"Oh God, Trent!" he cried. "I'm coming! You're making me come! I can't hold it back any longer. It all just feels too fucking good!"

* * * *

"Don't even try to hold it back," Trent urged. "Don't hold anything back! Come if you have to! Come!"

Trent pushed back against Brandon's groin to receive him completely. He called out Brandon's name hoarsely and repeatedly, liberally punctuated with gasps of "Fuck!" He tightened his spread legs around Brandon's, his hands groping back to grip the bodybuilder's ass muscles and press his thick, bursting cock even further inside his well-fucked butt.

"That's right, big man," Trent rasped. "Take me! Fuck me! I'm yours!"

Many a true word is uttered in the heat of passion. This was indeed what Trent wanted, what he had secretly longed for, for so long, to be completely possessed by another man, to give himself without reservation.

Chapter Nine: On the Prowl

Zerk, after Trent hung up on him that same evening, was also angry and horny.

Goddamn rookie. Still wet behind the ears, but he thinks he can act like a big man around me! I'll show him! I'll break the little bastard and make him my bitch, if it kills me! I'll have him on his hands and knees, begging, begging for my dick, before I'm done with him!

On the other hand, the kid was hot. Zerk couldn't deny that. Zerk wanted him. Either way! He'd gladly play either top or bottom man with Trent Carothers, whom he sensed had real potential as a fellow leather enthusiast.

No, I'd rather be Trent's bitch. Naked with my hands tied behind my back, handcuffed, maybe, yeah, handcuffed, like a goddamn perp! And that big blond bastard standing over me, force-feeding me his prick—making me choke on it!

"I'm going to go out of my freaking mind if I keep thinking about it," he said aloud. "If I don't get laid—!"

Then he did the only sensible thing, in the circumstances. He stopped thinking and acted by pure, animal, self-serving instinct. As though he'd rehearsed the actions carefully well in advance, Zerk got his jacket and his car keys, left his apartment, got into his car, and drove unerringly into the downtown section of the city. At this time of night, with so many of the businesses closed, there was comparatively little traffic.

He took an off ramp and a road that wound through a small business district off the freeway then changed to a narrow, two-lane road that ran through a thick, wooded area with several dirt side roads where picnickers and campers could go. Signs posted prominently warned that these activities were limited to the daylight hours, unless one obtained a special permit. Zerk took one of the dirt roads, driving for almost a mile off the paced highway before he stopped the car in a gloomy, heavily wooded, deserted area. Deserted, that was, except for the kind of gay men who were into quick, anonymous pickups and sex in the open air. Even some of the local straight men knew about this secluded area and kidded each other about it as a notorious homosexual cruising spot.

Zerk turned off the engine and just sat there, not sure of what his next step should be. He still found it difficult to concentrate on anything but Trent Carothers and the fight they'd just had on the phone. Zerk's imagination was tormented by obscene visions of his handsome young blond partner, of his enormous, thick cock, which Zerk had sucked so passionately, of the pleasure he'd experienced when it had fucked him in his ass. Zerk's dick became fully erect in his pants, almost touching the lower rim of the steering wheel, when he thought about the salty taste of the young bearded cop's hot cum in his mouth, about kissing Trent on the lips!

Another car was driving very slowly down the dirt track, a battered coupe, driven by a handsome, slightly surly-looking young man with carelessly tousled long brown hair. As his car passed Zerk's, the driver turned his head and smiled at him in open, blatant sexual invitation. The driver hit the brakes and slowed down even more, to a crawl, before pulling over a few hundred feet ahead of Zerk's vehicle and stopping altogether. His brake lights flashed on and off several times, and well acquainted with cruising techniques as he was, Zerk recognized this as a signal, a come-on. Impulsively, he blinked his own headlights, then waited, his heart pounding in his chest, his hands cold and clammy as they caressed the steering wheel nervously, for lack of anything better to do.

The young stud opened his car door and got out. He was wearing the tightest jeans Zerk had ever seen. The taut fabric followed every contour of his slender, firm body, and the outline of his cock showed plainly through the staring crotch of the pants. Quite a long, thick outline, Zerk noticed. Compared to this exhibitionist, he was a model of modesty when he dressed the part to go out cruising as part of his undercover work. Zerk stared lustfully at the guy's big basket as he strolled toward him, trying his best to look casual about it.

"Hi," the young man said, in a surprisingly deep, masculine voice, as he leaned against Zerk's car door to look in at him. "Been here long?"

"No, I just got here."

"It looks like it's going to be kind of slow tonight."

"Yeah."

"Yeah," the other guy agreed, placing his thumb in his left front pocket and lightly rubbing the outline of his dick through his jeans with his fingertips. Zerk choked at the sight of the growing bulge in the guy's pants as he continued to massage it slowly and teasingly with his palm. "Want to go for a little ride?" the young number asked when Zerk didn't say anything.

"Sure, get in."

The guy got into Zerk's car, and Zerk managed to get it started and in gear, despite his trembling hands.

His passenger was looking in the rearview mirror.

"What's the matter?" Zerk asked.

"Nothing. I just wanted to make sure nobody was following us. For a minute there, when I first got a good look at you, I thought you might be a cop."

"Me? A cop? That's a laugh. What made you think that?"

The passenger shrugged. "Oh, I don't know. They always seem to send the really butch ones out trolling to catch us. Turn down here," he told Zerk, indicating another side path. "Stop here. Jesus, man, don't go too far, or they'll be able to see us from that overpass! What's the matter, haven't you ever done this before?"

"Done what before?"

"Taken a guy out here in the bushes for a blow job," the young man said, matter-of-factly.

"Uh, not in this exact place. I'm new in town," Zerk lied. "I heard this was a good cruising place."

"You heard right. You ready?"

"I guess so."

"Let's give ourselves a little more room," the young number suggested as he quickly opened the door on his side and stepped out of the vehicle. "Come here, toward me."

Zerk slid over on the seat and sat on its edge, with his feet on the ground. His pickup was standing facing him, his crotch just a few inches from Zerk's face. The cop leaned over and placed his mouth over the outline of the young guy's cock through those tight jeans. He mouthed the worn denim, closing his lips around the lump the stud's dick formed underneath the fabric, as though he was already sucking it. The warmth of his mouth seemed to penetrate the worn denim, and the pressure from his lips sent a shiver of excitement through his pickup's body. Zerk was already getting off on licking, sucking, and gently biting that rapidly growing meat through the thin, soft, denim cloth.

"Take it out, buddy. I really want to suck on it." Zerk panted, excited by the mere fact that he was actually saying such a thing to a complete stranger. "Show me your naked dick!"

His trick's only response was the one he wanted. He unzipped his jeans and pulled his long, thick cock out of its tight confinement. Gasping at the size of the piece of meat being offered to him, Zerk unfastened his own pants, then raised his ass slightly off the car seat and pulled them down to his knees. His dick stood rigidly erect, its thick head pointing directly up from his crotch as Zerk bent over and took the head of the other guy's hard dick into his mouth. The cockflesh felt hot, instantly transforming his breath around it into the fiery blast from a furnace, and he began easing more and more of the long, pulsating ramrod between his lips, licking hard and fast with his tongue around the entire thickness of its head.

"Oh shit, man, you suck good." The younger man moaned. His cock had disappeared halfway into Zerk's mouth, the head beginning to enter the cop's hot, moist, hard-suctioning throat.

As Zerk continued taking more of his trick's considerable length into his mouth very slowly, relishing every solid inch, he reached up with both hands and unbuckled the guy's belt. With that done, he slid the jeans down around the young stud's ankles, still sucking his cock the whole time with undiminished hunger.

Zerk's hand slid upward on one hairy, muscular thigh until it reached the base of the prick he was sucking. He took a firm hold on the base of the erection and wrapped three fingers of his hand around the balls below it. His other hand went down into his own lap under his bent-over, hard-sucking torso, and with rapid up-and-down motions of his right arm, Zerk beat himself off while he sucked the young punk.

Suddenly, backing up to pull the cock out of his mouth, Zerk gasped, "Let's lie down to do it."

Without waiting for an answer, he opened the door on the other side of the car as well then stretched out across both of the front seats on his back with his legs spread widely apart. The other man was quick to follow. He crawled in between Zerk's legs and, somewhat to the older man's surprise, he took half the length of Zerk's cock inside his mouth. Zerk hadn't really expected this hot young number to reciprocate. He'd assumed the guy was trade, more or less.

"Bring your dick up by my face so I can watch you beat it off, before you shove it back in my mouth," Zerk demanded. "Jack off for me, you fucker!"

The cocksucker swung his body around, never taking his mouth off Zerk's tool, so that his legs were straddling Zerk's chest. His prick hung straight down, just inches above the other man's eager face.

"Now stroke it, man," Zerk whimpered. "Stroke it and suck me off, and then I'll suck you, too. Let's sixty-nine."

"Sure, Daddy. Whatever you say."

As the other guy held Zerk's dick in his mouth with his left hand, he reached downward with his right hand and began to flail himself, slowly but energetically stroking and squeezing the entire hefty length of his thick, uncut cock. Zerk's eyes were glued to that fat, round cockhead emerging from its retracted sheath of foreskin. It reminded him of Trent's uncircumcised penis. The younger man's slowly moving fist was manipulating the foreskin. His restless hand action would first cover, then uncover, the head of his cock in a steady pumping rhythm of masturbatory intensity.

The young stud was gradually taking more and more of Zerk's lust-swollen cock into his mouth and down his throat. As he sucked, he lowered his body so that the head of his cock could touch Zerk's panting lips. He jabbed blindly, obviously hoping that Zerk would soon start sucking him again. He was jacking himself off much faster now, and his fast-moving hand would occasionally touch Zerk's face in its eagerness to squeeze the cum from his balls. His mouth was now going up and down on the full length of Zerk's hard-on with ever-accelerating urgency. His tongue licked the head of the dick as it went in and out of his hot, wet, slippery mouth, just before it was driven deeply back into his voraciously receptive throat.

"Jack off, you cocksucker, I want to see you come." Zerk gasped. He could feel the expert cocksucking beginning to have its inevitable effect on his own pulsating prick. His trick could surely feel Zerk's nuts constrict in his left hand, and he must be aware that he would soon be getting a mouthful of the older guy's too-long-pent-up jism. He started sucking with the speed and eagerness of a wild man, at the same time speeding up his fist's pounding of his own prick.

"Suck it, buddy. Eat it, you horny little cocksucker," Zerk demanded. He felt his balls beginning to pump their unbearably hot liquid up into his cockshaft. "Oh God, I'm going to shoot! Put it down your fucking throat, baby, get every drop of it! Suck it! Suck it *off!*"

Then Zerk let out a wild, incoherent cry of lust as he saw the cock above his face explode a stream of thick white cum, and he felt the first wad of the hot, sticky cream strike his lips. Desperate to taste that semen, Zerk opened his mouth wide and began sucking the hot torrent of jism that was now spurting into his mouth and down his throat in such generous quantities.

With his mouth filled by the gushing load, he groaned loudly from deep within his throat when he felt his own meat erupting its load deep into his pickup's hot, suctioning throat. It seemed to Zerk that the two of them were never going to stop filling each other's hot, wet throats with cum. Their cocks continued to pump wave after hot, searing wave of fuck fluid into their eagerly drinking mouths and desperately swallowing gullets.

Finally, though, Zerk lay on his back on the car seats with his mouth wide open and panting for breath, his tongue sticking out of his lips and trying to lap up the last few drops of sweet-tasting sperm as they dripped from the other guy's thoroughly depleted but still rigidly erect cock.

Both men remained motionless for several minutes, the younger guy straddling Zerk's body with his now-spent prick dangling in front of the cop's flushed face, his own mouth still tightly surrounding the soft cock he'd just sucked dry. At last, though, the stud removed his lips from Zerk's tool, swung his body around, and, with considerable agility, managed to wriggle himself free from the front seat of the car. He stood beside it and pulled up his jeans.

"Thanks, man," he muttered as he zipped up. "But we'd better get the hell out of here before some stinking cop comes along and catches us!" He walked away, back toward his own car, without looking back at the hard-breathing man sprawled across the car seats. "I really needed that," he called. "I'll see you around."

Zerk wasn't able to summon the energy to do more than grunt in reply. He struggled to clear his throat of the wad of thick, salty cum the young stud had just deposited there, savoring its acrid taste on his tongue and thinking about Trent Carothers—what *his* cock felt and tasted like in his mouth, and how *his* semen tasted on his tongue, filling his mouth, sliding down his throat.

He was about to maneuver himself back into the driver's seat when the harsh white beam of a flashlight struck his face, blinding him. At the same instant, before Zerk had time to react, a voice barked, "Freeze! You're busted, you cocksucker!"

He recognized the voice, and then, when he struggled to sit up and blocked the flashlight's glare with one upraised hand, he recognized the face, as well.

"De Soto! You son of a bitch!" Zerk hissed. "You nearly gave me a heart attack!"

His fellow cop, who was also dressed in civilian clothes, turned off the flashlight. "You're getting careless in your old age, Kostopoulos," he taunted. "Anybody could have wandered over here and seen you and that punk sucking each other off."

"Are you working?" Zerk asked, a little nervously. "Trolling the bushes for queers?"

"No, not tonight. Luckily for you."

"Where's your car? I didn't see it when I drove in here."

"It's parked over there." De Soto jerked his thumb to indicate the general direction. "I've been hiking around."

"Hiking around, my ass. You're cruising for dick, the same as me."

"So what if I am?" There was an edge of belligerence in De Soto's voice.

"So don't act like you're any better than me," Zerk said.

"Okay. I won't."

"Well, don't just stand there. Get in the car."

De Soto did so, and Zerk put the car in gear. But he didn't drive to where the other police officer's vehicle was parked. Instead, he followed one of the winding dirt tracks deeper into the undeveloped land.

"Where are we going?" De Soto asked.

"Oh, nowhere in particular. I thought maybe you'd like to talk."

"Sure, Zerk." But they didn't talk. Suddenly, Zerk braked to a halt, where the dirt road came to an abrupt dead end, next to the fields. In the distance, a row of low hills could be glimpsed through dense growths of trees, clearly outlined against the moonlit horizon.

"So," Zerk said, with a hint of a challenge in his voice. "What've you been up to lately?"

"Oh, nothing much. I have been doing some research on that leather shit you're so interested in."

"Oh, really? You?"

"What's so funny about that?" De Soto demanded.

"You're so white bread, man, you're practically toast."

"I ought to make you eat those words."

"I'd like to see you try."

"Kostopoulos, are you daring me?"

"Yeah. I'm daring you to act like a man for a change, instead of like some pathetic closet case."

"Don't get me pissed off," the other cop warned.

"Go ahead," Zerk taunted. "Get pissed off. Get good and pissed off. What do I have to be worried about? It's not like you're man enough to top me."

"You bitch. You fucking bitch. You challenging me? We'll see. We'll see who's man enough. Take off your clothes. I'm going to fuck you right here, out in the open, where anybody can see us, and you're going to love it!"

"You haven't got the balls."

"No?" De Soto opened the car door on his side. "Let's see who backs down first. Get out," he ordered, curtly. "Get out and strip naked, boy. Now!"

This was exactly the sort of dangerous, exciting game playing that Zerk enjoyed the most. As he obeyed, getting out of his side of the car slowly and with a reluctance that both men knew was feigned, De

Soto got out, too. He unbuckled his belt and slipped the wide length of leather from his jeans. He doubled up the belt, letting it hang loosely at his side.

"Drop your pants, punk," he grunted.

"I'm not your punk. Not yours, not anybody's," Zerk boasted.

"No? We'll see about that, big man. We'll see. I think you're going to drop your drawers, right now. I think you're going to submit to me and get a little discipline. I think that blow job you just had was only a warm-up, wasn't it? You want more, don't you? That dumb young kid didn't begin to satisfy you, did he? Hell, no. You need some real man action—some *cop* action. Don't you?"

"Yeah," Zerk breathed.

"Drop 'em. Now!"

Zerk unfastened his own belt buckle, then his pants, with trembling hands.

"Lose the shirt, too," De Soto told him.

Zerk stripped his shirt off and tossed it onto the hood of the car. He stood there, his bare torso gleaming palely in the moonlight.

"Keep going," De Soto sneered. "Get naked."

"But it's—"

"Shut up! I thought a slave isn't supposed to speak to his master unless he's spoken to."

"You, my master," Zerk jeered. "You, anybody's master! That's a hot one. I ought to—" And then Zerk let out a yelp of pain as De Soto's belt slashed through the air and landed flat and loud against his chest. Then De Soto hit him again, on the ass. Finally, enraged by the way the other cop just stood there gaping at him, defying his orders, De Soto brought the belt upward between Zerk's legs and struck him in the crotch.

"Owww! You fucking sadist!" Zerk howled.

"Look who's talking," De Soto jeered. "Now, I've had about all the lip I'm going to take from you, boy! You better shuck those pants *now*."

His body burning with the belt lashes, his gasps catching in his throat, Zerk quickly pushed his jeans down to his ankles.

"All the way off," De Soto commanded. "And your boots, too. Everything, slave boy. I want that body of yours bare-assed naked."

When Zerk hesitated, the belt landed on him again. He shed his few clothes as quickly as he could. Then he stood in front of De Soto naked, his cock already stiffening with anticipation of what the other man might do to his exposed and vulnerable body.

Feeling his own cock bulging between his legs, De Soto unzipped his pants and pulled it out into the open air. "Get down on your knees in the dirt in front of me and suck it."

Zerk approached, wary of the belt dangling from De Soto's fist, but he was excited and getting even harder now. The husky Greek-American stud fell to his knees and put his hot, sweet, juicy mouth around the head of his prick, letting out a single loud moan of satisfaction at its size and taste before he opened his lips wider and stuffed the rest of the cock inside.

"Suck it, Xerxes," De Soto urged, panting. "Oh, you always were good at giving head!"

Zerk was good at it, all right. Very good. *I'm a hell of lot better at sucking dick than you are at being a top man!*

Still, even the token gestures toward dominance which De Soto had made had gotten Zerk wildly excited as he slipped naturally into a subservient role. He deep-throated De Soto with an easy expertise that he was smugly confident few other cocksuckers had ever demonstrated for the Puerto Rican stud's benefit.

Zerk could hear De Soto grunting as he stood there and got blown. The other cop's passivity didn't fool Zerk. He knew his mouth was giving the man intense pleasure, the kind of pleasure that no man could resist—or enjoy for long without being in danger of coming. He wasn't surprised when De Soto suddenly let out a gasp, and pushed Zerk away from his groin.

"Get back up on your feet," De Soto commanded. "Go over there and lean against that tree trunk. I'm going to warm up that butch ass of yours before I fuck it!"

"Don't get too carried away," Zerk advised, even as he began to obey the command. "You don't exactly know what you're doing. You're just a fucking amateur."

"I think I'll get the hang of it, fast enough. And you'd better stop mouthing off to me, boy!"

"Don't hurt me, master. Please don't hurt me too much." Zerk had intended the plea to be sarcastic. But his voice, as he backed against the rough bark of a large tree nearby, sounded more imploring and passionate than ironic, let alone truly fearful, even to his own ears.

"No one gave you permission to speak, slave. Turn around," De Soto demanded. "Face the tree. Get your arms around it. Hug it. Spread your legs some. Rub your dick against the tree trunk." Then De Soto raised the belt again.

He had a target now—Zerk's beautiful, hard-muscled, butch ass, which he proceeded to beat with the leather strap until the big guy collapsed to his knees, still hugging the tree with both brawny arms and moaning in genuine pain.

As though possessed, De Soto continued to lash him, snapping the belt back, lifting it high, bringing it down hard on Zerk's moonlit, pale, naked body, which cringed and writhed at each fierce blow. At last, Zerk fell away from the tree and lay on the grass screaming, trying to protect his face and crotch and newly welted ass from the rain of blows, cursing in a polyglot mixture of English and Greek, and raising a cloud of dust in the shadows. Suddenly, amidst the hail of leather, Zerk sprang up with a choked cry of "No! No More!" and ran out from under the tree and across the empty field behind it.

De Soto flung the belt aside and pursued him. He must've found it rough going through the uneven, grassy terrain, but Zerk was barefooted, so it was an unequal contest, and De Soto quickly caught up with him, right there in the middle of the field under the full moon. A flying tackle brought the naked police officer crashing to the dirt.

Clods flew in all directions as De Soto roughly mounted Zerk, forcing him to lie face down when the other cop tried to throw him off and escape. They wrestled, De Soto pushing Zerk's face into the soft moist soil until he stopped struggling and lay beneath De Soto passively, surrendering. De Soto let go then, which allowed Zerk to get his breath back in great, racking sobs.

De Soto reached into his pocket and pulled out a condom, then pulled his pants down, put on the rubber, and prepared to enter Zerk.

"Feel that, punk?" he demanded viciously, jabbing his unlubricated but fully erect and condom-sheathed cockhead between Zerk's squirming buns, searching for his asshole and finding it at once. "That's a man's prick going into your ass, getting ready to fuck you shitless, man!"

"You fucking amateur," Zerk taunted.

"I'll show you." De Soto lunged. His cock sank into Zerk's ass.

"Go ahead and fuck me, you dirty bastard. But not so rough, for Christ's sake! You're hurting me!"

"Bullshit. You love it like this, don't you? You like it rough and nasty. And besides, who could hurt a whore like you? This must be nothing compared to what some of your leather buddies do to you. Can you feel me in there, Zerk? Can you feel my big dick inside you, fucking you?"

Without waiting for an answer, De Soto plunged deeper into the hot, moist, responsive interior of Zerk's body, going in faster and harder with each new lunge.

"Take it! Take my cock!" he chanted, jerking his loins harder against the other cop's prone and shuddering body, slamming it down into the dirt, feeling how the muscles beneath him were taut with agony and pleasure! "I'm fucking you, big man. How's it feel?"

"Good," Zerk groaned. "Oh, you know it feels good, motherfucker, you know how much I like it. Yeah, fuck me, fuck me hard!" His outstretched hands dug into the loose earth and scattered it in clumps. "Harder," he demanded. "Fuck me harder, fuck me until it hurts! You hung son of a bitch! You fucking stud!"

Zerk had succeeded in goading the other cop to the point at which De Soto got really rough with him. De Soto seemed to cast aside his last vestiges of restraint. He fucked Zerk as, Zerk flattered himself, he had never fucked any other guy, with an insane abandon and a bruising, unrelenting energy. Zerk accepted everything that his fellow police officer was doing to him, with a greedy subservience that only inspired De Soto to jab his cock even harder, even deeper, into his convulsively responsive asshole. De Soto began to curse in Spanish as he abused the naked man who was sprawled beneath him in the dirt.

"Harder," Zerk urged. "Fuck me harder!" Then, no longer capable of coherent speech, he began to emit strangulated grunts.

De Soto got there fast. Too fast. With a yell of frustration, he tore his dick out of Zerk's butt, stripped off the rubber and flung it away, grabbed a fistful of Zerk's hair, and wrenched the other cop's head around toward him.

"You whore," De Soto cried. "You filthy, fucking whore. You dog in heat. Take my goddamn cum! Yeah!" De Soto came violently, spraying his white scum all over Zerk's handsome face, which was now almost unrecognizable beneath the sweat and dirt streaked over it. Then, exhausted, De Soto flung Zerk aside and collapsed onto the cool, moist earth and grass. The two men lay there gulping in air, breathing loudly, staring up at the night sky and the stars.

"You all right?" De Soto gasped, finally.

"*Now* you're worried?" Zerk retorted. He turned onto his side to reveal the muddy streaks of his own cum on his belly and thighs. His cock was still dribbling the last of its load. "I've got to give it to you, buddy, that was some scene, for a beginner. But we'd better get our asses out of here before we push our luck. If anybody were to come along and see us—"

"What do you mean, *us*? You're the one who's naked. Anyway, it's not as though they could bust us. But come on." De Soto helped Zerk get up, and they went back to the car. Zerk got dressed, fast.

De Soto gave Zerk directions, and Zerk drove to where De Soto's car was parked. De Soto didn't get out of Zerk's car right away, though.

"Let's talk for a minute, Zerk," he suggested.

"Sure."

"This was nice. This was almost like old times. Well, maybe it was a little wilder than what we used to do."

"I thought you couldn't get into the rough stuff."

"I'm full of surprises, I guess. Anyway, how are you and that sexy partner of yours getting along?"

"Fine."

"Have you nailed him yet?"

"None of your business, buddy."

"I'll take that as a yes," De Soto said, with a laugh. "I'm jealous. I'm still a little in love with you, Xerxes."

"No, you're not. You're in love with your wife and your kids. I thought we agreed to can all that love talk."

"Sorry. God, you're such a hard ass."

"What do you want from me? Okay, maybe I'm a little in love with you, too, in a guy way," Zerk admitted. "But you're married. Sneaking around, always getting together in secret, always watching the clock, never being able to sleep together because you always have to get out of bed when we're done and head home…that's not for me."

De Soto sighed, then consulted his wristwatch. "Well, speaking of watching the clock, I admit it, I've got to get home. How about a good-night kiss?"

"You've got some nerve," Zerk said, humorously. "Most guys kiss me *before* they fuck me, at least. Come here, you big dumb lug."

They kissed, lingeringly. Then De Soto went to his own car. Zerk followed him out of the park. On the street, they went their separate ways.

Chapter Ten: Role Playing

Trent dreaded facing Zerk the next day. He wasn't comfortable with the uneasy truce he and his partner had established. Trent's only consolation was the fact that he had Brandon's business card tucked away inside his wallet. The bodybuilder had given him a standing invitation to call him so they could get together again. The sex had been great, and Trent was already looking forward to repeating the experience. And he liked Brandon. Now, there was the kind of guy Trent could give some serious thought to hooking up with, for something more substantial than the occasional fuck-buddy get-together.

All this Dom and sub stuff was just me going through a phase. I had to give all that kinky stuff a try to find out what it was like and get it out of my system. Now I'm past all that. I'm ready to start looking for some decent, ordinary guy to maybe get involved with.

He met Zerk at headquarters.

"About what we said last night, on the phone —" Trent began.

"Later," Zerk said dismissively. "Right now we've got work to do." He looked at Trent with the slightest hint of a smug grin on his handsome face. "They brought your buddy, Marco, in."

"Brought him in? You mean they busted him?"

"Sure."

"Why?"

"Why not? I discussed it with the captain yesterday. We decided we've got enough on Marco. We decided it was time to drop the hammer on him."

"You might've consulted me," Trent pointed out.

"Why should we? It wasn't your call to make. What's the matter? This guy Marco isn't anything special, is he, as far as you're concerned?"

"Of course not," Trent lied.

"I mean, it's not as though he got past first base with you or anything."

"No," Trent agreed, lying again.

"Okay, then. He hasn't lawyered up yet. So let's start working on him. You want to play a little 'good cop, bad cop' with him?"

"Sure. I assume I'm going to be the good cop?"

Zerk grinned. "Naturally. You're the one the dude has the hots for. So you've already got an edge."

They entered the interrogation room where a very nervous, belligerent-looking Marco was seated on one side of the desk. He groaned at the sight of Trent.

"I should've known," Marco said. "I should've known you were nothing but a lousy cop. You dirty bastard. You stinking Judas!"

"You'd better can that kind of talk, if you know what's good for you, punk." Zerk growled.

"Fuck you, cop!"

Zerk smirked. "I'm not the one who's fucked, here. You are."

"You got nothing on me," Marco blustered.

"That's a laugh. We've got plenty. Enough to put you away."

Marco began to look a little less sure of himself. "I want a deal."

"You've been watching too many cop shows on TV," Zerk jeered. "Why should we cut a deal with you? You've got nothing to bring to the table."

Trent spoke up. "Let's not be too hasty, Kostopoulos."

"That's right. I can tell you plenty," Marco insisted.

"You're bluffing. You've got nothing," Zerk scoffed. "You think you're going to talk your way out of doing some hard time, don't you, punk? Well, I've got news for you. You're going down, taking the fall for those guys you work for, and the other cons, the other bastards doing hard time in the slammer, they're just going to love you. It's gonna be give-away day at the butcher shop, and you're gonna be the fresh meat."

"Shut up," Marco said.

"I hope you like being fucked up the ass, punk. Not that it matters much whether you like it or not, right now. You'll have to learn to like it, soon enough. And you won't be able to pick or choose which dude slams it to you. They're all going to nail you."

"Shut up. You're just trying to scare me."

Zerk, ignoring Marco for a moment, smiled at Trent. "Hey, Carothers, did I ever tell you about that special way the cons have of breaking in the new piece of ass on the cell block?"

"Yeah. It's kind of a dirty story, Kostopoulos," Trent protested, playing his part. "You know I don't like to hear that kind of talk."

"Jesus, you're a wuss! Stupid fucking dumbass rookie. Well, maybe I ought to tell it again, for Marco's benefit. You see, Marco, when a new punk like you is dumb enough to try to put up a fight, the other cons just gang up on him. One of them grabs him by the throat, like this." Zerk suddenly reached out and demonstrated by putting his hand on Trent's windpipe.

"Cut it out, Kostopoulos!" Trent demanded, slapping his partner's hand away.

"And he just starts squeezing, to cut your breath off. If the bastard squeezes too hard, you can actually pass out. Hell, if he really gets carried away, you never wake up. You're dead. But if you're lucky, you eventually come to, and you've still got the first guy holding on to your throat while one of his buddies already has his dick shoved up your ass. They usually pick the dude with the biggest dick to go first, to loosen your ass up for his buddies."

"Shut up," Marco cried. "Stop trying to scare me. I don't have to listen to this crap."

"I'm just trying to do you a favor, kid, let you know ahead of time what you're going to be in for once those horny motherfuckers get a look at you. Usually, when they first start to work on you like that, to break you in, two of them team up with a third guy. He grabs you by the balls, so if you try to put up any kind of a fight, all he has to do is start squeezing your balls, the same way the first guy is squeezing your throat, to keep you in line. I bet you don't do much struggling when you can't breathe and your nuts feel like they're being crushed. I bet the most macho stud there is would give it up real fast, and turn into just another jailhouse bitch, sucking dick and taking it up the ass and begging all those dirty, horny cons for more. Before you know it, he's being passed around the cellblock like a roll of toilet paper."

"You bastard," Marco whispered, his voice now tight with fear. "You dirty cop bastard."

"I've heard that when you start to strangle a guy, his asshole starts to tighten up and twitch in this real special way. He doesn't have any control over it. That's why some of these crazy serial killers, who are into raping and killing, strangle their victims to death while they're fucking them. These cons know that, you see, so they keep on choking the punk they're raping to make his ass tighten up and squirm like that and give their dicks a real good, hot ride. No wonder the horny sons of bitches get carried away sometimes and squeeze the punk's throat too hard, and the poor guy ends up getting fucked to death." Zerk let out a raucous laugh. "Hell, I bet some of those cons are so busy getting their rocks off they don't even realize they've killed the guy they're fucking! They probably just keep going, humping away, fucking him after he's dead!"

Marco was shaking. "Liar," he said. "You damn liar. You're just making it up, I know you are. Making the whole thing up to scare me."

"Yeah? Well, you'll be finding out for yourself, soon enough," Zerk said. "Hey, listen, Carothers, I've got to go take a piss. You keep this dumb punk company for a while. I've got nothing more to say to him, and I'm sick of wasting my breath on him. Let the hard-timers have him!"

Zerk left the room. Trent knew, of course, that the interrogation room was equipped with a video camera and a microphone, and that Zerk was no doubt now seated in front of the monitor in the next room, seeing and hearing everything that transpired between Trent and Marco.

"That Kostopoulos is a mean bastard, isn't he?" Trent remarked, shaking his head as he seated himself opposite Marco. "Nobody wants to work with him," he added, more than a little maliciously, for Zerk's benefit. "That's how I got stuck with him. There have been all sorts of complaints about him getting rough with guys who are in custody. He gets a real kick out of humiliating prisoners. Don't let him get to you."

Marco was looking at him, accusingly. "You set me up."

"I'm sorry about that. I didn't have any choice. I was just doing my job."

"You set me up," Marco repeated. "And here I—I liked you. And I thought you liked me. But no, you were just playing me, you bastard. Using me."

"I do like you, Marco. That's why I want to help you out here, if I can."

"You've got to help me. If you don't, I'll tell. I'll tell your boss about how we slept together. How we had sex."

"Go ahead and tell him," Trent bluffed. "He already knows. Who do you think told me it was okay for me to do it?" This was a lie, but Trent was counting on Marco having no way of knowing that. He leaned forward, across the table. "Now, listen, Macro. Threatening me isn't the way to go. You've gotten yourself into a real jam, and the only way you can get out is to cooperate with us. You tell us what we want to know, and I bet I can talk that bastard Kostopoulos into changing his mind and letting you make a deal. I didn't want to say anything while he was still here in the room with us, because I didn't want him to think I was agreeing with him or that I was on his side. But it's true what he says. Every decent-looking guy who ends up in the slammer gets gang-raped, and there's nothing the guards can do about it. I heard a story about this one guy who had his asshole torn apart so bad they had to put stitches in it. And all the time, while he was healing up, the other cons were just waiting for him to get out of the prison hospital so they could fuck him again. They'd make these sick jokes about it, telling each other how they hoped the prison doc had put a few extra stitches in, so the guy's asshole would be nice and tight when they finally got another crack at it. So he'd feel like a virgin when they screwed him. They said when they were done with him this next time, his shitter'd be torn up so bad, not even the doc could sew it back up again. I'd sure hate to have anything like that happen to you."

Fifteen minutes later, Marco was using a pen and a pad of lined paper to write out his "voluntary" statement, spilling his guts about every detail he knew about the operation he'd been involved in. Trent, still in his role of "good cop," had provided Marco with a paper cup of coffee and a box of tissues, since the thoroughly cowed Marco kept breaking down and crying, choking back sobs, as he wrote.

Afterward, Zerk was gleeful.

"I've really got to hand it to you," he told Trent when they were alone together. "You really played that poor dumb bastard. You really did a head trip on him. That bit about the torn asshole and the extra stitches, man, that was sheer genius."

Trent's own mood was less than jubilant.

"I don't feel good about leading him on and setting him up like that," he confessed.

"You'll get over it. You did your job. That's all."

"Maybe. That doesn't mean I have to enjoy it."

Zerk gave him an appraising look. "All right, now that it can't make any difference, are you finally going to tell me just how far you and that guy Marco went?"

Trent met his partner's gaze unflinchingly. "What makes you think—? Oh, hell, Zerk, I suppose I should know better than to think I can pull anything on you. We went all the way, and you damn well knew that already, didn't you?"

Zerk laughed. "Well, let's just say I wasn't one hundred percent sure until now."

"You all but told me to go ahead and do it, if I had to."

"You don't hear me criticizing you, do you?"

"No."

"So that's the end of that discussion, as far as I'm concerned. Oh, maybe just one other thing, before we drop it. Was he any good in bed?"

Trent struggled to suppress a lewd grin. "Sure. Just because he was a perp doesn't mean he wasn't a good fuck."

"Better than me?"

"Let's not go there, Zerk."

"Okay. But stop beating up on yourself, will you? Hey, I've got an idea. Why don't you come to my place tonight, and I'll cook dinner for us? You deserve a little treat."

Zerk was in such a good and obviously conciliatory mood that Trent didn't want to risk offending him by refusing. He knew that accepting the invitation was tantamount to agreeing to get intimate with Zerk again, to a greater or lesser extent. Oddly enough, despite their recent quarrel, Trent didn't find the prospect particularly repugnant. Quite the opposite, in fact! It looked as though he and his big, butch partner were going to kiss and make up. Trent was rather looking forward to it.

I must be oversexed, or something. I don't seem to have any kind of self-control lately, at least not in my personal life. The minute I see a good-looking man, I want to make out with him. Of course, Zerk isn't just any good-looking guy. We know each other. We're partners. He's kind of special. Shit! I'm not getting all soft on the guy, am I? That would be crazy. That would be setting myself up for a hard fall.

Later, on his way to Zerk's apartment, he stopped at a liquor store to buy a bottle of wine. After perusing the shelves, he bought a bottle of ouzo, as well. Trent had never tasted ouzo, but it was Greek, so he supposed a Greek-American such as Zerk drank it.

Trent had underestimated his partner's cosmopolitanism. Dinner turned out to be not Greek, but Italian—antipasto, a salad, shrimp scampi, even gelato for dessert. Zerk, Trent saw, had gone to a good deal of trouble to please him. As they ate and drank, the two cops talked shop. Zerk was perfectly pleasant, as though nothing had happened between them, but Trent still felt rather nervous. He quickly got semi-smashed on the potent ouzo.

"This stuff seems to go right to my head," he declared.

"Have another one," his host urged.

"Are you trying to get me drunk?"

"Absolutely."

"Well, I can't get drunk. I have to drive home."

"No, you don't. I can drive you home, or you can just sleep here tonight."

Trent grinned drunkenly at Zerk. "You'd like that, wouldn't you?"

"I'd like that just fine. And so would you, wouldn't you? Who do you think you're kidding with this hard-to-get routine of yours?"

They ended up, as Trent had known all along they would, naked in Zerk's bed together.

Trent became, for the time being, the aggressor, kissing Zerk on the mouth, then on the chest, sucking on his nipples, one after the other. Moaning, Trent kissed his way down the other man's torso to his pierced navel. His tongue-tip flicked out of his mouth, serpent-like, to tease the barbell stud inserted in the piercing, sliding it back and forth within the aperture.

"You like that, huh?" Zerk asked. "You like the belly button piercing?"

"It turns me on."

"Me, too, I'm really sensitive there. Lick it, baby. Stick your tongue in there."

Trent extended his tongue and pushed it inside Zerk's navel, pretending that his tongue was a cock and the little pierced depression was an asshole it was fucking. Zerk gasped and squirmed. He finally grabbed Trent by the shoulders and pulled him into the new position he wanted, with their faces at one another's groins.

"Let's suck each other," Zerk begged. "Let's suck some cop cock, partner!"

They were locked together in a sixty-nine, and had been for some time, when Zerk broke away from Trent and sat up, panting for breath.

"Wait a minute," he gasped. "Before we go any farther—"

"What?"

"It just occurred to me. Am I going to regret this in the morning?"

"Huh?" Trent stared at him, confused.

"You're not gonna cry rape, are you? Not gonna tell me I was the 'instigator' who talked you into doing something you didn't want to do?"

"I guess I deserve that."

"You know damn well you do. So are you planning on having second thoughts after you've shot your wad?"

"Hell, no," Trent blurted out. "I want to have sex with you, Zerk, any way you want! And I'll prove it to you. Come on, lay back and I'll suck you some more!"

But Zerk now had other ideas. "No! Let me rim you!" he gasped, his hesitation replaced by renewed excitement as he lunged for Trent's body.

"Jesus, you're something else!" Trent exclaimed. But he let Zerk twist his big body around and bury his hot, flushed face between his buttocks. Trent felt Zerk's hot breath on his butt, and then his whole body tensed as his taut, puckered anal ring was invaded by a wet, flexible piece of flesh. Zerk drove his tongue right into Trent's anus and began to lustily rim the asshole, turned on by the faint musky taste on his probing, eager tongue. He rimmed that hot ass until he had Trent squirming and cursing with excitement on the bed beside him.

"Eat it, you bastard, eat that ass. Clean me out. I want to feel that hot tongue all the way up my ass!" Trent chanted in a fever of arousal. That relentless tongue was thrust into his hole again and again. His cock got even harder than it had been when they'd been sucking each other, and, groping between Zerk's thighs, he quickly confirmed his suspicion that Zerk was getting as turned on as he was by what they were doing. "Eat that ass, you son of a bitch!" Trent shouted. He began to jack off in a frenzy of lust as Zerk tongued his anus again and again, insatiably.

Despite his intense arousal, Trent was grinning insolently as he used his fist on himself and pushed his ass back into Zerk's face to drive the other man's tongue deeper into the hole. When they'd first met, Trent had been the ignorant rookie, and Zerk had taught him. Now their roles were reversed, and Trent knew how to push Zerk's buttons. He had Zerk where he wanted him, and the big, dark-haired cop would do anything Trent wanted him to, at least in bed.

Chapter Eleven: Cops in Cuffs

The two undercover cops became inseparable, working together, often putting in hours of overtime, sleeping together, and, of course, having sex together. They took turns binding and disciplining each other, and after alternating roles in several such S and M scenes, they developed a kind of mutual bondage play that carried them through their succeeding sessions with unabated lust.

They used their handcuffs to lock their cocks and balls together. They even slept like that, some nights, awakening at frequent intervals, exceptionally aroused by their close, enforced confinement, and by the constant binding pressure and friction of the metal hoops against their crotches.

Trent remembered the first night they'd tried the handcuff trick. They'd had frenzied sex, taking turns fucking each other up the ass, emptying their balls of sperm again and again until an exhausted Zerk finally suggested that they get some sleep.

"Come on," he murmured insistently. Trent writhed and groaned, still turned on, as the other man ran his hands all over his naked, sweaty, jism-smeared body. "Lie down next to me." Eagerly, Trent obeyed. Zerk stretched out on the mattress beside him and rummaged through some objects in the "toy box" he kept on the floor next to his bed. To Trent's astonishment, Zerk produced two sets of regulation police handcuffs, made from heavy steel.

"Turn around, Trent," Zerk whispered urgently. "Let me cuff you, man!"

"Shit!" Trent started to protest that he'd had enough for one night, but one look at his partner's rugged, coldly determined face warned him that he might be missing out on something good if he demurred.

Zerk usually preferred to play bottom man, but Trent knew from the couple of times they'd switched roles that the hot Greek-American cop could be one hell of a tough master! Quickly, Trent turned his body around and put his wrists together behind his back, moaning with anticipation as the cold metal hoops closed tightly around his wrists with a loud, sinister double click.

Like a perp. Got my hands cuffed behind me, like some goddamn punk perp caught in the act! Only this cop isn't going to take me in and book me. He's going to keep me for himself, for his sex toy, and do whatever he wants to me, sexually!

Satisfied, Zerk took the second pair of handcuffs and carefully snapped one of the hoops shut around his own cock and balls, as though it were a cock ring.

"Now roll over, facing me."

"What for?" Trent demanded, staring at the grotesque sight of the handcuffs swinging between Zerk's muscular thighs.

Zerk slapped his face lightly, playfully, but hard enough to remind him of their respective roles as top and bottom.

"When I give you an order, you'd better obey me, boy." Zerk growled.

Trent rolled away from the other man and felt the links between the cuffs on his wrists cut into his spine as he rolled onto his back. It was a vivid reminder that he was now restrained, that he was Zerk's willing and vulnerable prisoner, for as long as the other guy cared to use his body.

"You'd better do what I tell you to," Zerk threatened. "Don't worry, asshole, it won't hurt. Not *too* much, anyway!"

And it didn't hurt too much, since Zerk was careful not to pinch Trent's scrotum as he snapped the other hoop of the handcuffs shut around Trent's cock and balls. But it was certainly uncomfortable, and Trent's dick, like Zerk's, began to swell to full, throbbing erection almost immediately, making the cuffs feel even tighter as they pressed around the bases of the two hard cocks.

Zerk took Trent's left wrist, opened the cuff, and locked the open hoop around his own right wrist. Then he leaned over and turned out the light beside the bed.

It was a strange sensation, lying there in the darkness broken only by the faint moonlight that penetrated the window shade, locked wrist-to-wrist and cock-to-cock to Zerk. They were lying face to face, their bodies pressed close together, and the slightest movement of their hips exerted enough friction on the lower pair of handcuffs to keep their pricks in a state of constant arousal, and neither of them, of course, could shift his position on the mattress without pulling the other man along with him, sometimes painfully.

"How do you expect me to get any sleep like this?" Trent demanded boldly, after a while.

"You'll get used to it," was Zerk's cool answer. He had laced the fingers of their cuffed hands together, and his sweaty palm was pressed against Trent's. Zerk had his other, free arm around Trent's waist, stroking his broad back, his buttocks, and his thighs, with languid motions of his hand. There was something strangely comforting about this relaxed intimacy, bizarre though the circumstances were, and Trent finally rested his head on Zerk's chest.

"Oh, man," the Greek-American stud murmured, running his hand up Trent's back to caress the damp, disordered hair that tumbled down over the back of his neck. "You're so beautiful, Trent. You're about the most beautiful man I've ever been with. You get me so hot, so horny, I can't stand it, sometimes."

"And you're very sexy," Trent whispered. "The very first time I saw you, there in the precinct, I thought to myself, 'Oh God, what a sexy man!' And when I found out you were going to be my partner, I thought, 'Oh shit, I'm never going to be able to concentrate on the job. I'm going to be thinking about sex, all the time.' That's how you'd already started to get to me, Zerk, even back then."

Long minutes passed. The pressure of the handcuffs around their cocks became more insistent, impossible to ignore.

"Let's jerk each other off," Zerk suggested in a whisper.

"Okay," Trent replied.

He was startled by his unhesitating agreement. It didn't sound all that exciting, compared to some of the heavy BDSM play they'd done together, but suddenly he was wildly aroused by the idea of beating off while coaxing an orgasm out of Zerk's big, throbbing dick.

Zerk had already dropped his free hand down between their sweaty bodies and wrapped it around Trent's cock. A thick vein, swollen and pinched off by the pressure of the handcuff, throbbed strongly beneath his touch. He began to stroke the tremulous shaft. Groaning as his tired body responded, surrendering to the pleasurable excitement, Trent groped for Zerk's cock and began to reciprocate energetically. The handcuffs clanked together as they worked furiously on each other's hard-ons.

Zerk's prick became slick with dribbled preliminary emissions in Trent's fist. Suddenly indifferent to the discomfort, in fact, rather turned on by it, Trent began to hump his hips hard, determined to create enough gritty friction so that he'd come when Zerk came.

Zerk emitted a guttural sound from deep in his throat and crushed his mouth down upon Trent's, thrusting his tongue into the other man's eagerly accepting mouth. Panting hoarsely, they ground their muscular bodies together and began to unload, spraying spurts of hot slippery cum over each other's bellies and chests until their pumping fists were smeared with the slimy jism and their sweaty, embracing bodies stuck together as though glued.

The violence of their simultaneous orgasms died away, to be replaced by a delicious, voluptuous languor of fatigue and sexual satiety. Clinging to the other gay cop who had introduced him to this bewildering new world of pain and pleasure and perversity, Trent slept. His cheek rubbed against the sleek mound of Zerk's pectoral muscle, and their cuffed hands were still locked together by their interlaced fingers as well as by the metal restraints around their wrists.

After that, the handcuff routine became a frequent ritual for them, part of sleeping together.

One morning after a night of intense sex, they lay naked on the bed, saying little to each other, although they communicated simply by being together. Trent had enjoyed himself immensely. He always got off on having sex with Zerk. But it lacked one thing, perhaps—that peculiar thrill of the unknown that came from the anticipation and suspense of tricking with a new, unfamiliar partner. Zerk had felt a similar lack recently, too, Trent suspected. Zerk was too lusty a man to be easily domesticated. As they lay there, their naked bodies entwined on the semen-sodden sheets, Trent felt Zerk's warm hand come to rest against the small of his back. His long, thick fingers teased the crack of Trent's ass, where the sphincter rim still smarted from Zerk's thorough fucking of it earlier.

"You've got something on your mind, Trent," he said. "Haven't you?"

"Yeah, I guess I do."

"What's the matter, you getting tired of me already?"

"Of course not. You know better than that."

"Do I? I thought maybe you were thinking about finding yourself a new boyfriend."

"I've already got a boyfriend. You." Grateful that they could discuss their relationship frankly, Trent rolled onto his side, facing Zerk, who did the same. They pressed themselves together, their limp, deflated cocks rubbing against each other. Trent kissed Zerk on the mouth.

It was true. Zerk was his boyfriend. Almost, although for some reason Trent still felt hesitant about using the word, his lover. They were more than partners, more than friends. They shared a bond that went deeper than that. It was dependent on more than physical sex, although it was never completely independent of lust.

"What is it, then?" Zerk asked quietly.

"It's tough to explain." Trent sighed and hugged the other man closer to his chest with both arms. "We're partners at work. We're fuck buddies, and I like that. I wouldn't want it to be any other way. You've taught me so much, and not just about police work. You've taught me in bed, too. But I'm used to fucking around with a lot of different guys, not just one all the time. I like a little variety, now and then. Does that make me a whore?"

"No. It makes you an honest gay man."

"But I like to share things with you, Zerk, because that always makes it seem more special. So what would you think about the two of us getting into some sort of scene with a third guy, every now and then, and working him over together?"

The question caught Zerk off guard. Trent could feel his muscles tense, involuntarily. But then Zerk nodded his head thoughtfully, and he looked Trent directly in the eye. "Yeah," he said, slowly, with a little laugh. "I think that could get very interesting! Did you have any particular guy in mind?"

"No," Trent admitted. Zerk had told him which of their fellow cops he knew for a fact, or strongly suspected, were gay, so he added, "I don't think it would be such a smart idea to seduce any of the other guys down at the precinct, not yet, anyway. I was almost hoping something might come up on the job some night, if you know what I mean."

Zerk grinned salaciously. "Oh, I know exactly what you mean! All those hot guys we run into in the bars, for example, who are constantly cruising us—sometimes I'm tempted to cruise them right back, and not just as part of the job, either. I want to cruise them back, for real." He leaned over to kiss Trent again, and to play with his stiffening cock. "Yeah, I know *exactly* what you mean," he repeated. "You give me a little time to think about it, and I can just about guarantee I'll come up with something. Something we'll both like!"

Chapter Twelve: A Massage with Extras

And Zerk did come up with something, sooner than either he or Trent anticipated. At headquarters, that very afternoon, Zerk came over and sat down in the chair beside Trent's desk after a brief consultation with their captain.

"We're expanding our operation again," he informed his partner. "You heard about those all-male massage parlors downtown?"

Trent nodded. In the past year, some of the massage parlors that employed women to cater to male customers had changed management and had switched to an "all-male" policy, ostensibly as part of a local clean-up campaign after repeated vice raids and busts. The new masseurs were, of course, all male prostitutes, and the customers were now gay men, looking for only one kind of service.

"They suspect there's mob involvement?"

"For sure. We've got a way inside this time, though. One of the property owners is so nervous about what's going on in his building that he's willing to cooperate. If we keep his name out of it, he's willing to let us go in there and install hidden cameras to film what goes on in there. Then we can shut the massage parlor down, and he can rent the property to a new tenant. There's an empty apartment in the same building, upstairs. Our technicians can install the cameras and the microphones in the masseurs' cubicles during the night, after they close. When the place opens for business the next day, we'll be all set to start making our own little homemade porno movies, complete with soundtracks."

"It sounds like a pretty simple, straightforward job, Zerk."

"Yeah." Zerk seemed intrigued by the prospect. "Right up our alley, so to speak."

A few days later, after the monitoring equipment had been installed, they reported to the stakeout to check out the late afternoon action in the massage parlor. They entered the building in plainclothes and took the service elevator up to the third floor. Zerk knocked lightly on a door. It opened to reveal a studio apartment, with only a few pieces of furniture, but littered with cables and two laptop PCs, each connected to a recorder and a video monitor.

One of the cops in the room was wearing an earphone plugged into one of the PCs, and the other was busy changing the digital tape in one of the recorders. Trent recognized them from the precinct and greeted them casually.

"So what's the deal?" Zerk asked.

"They've got two cubicles," the cop manning the recorder explained. "We've got a camera and a mike in each of them. But they usually only have one whore on duty at this time of day. At night, when it gets busy, they have two. Two cocksuckers, no waiting," he joked. "We've been recording everything that goes on, and we can play it back on these laptops if we want."

The guy with the earphone grinned. "A customer just left. Big tipper. There ought to be a new act along in a minute."

"The first shift masseur just quit for the day," the first cop said. "He developed a sore mouth."

Everybody laughed.

"Has anybody come in and asked for *just* a massage?" Zerk asked.

"Are you kidding? Not so far. This dump is a gay whorehouse, pure and simple."

Trent looked at the monitor that was on at the moment. The camera, obviously mounted somewhere in a concealed location in a wall, showed a small room in which there was a folding massage table, set parallel to the wall, with a small pillow on it. There was an upholstered chair, a locker, and a washbasin with a soap dispenser and a stack of fresh towels. A large mirror on the wall opposite the camera

Good Cop, Bad Cop

completed the décor.

A young man wearing a pair of very snug-fitting white sweatpants, with rubber flip-flops on his bare feet, and a white tank top undershirt that displayed big shoulders and brawny arms entered through the cubicle's door. He was in his mid-twenties, reddish-blond and good-looking, with his cock stuffed visibly down one leg of the tight sweatpants. It was quite obvious that he wasn't wearing underwear. He had a heavy gold chain around his thick neck, matching the hoops in his pierced ears.

"See? The changing of the guard. The new masseur has reported for his shift," the cop with the earphone remarked, licking his lips with lewd anticipation. He removed the earphone and pushed a button on the PC's keyboard. "Here, I'll turn the sound on, so we can all hear."

The blond masseur moved with a sulky litheness around the cubicle. The cops could hear the muted slap of his rubber sandals against the floor.

The door opened again. The man who came in was paunchy and barrel-chested, with a slightly jowly face and a carefully oiled pompadour hairstyle. He had "small-time businessman" written all over him, and he was wearing a wedding ring. He exchanged greetings with the masseur, who introduced himself as "Larry." Larry then suggested that his customer might want to take off his three-piece suit and hang it up on the hooks provided for that purpose on the wall. The customer eagerly stripped naked and stretched out face-down on the massage table.

The masseur began kneading the guy's back, actually quite expertly, from the looks of it, while the customer turned his head toward him, every now and then, to make some innocuous, just-being-friendly remark. The masseur merely smiled and continued his manipulations, his arm and shoulder muscles rippling with easy power as he worked.

"I'd like you to work on my front," the customer said suddenly, in a faintly wheedling tone of voice. "That's where I'm *really* tense, where I really *need* it." He rolled over, displaying a thick, stubby erection jutting straight up from his hairy groin. The masseur worked on in silence, a silence that gave an air of a pantomime, or a silent movie, to the whole performance.

"He can't make the first move," Zerk explained, for Trent's benefit. "If he does, that's soliciting, and for all he knows, that guy could be a cop."

The masseur appeared to finish. He took a towel, and began to wipe the oil off his hands.

"Is that all?" the man on the massage table asked.

"That's our standard massage, sir."

"The guy at the front desk told me I could pay extra for a 'special' treatment."

"Oh? Did he give you a ticket for that?"

"Yes, it's over there, in my pants pocket."

The nude customer retrieved the ticket, which he handed to the masseur, who glanced at it.

"What would you like me to do for you, sir?" he asked.

"Just make me feel good."

The masseur smiled knowingly. "I'm afraid you'll have to be a little more explicit."

"Oh, come on," the customer said, a bit testily. "I've been waiting all day for this. Look at me. Look at how *tense* I am. You know what I need."

The masseur approached the table again. "Maybe this will help to relieve some of that tension." He dropped his hands lightly onto the paunchy, pale abdomen of the other man.

"Oh, yes."

He made lower circles, stroking harder, very slowly. "Does this feel good?"

"God, yes. You're so fucking hot!" the customer moaned, shuddering from head to foot with lust. "But the guy at the desk, he said you'd give me a *nude* massage. That you'd get naked, too."

"Sure." It took the masseur only a few seconds to pull his tank top up over his head and off, kick off his flip-flops, and step out of his sweatpants. Naked except for the gold chain around his neck and his earrings, he resumed the massage, taking his customer's cock in his hand this time.

Trent watched the monitor, fascinated. The recorder hummed barely audibly nearby, preserving the scene for posterity. In the little room, the masseur had begun to kiss the chubby man on his throat, then on his nipples, while slowly and expertly his hands caressed the customer's penis. His fingers tangled in the guy's coarse pubic hair.

Next, the masseur's head went down against the flabby muscles of his customer's belly. He licked the tautening skin of the man's cock with his agile pink tongue. The other naked man groaned ecstatically.

"If only I could get my wife to do this, but she thinks oral sex is dirty. I'm not ashamed of anything I do with *you*, Larry," the john told the masseur. He giggled as a thought struck him. "I wouldn't even care of somebody walked in here right now and caught us. I wouldn't care if a whole *bunch* of other guys were watching us get it on together!"

Mocking laughter in the studio apartment broke the growing tension, as all four cops reacted to this ironic boast. They were all gathered around the monitor, staring at the obscene spectacle of Larry licking the fat man's erection, wetting it thoroughly with his saliva from its tip down to the balls. Trent glanced nervously at Zerk to see how his partner was taking all this. Zerk was a good actor—a vice cop had to be—but Trent could see that, right now, his guard was down. His face was almost feral with suppressed lust, and his eyes glinted like those of a wild animal glimpsed by firelight. Trent winced. What would the other two cops in the room with them think and say if they knew that he and Zerk had sex together, just like the two men in that cubicle? That he and Zerk liked nothing better than taking turns sucking each other's dicks, at least, as a prelude to other, even grosser, activities!

The customer was groaning now as Larry slipped his cock inside his mouth and began to suck. He allowed the john's hands to roam over his nude body, caressing him.

"Oh, you're good. You're beautiful. Suck it, baby, suck it for me, good!"

"Look at that horny cocksucker go to town on that fat bastard's dick," one of the cops jeered. "He's not just doing it for the money. The lousy whore is really getting off on it. The cocksucker. The dirty cocksucker!"

The married man suddenly sat up and tugged on Larry's shoulders, trying to maneuver him into another position.

"Wait!" he gasped. "Let me suck yours, too! Let me suck yours while you go down on mine!"

Larry clambered up onto the massage table next to his wildly excited john. The two naked men slid into a sixty-nine position, embraced each other around the waist, and shoved their cocks down each other's throats. Their slurps and moans of mutual oral passion came through the monitoring equipment loud and clear, and Trent could feel his own prick pulsating madly with envy and frustration inside his suddenly too-tight pants. Even the two supposedly straight cops, there in the room with Zerk and him, seemed, he noticed with a perverse satisfaction, to be getting turned on by watching the two men suck each other so hungrily, with such animal abandon.

The equipment hummed and blinked on, mechanically recording the sex act, impervious to the emotions and responses that agitated the four human viewers, as the cocksucking quickly built to its inevitable double climax. The two naked men had been feeding at each other's crotches for no more than five minutes of intense sixty-nining when Larry grunted loudly as he must have felt his customer's cock twitch extra-hard inside his mouth. A moment later the first spurt of the john's cum slammed against the back of the masseur's throat. Larry pulled back until only the pulsating head of the fat man's prick was still caught between his expertly suctioning lips. He swallowed noisily, but his john was coming so hard, so copiously, that the excess flow of the warm, thick cum poured over his swabbing tongue and escaped from his mouth, dripping down his chin.

Then Larry's hard-muscled body shook as a violent spasm of intense pleasure seemed to hit his own cock. His customer soon got what he wanted, what he was paying for, a mouthful of a potent young male's jism. Gasping, slurping, sucking hungrily on each other's shafts, the two naked men clawed at each other's writhing bodies as they rolled over on the table shooting and sucking and swallowing.

"Whore!" one of the cops gasped. "Dirty, cocksucking whore! Look at that! Isn't it disgusting?"

"Yeah," Zerk lied. "It's hard to believe one guy would want to do that to another, isn't it?"

At last it was over, and Trent watched, numb with lust, as the masseur casually rinsed out his mouth and washed his hands at the washbasin and the customer sheepishly put on his clothes, kissed him good-bye, and left, not without first slipping him a generous tip. Larry, looking quite unperturbed by the orgasm he'd just experienced, got dressed again, barely in time before his next customer knocked on the door of the cubicle and entered. Then Trent got the shock of his life when he recognized the big, ruggedly good-looking man who had just come into the room for his "massage!"

"Jesus Christ!" he exclaimed, under his breath. "I can't believe it!"

"What?" Zerk asked.

"I know that guy!"

"Oh? Friend of yours, Carothers?" one of the other cops taunted.

"No, asshole. Don't you recognize him?"

Zerk leaned in closer to the monitor to scrutinize the image. "He *does* look kind of familiar."

All four of them studied the new customer intently. As the big man walked into the cubicle, it would have been obvious even to a casual observer that he was very athletic. All of his muscles, even in the loosely tailored clothes he wore, were evident, projecting a sense of quiet strength. His shoulders were broad, and the quartet of cops could see that his slacks, though not particularly tight, hugged his thighs.

"Wouldn't you like to get comfortable?" Larry was suggesting. He sounded a lot more eager to get down to business with this attractive number than he had been with his previous customer.

"Oh, sure," the big guy said, a little awkwardly. "I guess so." He pulled off his jacket and shirt and draped them over the chair near the table. Every muscle in his hairy chest seemed to ripple as he completed this slight movement. His arms, and especially his biceps, were enormous.

"Okay, Carothers," one of the cops demanded. "Give! Who is he?"

"He's Cornell Jaeger," Trent explained, smugly.

"No!" the other cop gasped.

"You have got to be shitting me," the first cop said. "Not Cornell Jaeger, the football player? The one who makes those action movies, now?"

Trent grinned. "Exactly. It's him, all right. He was a big hero of mine when I was in college, I..." He broke off, remembering that he and Zerk weren't alone in the room, just before he would have gone on to say that he'd not just admired Cornell Jaeger and followed his career, he'd practically worshipped the guy. Trent had jerked off countless times in his dorm room bed while fantasizing about the husky NFL star, whose photos he'd religiously torn out of sports magazines and taped to the wall as erotic inspiration in those comparatively more innocent days.

"Another illusion shot to hell," Trent said coolly, for the two straight cops' benefit. "He's taking quite a risk, coming to a place like this to get laid."

Zerk grunted, sounding amused.

In the cubicle, Larry was indeed getting right down to business.

"Come on," the masseur urged Jaeger excitedly. "You get undressed, and I will, too, and then I can give you a real rubdown, with both of us in the nude." Cornell got naked and lay down, and Larry, also nude and already developing quite an erection despite his recent ejaculation, began working on him, obviously trying to put him at his ease as he stroked him from head to toe with oiled hands.

"Oh, you're really tense. There's nothing to be nervous about. You don't have to be embarrassed around me," Larry purred. "I've seen a lot of jocks in here. I know what you guys need to relieve all that tension. And I'm very discreet."

"I'm just a little bit uptight, I guess, at this whole scene," Cornell admitted. But as Larry rubbed his shoulders, he seemed to relax. Then, without a word about sex or money, Larry ran his hands down the husky former linebacker's torso, leaned over, and took his cock in his hand, caressing it with his fingers.

"I bet that feels good, doesn't it, big man?" he asked Cornell, as though eager for his approval.

"Yeah," Cornell gasped, his voice fading away with pleasure.

Larry kept on playing with him until his cock was stiff, then he bent over and took it in his mouth, sucking it passionately and masturbating himself with one hand as he did so. Zerk was snickering, and Trent felt aroused but uncomfortable watching his one-time idol being sucked off by the blond masseur. After a few minutes of fervent cocksucking, though, Larry seemed to sense that Cornell wasn't enjoying it all that much.

"Is something wrong?" he asked, his lips still poised an inch from the head of Cornell's throbbing hard-on.

"Could you, would you mind doing it a little more roughly?" Cornell asked Larry, very hesitantly. "I mean, could you massage my body real hard *while* you blow me?"

"Whatever you like," Larry replied. He started kneading the

football player's shoulders and pecs again as he sucked his dick, and Cornell seemed to get off on it more. Then, quite by accident, Larry's fingernail scraped across his skin near his nipple, leaving a long red mark. Before he could stop sucking to apologize for scratching Cornell, though, a strange look came over the big man's face. He let out a grunt of pleasure and, to Larry's apparent surprise, he made it clear that he had enjoyed it!

"Yeah, like that," Cornell gasped. "Do that again! Only do it harder this time! Please!"

Larry arched his fingers into claws so that his nails would scratch Cornell's chest, and he started massaging and blowing him again. He left a trail of red marks as he worked his way down Cornell's torso, but the more pressure he exerted, the more Cornell seemed to like it! His cock was getting very hard inside the blond's mouth, and his breathing was labored. It was blatantly obvious that he was enjoying his "massage" a lot more now that Larry had put a little pain into it!

"Will you do something else for me?" Cornell demanded abruptly.

"Maybe, but I'll have to get more money for extras," Larry said warily.

"No problem, I'll pay you whatever you want."

"It all depends on what you want me to do." Larry was about to quote his prices when Cornell interrupted him.

"Hurt me! Beat me! Beat me with my belt—with anything! I want to be a slave!" Cornell shouted, suddenly looking and sounding positively frenzied with lust. "Beat the shit out of me!"

"Jesus," Zerk laughed. "Who'd ever have thought that Cornell Jaeger could be such a sex freak?"

Larry was every bit as shocked as Trent and the other two cops were by this unexpected revelation that Cornell Jaeger was a masochist. In fact, the masseur, who thought nothing of sucking guys' cocks for money, seemed downright disgusted by what was now being asked of him!

"I'm sorry, man," he said firmly, backing away from Cornell, his hard-on suddenly drooping. "I really can't get into that sort of sick, perverted shit."

"Fuck," Cornell groaned. He jumped off the table, hitting the floor with a thud, and snatched up his clothes. He was still only half-dressed when he literally ran out of the cubicle, tossing Larry a twenty dollar bill over his shoulder, no doubt as hush money, as he fled in confusion and shame. Zerk doubled up with laughter as Larry greedily retrieved the bill.

"He's not only a whore, he's a dumb whore," Zerk said. "The guy was all set to pay him whatever he wanted—he was really hot for it." He paused, catching Trent's eye and staring intently at his partner, a slow, lewd smile spreading across his face. "I don't think we're going to see anything to top that for quite a while," Zerk said casually. "Let's go get some coffee, Trent, and bring it back. You guys want us to get you anything?"

They took their fellow officers' orders for coffee and sandwiches, and Zerk fairly hustled Trent out of the apartment.

"What's the big hurry?" Trent asked irritably as they rode down in the elevator.

"Meet me at the coffee shop around the corner," Zerk said breathlessly as he dashed out of the building and into the street. "I won't be more than a minute." He began to run down the sidewalk.

"What the fuck?" But Zerk didn't answer or even look back at Trent, who, shaking his head, slowly walked down the street in the opposite direction. He caught himself wondering for approximately the hundredth time since he'd first started working with his partner whether all Greek-American cops were crazy, or just Xerxes Kostopoulos.

Chapter Thirteen: Negotiations

Zerk was gone for more than a minute. It was more like ten or fifteen. Trent was already thinking about heading back to the stakeout with the coffee and sandwiches when his partner hurried up to him in the coffee shop, grinning insolently—and sporting a noticeable hard-on tucked down one leg of his tight pants.

"So—what was that all about?" Trent demanded. "Did you get so hot and bothered watching Larry suck those two guys off that you had to go beat off, or what?"

Zerk ignored his taunt. "It's all set up," he said, enigmatically.

"*What's* all set up?"

"Us and that big guy, Cornell Jaeger. We're both going to fuck him tonight." Trent almost dropped the things he was carrying, and Zerk's grin broadened. "That is, if you're interested," he teased his fuck buddy.

"You can't be serious, Zerk!"

"You're *not* interested?"

"Of course I'm 'interested!' I've had the hots for that guy ever since the first time I saw him play! But I can't believe—what did you do, go right up to the dude and ask him if he'd like to get into a three-way with two vice cops?"

Zerk laughed. "More or less. You're the one who gave me the idea, you know. You were practically coming in your pants while you were watching Larry blow him, and since Jaeger didn't stick around long enough to get his rocks off, I figured he'd still be horny enough to try just about anything. That's how these fucking masochists are, you know."

"Yeah, you ought to know!"

"Watch your mouth, rookie. Anyway, so I caught up with him and pretended I was a football fan who wanted his autograph, at first. We cruised each other while we were chit-chatting, and then he propositioned me. And then I whipped out my badge and told him all about how'd we just watched him having sex with Larry inside the massage parlor and taken it all down on videotape."

"*Jesus*, Zerk! You *didn't!*"

"Don't sweat it, Trent, it's cool. He was pretty pissed off and bent out of shape at first, as you can imagine, but once I explained to him that it was okay because my hot little partner and I are both gay and into light bondage and S and M, and we just might be willing to make sure that certain sections of that videotape get erased accidentally on purpose...Well, I guess you get the general idea of how the conversation went from there, don't you?"

"I can't believe it!" Trent exploded. "I can't believe that you actually tried to blackmail a guy into having sex with us, let alone that you offered to destroy evidence!"

"What evidence? We're not going after the customers, remember? And I not only tried, I succeeded. He's coming over to my place at ten tonight, and he's going to do anything we want, as long as it's sexual and, as he put it, as long as my partner's as much of a hot, dirty sex pig as I am."

"Who are you calling a sex pig?" Trent protested. "Speak for yourself, man!"

"Who do you think you're kidding? This is me you're talking to," Zerk retorted.

Trent glowered, but said nothing.

"I described you to him and told him what you like to do in bed with that hot mouth and ass and big dick of yours, and he practically came in his pants, too, he was so fucking turned on. So get off your high horse, Trent. I didn't have to force him into agreeing to anything. Hell, we'll be doing the poor bastard a favor! He can't afford to get involved in a sex scandal. He's probably afraid to go to the bars or the baths very often because he's likely to be recognized, and he's going to have just as hot a time with us. Probably hotter! It'll be a hell of a lot safer than paying for it in a sleazy dump like that massage parlor.

"Besides, this is every bottom man's fantasy—to get worked over by a couple of hot cops. He may think he hates my guts right now, but I'll bet you anything he's already getting all hot and bothered, and he's already just about ready to jerk off, thinking about what's going to come down tonight. Man, if we play our cards right, this could be one wild session. And you're the one who wanted us to find another guy for both of us to work over, remember?"

"Sure, some guy who wants to get into a threesome with us of his own free will," Trent insisted. "Not a dude who has to be forced into it!"

"'Forced,' my ass! You still don't understand how these fucking masochists' minds work, do you, partner?"

Trent still wasn't entirely convinced, to say the least, and they argued about it all the way during the walk back to the stakeout, and then again after they got off duty early that evening. Trent pulled out every argument he could think of. Cornell Jaeger wasn't just any celebrity, he tried to point out to his partner. Jaeger was a local boy who hadn't forgotten his roots. He maintained a house here in the city where he'd grown up. He was always making personal appearances to raise money for charity. He'd even insisted that one of the movies he'd recently starred in be filmed here, to give the local economy a boost.

"All right, the guy's a saint," Zerk jeered. "Well, we'll see how saintly people still think he is, if this gets out. Imagine how much money one of those scandal sheet newspapers would pay to get their hands on that tape. It could be the start of a sweet little extra retirement fund for both of us, kid."

"Don't even joke about such things."

"What makes you think I'm joking? I'm just considering all the options before I commit myself to doing anything."

"We're not going to do *anything*, Zerk," Trent tried to bluster. "We're going to forget about this whole thing."

"You're really bent out of shape at the thought of your football hero taking a dive, aren't you?"

"The guy's still in the closet. He got horny and wanted to get his rocks off. None of that's a crime."

"Oh yeah? I was under the impression it started to be a crime the minute money changed hands for sex, back there in that dump," Zerk retorted.

"You'd better keep that in mind, the part about it being a crime when money changes hands or when sex gets traded for something, for that matter. Anyway, he'll never show up," Trent concluded haughtily, although he half-hoped he was wrong.

Zerk chuckled. "Oh, he'll show up. You'll see! And so will you! You're already thinking about it, aren't you? Trying to decide exactly what you want to make him do for you. I can read you like a book."

"You smug bastard."

Zerk at least had the decency to invite Trent over to his place and make dinner for them. They continued to bicker, all through the meal.

At nine-thirty, Zerk got a call on his cell phone.

"He's on his way," he reported, triumphantly, after he hung up. "He wants to get here early, he said. He's worried about finding a place to park. He sounded nervous and eager, and horny. Come on, help me get everything ready."

Cornell rang the doorbell fifteen minutes later, a quarter-hour ahead of the ten o'clock rendezvous. He was wearing casual clothes—a tight pair of faded jeans, a sweatshirt with the sleeves cut off at the shoulders, tennis shoes, and, in an attempt to conceal his identity, dark sunglasses, even though it was nighttime.

"Come in," Zerk said.

* * * *

Cornell recognized the cop's voice from their previous encounter. He forced himself to take a deep breath before he turned the doorknob, pushed the door open just far enough to give himself room to squeeze through the crack, and shut it behind him. Zerk's living room was almost pitch black, and for a moment Cornell's eyes, after he'd removed his sunglasses, could make out nothing.

"Lock the door," Zerk instructed him, coldly.

Cornell fumbled in the gloom for the button on the doorknob and the security bolt higher up on the jamb. "Can't you turn a fucking light on, man?"

"I will now." Cornell heard the scratch of a match being lit. A moment later the flame touched a candle's wick, and he could see Zerk sitting in a leather armchair wearing jeans, motorcycle boots, and a black leather vest. Zerk lit a second candle and set it on the table beside his chair. Together they gave the immediate area of the room adequate illumination, and as Zerk positioned the candles, Cornell noticed for the first time that Trent was in the room, too. Trent was lounging in another overstuffed armchair across from Zerk's, stripped to the waist, his heavy, athletic body sheathed only in a pair of tight jeans that were even more revealing and in need of repair than Cornell's. He, too, wore heavy boots on his feet. He looked up at Cornell and grinned lewdly, his rugged face almost demonic in the flickering light and shadow patterns thrown by the candles.

"Hi, Mr. Jaeger," Trent greeted Cornell softly. "Glad you could join the party."

"The orgy, you mean." Zerk laughed. "And what's with this 'Mr. Jaeger' shit? What do you think this is, a lawn party?"

"So you're the other shakedown artist," Cornell said, ignoring Zerk for the moment as he gave Trent the once-over. "At least you're good-looking. Your con artist buddy wasn't lying about that."

"Watch your mouth," Zerk warned.

"I ought to report you, both of you, to your bosses," Cornell threatened. "And maybe I will. Then we'll see how tough you talk, cop."

"Go right ahead. You got your cell phone on you? Need the number?" Zerk asked.

"You bastard. You know I won't—you know you've got me, right where you want me."

"Not quite. Not yet."

"This is a business deal. A business deal, pure and simple. So maybe—just so there won't be any misunderstandings—maybe we'd better establish a few ground rules, first," Cornell said, softly. "You know," he added, looking and sounding increasingly nervous. "Before we actually *do* anything."

"I wasn't aware that you were calling the shots," Zerk taunted him.

"I can still walk out of here, tape or no tape."

"Okay," Zerk said. "Then I guess you might as well walk out of here with it."

* * * *

Nonplussed, Trent watched his partner go over to his desk. He opened a drawer, took out an object sealed inside a manila envelope, and tossed it to Cornell, who caught it without thinking, with a former football player's quick physical responsiveness.

"What the fuck is this?" Cornell demanded.

"It's the tape."

Cornell tore open the flap of the envelope and looked inside. "Okay, I can see it's a tape. How do I know it's *the* tape?"

Zerk shrugged. "Pop it into my player over there, if you want to, and see for yourself. Take your time. My partner and I aren't in any hurry. We're not going anywhere. I wouldn't mind watching a little porn."

Cornell hesitated. "Are you bullshitting me?"

"As a matter of fact, no. That really is the tape of that guy Larry sucking you off, and you begging him to beat your ass."

Cornell winced. "Why are you giving it to me?"

"I don't really have much choice. My boss called me into his office this afternoon. He told me he'd discussed the issue with the top brass. Once word started to get around that we had a video of a hot-shot celebrity, caught in the act, patronizing a male prostitute in a sleazy massage parlor, well, people started getting nervous. And since we already have all the evidence we need to bust the guys who run that place, it was decided we'd be better off leaving you out of it. No need to complicate matters, if you know what I mean." Zerk grinned. "So I volunteered to deliver the tape to you, in person, to explain what happened and extend to you the department's sincere apologies for the whole unfortunate incident. My boss even gave me your home address."

Cornell stared at Zerk, warily. "But you still let me think—you still had me come over here."

"Sorry about that. I have to admit, I was a little curious about whether you'd really have the balls to show up. So, since we'd already set up this little appointment, I didn't see any need to cancel it. If you'd stood us up, I'd have paid you a visit at your place, later on tonight. Which probably would've thrown one hell of a scare into you, at first."

"You bastard," Cornell spat.

"Now, that's no way to talk. Be nice. You're getting off pretty easily."

A thought occurred to Cornell. "You didn't have to tell me your boss wanted you to give me the tape. You could've shaken me down first, made me have sex with you, even told me you wanted money from me."

"I could've done that, I guess," Zerk admitted with an infuriating cheerfulness. "But, for one thing, I'm really a nice guy, believe it or not. And, for another, my partner, here, is a big fan of yours. He used to jerk off thinking about what it would feel like to suck your dick."

* * * *

As he spoke, Zerk glanced at Trent, who hadn't told Zerk any such thing. Zerk had thought he was making it up, just to yank Cornell Jaeger's chain. But now, judging by the guilty look on Trent's face, Zerk strongly suspected that what he was telling Cornell maybe just happened to be true!

"So he'd never forgive me or let me hear the end of it if I tried to shake his idol down," Zerk went on, smugly.

"You're an asshole, Kostopoulos," Trent fumed. "A complete asshole."

"Don't make me regret I just handed over that tape, Carothers," Zerk said.

"I want you to know, Mr. Jaeger, that I wanted nothing to do with this," Trent protested. "Nothing to do with any part of it!"

"Yeah," Zerk drawled. "That's why you're here—that's why you ran over here, like a dog in heat, with your tongue hanging out of your mouth and your dick getting hard in your pants. Because you wanted nothing to do with it. Because you *weren't* all hot to trot at the thought of fucking your boyhood hero! Don't make me laugh."

"Son of a bitch," Trent hissed. "Playing me. Playing me, like I was some kind of a goddamn perp!"

"You'll get over it," Zerk predicted. "And so will you, Jaeger. Now, as far as you're concerned, the only question is—are you going to take your little party favor and go, or would you like to stick around and get laid, after all? It's your choice."

Cornell looked flustered. "I just came here to get the tape."

"Bullshit. You came here to get worked over by two cops. You were scared, weren't you? You were disgusted. Maybe you still are. But the idea really turned you on, didn't it? Deep down inside, you were looking forward to it."

"No," Cornell whispered.

"No? Well, then there's no real harm done, is there? You can just turn around and walk out of here. I will admit I'm a little disappointed. I was kind of looking forward to a really hot three-way session with a willing bottom man, myself. I guess, after you're gone, Carothers and I will have to kiss and make up. Maybe I can talk him into working *me* over the way the two of us were going to work over you. Carothers is really pissed off at me right now. I'd better let him take out some of that aggression on me before he freaks out. It ought to be a really hot session. Too bad you can't stick around and play, too."

"I...I don't want—!" Cornell stammered.

"You don't want to play, is that it? That's okay. You don't have to. Nobody's going to force you." Zerk lowered his voice. "But you *do* want to, don't you?" he suggested, in a soft, insinuating whisper. "You want to be a sex slave, don't you? You want to be worked over, good and hard, by a couple of cops."

"No," Cornell protested. "I don't want anything like that!"

"You don't have to lie to me. You can stop lying to yourself, too. Let me offer you a little unsolicited advice, man. You got off easy, this time. No headlines in the tabloids, no TV commentators shaking their heads about the latest celebrity sex scandal. But do the math. The police commissioner and a couple of the other higher-ups know about this. So does my boss. Me and my partner, of course. And there were two other cops on that stakeout with us who saw you with that whore. They've been told to keep their mouths shut, but who knows? So quite a few people are already in on your little secret, even though none of them will supposedly ever say anything. But the next time, you might not be so lucky. You might get found out. Unless you wise up and figure out how you can find some guys to fool around with, guys you can count on to be discreet and not blow your cover. You know, maybe I could help you hook up with some hot men like that, right here in town. I have my contacts."

"Shit," Cornell exclaimed.

"I know you're nervous," Zerk purred. "There's nothing to be nervous about. Not here, not with us. We're the good guys. We're good cops. We want to be your friends, we want to help you out, help you to explore some of those fantasies you've been thinking about that have been driving you crazy because they turn you on so much. Because they get you so fucking hard. But, if you want us to, we can be bad cops, too. Dirty, nasty cops. The kind you've always wondered what it would be like to have working you over. Making you do all of those dirty, nasty things you want to be 'forced' to do. Well, there's my proposition. Make up your mind. You want to leave? Or would you rather stick around and play some games?"

"Yes," Cornell gasped. "I...I want to! I want to stay here."

"It's all right. My partner and I are very experienced. We know what to do. We know what you want."

"Do you?" Cornell asked, his breath catching in his throat.

"Yeah. Come on, man. Come on into the bedroom."

* * * *

Zerk picked up the two lit candles and led the way with Cornell following him, moving instinctively, like an automaton, while Trent brought up the rear. In the bedroom, the bed itself was unmade and looked inviting enough, ready for sexual activity, but Zerk ignored it and walked across the room toward a large black rubber mat spread out on the floor, and Cornell saw that this improvised bed was equipped with a number of accessories, all of which proclaimed Zerk's intention to get down to business right away. There was a folded trick towel, a box of condoms, a tube of lubricant, a long, coiled length of black rawhide, and a somewhat sinister-looking black metal box or storage trunk.

"Take your clothes off, and get that butch ass of yours over here,"

Zerk commanded as he set down the flickering candles, then shed his leather vest.

"Don't you even have a decent dungeon or playroom?" Cornell asked as he stepped out of his shoes. "Some top man you are!"

"I warned you about that mouth, slave boy. You'd better adjust your attitude, right now. I've got everything we need to discipline your butt, right here," Zerk declared. "I don't need a lot of fancy equipment to work a guy over and make him beg for more!"

"All right, let's get this show on the road." Cornell decided not to waste any time with a display of false modesty or feigned reluctance. Better to get it over with as quickly as he could, let these bastards have their way with him, get his own rocks off, and split. Despite his embarrassment, his nervousness at the prospect of having sex with two total strangers, he had to admit that he liked what he saw, on a purely physical level. Both cops were hot numbers, handsome, well-built, obviously well-hung, and their air of arrogance, of being in control, only heightened the appeal they had for him. He was completely at the two horny motherfuckers' mercy, at their sexual disposal, and the thought of submitting to them and being their sex slave excited him.

"You're taking a hell of a long time getting those clothes off. What's the matter—our strip show not turning you on?"

Zerk and Trent were both naked as the latter spoke, although they then slipped their boots back on. Angrily, Cornell threw off his sweatshirt and jeans and tossed them onto the floor, his nude body trembling with lust. He didn't wait for further commands, but walked boldly across the room toward the two fuck buddies, holding himself erect, his cock swinging heavily from side to side between his legs each time he took a step.

For an instant, at least, he had gained the upper hand. Both of the other men were staring at him with undisguised curiosity and lust, their hands straying down to their own crotches to grasp their pricks and fondle them into near-erections as they examined Cornell's superb body and magnificently proportioned cock.

"Now listen, you two," Cornell insisted. "There's going to have to be some limits."

"All right," Zerk agreed. "What do you want to suggest?"

"You can't do anything that'll leave marks on my face. I begin shooting a new movie next week."

"Agreed."

"We need a code word, a safe word. I don't have many limits, but I do have some."

"How about 'sex tape?' You say 'sex tape,' and whatever we're doing to you, we'll stop," Zerk suggested.

"Smart ass. All right."

"Anything else?"

"I guess not."

"Then come here," Zerk commanded. But he betrayed his own eagerness by taking a quick step himself, in Cornell's direction, so that he met him halfway. Cornell approached him warily, his arms at his sides. Zerk suddenly reached up, grasped them by the bulging biceps, and held Cornell in place in that way as he moved right up against him until the two men's chests touched—as did the heads of their rapidly stiffening pricks. Cornell could feel Zerk's hot breath on his face as he returned the vice cop's penetrating gaze without flinching.

"Don't look at me unless I give you permission to," Zerk warned in a fierce whisper. "A submissive doesn't do that, during a scene with a top man."

He was already trying to ease them into their roles as top and bottom, respectively, but Cornell resisted. "I'll look at you if I fucking want to," he said—nervously, but with a show of bravado.

"A smart ass, huh?" Zerk grunted, and Trent, too, let out a grunt of amused agreement. "A real smart ass slave—that's what you are. Maybe, just maybe, you'd benefit from being taught some manners. I think you need a little discipline. And my partner and I are just the men to give it to you."

"I don't need anything from you. I already have that tape." Cornell was finding it difficult to keep his voice steady, though. As he spoke, Zerk began to run his hands down the length of his nude body from his shoulders to his hips, then around Cornell's waist to caress the sleek muscles of his ass. Cornell clenched his buttocks in an involuntary gesture of self-defense as he felt the tip of Zerk's middle finger slip between them and probe at the delicate flesh of his sphincter muscle. "No," Cornell gasped. "Please. Please, don't."

"I don't hear our code word coming out of your mouth, slave. So I guess when you say 'don't,' you really mean, 'go right ahead.' Nice ass. Real nice! Tight, butch ass!"

"You made me come over here to have sex with you, so get it over with," Cornell said, tensely. "I'm not interested in your pathetic little tough cop act. Just let me have your cock. In my mouth and in my asshole—I want to suck and fuck. I don't want to stand here with you playing with me and teasing me all goddamn night! Let's get right down to it—if you've got the balls, which I'm beginning to doubt!"

Grinning, Zerk shook his head and glanced over Cornell's shoulder at Trent, who had moved behind him. "A real smart ass," he repeated. "Always mouthing off. Well—let's find out if that's *all* this fucker's mouth is good for!" His hands shot up to Cornell's broad shoulders again, gripping them hard as Zerk pushed down with all his strength. "Get down on your knees and start sucking my dick, if you want to 'get right down to it' so fast!" he ordered. "Blow me, and then maybe I'll be in a better mood—maybe I'll go easy on you instead of really working you over the way you deserve, you mouthy bitch!"

Cornell allowed the other man to shove him down to his knees on the floor. He licked his lips to wet them and took a deep breath to calm himself as the weighty mass of Zerk's fat prick slapped lightly against his cheek. The musky sex smell of Zerk's crotch filled his nostrils and was like a potent aphrodisiac. Suddenly Cornell wanted to suck it, and he hated himself for responding so helplessly to a bastard like this cop, even if it was only a response on the crudest, most basic physical level.

* * * *

"Get busy," Zerk barked, misinterpreting Cornell's hesitation for a sign of reluctance or rebellion. "Suck it, or I'll make you wish you had, in a moment! I want it in your hot, cocksucking mouth, and I—oh, yeah! Suck that cock!" he moaned, tensing all over and changing his harsh tone of voice to a groan of complete sensuous satisfaction when Cornell abruptly lunged forward, buried his faced in Zerk's crotch, and sucked the head and most of the shaft of his throbbing hard-on deep inside his warm, juicy mouth in a single effortless gulp.

Cornell's sudden submissiveness took Zerk completely by surprise, and the cop's knees buckled as the first wild thrill of being so expertly fellated—and by a man he'd no doubt expected he would have to browbeat into submission, first!—shot through him. He had to lean forward and rest his hands on Cornell's shoulders to steady himself as Cornell continued to kneel abjectly in front of him and exerted his mouth and tongue in an attempt to drive him frantic. Cornell sucked the last few inches of solid shaft into his mouth, letting the bloated head of Zerk's penis slip down into his carefully cleared throat, and then—breathing rapidly but regularly, through flared nostrils—he began to give his tormentor the deep-throating of his life!

* * * *

Trent, awestruck, envious, watched from a few feet away, exulting in the wanton spectacle of Cornell blowing his buddy like that, with such animal abandon and hunger. In the warm, wavering glow cast by the two candle flames, the exhibition was one of the hottest things Trent had ever seen.

"Suck it, man! Suck his dick! Get it all down your goddamn cocksucking throat!" he told Cornell, and he seized his own tool in his fist and began to masturbate with rough, overeager strokes.

"He is, partner—believe me, he is!" Zerk gasped. "He's terrific! The hottest mouth I've had swinging on my joint in a long while—no offense, pal! Christ, I'm going to blast any minute, if keeps this up! Get the rawhide—!"

His voice trailed away into another loud gasp of passion as Cornell's wet tongue sped up its tempo, but Trent understood what Zerk wanted him to do. Trent grabbed the length of black rawhide cord from the mat, stooped behind Cornell, and seized one of his wrists, looping the rawhide around it and tying it snugly before Cornell knew what was happening to him.

* * * *

Still sucking, Cornell put up a token struggle, but he finally let Trent lash his wrists tightly together behind his back with the rawhide. He was now effectively the two men's prisoner, naked and helpless, completely at their sexual disposal, the tight bindings making his biceps swell out when he flexed his arms in a useless attempt to find a loop in the rawhide encircling his wrists and slip his hands out of the restraint.

He sensed that Trent had fallen clumsily to his knees on the floor behind him—and then the other guy was pressing his solid torso against Cornell's back, his arms going around Cornell's waist to fondle his pecs, his nipples, his flat belly, his thighs, his cock and balls.

Trent's hot, sweaty hands lingered there for several minutes while Cornell blew Zerk, Trent's fingers groping him frantically. Cornell got hard quickly, and it was useless to pretend to himself or to his two molesters that he wasn't getting turned on. Within a very few seconds the familiar hot, flushed sensation of total arousal had flowed down through Cornell's sweating body to his crotch, and a hot, buzzing feeling of fullness and excitement pulsed away, deep inside his cock. He was hot, all right. Hot for cock! For Zerk's cock! The slimy cop bastard was turning him on!

He lunged forward to try to force even more of that huge, hard fuck tool down his throat. His lips caressed the thick shaft, and his tongue lashed out at the throbbing meat he was sucking like a fleshy whip. Saliva escaped from his mouth and drooled down his chin.

Trent wrapped both arms around Cornell's body from behind and rubbed his cock back and forth within the warm, sweaty cleft of Cornell's anal crack, dry-humping him without attempting to actually insert his dick between Cornell's buns.

"That's enough—I don't want to come yet." Zerk moaned, prying Cornell's mouth away from his prick just in time to fend off a premature eruption. Cornell was disappointed. He desperately wanted to take Zerk's load in his mouth, to taste the cop's cum! But he had little time in which to think about that. Zerk grabbed a handful of Cornell's hair and tugged on it to make him struggle up from his knees. Trent, who was still embracing Cornell tightly, rose, too.

"Lick and suck every part of my body," Zerk instructed. He pushed Cornell's face into his chest, and the horny bottom man blindly opened his mouth and thrust out his tongue, running its slick surface quickly over one of Zerk's pectoral muscles until it found his stiff nipple and began to tease it.

Cornell closed his lips around the tit and as much of the surrounding muscle as he could cram inside his mouth and began to lick and suck, as he had been told to do. Zerk let him work on one nipple for a long time, then pushed his mouth over to its twin. Then back again. Then down lower, so that Cornell's tongue-tip could toy with his navel piercing, drill its way into the deep pit of the navel itself, and slide wetly down the flat plane of his belly, toward his pubic bush and the root of his cock.

Cornell licked the slightly sweat-salted skin, getting more and more turned on as he strained uselessly at his bonds and his own untouched hard-on throbbed so violently it leaped up to smack his belly every now and then.

Meanwhile, Trent hadn't been idle. The blond cop had been playing with Cornell's vulnerable ass, crushing the cheeks together and then pulling them wide apart to expose the hairy valley that ran between them, with its rosy pink hole. Cornell wriggled his fingers, but his tightly bound hands could reach down no lower than the base of his spine, and he was powerless to push Trent's exploring digits away from his asshole. The blond cop pressed the tip of one blunt finger against the taut muscle, then through it, working it around inside and getting Cornell hotter and hotter as his anus constricted to bring pressure to bear on the finger that had begun to fuck him, gently but insistently. He finally groaned in mingled lust and despair, and his wet tongue swabbed over the base of Zerk's pulsating hard-on.

"Oh, yeah! He's tight! Tighter'n hell!" Trent told Zerk excitedly. "You can tell just by touching his asshole that he's going to be one wild fuck!"

"That ass is mine, partner," Zerk reminded Trent in mock anger. "Or at least the first crack at it is—so keep your hands off it for the time being. I'm going to fuck him myself in about a minute—I can't stand much more of this tongue-bath he's giving me without popping my wad! You can fuck him after I'm done with him."

"Let me get him nice and warmed up for you, Zerk!" Trent begged. "Let me rim him!"

"Yeah, go ahead, eat his ass. Get him so hot for my cock he'll beg me to fuck him," Zerk agreed with savage approval. "Rim the fucker, and rim him good! Show him he's not the only stud around here who's got a hot tongue! You know how to use yours to turn a guy on, too. You've rimmed mine often enough—do him half as good as you've done me, and he'll be screaming for hard, hot cop cock up his stud ass!"

Still forced, willy-nilly, to use his tongue and lips to arouse Zerk's cock and balls, moving his mouth from one side to the other and then back again at the cop's grunted command, Cornell tried to keep his buttocks clenched tightly together to repel Trent's advances—but he felt the cheeks being pried apart by Trent's strong fingers. Hot breath touched the moist hole, and a moment later a wet, flexible piece of flesh—Trent's tongue—ran over it then wormed its slippery way inside, despite Cornell's wriggling struggles.

He groaned and shoved his ass backward, pressing his parted buttocks right against Trent's face as he felt the stiffened length of the young cop's tongue plunge deep into his anus and begin to dart back and forth, then lick out the inside of his anal aperture with fast, deft sweeps. It was useless to resist. Trent was just too good at this, and there were few things that turned Cornell on more than a really good, deep rimming could. He shoved his ass into the blond cop's face, and Trent ate it with the same passion that Cornell was exhibiting as he sucked and licked Zerk's crotch at his command.

"Okay," Zerk said at last, tearing his body away from Cornell's so abruptly that he almost stumbled and fell as he took the backward step in the ill-lit room. "That's enough! I can't stand it. I can't wait any longer! I just have to fuck this hung bastard's butch ass! It's all I could think about today—is he getting there, Trent? Is that tongue of yours getting him hot? Is he hot for cock, hot for my cock?"

"Yeah," Trent assured him. He pulled his mouth away from Cornell's well-tongued asshole and stood up. He pulled Cornell to his feet as well, then shoved the bound man toward the floor so that Cornell lost his balance and sprawled across a corner of the mat, cursing as his thigh banged into the hard floorboards.

He expected, after what Zerk had just said, to be turned over onto his belly and screwed, and he was just about to plead that they use a rubber and some lubricant on their dicks before they took him when he realized that Zerk had some further refinements of cruelty in mind. Despite his eagerness to fuck Cornell's butt, Zerk was pulling a box toward the mat. He opened it, and, in the light thrown by the two candles, Cornell could see that the box was loaded with an impressive collection of sex toys—restraints, dildos, collars, cuffs, a blindfold, and so forth.

"A night in hell, baby," Zerk taunted Cornell as he began to rummage through the box, selecting which implements he wanted to employ first. "That's what you're in for, what we're going to treat you to. Every dirty, filthy thing you've ever fantasized about—you're going to experience it now. And the best part is you won't have to feel guilty about it afterward. Because you're not going to have any choice in the matter. You're going to do everything we tell you to, whether you want to or not!"

Chapter Fourteen: A Night in Hell

Cornell couldn't imagine how he'd ended up in this predicament.

Well, as a matter of fact, if he was honest with himself—he knew exactly how it had happened. It had all started when, desperate for some quick, anonymous sex, he'd gone to that crummy massage parlor and allowed himself to do his thinking with his dick!

Now, he was naked in this sadistic cop's apartment. Technically, he wasn't completely naked. He was now wearing an uncomfortably snug-fitting body harness, buckled and snapped around his torso, and an equally uncomfortable dog collar was buckled tightly around his neck. An elaborate cock and ball harness, made from chrome and leather, was fastened around his genitals. A separate leather strap, with adjustable snaps, connected the genital restraint to the front of the body harness. It pulled his testicles up and away from his groin and kept his penis in a state of continual arousal. Finally, his wrists were handcuffed behind his back.

Kostopoulos, that fucking sadist, whom Cornell had now begun to suspect must be literally insane, had a massive structural beam running across the ceiling of his bedroom. It was an odd architectural feature, and the cop had taken advantage of it. He'd screwed a row of several heavy-duty industrial steel eyelets into it. Cornell was suspended from four of these by means of heavy chains fastened to D-rings incorporated in his body harness. He dangled there in mid-air, helplessly, with his feet about a yard off the floor. The two lousy cops had needed to haul out a little stepladder, which Zerk kept handy in his closet, to get their victim that high off the floor!

Hanging there, *per se*, wasn't all that uncomfortable, Cornell had to admit. His weight was reasonably well distributed, although the straps of the harness had now begun to dig into his flesh. It was humiliating to be swinging from the ceiling like that, like a trussed-up turkey on display in a butcher shop. But Cornell might have been able to withstand the suspension, for a while at least, without complaint.

What he was having difficulty enduring was the pinch of the alligator-toothed metal nipple clamps Zerk had fastened onto his tits. They bit into the tender cones and felt searing hot. But that heat was nothing compared to the fiery smart that lingered in Cornell's buttocks as a result of the fierce flogging Zerk had just given him with a belt. The bastard had really laid it on, and worse, he'd made Cornell beg for it—beg to be beaten. Then he'd forced him to count each blow, and then, when the cop's arm got tired of swinging the belt and he took a breather, Cornell had been forced to thank the top man, effusively and at length, for flogging him!

Then the other cop, Trent, got into the act. He selected a toy from his partner's well-stocked box of sex aids, and, like a kid on Christmas morning, got all excited as he asked Zerk to show him how it worked. It was a violet wand, an innocent-looking tool with a rounded glass tip that sent a buzzing electric shock through whatever part of the body it was applied to. Cornell screamed when Trent used it on his chest, but that was nothing compared to the cries and pleas he emitted when the bearded blond cop touched the device to the head of his cock, and then to his balls!

When they had tired of this particular torture, Zerk and Trent turned to another. Zerk started fastening additional leather straps around the swaying, naked body of their muscular victim around his thighs, to serve as anchors for several heavy iron weights, and he also attached chains to the waistband and the chest strap to permit suspension of a pair of lead cylinders. He placed a second, adjustable cock restraint around the slave's genitals, buckling it tightly into place and hanging a boot from a length of slim chain fixed to its underside. Cornell bit his lip and felt sweat running down his face, blinding him as Zerk began to fill the boot hung from his cock and balls with large steel ball bearings, each of which seemed to weigh a pound as it added to the pressure on his genitals, forcing his scrotum to stretch—and stretch—and *stretch!*

"No! No more! Don't! Please—no more!" Cornell gasped, each word costing him an effort. "It—it hurts too much. I can't take it, sir! No! Let me down! I'll do anything! Anything you want! You can fuck me—fuck my ass—both of you! All you want! Anything, but this! You're torturing me—you're killing me! Jesus, I can't stand any more! Please—please—please!"

"Forgot your safe word, slave?" Zerk asked. "You need me to refresh your memory for you?"

"No—'sex tape, sex tape!'"

"That's just what I've been waiting to hear, fucker," Zerk said, triumphantly, although he immediately detached the heavy boot from the genital restraint. Cornell moaned with relief as the agonizing pressure on his scrotum ebbed away. "You all right?"

"Yes—yes, sir."

"You want me to stop altogether? Want me to untie you?"

"No! God, no!"

Zerk laughed. "I didn't think so. All right, now that we've tested your limits, and you've lost the attitude, and you've decided to be a little more cooperative—beg for it. Beg me to fuck your butch ass for you. Beg me to fuck it good and hard!"

"Fuck me, cop," Cornell panted. "Please fuck me—please fuck my ass!"

"Louder, slave. Say it like you mean it."

"Please, please fuck my ass for me! Please fuck me, sir! My ass, fuck my ass, please fuck my ass with your big, hard cop cock!"

"Louder! Still not sure you mean it, slave!" Zerk taunted.

"*Fuck me! Fuck me! Fuck me!*"

"That's better, slave," Zerk said. "That's a lot better. You want to get fucked? Well, I'm going to fuck you, right now. I'm going to give you a fuck you'll never forget—one that you'll remember for the rest of your life and jerk off thinking about." He turned back toward the bed and snatched up his discarded belt. It was leather, with three rows of pointed metal studs. "Take this, slave! This ought to warm up that horny butt of yours!" Zerk growled as he swung the heavy belt and landed a moderate blow across Cornell's solid buttocks, making his hanging body sway wildly back and forth in the doorway as he reacted to the blow with a shriek.

"Ow! You fucker! I told you, you could screw me! What more do you want? You fucker!" Cornell cried out as Zerk struck him a second and a third time, harder each time.

"I like a man's ass to be burning hot when I shove my dick in it," Zerk informed Cornell as he deliberately aimed the belt across the front of Cornell's thighs for the fourth blow, just grazing the lower portion of his traumatized scrotal sac. To add to Cornell's humiliation, he saw that Trent was observing them intently. The blond cop laughed cruelly as he admired his friend's skill with the belt—and Cornell's helpless reaction.

"You fucker," Cornell moaned, writhing uselessly against his bonds. "Fucking sadist!"

"Give me a hand here, partner," Zerk requested. "Help me warm up this punk's ass!"

* * * *

Trent moved to the side and let Cornell have it across the ass with a second leather strap he'd taken out of the box with the sex toys, noticing with satisfaction that, despite the expression of sheer agony that contorted their handsome victim's face, Cornell's cock had jumped back to proud, total hardness when Zerk had grazed his nuts with his belt. The guy was definitely into pain, big time!

"Aren't you forgetting your manners, slave? I think you meant to say, 'you fucking sadist, sir!,' didn't you?" Trent taunted.

"No! I meant what I said! Dirty pigs!" Cornell cried, in a final flash of defiance.

"Address us properly, both of us, as 'sir' or 'officer' at all times—or I'll let you have it right between your legs this time!" Trent hissed. "I'll bust your balls, slave!"

"No! Please! I'll say it—sir, officer!" Cornell babbled, giving in.

After that, he offered no resistance, no matter how outrageous the demands they made upon his body. Nor did he utter his safe word. Zerk replaced the boot, filling it with only a few of the ball bearings this time, until it once again forced Cornell's cock and balls to pull down, away from his groin. Zerk made the boot swing, pushing it back and forth between Cornell's legs and increasing the bottom man's misery considerably.

Cornell saw Trent step back. He turned his head toward the young blond cop and gave him an imploring look. But if Cornell hoped to receive any sympathy from Trent, he was immediately disillusioned. From his vantage point, Trent watched Zerk bind their prisoner with a variety of leather straps, increasing the weights hung on each one until Cornell could not have continued to stand up had he not been supported by the chains. Zerk worked on him for a long time, running his palms across the hard, tightly stretched flesh of Cornell's swollen, empurpled cock, playing with it, with his aching balls, setting the weighted boot into wider and wider swinging arcs—which Zerk maintained, instead of suggesting that Cornell do it himself.

"How does that feel, slave?" Zerk demanded.

"Oh God, sir! It hurts—it hurts!"

"Shit! This is nothing. I ought to load up that boot with enough weight to stretch your ball sac all the way down to your knees. Then you'd have something to complain about."

"Please, sir. Please don't!"

"Our boy, here, seems to be developing a more cooperative attitude," Zerk remarked to Trent.

"Yeah," Trent agreed. "I think it's about time we started to turn the tough guy into our bitch. I don't know about you, partner, but this is getting me hot. Hot and hard. I'm going to have to stick my cock into something before much longer."

"I feel like doing some fucking, too. Hey, slave! Let me know when you're ready to take my cock up your ass," Zerk invited. "You can have your choice. You can have some more weight in that boot, and get fucked later—or I'll stop stretching your balls, and fuck you right now."

"Now, sir!" Cornell pleaded. "Please, officer! Please, please fuck me right now, sir!"

"You've been a pretty good slave," Zerk deigned to admit. "Hasn't he, partner? I think he deserves a good, hard fuck. Come on, let's take him down."

They freed their victim from his doorway suspension, and eased his trembling body down onto the floor. They detached the boot from the cock restraint around Cornell's genitals.

Now that Zerk had finally decided to fuck him, he wasted no more time in preliminaries, but straddled Cornell's hips at once. He reached for a condom.

"Fuck him in the mouth while I shove mine up his ass," Zerk instructed Trent as he grasped his slick cock in his fist and bent it down to press the head between Cornell's parted ass cheeks, which were still red from the blows of Trent's leather strap. Trent immediately squatted beside Cornell's head, gripped it between his hands, and raised it, pulling Cornell's mouth toward his jutting, dripping erection.

"Suck it, slave," Trent told Cornell urgently, pressing the knob of his fuck tool against the bottom man's moaning lips. "Suck it while you feel your master's dick going up your ass!"

* * * *

Cornell opened his mouth wider and went down on Trent's thick length of rock-hard manhood. He had just pursed his lips around the middle of the shaft and begun to suck when he felt his asshole being forced open by the steady pressure of the huge, latex-sheathed hard-on that Zerk was trying to drive through it. There was pain, and then an incredible bloating, full sensation as the head and several inches of the shaft of the well-lubricated dick pierced Cornell's tight sphincter muscle and sank into the hot, tensed depths of his ass, pushing the curved walls of his anus wide apart to make room for the mighty phallic weapon that the hot Greek-American cop was violating him with.

Zerk grunted and pushed again, more insistently this time, using his weight to back up the thrust. Two or three inches of cockshaft slipped into Cornell's butt, and he shivered with agony as his asshole was forced to stretch still wider open by that massive prick!

"Oh, yeah—what an ass!" Zerk marveled, preparing himself for the third and final thrust that would complete his possession of Cornell's body. "It's even better than I thought it would be! I can't begin to describe it, Trent. Wait'll you feel it around your cock! Wait'll you fuck him, partner. Wait'll you come inside this hot, tight ass, buddy! It's like every wet dream you ever had, all rolled into one! He's prime ass, all right—a good fuck boy, a good ass slave! I don't even have it all in him yet, but already I can tell that this is going to be one hell of a hot fuck. I don't have it all in him yet—but I will—*now*, right *now!*"

As he spoke he thrust, and Cornell almost choked on Trent's cock as a shriek of agony welled up in his throat and he tried to heave himself up from the floor. But, pinned down as he was by Zerk's body, to say nothing of the grotesque assortment of heavy weights which clanked and rattled every time he tried to move a muscle, there was nothing he could do except lie there and take it.

He couldn't even grit his teeth—not with Trent's nine inches of cock rammed into his mouth! Zerk's cock felt just as big, if not bigger, as it reamed him out.

Cornell's ass flexed involuntarily in protest at the terrific bulk and pressure and friction that it was being forced to absorb. Perversely, Cornell found that he was beginning to enjoy it! Beginning to respond to Zerk's brutal thrusts with hip movements of his own! Beginning to suck on Trent's colossal cock with more enthusiasm than desperation! Beginning to want more—and more, and more! Even if it did kill him or transform him beyond recognition into some sort of an insatiable, sexual monster, whose masochistic appetites no amount of depravity, no quantity of cock, could glut!

Cornell's bound and harnessed body shuddered convulsively in wave upon wave of frenetic eroticism. Zerk was jerking him off again with a rough hand slicked with another scoop of the lubricant as he screwed him, and Cornell could no longer distinguish the sensations in his well-fucked asshole from those that shot through him each time his fucker pumped on his cock.

The prick that was being rammed down his throat with such fiendish brutality seemed like a part of his own body now, too, and provided further lewd sensations that only excited him more. One thing, though, was for certain. The three of them were steadily pushing themselves and each other nearer and nearer to the edge of an explosive sexual release, a triple orgasm that was guaranteed to blow the three panting, sweating studs' minds, as well as their nuts!

Cornell knew that things could never be the same for him after this experience. He would never be the same. If he survived, that was! If the sheer intensity of the orgiastic delight that was about to engulf him didn't turn out to be too much for any man to take! Fucked to death? Cornell almost suspected that such a thing was possible, now, the way he felt at the moment, impaled on Zerk's tremendous prick. But what a way to go! He literally wouldn't know whether he was coming or going—because he'd be doing both at once!

"See?" Zerk laughed breathlessly as he paused between thrusts and felt Cornell lunge upward from the floor to force him to start his fucking rhythm again. Cornell couldn't endure the slightest delay. He had to have it! He had to feel that stud cop cock going in and out of him—fucking him! "It's not so bad now, is it, slave? No, it's not so bad at all! I even think you're beginning to like it, to like being a cop's bitch—and this is only the beginning, slave, only the beginning—of something that could turn out to be real good for both of us!" He began to fuck Cornell again—hard and rough. The way the other man had learned to like it!

"You mean all three of us—don't you?" Trent panted as he fucked Cornell's face and throat. "You're going to share your submissive little bitch with me, aren't you, partner? Oh, shit—I'm coming! Take it—here it comes!" His big body tensed as he began to ejaculate with exceptional force.

But Cornell didn't even hear him as he instinctively cleared his throat and got ready to swallow the load of hot cum that was being shot into his mouth from the blond cop's huge dick, which went off like a pistol in his mouth, firing volley upon volley of thick, clotted scum down his desperately swallowing throat.

Cornell was thinking, even as he sucked and swallowed, about what Zerk had just said, and he had to agree. This was just the beginning, all right. The end of one stage of his sex life and the beginning of another, more intense level of response. Beyond that, though, he didn't know what the future had in store for him, now that he had willingly become a complete masochist. But, no matter how it turned out, Cornell was fairly certain about one thing. It wasn't going to be dull!

Trent and Zerk grinned at each other as, sweating, straining, and groaning, they emptied their loads of sperm into their slave's writhing, bound body, filling his throat and his asshole simultaneously with the liquid outpouring of their too-long-pent-up lust. The two cops knew that for them, too, this was only a beginning—that they'd have just this kind of rough, savage, wildly satisfying man-to-man sex, with each other and with a third partner, any number of times after tonight—and that it could only get better!

Chapter Fifteen: Fantasy and Reality

Trent knew that he was dreaming again—another sex dream, of course—and an unusually vivid and detailed one. This time he was a prison guard, wearing a drab brown uniform. He seemed to be both a participant and an observer, acting out the lurid fantasy while, at the same time, remaining detached enough to see himself going through the motions, from a distance.

Trent went to the cell and found the prisoner on the floor, completely naked, doing push-ups to relieve the monotony of incarceration and keep himself in shape. It was quite a display of raw athleticism. But, when Trent stepped up to the bars of the cell door, Marco paused, poised in mid-air, his broad back arched and shiny wet with sweat, his hard, round buttocks flexed.

He stared at the guard through slitted eyes, returning his hard gaze coldly for a few seconds, and then resumed his exercises.

It was a deliberately provocative display, and as Marco's muscles flexed, relaxed, rippled, and bulged, Trent felt a corresponding tension in his own loins.

After several minutes in which the only sounds in the room were Marco's deep breathing and the guard's own effortful respiration, Marco got up and faced him, his hands relaxed by his sides, his naked dick swinging out in a heavy arc from between his legs. His equipment, even in repose, was large and impressive, a good match for his well-developed physique.

"What do you think you're looking at?" Marco asked, mock-innocently.

"I'm looking at you, you piece of shit," Trent retorted.

"Nice mouth—officer," Marco said, with a sneer. "Don't you have anything better to do than hang around here, checking me out?"

"No, I don't. So I'll hang around here, checking you out, as long as I damn well feel like it. And there's not a damn thing you can do about it, is there?"

"Come on, Carothers, knock it off. What do you want?"

"You know damn well what I want, punk." Trent growled, unlocking the cell door and sliding it back just far enough for his big body to ease through the gap. "I think it's about time you and me started getting acquainted—so you'll know who's the boss around here. So you know your place. We don't want any misunderstandings about that, do we, now?"

"Get lost," Marco said, a little nervously.

He was a hot little bitch who had all the makings of a first-class submissive, Trent had to admit. Marco was looking at Trent with just the right degree of calculation and apprehension, which, at the same time, he was trying—not completely successfully—to cover up with a display of macho bravado. Damn, but the guy was sexy! Trent was going to have no difficulty whatsoever playing his own part. He could already feel himself getting into the spirit of the scene. He was the one who was in charge—and this defiant little bastard had better understand and accept the fact, if he knew what was good for him!

"I'll yell," Marco threatened. "I'll yell for the other guard."

"Go ahead. Go right ahead. You yell for him, and I swear to God it'll be the last time you yell—ever."

"I'm not afraid of you."

"Sure you are. You're a smart ass, but you're smart enough to be scared. And you are scared of me, aren't you, punk? I can smell the fear coming out of you, like your sweat. Just oozing out of you. And you know what? It turns me on."

"Please! Please, just let me alone."

"Yeah, that's better. That's much better. Much more of the right attitude. Come on over here and get down on your knees." As he spoke, Trent sat down on the edge of Marco's bunk and waited.

Naked, breathing hard, dripping sweat, Marco walked over to him and knelt between his spread legs, leaning his forearms on Trent's thighs, which were as hard as those of a marble statue of some Greek god in a museum.

He unzipped the fly of the guard's tight brown uniform trousers, pulled out his unexpectedly long and thick, uncircumcised dick, freeing it from his undershorts, and took it in both of his hands, fondling it eagerly into full erection. Trent responded immediately by throwing his head back and letting out a muffled groan of lust.

Marco wet his lips and brushed them back and forth over the head of the guard's penis, squeezing the shaft with his hand and making it pulse even more strongly in response to the pressure. Then he gave Trent what he wanted—a hot, impassioned blow job, taking all of his uncut meat inside his mouth and working up a mouthful of lubricating saliva around its bulk as he eased it slowly in and out of his mouth and down into his carefully relaxed throat.

"Take your time, punk," Trent commanded. "Get your mouth all the way down on my prick and keep it there. Deep-throat the motherfucker. Choke on it, if you have to. I don't give a damn! If you can't take it all, if you can't handle it, that's your tough luck. And don't waste my time by pulling your tough-guy act on me, bitch. You know you want that cock in your mouth. You know you want to suck it!"

Marco sucked it, with a concentration and enthusiasm that his tormentor found not only gratifying, but rather suspicious. The prisoner was willing to be his bitch, all right! And Trent was just the man to take full, selfish advantage of the fact!

Trent didn't stop Marco from caressing his thighs, his taut, ridged belly under his uniform shirt, his muscular yet resilient pectorals and the hot spikes of his stiff nipples. He unbuttoned his shirt and pulled the T-shirt he wore under it up to his armpits to give Marco's busy hands free access to his magnificently developed torso as the stud prisoner sucked him.

He was responding hotly to Marco's oral lovemaking, breathing very deeply and suppressing gasps as the naked young man worked on his meat.

Marco knew Trent was coming close to ejaculation. He felt Trent's hands on his bare shoulders, and he thought for a moment that the guard's tough-guy, rough-trade act, which had already been stretched to its breaking point by the hot blow job, was going to collapse altogether, and that Trent might even seize him in a lustful embrace. But, instead, he took Marco's shoulders in a vise-like grip and pushed his cocksucker away from him.

Marco looked up, gasping, saliva drooling from his lips.

"You've got a hot mouth." Trent grunted appreciatively as he pulled off his T-shirt altogether, then dropped his pants to his ankles and pulled off his shoes and socks, so that he, too, was completely naked. "No wonder you're so popular here in the slammer! Now, you lie down on that bunk. I want to check out that hot, butch ass of yours that you've been spreading wide open for every con in the quad, and that your cellmate's been plugging every goddamn night with his big stud prick!"

"Yes, sir," Marco said, lying down on his belly and spreading his muscular legs wide.

"Put your hands behind your back." Trent retrieved his handcuffs from the belt of his discarded uniform and snapped them around Marco's wrists, pinning his arms behind his back, just above his butt.

"What's that for, man?" Marco protested.

"Just a little safeguard. Plus, it turns me on. Now shut up. I've had enough of your mouth for now. I want your ass!"

Trent didn't waste any time. He climbed onto the muscular prisoner's back and simply rammed himself forward and down, parting Marco's buttocks with his hands and driving his wildly excited prick—which was lubricated only by a thin film of spit from Marco's sucking mouth—through the guy's sphincter rim and then deep into his ass, rending his anal muscles so brutally that his victim had to bite into the pillow under his face to stifle a scream of pain!

"Yeah," Trent grunted. "Nice, tight ass!"

But Marco was fighting him, writhing under him. Trent eased more of his weight down upon the prisoner's body, to hold him down on the narrow bunk. Marco continued to squirm under him, and Trent felt Marco's fingers rub up against his own hard belly as Marco tried to move his wrists, to get free of the handcuffs or at least push away the guy who was lying on top of him, to urge him to enter him more gradually. But Trent wasn't having any of that!

"Settle down! You lie there and spread it, punk!" he growled, slamming his prick even more roughly into Marco's manhole.

Trent's brawny arms went around Marco's chest and belly, and he shoved and pumped until his hipbones were battering Marco's buttocks quite painfully. He thrashed about like a wild, rutting animal as he fucked, again wasting no time, driving himself steadily toward orgasm.

Just as Trent sensed that Marco was beginning to adjust anally to the massive size of his cock and had begun to enjoy himself—to get off on being humped so roughly—it was all over. There was an explosion of hot, thick sperm like a creamy enema being forced deep up into his burning, spasming rectum, filling his asshole completely with the liquid proof of the other man's potency and lust.

Trent lay on top of him for a moment, panting, and then he got up. He pulled his big prick out of Marco's asshole quickly and callously. If the withdrawal hurt the prisoner as much as the actual screwing had, then so much the better!

Marco rolled over, groaning, flexing his arms as though he was trying to relieve some of the ache in his shackled wrists.

Trent was standing over him, looking down at him again, a glare of triumph in his eyes, positively gloating with lewd animal satisfaction and sexual conquest.

"Well, punk?" he demanded, roughly.

"Well, what?"

"Did it hurt when I fucked you like that?"

"Yeah, man, of course it hurt. It hurt like hell, as a matter of fact. I don't like that kind of rough fucking very much, anyway," Marco lied, "and you're hung like a goddamn horse, and you fucked me like a pile driver going into my butt!"

Trent shook his head, grinning. "Tough shit, man. You'll get used to it—you'd better get used to it, because that fast fuck didn't begin to satisfy me. I'm going to want to plug that hot ass of yours again sometime—sometime real soon."

Marco writhed impatiently on the bunk, biting his lower lip. "Okay, officer. Whatever you say, sir. You can have me any time you want, and you can have my cellmate, too, if you want. Hell, we can even get into a threesome sometime. But take these fucking handcuffs off me, will you? My wrists are starting to kill me!"

Trent only snickered. "Fuck! I ought to leave you here like this—lying there bare-assed naked, handcuffed, with a load of jism up your ass and the door wide open. I bet the other cons would love it. If they walked past and found you waiting for them like that, there'd be one hell of a gangbang, wouldn't there?"

The fantasy excited Trent all over again, and he fondled his prick roughly for a moment before, with obvious reluctance, he started to pick up his clothes and put them back on.

He let Marco stew for several minutes, but when he was finally dressed, Trent pulled out his key ring and unlocked the cuffs.

"The only reason I'm letting you off easy this time is because you're such a good fuck," he said, slapping Marco on the ass. "I think you and I might be able to work something out on a regular basis. I'm sick of humping these young nelly punks who can't take a little punishment. I like to fuck around with a real man, the kind of guy who can take it rough and beg me for more. That's why I think you're going to make me one fine, submissive little bitch!"

And, with that ominous pronouncement, he went about his duties, *leaving the naked and exhausted Marco to speculate about just what further humiliation and abuse were in store for him.*

Trent jarred awake. The dream had left him with a hard-on, of course, and he tried to ignore the insistent throbbing in his groin as he relaxed in his bed, mulling over the possible implications of what had just happened.

The sex dreams seemed to be getting dirtier, more pornographic each time. At least this time he'd been the top!

But the idea that Marco would welcome him into his bunk—or rather, his bed—was now absurd. Marco, after all, had called him "you stinking Judas," the last time Trent had seen him, and Trent wasn't sure he didn't deserve the insult. He was sacrificing some things willingly enough for his job as a cop, his time and his energy. He wasn't sure he wanted to sacrifice his self-respect, as well.

Was there, when it came right down to it, *anything* he wasn't willing to do, for Zerk Kostopoulos?

Trent was confused.

He supposed he ought to be satisfied, and that in some sense he was being ungrateful by harboring these vague feelings of dissatisfaction. Things were going well at work. And, to put it bluntly, he was getting plenty of sex. He and Zerk were—what, exactly? Fuck buddies? Friends with benefits? Lovers? Well, hardly *lovers*, in the way Trent had always thought of the term. Zerk, like any other guy, had his good qualities and his bad, but one thing was for sure, there wasn't anything particularly sentimental or romantic in his personality. Trent could only too easily imagine how Zerk would react, how he'd scoff and sneer if Trent ever worked up enough nerve to make some sort of a declaration of love for him. The bastard would never let Trent live it down!

If only he had someone to talk to. Trent realized that he'd been spending so much with time with Zerk, both on and off the job, that— with the obvious exception of Alejandro De Soto—he hadn't yet developed any real friendships with any of their fellow police officers.

Trent liked most of them, and he hoped they liked him, but there was no intimacy between them—not even the non-sexual intimacy that could exist between two guys who worked together. Trent made a mental note to try to correct this situation. It wasn't healthy for him and Zerk to have such an exclusive one-on-one relationship. It bordered on the obsessive.

What Trent needed, he thought, was a sympathetic gay friend, someone he could confide in. He could always give De Soto a call. The married cop definitely wanted to get together with Trent again. They could have sex. But Trent wasn't sure he'd feel comfortable discussing his ambivalent feelings toward Zerk with De Soto. After all, Zerk and De Soto had once been fuck buddies, and Trent sensed that De Soto, who had wanted more from that relationship than Zerk had been prepared to give him, might still be carrying the torch for Zerk.

Trent was sitting at home one night, stewing these things in his mind, when inspiration struck. After all, he had met at least one extremely attractive and congenial gay man recently, a guy who, in addition, had an advantage in that he was definitely *not* a fellow cop—so there'd be no need to waste time on talking shop with him first, before getting into a more personal discussion. That stud bodybuilder, Brandon, with whom Trent had enjoyed such a memorable one-night stand—he'd raised the possibility of getting together with Trent again. He'd given Trent his business card. Where was it? Where had he put it?

Oh yeah, in the top drawer of the nightstand, where I keep most of my sex-related stuff.

In his bedroom, he retrieved the card and was about to pull out his cell phone when he saw the freebie gay magazine he'd saved in the open drawer. Trent hesitated. It was as though he could visualize two isolated pieces of a jigsaw puzzle, which he could now picture fitting together in his mind.

He pulled out the magazine and turned quickly to the section with the classified ads. He stared, hard, at the ad of the escort named Royce.

That broad, muscular back. That ass. Those thighs. That hair, and that thick mustache. Even though the photo deliberately didn't provide a real look at the guy's face, it was remarkable how distinctive—how recognizable—those other physical attributes could be. Trent was suddenly very sure that he'd run his fingers through that hair, had run his hands along that back, that ass, and those thighs, and had kissed the mouth underneath that mustache.

He was sure the photo was of Brandon.

"Fuck!" he exclaimed.

He pulled out of the drawer the business card Brandon had given him, the night they'd tricked together. You didn't have to be a cop to do a little simple detective work. The phone number and the website name on the card didn't match the phone number and the website name in the ad.

Trent went to his computer. He turned it on and pulled up the website listed on the business card. It was straightforward enough, with a photo of admittedly shirtless Brandon, advertising his services as a personal fitness trainer and photographers' model. There wasn't anything sexually suggestive, although a gay man who might stumble across the website while browsing the Internet would probably pause to take a second look.

Next, Trent pulled up the website listed in the classified ad. Before he could access it, he had to click on a box, agreeing that he was over twenty-one and was not offended by material of a sexual nature. And then, when the site opened, there was "Royce"—or rather, Brandon—in several provocative photos. In all of them, he was nude, smiling seductively at the camera, and very, very erect. Erect, that is, except for the one shot in which he once again had his back turned toward the camera so the viewer couldn't see his cock—only his buttocks, which he was spreading wide open with both hands to expose his ass crack and his sphincter.

"Whore!" Trent exploded. "Dirty, stinking whore!"

He stomped off into the kitchen and grabbed a beer from the fridge. Sucking it down rather quickly and recklessly, he calmed down enough to return to the computer and continue to look at the website. It included a schedule of "Royce's" fees, which varied, depending on how much of his time a customer was willing to pay for.

Between his day job down at the gym and his extracurricular activities, the guy must be making out all right, if he could afford to maintain two separate phone lines and two separate web pages. Brandon, apparently, was leading a classic double life—personal trainer and model by day, male prostitute by night.

He must have been on his night off when I met him. Handing it out for free. I guess I should be honored that he didn't present me with a bill afterward!

He sat there and drank more of the cold beer, which began to help him cool off in more ways than one.

Well, am I any better, when you come right down to it? I pretend to be someone I'm not all the time, for the sake of the job.

He found his cell phone, and, out of curiosity, called the number in the ad. He got an answering machine.

"Hi, this is Royce. I'm not in right now, but if—"

The cheery voice was definitely Brandon's. Trent hung up without listening to the rest of the recorded prompt, let alone leaving a message.

He hesitated, drank more beer, and then tried the number on the card. Brandon, somewhat to his surprise, answered after the second ring.

"Yeah? This is me, Brandon. Who's calling?"

"Ah—Brandon, it's me. Trent. From the other night. Maybe you don't remember?"

"Of course I remember. It's good to hear from you. What's happening?"

"Oh, not much. I was just wondering—?"

"You sound a little hesitant, Trent," Brandon said, smoothly. "What's on your mind? Come on, tell me."

He's used to dealing with nervous potential clients, Trent couldn't help thinking, with a flash of resentment. He suppressed it.

"I was hoping I could see you again sometime," he said.

"Sure, Trent. I'd like that. When? How about tonight?"

"Tonight?" Trent was tempted to add, a little spitefully, "Oh? You're not working tonight?" But he didn't say it. He immediately felt ashamed of himself for thinking it.

"Yeah, right now, if you're free," Brandon was saying.

"Okay. Can I come to your place?"

"Of course."

"All right. I'm leaving right now. I'll be there in, oh, maybe half an hour."

"Hurry." There was a seductive urgency in Brandon's voice.

"I will," Trent promised, before he hung up.

He's so hot. I don't care. I don't care if he is a hustler. I like him. I want him. And I have to talk to him. I've got to talk to somebody, before I explode!

Forty minutes later, Trent was comfortably installed in Brandon's living room with a beer in his hand. They were making small talk— rather clumsy, strained-sounding small talk, on Trent's part. It didn't take Trent long to run out of casual things to say.

Brandon was looking at him with a curious expression on his handsome face.

"What's the matter, Trent?" he finally asked. "What's bothering you?"

"I don't know what you mean. What makes you think anything's bothering me?"

"Listen. Maybe we haven't known each other very long, and maybe we don't know each other very well, yet. But I can tell you have more on your mind right now than just sex."

"Don't get mad, Brandon, but—"

"Why should I get mad at you?"

"I saw your ad. And your website. The one where you call yourself Royce."

"Oh. So that's it." Brandon didn't seem particularly surprised—or the least bit defensive.

"Well, is that all you've got to say?" Trent asked.

"That's all I've got to say for now. I'm waiting to find out which of the categories you fall into."

"Huh? Categories? What are you talking about?"

"It's simple. Whenever I tell a guy that I work in the sex industry—all right, that I hustle, to make a few extra bucks—he always reacts in one of three ways. Either he's disgusted, totally turned off, and wants nothing further to do with me, or he's really turned on, sometimes to the point that it's all he wants to talk about, and he starts seeing me as nothing but this hot, porno, fantasy sex object. I prefer that to the disgust, but it can get kind of tired real fast. The third category—that's the guy who can handle it, take it in his stride, without being all judgmental about it. Who can still treat me as though I'm a human being, not some kind of a freak."

"I'd like to think I'm in that third category," Trent said. "But I'm still trying to get used to the idea. You may have to give me a little time."

"Sure. I think you're worth it."

"Where'd you come up with the name Royce, anyway?"

"It happens to be my middle name. It's a family name, in fact."

"Let me ask you something—"

"Sure, anything."

"When you're with these guys—do you get turned on?"

"Usually. I hardly ever have to fake it. I've got a pretty strong sex drive to begin with, which is an advantage in this line of work. And I've got a good imagination, too. Unless a guy is actually physically repulsive, which is rare—thank God!—I don't ever have much trouble really getting into it."

"That's one of the things I'm having trouble understanding, Brandon. How you can get aroused with a guy you're not attracted to. I don't think I could do that."

"Is it really all that different from being really horny, so horny that you go out and pick up some guy just for sex, even though you know from the get-go that you really don't have much in common with him, and it's not going to be anything but a one-night stand?"

"I guess not."

"And I'll let you in on a secret. A guy can be not all that good-looking, and not have such a great body, and you can still have a lot of fun with him in bed. And enjoy his company, before and afterward."

"I suppose that's true. Even though I'd have to point out—well, that it's easy for *you* to say that. You're gorgeous."

"Thanks for the compliment. Right back at you, by the way. I'll admit that what's on the outside can be kind of important. It's the first thing you see, after all. But it's not everything." Brandon smiled. "Maybe I should've been upfront with you the night we met. But I don't usually confide in a guy about my alter ego, 'Royce,' until I get to know him a little."

Trent finished his beer. "I understand. I haven't been entirely, ah, upfront, as you say, with you, either."

"Oh, really? And what deep, dark secret are *you* hiding, Trent?"

"The night we met, you never got around to asking me what I do for a living, and I didn't volunteer the information. Deliberately. I didn't want to be pigeonholed and judged right off the bat, either, I guess."

"No, I was too hot to get you back here and into bed to be too curious, I'm afraid."

"Brandon, I'm a cop."

He'd succeeded in startling the other man.

"Holy shit. You don't look like one. I mean, God knows you're really butch, but with that long hair, and that beard—! I'd never have guessed."

"I'm working vice, right now. I usually work undercover. That's why I don't have to wear a uniform or look too yuppie-ish."

"Oh, this is great, just great. I just admitted to a cop—and to a vice cop, at that!—that I'm a male prostitute."

"I'm not going to bust you, Brandon. Give me a little credit."

"Well, that's a relief."

"We go after the guys who work the streets or who make a nuisance of themselves in the bars and other public places. The department isn't interested in guys like you, who run a little private business on the side, as long as you're discreet."

"But suppose you were told to bust me as part of your job—you'd have to do it, wouldn't you?"

"That's kind of an unfair question, Brandon."

"Well, let's table that whole issue, as they say, for future discussion. Now I understand something else. This guy you had the fight with—which is why you were out cruising the night we met in the first place—I remember you telling me you work with him."

"He's a cop, too. He's my partner."

"Well, now that we've started being honest with each other, don't stop now," Brandon said, humorously. "I'd better get us a couple more beers. Come on, Trent. Tell me all about this hot cop romance of yours."

Trent told him—at length and in considerable detail.

"It sounds to me like you're in love with the guy," Brandon said, when Trent had finished.

"Maybe I am."

"No offense, but I wonder if part of it is because he's the first guy you've ever been this close to. Working together in such a high-stress job—that can bring two guys close together. Even if they're not having sex. I'm not sure these office romances are such a great idea. That's why I might date a guy I knew from the gym, but I sure as hell wouldn't let myself fall in love with him—let alone with another escort. Well," Brandon added, with a laugh, "unless he was incredibly hot, then I might reconsider. Let's face it—we're all hypocrites, and I don't claim to be better than anybody else. As for your buddy, Zerk, he sounds like the macho type who has trouble expressing his feelings. Except in bed. When two guys are naked and fooling around together, the truth usually starts to come out." He glanced at his watch. "It's getting kind of late."

Trent stood up. "I guess that's my cue to leave," he said, a bit awkwardly.

Brandon smiled at him. "On the contrary. That was a not-so-subtle way of suggesting that maybe we've done enough *talking* for one night. Let's fuck. Unless you're turned off by the thought of having sex with a whore."

"You're not a whore, Brandon."

"Sure I am. Technically. But I don't want to be one, with you. My mouth and my dick and my ass are for sale, when I choose to peddle them. My friendship's not for sale. It's yours, if you want it, Trent. And so am I."

"Let's go into the bedroom," Trent suggested.

This time, the sheets and pillowcases were powder blue. Trent realized that since "Royce" did both in and out calls, a lot of johns had no doubt enjoyed themselves with him in that bed. Brandon probably had to change the sheets more often than most other guys did—an occupational necessity. It was probably smart for a high-class hustler like him to maintain a well-stocked linen closet.

Oddly enough, the thought of Brandon's promiscuity, of his whoring around for cash, no longer bothered Trent. On the contrary—it excited him!

They were naked on the bed, kissing, when Brandon grasped Trent's prick is his hand and began to jerk him off with a rapidly increasing urgency.

"So you like it a little rough, do you?" Brandon gasped.

"Sometimes."

"I can get into it, a little. Why don't we get a little kinky? I know I'm not as experienced in such things as you and your partner are, but maybe some light bondage to spice things up?"

"Sure," Trent agreed. "What've you got to tie me up with?"

"Not you. Me. I want to be restrained while you fuck me."

"Wow."

"I'm sure I'm not the only guy who's fantasized about being fucked by a cop. I don't want you to think you're just a sex object, Trent, but do you think you could get into that?"

"Just give me a chance. You'll see."

Brandon opened the top drawer of his nightstand and pulled out a strip of condoms and a tube of lubricant, setting them on top of the nightstand. Then he opened the second drawer, rummaged around inside it for a moment—and produced a set of regulation police handcuffs!

"Jesus," Trent exclaimed.

"Some of my customers—" Brandon began to explain.

"Never mind, I get it. You got the key?"

"Right here." Brandon deposited it on top of the nightstand, as well.

"Fuck. This is going to be hot," Trent prophesized.

The two men embraced and kissed again. Gripping Trent's cock hard now, in a tight fist, Brandon lay half on top of him, opened his legs, and pulled Trent to him. He lowered his head to Trent's crotch, his arms going around Trent's body to grasp his buttocks, holding on to him tightly. The musky heat of Trent's groin blended with Brandon's hot, panted breath as he drew the cop's cockhead into his mouth. A thrill shot through Trent as his buddy sucked him into his mouth deeper and deeper, filling his oral cavity with the turgid meat.

With one hand, Brandon held Trent's huge balls away from his body, rolling them rapidly around in his fingers as he moved his head up and down on the throbbing shaft of that big cock, his wet lips caressing it, his hot tongue playing over the swollen, smooth-skinned head, drilling down into the pouting piss slit, driving Trent wild. After long, delightful minutes, Brandon pulled his mouth away and looked up at his new sex buddy, his hands traveling up Trent's chest to rub over his shoulders.

"Shit," Brandon moaned. "As much as I love touching you—go ahead. Cuff me." He lay on his back on the bed, with his head on one of the pillows, and raised both of his arms over his head, holding his hands close together on the edge of the mattress, underneath the "headboard" of the bed, which was really no more than a long, horizontal square metal tube joined to several short, matching, upright sections. Trent cuffed Brandon's wrists together, taking care to loop the chain between the cuffs around one of the short metal posts.

"Now you're my prisoner," Trent said.

"Yeah," Brandon replied, staring up at Trent. "What're you going to do to me?"

"Anything I damn well want!"

Aroused, Trent got on top of Brandon and embraced him furiously, his hands roaming all over that hard-muscled body, rubbing their naked flesh together with such urgency and lustful enthusiasm that Trent was afraid, for a moment, that it would be all over for them right then and there. Their overexcited cocks threatened to gush immediately. Their powerful bodies fitted together with a frictionless ease. Brandon's wrists were restrained, but his hips started thrashing from side to side, his loins pushing up into Trent's. Their mouths were glued together, hurting a bit when their teeth came into contact through their crushed-together lips. Trent's hands were thrust into Brandon's dark hair, moving his head insistently from side to side as they tongue-kissed furiously.

"My prisoner," Trent repeated, in a gasp, against Brandon's lips. "My stud prisoner!"

"Fuck me. Fuck me, cop!"

"You're not the one giving the orders here. I am. But I'm going to fuck you, all right. I'm going to fuck you like the horny little bitch you are!"

Trent slid down Brandon's torso and sucked his cock. He pulled his mouth away from the saliva-coated hard-on after feasting on it for several minutes, letting the head slip out and slap back against Brandon's belly. Then Trent's hands went around Brandon's hips to his ass, lifting his lower body up. Brandon cooperated. Those muscular legs of his shot over Trent's broad, sunburned shoulders, gripping him firmly around the neck. Brandon's eyes were squeezed tightly shut as he surrendered his ass to the other man to use—or abuse!—as he wished. The handcuffs rattled against the bed frame when Brandon strained instinctively at his bonds, his shoulder and arm muscles bulging from the useless effort.

"Fucker," he moaned. "Fucking stud cop!"

"Shut up," Trent warned him.

His mouth was watering for a taste of Brandon's flesh. He leaned down and bit, none too gently, into Brandon's thigh. The bodybuilder's leg was so muscular that Trent's nipping teeth had difficulty obtaining a purchase on the taut skin. He finally managed to compress a mouthful of the flesh between the edges of his teeth, however, and he bit down hard. Brandon let out a yelp.

"I told you to shut up," Trent reminded him. He slapped Brandon's ass—hard!

Brandon jerked in response to the butt-reddening blow. His thigh muscles were rock hard and stood out in cords along his sleek, tanned limbs as he strained his butt up against Trent's groin in a silent gesture which unmistakably meant, "Fuck me now!" Trent inhaled sharply, giving himself a good whiff of Brandon's body aroma—a clean, musky smell that was as rawly masculine as his body looked and felt.

Trent pressed his mouth lower down, traveled around between Brandon's thick upraised legs with his lips and tongue, and found the especially warm area beneath his balls. Brandon sucked in his breath in a series of pained rasps when Trent's wet, squirmy tongue hit that crevice. He shoved his legs even higher on Trent's shoulders. His body tasted sweet down there. Trent found the cleft of the other man's hairy asshole at last and lapped at it delicately with his tongue, sending shivers of delight through the big stud he was preparing to rim. His fingers grasped those magnificently developed male buttocks and hoisted that ass even higher, pressing the hole against his lips.

"Yeah, Trent—rim it." Brandon moaned. "Lick my ass—get it good and hot and loosened up for your cock. Eat it out for me!"

Without hesitating for a second, Trent gathered saliva in his mouth and drooled it into the rosy pucker-muscle he was nuzzling with his lips, at the same time letting some of the spit dribble onto his fingers. He quickly dropped his hand to his hot, pulsating cock and massaged the spit over the head and the upper part of the shaft to lubricate it. As he worked the spit around on his cock, Trent speared his tongue deep into the writhing hole of Brandon's ass again and again, getting it ready for his cock.

His hands then moved up to Brandon's sides and pulled the man's body down tight against his crotch. Brandon slid into the proper position and waited, tensely. He didn't have long to wait. Trent's knees were now on the bed on either side of Brandon's waist, and he was sitting back on his heels as he grabbed a condom and the tube of lubricant. His gloved dick was aimed perfectly at a forty-five degree angle as Brandon's sensuous, butch ass pushed down against it with blind desire. Trent reached under to grasp the two firm cheeks of the other man's incredible glutes and yank them wide apart as his cock ground into the warmth and soft-skinned vulnerability between them.

"Are you ready?" Trent asked.

"Yeah—let me have it," Brandon groaned.

Trent paused a second, inhaling deeply. Then Trent felt Brandon's ass press more tightly against the tip of his cock. Trent felt the head of his thick tool push through Brandon's hole, enter him easily, and move, more slowly, foreword, deeper into that lush, hot ass that was opening itself up for him. Brandon breathed in with quick, nervous gasps as Trent slid deeper and deeper into the tight sleeve of his asshole. He could feel the head of his cock press against some barrier deep inside, and he knew he'd reached the bend in Brandon's rectum.

"Fuck me, cop!" Brandon urged. "I can't stop you, can I?"

"Yeah, you're mine, stud!" Trent grunted as he concentrated on forcing the rest of his cockshaft into that tight, resisting hole. "So you'd better stop fighting me. You'd better just relax and take it. *Now!*"

He shoved harder, and the obstacle yielded and his cockhead passed through it. Now he could shove himself completely inside Brandon's anus—and Trent did so, before Brandon could tense up again and make it harder to penetrate him fully.

"Oh, it's in me now, man. It's filling me up," Brandon gloated. "It's stretching me wide open. Fuck me, cop. Fuck me hard."

"I'm fucking you, all right. Feel that, big man? Do you like the way that big dick of mine goes in and out of your hot stud ass?"

"Yeah! Yeah!"

There was no need for further words. Breathless, blinded by his own sweat that was streaming down his face, Trent pistoned his prick in and out of Brandon's butt, without a care for the other guy's pain or pleasure. He knew Brandon was getting off on this rough treatment. And Trent was selfishly enjoying Brandon's body now, using it callously for his own sexual relief—relief which, he sensed, was already well on its way. Trent could feel his orgasm building up deep inside his pelvis, inside his balls. His cock was burning with friction and from its need to unleash its sperm. Trent's swinging balls smacked against Brandon's ass cheeks with a loud report as he plunged as far into him as he could force his fuck tool. Brandon only groaned loudly with undisguised masochistic pleasure and shoved his ass back and up to meet the aroused young police officer's impaling thrusts.

Trent raised himself up on his hands to look down at the beautiful male body he was molesting with such violence—and that did it. The sight of his cock pumping in and out of that yielding manhole was just too much for him to take! As he stared down at his prickshaft sunk deep between those two ripe buttocks, Trent came, as violently as he could ever remember having lost his load. He shot and shot inside that tight butch ass he'd fucked so hard.

"Oh, God!" he cried as he felt the first hot spurts escaping from his pisser and lubricating the inside of the condom. Brandon's hole twitched obscenely around his pulsating bulk. "I'm coming, you son of a bitch," Trent informed his sex partner, his shouts and gasps for breath drowning out Brandon's own loud cries of passionate satisfaction. "Fuck, does it ever feel good, coming like this inside your hot ass. Take it! Take it, man, take all my hot come!"

"Give it to me!" Brandon howled.

Trent kept plunging into him, even after he'd finished spurting. He could hear Brandon yelling incoherently, could feel the big man's hot, sweat-wet body thrashing about on the bed beneath his own. He pounded his prick into Brandon's butt several more times before he dropped down onto him, exhausted, his spent but still rock-hard cock once more sinking as deeply into Brandon's asshole as it could, but staying in there immobile this time. Trent was drained, and he could feel Brandon's well-fucked anal muscles close around his dick tightly, jerkily contracting themselves against the heat and rigidity of his cockshaft.

"I want to come, too," Brandon pleaded, his powerfully muscled arms straining as he tugged uselessly at the handcuffs.

"I bet you do."

"Come on, Trent. Let my hands loose. Let me jerk off."

"Not yet." Trent reached for the lube, applied a little of it to his palm, and began to toy with Brandon's grossly turgid cock. The bodybuilder moaned when he saw and felt the cop's fingers begin to stroke it lightly, with just enough pressure to increase the level of erotic stimulation, but not hard enough to make him shoot.

"Harder," Brandon begged. "Jerk it harder."

"Not yet," Trent repeated. "I think we'll take it nice and slow—see how long you can hold out before I finally let you shoot. You made a big mistake, fucker, when you let me cuff you like that. You're mine now, remember? Mine to play with, for as long as I want. I may even fuck you again before I let you come!"

Brandon groaned. "You sadistic bastard!"

"That's 'Officer Sadistic Bastard' to you, boy. You'd better start demonstrating some respect for the law, if you know what's good for you!"

Chapter Sixteen: Games Cops Play

Zerk and Trent, along with some of the other officers on the vice squad, were in the precinct house when their boss opened his office door.

"Hey—Kostopoulos, Carothers," the captain said, gruffly. "Get your asses in here, will you? On the double."

"What'd you do this time, Kostopoulos?" De Soto teased Zerk.

"Aw, go fuck yourself," Zerk retorted.

The two partners went toward the office.

"I told you we'd get into trouble for that stunt we pulled." Trent hissed, only loud enough for Zerk to hear.

"Calm down. Let me do the talking."

Inside the small, cramped office, they closed the door behind them, at their superior's request. They stood there, waiting, while the captain, who was seated behind his littered desk, studied a file that was open on the desk in front of him.

Finally the captain looked up at them and spoke. "Guess who I just got off the phone with."

"I can't imagine, sir," Zerk said.

"The police commissioner, no less."

"Really?"

"Really. And guess what he had to say?"

"I can't imagine, sir," Zerk repeated, while Trent stood beside him, in an agony of suspense.

The captain finally cracked a smile. "He wanted to congratulate me on the whole way we handled this Cornell Jaeger business."

"Really?" Zerk tried hard to keep his relief from sounding in his voice.

"Yeah, really. What is there, an echo in here? And what's the matter with your partner, Kostopoulos? Can't he talk?"

"I was, ah, waiting to speak until I was spoken to, sir," Trent fumbled.

"Well, I'm glad to see that some of your partner's bad habits haven't rubbed off on you—yet. God knows, Kostopoulos is usually mouthy enough for two people. Anyway, Mr. Jaeger seems to have written a letter to the commissioner, thanking him for the tact the department showed in keeping his little sex tape under wraps and preventing a scandal from breaking out. He even enclosed a fat check, made out to the Police Benevolent Association."

"Oh? That's wonderful, sir," Zerk said.

"Yeah, well, in a way it could almost be interpreted as hush money, after the fact. But let's not look the gift horse in the mouth. I understand Jaeger was particularly impressed by the way you two men conducted yourselves the other night when you went to his house to explain what had happened and hand over the tape to him."

Now Trent was the one who was tempted to blurt out, "Really?" To his knowledge, nothing of the sort had happened. He'd never set foot in Cornell Jaeger's house. He knew the football star turned actor *had* a house somewhere in the area, but he had no idea of exactly where it was located. As for the infamous videotape, Trent had been present when Zerk had given it to Cornell Jaeger, all right—in Zerk's apartment, before they'd both worked Jaeger over, then fucked him shitless. The limp-dicked Cornell had barely been able to find enough strength to pull his clothes on before he'd staggered out of Zerk's place after willingly enduring hours of abuse, mumbling barely audible thanks.

"Good work, men," the captain was saying.

"We were just trying to do our bit to promote good public relations," Zerk replied. He was, Trent noticed, somehow managing to maintain a straight face—the sanctimonious bastard!

"I understand Jaeger's house is really something. What's it like, Carothers?"

"Oh, it's—very impressive, sir. As you might imagine."

Zerk came to Trent's rescue. "Mr. Jaeger was such a gracious host, and was so nice and understanding about the whole unfortunate incident, that we got all caught up in talking to him and hardly noticed the surroundings."

As relieved though he felt at the fact they were off the hook, Trent wanted to slap Zerk's smug-looking face. The son of a bitch had missed his calling by becoming a cop. He should've been an actor!

"Well, I'm just glad it all worked out okay. This is the sort of thing that, if mishandled, could've given the department a black eye. All right, go on about your business, men. But thanks again."

When the partners emerged from the office, the expressions on their faces revealed the fact that they hadn't been bawled out. As a result, their colleagues immediately lost interest, allowing them to converse together in comparative privacy.

"That was a close call," Trent observed.

"Yeah. Especially when he started grilling us about our buddy Jaeger's house. The captain wrote down the address when he gave me the tape and told me to deliver it to Jaeger and to take you along. We may have to drive past the place and take a look at it, in case anybody else asks. Then we can at least describe the outside."

"You're lucky you aren't struck by lightning for being such a hypocrite." Now that they were out of danger, Trent felt free to give Zerk a hard time. "'Promoting public relations,' my ass!"

"As I recall, you had your ass eaten out by your boyhood hero," was Zerk's crude rejoinder. "Among other things you made him do, or that he volunteered to do to you. So you've got nothing to complain about. Come on, let's go get some coffee."

They went to their favorite coffee shop. Trent knew his partner's various moods by now. He sensed that something was brewing besides the coffee. He waited, patiently, for Zerk to say what was on his mind.

"Something's been bugging me, Trent," Zerk finally admitted.

"A lot of things seem to bug you. What is it this time?"

"That night we invited Cornell Jaeger over to my place."

"The night you forced the poor guy to come over to your place by threatening to expose him, you mean."

"That's exactly what I'm talking about. That night, before I actually handed over the tape to him with no strings attached, you thought I was dirty. You thought I was capable of coercing the dude into having sex with us against his will in exchange for the tape. You even thought I might shake him down for money."

"Well, Jesus, Zerk! It's not like you did anything to discourage me from thinking that. You were bragging the whole time about how you had Cornell over a barrel. You were getting off on the fact that you had him at your mercy, at your beck and call."

"I was just playing him the whole time. Playing you, too. Seeing how far he'd go. And how much you'd be willing to put up with. I was testing you."

"I know that *now*. A hell of a lot of help that was to me, back then. These sick little head games you like to play, fucking with people's minds…I know you get off on them, Zerk, but—"

"Don't pretend you don't get off on them, too. You were hotter'n a firecracker that night with Jaeger. You couldn't get enough of it. I thought you were going to fuck the poor bastard to death before you were through with him. God, you were turned on."

"You don't hear me denying it, do you? Don't interrupt me. You're playing with fire, Zerk. One of these times, you're going to get us both burned."

"Okay. I'm sorry. Sorry if I pushed it too far. But one other thing—"

"What?"

"You seemed to go along with it. Oh, you argued with me, you tried to talk me out of it. But you didn't really do anything to stop me.

You didn't threaten to blow me in for what I pretended I was willing to do to Jaeger."

"What, now you're telling me you *wanted* me to threaten you? Zerk, you're my partner. I didn't like that whole setup at first, before I knew you were just bluffing. I wasn't comfortable with it. But I didn't exactly 'go along' with it. Not in the way you mean. I wanted to be there—because I thought, maybe right up until the last minute, I might be able to talk you out of it. I might be able to do something to protect Jaeger—and to protect you. Protect you from yourself. God knows you need somebody to watch your back, with all the crazy things you do."

"Was it only because I was your partner, or was it because you had certain personal feelings for me?" Zerk probed.

"Of course I have personal feelings for you. You know damn well I do. What are you fishing for, a declaration of undying passion? You want us to go shopping for wedding rings?"

"Shit," Zerk muttered.

"*Now* what's the matter?"

"Nothing. Everything. Shit," Zerk repeated.

"Come on, tell me. Is it me? Something I did? Or said? Have I done something wrong?"

"No. Yes. I don't know. Listen, Trent—can I talk to you seriously, man to man?"

"Of course you can. I thought we already were having ourselves a serious discussion this whole time."

"And you won't make fun of me?"

"I will if you say something funny—or something stupid."

"Sorry I asked. Well, I guess I might as well go ahead and take a chance." Zerk hesitated, then heaved a weary-sounding sigh. "I've always believed in playing the field, you know? Sure, there were some guys I've felt different about—guys who were special. Not just your average trick or just another good old reliable fuck buddy. You follow me so far?"

"Sure. I've felt the same way, about certain guys."

"This isn't going to be easy for me to say, Trent."

"Then for God's sake, Zerk, just say it and get it over with. Spit it out."

"All right. I think I'm in love with you." Zerk waited, avoiding Trent's gaze. "Well," he said, humorously, "at least you aren't laughing—not yet. That's something."

"You've kind of taken me by surprise, Zerk," Trent admitted.

"Why? No, really, tell me exactly why. I'm interested. Is it because you can't imagine me being in love with any one guy, or because you can't imagine yourself ever feeling the same way about me, in particular? Am I such a loser?"

"We work together, Zerk. We're partners. We get along pretty well—most of the time. The sex has been really hot—*all* of the time."

"I have a feeling there's a 'but' on the way."

"Not necessarily. I like you a lot, you know that. I'm very fond of you. I don't know if that's love, or not. But—oh damn, I *did* say 'but' after all, didn't I?—it's more than the way I usually feel about just another hot guy I'm having sex with. You're a lot more to me than that."

"Well, at least that's honest. I wasn't really expecting a big declaration of undying love from you, baby. But what you just said is a hell of lot better than nothing."

Now it was Trent's turn to feel hesitant. "Don't get too excited, Zerk, because—"

"Uh oh, here it comes. I knew it. Because what?"

"I met this guy. I like him. Almost as much as I like you, only in a different way, maybe. I'm kind of confused."

"Tell me about him."

"I thought you'd be mad."

"I'm furious," Zerk declared, but he smiled to show Trent that he wasn't being entirely serious. "Come on, tell me about this dude. I promise I won't be *too* jealous."

Trent told Zerk about Brandon, withholding very little.

"Okay," Zerk groused after his partner's lengthy recital, "*now* I'm mad. Now I'm jealous. *This* guy sounds hot. *This* guy sounds like he could be a real threat to me. If he were just some muscle-bound gym freak you picked up for a one-night stand—that would be different. I can tell from the way you talk about him that you want to see a lot more of him. Damn."

"I'm sorry, Zerk. When I said I was confused, I wasn't lying. I like Brandon. I like you. I'm all mixed up. I don't want to have to choose between the two of you. If I had to—I think I'd pick you. I can't imagine not—well, not being with you, the way we've been together."

"Maybe you don't have to choose," Zerk said, slowly and thoughtfully.

"What do you mean?"

"Maybe we could get some sort of a three-way thing going. I'd be willing to share you with this big muscle stud of yours. Let you have him, on the side. Even if he wasn't interested in me."

"Jesus, Zerk. I hadn't thought of that. Of the three of us getting it on together, I mean."

"Why not? I'd like to meet this guy. He might like me. I might be his type. He might even decide he prefers me to you, kid. You'd better watch out. I may steal your boyfriend away from you."

"You're welcome to try."

"That's the spirit, partner. You're pretty sure of yourself, aren't you?"

"Maybe. I have to admit it—now that you've brought the subject up, I wonder how Brandon would feel about it."

"You've come a long way since we first met. You were just another dumb rookie. Oh, maybe more willing to learn than most. Now you've started to man up. You're a lot more self-confident."

"Thanks to you."

"Oh, I may have had a little to do with it, but don't sell yourself short. Give yourself some credit."

"Zerk—?"

"Yeah?"

"I do love you, a little, in my own way. I hope you realize that."

"You are so fucking hot. You are so fucking sweet."

That night, after they'd made love, at Trent's place, Zerk got talkative again.

"I've been thinking. This boyfriend of yours—"

"He's not my boyfriend!" Trent was quick to protest.

"Whatever. Let's not quibble about the exact terminology. Anyway, I was thinking—your buddy Brandon. Why don't we play him?"

"Play him? What the fuck are you talking about?"

"You know, a little harmless head game, just to jack up the excitement." Zerk got out of bed and, still nude, went to his desk. He opened his laptop PC and turned it on. "What's this guy's porno website called again?"

"I'm not sure I want to tell you. What do you have in mind?"

"For now, I just want to take a look at it. Come on. Tell me. I can always just do a search. There can't be too many hustlers out there who use the name Royce."

"You fucker," Trent grumbled. "Okay, move over." He, too, got out of the bed and took over at the PC. He accessed Brandon's, or rather Royce's, website. "Satisfied?" he asked Zerk.

"Not quite." Zerk was looking at the screen over his shoulder. "Oh man, that *is* hot. That's some fucking body. I could go for him—big time." Zerk went in search of his cell phone and then, flipping it open, returned to Trent's side, at the PC.

"Don't even think about it, Zerk," Trent warned.

"Why not? It's what he does, isn't it—take calls from guys?"

Zerk's argument was hard to refute. Trent fell silent as his partner punched in the number he saw on the screen. Trent prayed that Zerk would get only Brandon's answering machine. But no.

"Hey, is this Royce?" Zerk asked, affecting a tone of wide-eyed innocence. He held the phone so Trent could hear both sides of the conversation.

"Yes. May I ask who's calling?"

Inwardly, Trent cringed as he recognized Brandon's voice.

"Ah, my name's Demetrios," Zerk prevaricated. "I'm looking at your website, man. It's really getting me excited."

"Well, that's not such a bad thing, now is it?" Brandon purred. "It's nice to meet you, Demetrios. That's an unusual name."

"I'm Greek-American. Do you like dark, hairy men?"

"I love them. The darker and the hairier, the better."

"I want to book you for a session. As soon as possible."

"Sure. I've got my appointment book right here—"

"Can I come to your place? Do you live here in town?"

"I live downtown. And of course we can set up an in call. How about tomorrow night? At ten?"

"I want a nice long session," Zerk specified. "I don't want to feel rushed. I want to take my time."

"Sure, as long as you want. I won't book anybody else after you."

"I want to do everything," Zerk said, breathlessly. He smirked at Trent, who shook his head in disgust. "You're not going to play me for trade, are you? You do reciprocate, don't you? I want to really make love with you. Suck, fuck, rim—everything."

"Whatever you like, Demetrios," Brandon assured him. "I'm very versatile. And I love sex. I promise you, you won't be disappointed."

"I have a lover," Zerk said. "He's kind of a dumbass, but he's a horny bastard, just like me. Suppose I bring him along—how much would you charge for a session with both of us?"

After Brandon named his price, Zerk covered up the speaker of the cell phone with his palm and grinned at Trent.

"Some high-priced whore," he whispered. "Is he worth it?"

"Yes," Trent said, a bit sullenly.

"He'd better be." Zerk retorted. He took his hand away from the phone. "That sounds great," he told Brandon. "Very reasonable. We definitely want to do it."

Trent listened, torn between arousal and disgust as Zerk and Brandon finalized their arrangements. Brandon gave Zerk his address and wanted Zerk's phone number. Zerk promised that he and his "lover" would show up at ten the following evening and that he'd pay in cash.

"I guess it's a date, then," Zerk told Trent after he hung up.

"You bastard."

"I can't wait to see the guy's face when you show up on his doorstep alongside me."

"What makes you think I have any intention of going through with this?"

"Oh, you'll go through with it, all right," Zerk said, with an infuriating smugness. "Who do you think you're kidding? You know damn well you wouldn't miss it for anything. I recall hearing this coy routine of yours before, when we hooked up with Cornell Jaeger. It isn't any more convincing now, baby!"

"I could call Brandon right now and tell him who this john 'Demetrios' really is," Trent threatened.

"Go right ahead. Tell him he was just talking to another cop. A cop you happen to be sleeping with. You think it'll make any difference to him, as long as he gets paid? I'm getting really hot, just thinking about this big, muscle-bound stud of yours. I'm going to keep that appointment tomorrow night, whether you come along or not."

"You bastard," Trent repeated.

Trent stewed over the whole situation, overnight and throughout much of the following morning. Then he came to a decision and made a phone call.

That evening, he and Zerk drove to Brandon's apartment building together. Zerk called "Royce" on the lobby intercom, and Brandon buzzed them in through the security door.

"You know, I've been thinking," Trent said, casually, as they rode up in the elevator together. "If you really want to play a head game with this guy—"

"Yeah? What?"

"Why go only halfway? Let's give it a little extra twist."

"Such as?"

"You go in first. Tell him I'm circling the block in the car, trying to find a place to park. Meanwhile, you get all friendly with Brandon. Tell him you can't wait to get it on with him. Make sure both of you strip down and get ready for action. Hell, even start sucking his dick, or let him suck yours, for that matter. Only make sure he hasn't bolted the door from the inside or put the security chain on it. Why should he, when he's expecting me to call from down in the lobby, any minute, to be buzzed in, too? So I can come up and join you two? Only I'll be right there, in the hallway, outside the door, the whole time. I'll give you guys a few minutes to get all warm and cozy together, and then I'll burst right in and take him by surprise. You said you wanted to see the look on his face when he sees me. Imagine how he's going to react when he sees me in the apartment, all of a sudden, without any warning."

"Oh, man. Now you're talking. You're learning fast how to play my kind of games. Let's do it. It ought to be wild!"

The elevator door opened on Brandon's floor. "Go on ahead," Trent whispered. "I'll hang back. Remember—act natural, and act really horny. Don't let him suspect anything."

"I won't. You think you're talking to an amateur?"

Grinning, Zerk went down the hall and knocked lightly on Brandon's door. It opened, and Trent heard Brandon greeting Zerk as he let him inside the apartment.

"Where's your friend?" he heard Brandon ask, before the door closed again.

Trent moved to the door and stood there, waiting and listening. He didn't have to wait long. Even through the door, he caught the familiar, unmistakable sound of belt buckles and zippers being unfastened, shoes being kicked off, and pants being shucked. After a minute or two of comparative silence, he heard further, more sinister noises—the sound of a scuffle.

"Shit!" he heard Zerk exclaim, his voice muffled by the distance and the closed door. "Who the fuck are *you*? Hey, let me go! Trent! Help me, Trent! Trent! Where the hell are you? Get in here! Help!"

Trent tried the door. It was unlocked, as he'd anticipated, and he let himself into the apartment, closing the door after him. He was confronted by a highly arousing sight. There, in the middle of the living room, was Zerk, nude except for his thick white cotton athletic socks. A very muscular young guy, in his early twenties, perhaps, with untidy long red hair and a reddish-gold mustache and goatee to match, had Zerk wrestled down on the floor, in an arm lock. The kid who had Zerk pinioned wore jeans, a sweatshirt, and sneakers. Kneeling beside them, helping to hold Zerk down on the floor, was Brandon—who was totally nude. Zerk's clothes, along with others, presumably Brandon's, were strewn across the floor nearby.

"Trent! Get this son of a bitch off of me!" Zerk bellowed.

"Jesus, Zerk," Trent replied, trying his best to sound surprised. "Where'd this guy come from?"

"He was hiding in the other room. He jumped me when my back was turned, when I wasn't looking. Get him off me!"

"Stop resisting," Trent advised, in his best police officer's "tone of command," as he pulled a pair of handcuffs from his pocket and approached the three other men. "Hold his arm for me, Brandon," he told his bodybuilder friend.

"Trent! What the fuck are you doing?" Zerk roared.

"Cuffing you," Trent said, as he snapped the cuffs onto his partner's wrists, restraining his hands behind his back. "Playing you, like you were going to play my buddy, Brandon, here. How's it feel, big guy? How's it feel to be the victim, for a change?"

"You son of a bitch! You cocksucker! You set me up!"

"Yeah," Trent bragged. "It wasn't difficult. You were so horny, so hot to trot, you walked right onto it, didn't you? You must've been thinking with your dick. And now look where it's got you. On the floor, naked and cuffed."

"You get these cuffs off me, Carothers. Right now. And that's an order."

"You're not exactly in a position to be giving orders at the moment, are you?"

"I mean it. You let me loose right now, or—!"

"Or what?"

"I'll get you. You'll pay for this. You'll pay for this, big time."

Trent studiously ignored Zerk, who continued to writhe about, face down on the floor, his arm muscles straining as he tugged, uselessly, at the cuffs. Trent turned toward the young red-haired man.

"I don't think we've been introduced," Trent said, politely. "I'm Trent."

"I'm Manny," the redhead replied.

"Manny is the buddy of mine I told you about," Brandon said. "When we talked on the phone today."

"I don't care if the motherfucker is your long-lost kid brother, you fucking son of a bitch!" Zerk shouted. "You guys better let me loose, right this minute!"

"Ignore him, Manny," Trent advised. "He's just a cock-hungry bottom who has delusions about playing top."

"He's got a hot body, though, doesn't he?" Manny remarked, looking down at the naked and still-struggling Zerk.

"Yeah, he's a pretty decent fuck," Trent conceded.

Zerk started to calm down a bit. Obviously assessing the situation and trying to sort out his options, he rolled over onto his side so that he could look up at all three men.

"Listen, you there, Manny," he said. "You'd better let me go. Right now. You're already in a lot of trouble, punk. You don't know who you're messing with. I'm a police officer. I'm a cop!"

"Sure you are," Brandon jeered. "And I'm the police commissioner, and this is the annual policemen's ball!"

"I'm telling you I'm a cop. So is the blond guy. He's my partner."

"Is he on the level, dude?" Manny asked Trent.

"Naw," Trent said. "He's bullshitting you. It's just this big sex fantasy he has, sometimes, of being a cop. He even likes to dress up in a fake cop uniform, sometimes, to act out his fantasies."

"Trent, you bastard. You sick motherfucker, you. You'd better set these guys straight, right now, before this goes any further. Or you'll pay for this, you little prick!"

"I wouldn't start calling other people names, Zerk, if I were you," Trent taunted his partner. "There are a couple you deserve, after the way you tried to set up my buddy Brandon, here."

Manny unzipped his jeans. "You told me I was going to get my cock sucked, man," he reminded Brandon.

"Sure, buddy," Brandon said. "Our buddy Zerk, here, is going to suck all of our dicks. He's going to be our fucking sex slave tonight. You might as well get comfortable, Manny. Take your clothes off. Then he'll blow you. Hell, he'll do anything you want him to."

"I'm not doing shit!" Zerk protested. "I'm not sucking your dick, or that punk's dick, or anybody's dick!"

"We'll see about that," Trent declared, ominously.

"I'd better go lock and bolt the front door, Trent," Brandon suggested. "We don't want to be interrupted while we entertain your buddy." He went to the door to secure it.

Manny was stripping, revealing a lean, pale-skinned body and—protruding from a dense bush of reddish pubic hair—an oversized cock. He took his impressive endowment in his hand and stroked it into full, throbbing erection.

"Put your mouth on his cock and don't take it off until we tell you to," Trent instructed Zerk.

"Fuck you, rookie!" Zerk retorted. "And fuck both of your asshole friends! You candy-assed little bitch! You're not man enough to even dream about topping me, you fucker. And neither is either of your cocksucking buddies! Punks! Dirty, stinking, no-good punks, all three of you!"

"It looks like the slave boy needs to be taught some manners," Trent said.

"Yeah, he sure does. And I'm just the man who can teach him," Manny declared.

He assumed a legs-spread stance directly in front of where Zerk half-lay, half-sat on the floor. He reached down, grabbed a fistful of Zerk's hair, and jerked him forcefully up onto his knees. Manny's hefty cock swung against Zerk's face, slapping his cheek.

"Don't make me hurt you," Manny growled. "You better start sucking. Put my hot, dirty dick in your mouth and get busy on it. And you'd better suck it nice. If I feel your fucking teeth, even once, I swear to God I'll knock 'em down your throat. Now suck!"

"Wait," Trent said. "Hang on just a minute, Manny."

"Don't make me wait too long, man," the young stud pleaded. "I'm really hard up! I really need to get blown!"

"You will be," Trent promised. "Either by my buddy, here—or by me." Trent leaned over Zerk, who stared up at him defiantly. "You want a safe word, Zerk? How about 'sex tape'? You remember that safe word, don't you? I think it'd be highly appropriate, under the circumstances."

"Fuck you and fuck your safe word," Zerk said.

"Now, now. Let's all play nice here, shall we? All you have to do is say 'sex tape,' and I'll uncuff you. You can get up, put on your clothes, and walk right out of here. You'll have to go home and jerk off all by yourself, though, because I'm going to have to stay here and let my buddies Brandon and Manny do to me what they were planning on doing to you. I'm going to have to let them work me over good. They're both pretty horny, so that's the least I can do. I'd hate for them to be disappointed."

Zerk glared at him but said nothing.

"I don't hear the safe word coming out of his mouth—do you, guys?" Trent asked Brandon and Manny.

"Fuck you, Trent. Don't rub it in," Zerk muttered, his voice barely audible.

Trent laughed. "I think our guest is ready to party, guys!"

"About fucking time!" Manny exclaimed. Once again, he seized a fistful of Zerk's hair, and jabbed the head of his cock against Zerk's lips. "Open your mouth and suck my dick!"

"Yes—yes, sir," Zerk moaned. And he licked the base of Manny's cock with his tongue before he opened his mouth wide and sucked the fat head deep inside his mouth. Manny maintained his grip on Zerk's hair, holding his head in place, while he fed more of his turgid ramrod between the naked, handcuffed cop's slavering lips. Zerk gagged but continued to suck passionately.

"You weren't kidding, man," Manny gasped, addressing Trent. "This dude is one cock-hungry little slut!"

He worked his hips hard to drive himself in and out between those pursed and loudly suctioning lips. Zerk sucked and sucked, hungrily, almost desperately, as though he was famished for the taste of man meat.

"Wow. It's just like you told me, Trent. It sure didn't take long to turn him from a mouthy dude with an attitude into a nasty little sex pig. Make him do more for you, Manny," Brandon suggested, with sadistic relish. "Make him lick and suck on your balls. Make him lick your ass."

"He'll do anything you tell him to do," Trent confirmed. "Or else! He's going to service all three of us. And he's going to get off on every minute of it."

"You freak," Manny taunted Zerk as he pushed the cop's face lower down and allowed him to use his tongue on the big, red-haired sac containing his nuts. "You fucking freak!"

"Let him smell your crotch," Brandon coached. "Push his face up under your balls and let him lick the muscle there. Make him lick your sweat. Now turn around and shove your ass in his face. Make him smell your man's ass, make him kiss it, make him clean out your hole with his tongue."

"Fuck, Brandon. And to think, when we first met, I thought you were only into vanilla sex," Trent told Brandon.

"Some of my customers are really into this kinky shit. I try to accommodate them. I've got to admit that this whole scene is starting to get me hot. Maybe I've been missing out on something all this time."

They watched, fascinated, as Manny reached behind himself with both hands and pressed Zerk's face between his buttocks. Zerk emitted an astonishing array of obscene, animalistic noises as he rooted around inside Manny's pucker with his lips and tongue. Zerk, like Manny, had a raging erection, but, with his hands cuffed behind his back, he couldn't even touch himself. Manny had no such problem. He took one hand away from Zerk's head, and began to masturbate—staring wide-eyed at both Trent and Brandon as he did so.

"Oh, shit, guys," Manny gasped. "I'm going to come!"

"Shoot on his face," Trent commanded the boy. "He likes that!"

Manny whipped around, got a fresh grip on Zerk's sweaty, disheveled hair, and held his head immobile while his fist savagely flailed his cock. It spat, spraying thick white clods of scum directly onto Zerk's flushed face. Some of the semen struck Zerk directly on his parted, gasping lips and flew inside his mouth. Grunting, Manny pushed his erupting manhood back inside Zerk's mouth and forced him to swallow the rest of his spurting load.

"Eat it!" he commanded. "Eat my scum!"

Then he pushed Zerk away from him, and Zerk, losing his balance, toppled sideways on his knees and slumped onto the floor.

"Cocksucker," Manny said, spitefully. "I guess I showed you!"

Trent went over to Zerk's discarded pants, searched through the pockets, and pulled out an envelope. He'd seen Zerk put it in there, earlier that evening.

"Here's the money my buddy agreed to pay you, Brandon," he told the male escort, after glancing at the bills inside the envelope and counting them. "He had it all ready for you. You and Manny can split it, like we agreed on the phone."

"No, give it all to Manny. He's earned it. I don't want any money. I'm enjoying this too much. This isn't work—it's pleasure."

Trent handed the envelope to Manny, while Zerk glared at them murderously.

"Don't you dare give him that money, Trent," Zerk blustered. "Not one goddamn cent."

"Why not? You made a deal. You arranged to come here for sex, and you agreed to pay for it. Now you're paying for it."

Manny was exultant. "Man, this is great. Not only did I get my dick sucked—I got paid for it!"

"I told you this could be a lucrative line of work," Brandon told him. "I've been trying to recruit Manny, you see," he explained to Trent. "I think he could make a pretty good escort. All he needs is an experienced guy like me to show him the ropes."

Manny began to collect his scattered clothes.

"You're not leaving, are you, Manny?" Trent asked.

"Yeah. Sure I am. That was the deal. I was supposed to help Brandon subdue this fucker, so you two guys could work him over."

"But the party's just got started. You're going to miss out on the real fun. Hey, I've got an idea." Trent helped himself to Zerk's wallet and pulled out a twenty-dollar bill. "As long as you've got all that money burning a hole in your pocket, why not take a sporting chance? I'll bet you this twenty you can't fuck him hard enough to make him yell for you to stop."

"Are you serious, man? I can screw him?"

"Sure. Why not? He's in no position to turn you down. He seems to have forgotten the safe word we agreed on. At least, I sure don't hear him saying it, do you?" Trent paused. Zerk looked as though he was about to say something, but he bit his lip—and lowered his head, avoiding Trent's searching gaze. "His ass is yours," Trent declared. "Go ahead. Fuck him."

"It's a sucker bet," the young thug boasted. "I'll make him beg me to stop, all right. I've had lots of bitches who couldn't take this big dick of mine. Once it's in them, they start screaming for me to take it out."

"But I bet you don't," a cynical Trent guessed. "I bet you just keep on fucking them, and the next thing you know, they're screaming because you're making them come."

"Yeah." Manny grinned at Trent. The two of them were now buddies, talking about sex, man-to-man.

"Make him scream like that. I'm in a generous mood tonight. I'll give you the twenty if you make him scream, either way—whether he yells for you to stop, or yells for you to keep on fucking him!"

"I'll hold him down for you," Brandon volunteered.

"If he gives you any trouble, take a belt to his ass," Trent suggested. "Smack his butt for him, good and hard."

Zerk was now so mad he began cursing—in Greek. Trent didn't know what his partner was saying, but he suspected it was highly uncomplimentary. He was probably saying terrible things about all three of the other men in the room—and about their mothers!

Brandon rolled Zerk onto his back on the floor and straddled his chest, grasping Zerk's thrashing legs by the ankles and hoisting them up and over his massive shoulders. Trent saw that his bodybuilder buddy had prepared for his tryst with them. There was a tube of lubricant and a strip of condoms on a table beside the couch. Manny was making good use of the sexual accessories, putting on a rubber and slicking himself up.

"Kneel down behind me and shove it up his ass," Brandon urged his young friend.

"Yeah, man," Manny gloated, as he complied. "This is going to be great!"

He applied some more of the lubricant to his fingertips then roughly inserted them into Zerk's cringing asshole, working the fingers around to lubricate it thoroughly.

"For a dude who's supposed to be such a whore, he's got a nice, tight ass," Manny reported.

"You bitch," Zerk shouted, reverting to English. "You miserable little bitch!"

"*You're* the one who's going to be *my* bitch, big man," Manny taunted the helpless cop. "Starting right now!"

Brandon, who was seated on Zerk's chest, lifted Zerk's legs even higher on his shoulders as he bent his rugged body forward, using his weight to keep Zerk pinned down. Zerk's raised butt was fully exposed and accessible to Manny, who took up his position behind Brandon, kneeling on the floor. The young tough guy grasped his slippery latex-sheathed cock in his fist and bent it down to aim its head between Zerk's inviting ass cheeks.

"Go ahead, take him," Trent urged. "I want to watch you fuck him. I want to hear him scream!"

"Oh, God! Oh—no!" Zerk cried as Manny pressed his cock into the crack of his ass and the thick, blunt head of the lightly lubricated tool touched his sphincter and ground into it, hard—hard enough to penetrate the ring of tight muscle, which resisted for only a second before it began to stretch and retreat, molding itself around the bulky knob of flesh that was being forced deeper and deeper into the cop's yielding fuck hole.

"Man, he's tight!" Manny gasped.

Trent was cynical. "Tight? Him? Don't make me laugh. He must be fighting you. He must be squeezing his shitter closed, trying to keep you out. Keep fucking him. That ought to loosen him up. Before you know it, that hole will feel like a hot, wet, juicy cunt working on your dick. Believe me, I know. I've been in there. I've had him. He loves it—don't let him fool you. He loves to get fucked! And he's going to be fucked, good and hard, isn't he, Brandon? We're both going to have him, once Manny's done fucking him."

"Yeah," Brandon replied, pushing the head of his cock against Zerk's lips and forcing the helpless cop to suck it. "We're all going to fuck him. We're going to show this horny buddy of yours one hell of a good time! Go on, rape his ass, man," Brandon told Manny. "Rape his ass!"

Not that the punk needed any encouragement. "I'm going to win that twenty—easy," he boasted.

And he did. No sooner was he fully immersed in Zerk's ass than the handcuffed cop stopped fighting and began to cooperate, obviously welcoming Manny's use of his hole. Zerk humped his ass wildly upward in response to each of Manny's urgent thrusts. If the violent repeated penetrations were costing him any discomfort, he certainly wasn't showing it.

"Fuck me, you dirty little punk!" Zerk shouted, letting Brandon's cock slip out of his mouth. "Fuck my ass!" He sobbed and quivered in response to the savage anal invasion. "Fuck me!" Zerk howled. "Fuck me, fuck me, *fuck* me! Fuck me *hard!*"

"I believe we have a winner, guys," Trent joked. He slapped the twenty-dollar bill into Manny's outstretched hand. Then, his eyes riveted to the spectacle of his stud partner getting fucked, Trent began to strip, too. He was eager to get his own turn at Zerk's mouth and ass and to enjoy himself with Brandon and Manny, as well. Zerk was going to be pissed off at him, at least temporarily. Trent might as well make the most of this opportunity. He might as well really give Zerk something to be mad at him about!

This little get-together had been Zerk's idea. Now Zerk was the guest of honor, the object of a gangbang. He seemed to be enjoying himself.

Chapter Seventeen: House of Leather

Zerk tried his best to give Trent the cold shoulder the day after the orgy at Brandon's place. Zerk's aloof performance wasn't very convincing, though. He'd obviously had too good a time! Before the morning was over, Zerk had given in and begun to talk to his partner again with his customary warmth. And, before too much more time had elapsed, Zerk was almost bragging about the incident—as though he'd been the one who'd thought it all up, planned everything, right from the beginning!

"I can't believe the way you played me, partner," he gloated. "The way you set me up. That was something else!"

"I learned from the master," Trent replied.

"Fucker." Smiling, Zerk reached out and affectionately ruffled Trent's thick blond mane, the way a guy might tease his kid brother. There was nothing fraternal, however, in the lustful way he was looking at Trent—unless you were talking about the kind of family in which a certain amount of inbreeding was tolerated, or indeed taken for granted!

Trent suddenly found himself in a confessional frame of mind. "You know why I played you, don't you, Zerk?"

"Sure. To pay me back for that scare I threw into you when we first met Cornell. And to take me down a peg or two, which I suppose I deserved."

"Yeah, but—maybe those weren't the only reasons," Trent faltered.

His partner looked at him. "What else?"

"Maybe—I was starting to feel as though I was falling in love with you. And I decided to back off, because I was scared."

"Scared? Scared of what, for Christ's sake?"

"I don't know. Of getting hurt, maybe, when we break up."

"Which you're assuming we will."

"Eventually. How many gay men really hook up with another guy and stay with him?"

"Aren't you willing to take a chance on me and just enjoy it for as long as it lasts?"

"I'm not much of a gambler, Zerk. Never have been. Either with money or with my feelings."

"Trent, as cops, you and I gamble every day. Every time we go on duty, we're taking a risk. We never know what could get thrown at us."

"That's true. I never thought of it that way."

"Well, maybe you ought to start thinking of it that way, and stop playing it so safe—not on the job, I mean, in your personal life. Maybe it's time you took a chance on another guy, for a change. I'm in love with you, asshole," Zerk went on. Despite the hint of impatience he heard in his own voice, to his ears it also suddenly sounded husky from emotion. He'd somehow made *asshole* sound like a romantic term of endearment! Embarrassed, he added, brusquely, "I don't think about how long it's going to last, or whether I'll get hurt in the long run. All I can think about is how crazy I am about you and what I can to do to make it work for us." Zerk grinned. Now that he'd finally said what had been on his mind, troubling him, for some time, he felt less nervous. "There. I've laid it on the line, as best as I can. Take it or leave it. Say something smart, if you're afraid to talk seriously about it."

"All right. I can lay it on the line, too. I'm in love with *you*, asshole. Even sharing you with other guys—occasionally—only seems to make me feel closer to you, for some reason. I get off on seeing you get off. I like it when you get off, watching me get off. Most of all, I like it when the two of us get off together."

"So what you're saying is we're already in some kind of a relationship, the two of us, aren't we?"

"Yes, we are. A weird one, but definitely a relationship."

"Okay, then. I'm willing to find out where it'll go, if you are."

"I'm with you, partner," Trent assured Zerk.

"That's settled, then. Now, that wasn't so hard, was it?" Zerk paused. "Now let's talk about how many kids we want to adopt."

"Jesus, Zerk!"

"Just kidding," Zerk teased him. "Or maybe not. Man, you should see the look on your face! Priceless. Some Daddy *you'd* make."

"Oh, I don't know. I bet I'd be good at discipline."

Zerk groaned. "You worry about disciplining *me*, fucker, and other guys who are over the age of consent—at least for the time being. Let's not get too carried away, here."

The only thing that now gave Trent any cause for concern was the very real probability that Zerk would find some way to pay him back—not right away, perhaps, but eventually. No doubt when Trent least expected it!

"I've heard from our buddy, Cornell," Zerk said a few days later.

"Oh yeah? Does he want to get together with us again?"

"Of course. Only he'd like us to wear our uniforms, next time. He's got this little fantasy scenario he'd like to play out, in which he gets arrested and gets roughed up while he's being interrogated. We'll have to set that up. It ought to be a really hot session. In the meantime, our friend Jaeger's apparently been keeping himself busy. I understand he's been cutting quite a swath through the local leather community. And I'm afraid we may have to take a lot of the credit, or the blame, for that. Looks like we were a bad influence on him. The catalyst that transformed him from a closet case into a die-hard bottom."

"I hope he's not taking any chances. Doing anything that might get him into trouble again."

"If I may be so immodest, I've done my small bit to help steer him the right way when it comes to that. I've suggested to the guy that he stay away from the bars, for one thing. He's too damn recognizable. I've shown him how he can meet up with guys through the Internet, and how to do a little common-sense screening of them before he even *thinks* about meeting them in person. He's also taken my advice to do most of his playing around behind closed doors, in private, and preferably in his own house."

Trent had to laugh. "So, in other words—you've been mentoring him, the way you mentored me when I first joined the force?"

"Exactly," Zerk boasted. "And it looks as though I've found myself another very apt pupil."

"You smug bastard. So fucking full of yourself. So full of shit is more like it."

"I love you, too, babe—especially when you start sweet-talking me like that. But, seriously, Trent, Cornell's throwing a big leather party at his house on Saturday night, and we're both invited. Lots of guys who are heavily into the scene will be there, including some out-of-towners. And Cornell's hooked up with one of them, this very well-known top man who calls himself Master Lambert. He's agreed to act as co-host, help get things organized and keep the party going. That was a smart move on Cornell's part. He's willing to admit that he's still pretty inexperienced with the whole leather scene, so he could use advice and help. So—should I call Cornell back and tell him we'll both be there? With bells on?"

Trent grinned. "You bet. Tell him we'll both be there—with leather on!"

"By the way—not that I like to spoil the surprise for you, but maybe we've had enough surprises lately. I talked to our other buddy, Brandon, too. I hooked him up with Cornell—told Cornell that, instead of taking a risk with cheap hustlers, he can afford the high-class talent, the kind he can count on to be discreet. Brandon's been invited to the party, too, so we'll see him there." Zerk shot Trent a sly, calculating look. "Just between you and me, partner, I think Cornell is already kind of smitten with our favorite high-priced male prostitute. You may have some competition there. Even though I suspect Cornell is paying for what you've been getting for free—so far."

"Don't even think about trying to play me, Zerk," Trent scoffed. "You're not up to it!"

The declaration made Zerk guffaw with laughter at his partner's expense.

* * * *

Cornell Jaeger's house was quite a surprise. Trent had pictured something impressive, but probably conservative in style. What he found, when he and Zerk drove up to it on Saturday evening, was a large, modernistic glass-walled box, set on steel stilts and surrounded by balconies on all four sides. The house, on a large landscaped lot, was isolated from its immediate neighbors. The parking area was filled with automobiles and motorcycles, and a smiling young man in full leather, brandishing a flashlight, was acting as a parking valet. He had a clipboard with the guest list, and checked the two cops' names against it.

"You can take the stairs, right over there, gentlemen, and go right up," he instructed the newcomers as he replaced Zerk in the driver's seat.

They climbed the steel staircase and found themselves inside the house. The structure, as large though it was, seemed to be filled with men, all of them obviously gay, all of them exceptionally attractive, and all of them with casual cruising expressions on their faces as they returned Trent's polite, rather shy, welcoming smile. The guests were dressed informally, to say the least, Trent noticed to his relief. He and Zerk had debated what to wear but had finally opted for conservatism—jeans, boots, T-shirts, and motorcycle jackets.

There seemed to be two distinct types present. There were the guys in leather, usually boots and jackets worn with Levi's, although

Trent saw a number of butch numbers who had on leather chaps or motorcycle pants, often without any crotch or ass pieces, so that the wearer's buttocks and genitals were fully exposed, hanging out free beneath the rawhide lacings or rivets that held the pants together. Leather vests or body harnesses, or both, worn over bare torsos, were also popular. Many of the men were tattooed, and many had adorned themselves with studded wrist and arm bands. Trent saw several dog collars and one beautiful stud sported two pairs of handcuffs, each one worn as a sort of massive double bracelet, one pair on each wrist. Another guy—tall, powerfully built, carrying himself haughtily erect as he surveyed the others in the large living room—had his eyebrow pierced, an earring in his pierced left ear, and two additional rings going through his nipples. The hardware was heavy, solid metal, not thin wire. He was unzipped and had his limp but thick cock dangling out of the V of his open jeans. A third ring, of massive surgical steel, pierced the head of his dick just beneath the piss slit, where the flesh was thick, but surely highly sensitive. Trent thought he had never seen anything quite so barbaric-looking—or so arousing!

"That's our co-host, Master Lambert," Zerk whispered.

"And how do you happen to know him?" Trent asked.

"Just from seeing his photo on the Internet. I can't wait to see him in action."

The second category of guests tended not to be so tough-looking, although there were enough attractive numbers to keep Trent's interest level high as he checked them out. Some of these men wore nothing but jeans, jockstraps, or leather briefs. A few were already completely nude, or wearing only boots, as they wandered around the house unselfconsciously. Many were adorned with the chains or leather bindings that seemed to be the uniform of the day—or, more accurately, of the night. Trent assumed that many of the guests in this second group were bottom men, either the slaves of the top men, or bottoms who had come to the party alone in search of a master for the night, and the thought that most of these men's bodies were probably readily available to anyone who showed any interest in them only excited him further.

But no one was doing anything overtly sexual just yet—the guests were standing around drinking, cruising, and talking. Everyone, even the butchest and most sullen-looking of the leather tops, was quite friendly. Several guys approached Trent and Zerk and introduced themselves to them. There seemed to be none of the cliques or private groups one found in bars or at most parties. Trent began to smell the sweet, strawy odor of marijuana drifting through the rooms, mixed with the sharper sting of the poppers that a lot of the guests were snorting.

"If we see anybody using any hard stuff, do we tell them to cool it, and threaten to bust them if they don't?" Trent whispered in Zerk's ear.

"Don't be an asshole," Zerk retorted. "We're off duty, remember? But, now that you've mentioned it—keep in mind that we *do* have random drug tests, occasionally, down at work. So indulge at your own risk. It'd be just our luck to be told to piss in a bottle, first thing Monday morning."

A familiar, smiling face appeared at their side—Cornell Jaeger's. The football star turned actor was extravagantly attired in a full black leather outfit that looked custom made. Trent couldn't even speculate how much it had cost. The chaps were of soft, thin glove leather that clung to Cornell's lower body like the proverbial second skin. They were slashed open at regular intervals up and down the legs to expose his bare, tanned flesh, and laced up with black rawhide thongs threaded through chrome eyelets in these gaps. Under the chaps, Cornell wore matching black leather bikini briefs, and he had highly polished motorcycle boots, with spurs, on his feet. He was stripped to the waist, but his torso was bound by a remarkably elaborate harness made of criss-crossed strips of leather and lengths of chain. Each of his brawny forearms was encased in a black leather gauntlet, secured by additional rawhide laces. As an accessory, Cornell had a small bullwhip coiled up and thrust through his belt. He was also as high as a kite from the poppers he was sniffing from a cylindrical chrome inhaler that swung on a matching chain around his neck.

"Officers Carothers and Kostopoulos," Cornell greeted them humorously. "My favorite members of the police force! I'm glad you could make it. Everybody is going to want to meet you." He silently offered them the inhaler.

"Maybe later," Trent said, cautiously, as Zerk, too, declined with a gesture of his hand. "This looks as though it could get pretty wild," Trent added, surveying the crowd.

"Could? It will, if I have anything to say about it," Cornell said with a laugh.

"I like your outfit," Zerk commented.

"Thanks. It's new. I'm trying to make up for lost time, as you see. Really immersing myself in the whole leather scene. It's amazing, what—and who—you can find on the Internet, if you know where to look. You guys' friend Royce, for example. He's amazing."

"I knew you and he would hit it off," Zerk said, giving Trent a knowing look. Trent returned the look but tried to keep his facial expression emotionless. He wasn't about to give Zerk the satisfaction of thinking he'd scored a point!

So obviously Cornell only knows Brandon, aka Royce, in his professional capacity, as a stud for hire. At least so far! Well, I'm not going to be the one to blow Brandon's cover.

"Is Royce here yet?" Trent asked.

"Yeah, he got here a little while ago," Cornell said. "I don't know exactly where he is at the moment—a guy as good-looking as he is has probably been snapped up already and is balling his brains out in one of the orgy rooms."

"Where are the orgy rooms?" Zerk asked eagerly.

"You're looking at them," their host retorted. "Any room in the house, as far as I'm concerned. Make yourselves at home. Oh, excuse me, I see a couple of guys who've just arrived, from out of town, who

I don't know—I mean, I don't know them face-to-face yet. I recognize them from webcamming them. I have to go over and introduce myself and make 'em feel welcome."

Cornell moved off. Trent and Zerk got drinks and chatted with several of the guests. Trent found himself playing one of his favorite mental games, trying to single out the men he wouldn't mind balling with before the night was over. With so many attractive numbers surrounding him, it was hard to narrow down the list!

Around them, guys were dancing in couples, as the music being piped in over an elaborate built-in sound system changed from upbeat hits to slower, more sensuous rhythm-and-blues numbers. Somebody had dimmed the already low lights in the living room to an even more intimate soft glow, and a lot more of the men had discarded their shirts and were dancing bare-chested, rubbing their hot bodies restlessly together as they embraced.

Trent looked around for someone to ask to dance. He didn't have to bother—a man came up to him with the same idea in mind. He had on tight jeans faded almost bluish-white by repeated washings, and full of holes and frays, with boots, and a black leather belt and tight-fitting torso harness as his only upper garments. A long mane of immaculately groomed dark hair gleamed dully over a brutally handsome face that Trent thought looked familiar in the poor light. He wondered if he'd seen this guy down at his gym—particularly when he noticed his exceptionally well-developed body.

The man, interestingly enough, smiled at Trent—but addressed himself, first, to Zerk. "Do you mind if I ask your partner to dance, sir?"

"No, go right ahead," Zerk replied. "Go ahead," he told Trent. "Dance with him."

Trent and the stranger began to dance, without conversing at first, arms flung around each other so that they could press their chests and crotches together, the way most of the other couples were doing. Trent wasn't surprised to discover that his partner already had a roaring hard-on trapped in those provocative jeans of his. He rubbed his own basket over the bulge again and again, to make his new friend even hotter, making it clear that Trent was open to suggestions.

"How'd you know we were a couple?" Trent finally asked.

"I saw you come in together, and I can tell when two guys are more than 'just friends,'" his dance partner replied.

"And what makes you think I'm the bottom and my buddy is the top?"

"Just an educated guess. He has that kind of possessive way of looking at you."

"We both go either way," Trent informed the other man. "I don't need his permission to dance with another guy—or to do anything else with another guy, for that matter."

"Good."

Marijuana cigarettes were being passed from hand to hand, but both Trent and his partner silently refused when one was offered to them. They swayed back and forth to the beat of the music, their heads resting on each other's shoulders. Men who weren't dancing were on the floor or on the sofas and chairs nearby, fooling around with each other. Some of the ones who *were* dancing were getting into some heavy action together, feeling each other up, with hands shoved inside pants, up crotches, or over ass cheeks or cupping pecs. Many men were tongue-kissing nonstop as they ground their bodies together.

Trent, getting more and more aroused by the proximity of the handsome stud he was dancing with, reveled in the open, unashamed sensuality of the scene. Cornell knew how to throw a party, all right, and the majority of the guests were obviously the type who preferred making out to standing around posing and cruising all evening. In the air of expectancy that flowed through the house, Trent sensed a crackling, electric, erotic charge being shared by every man in the place. All sexual hell might break loose at any moment now—and that would be just fine with him!

He breathed in his dance partner's strong, masculine leather aroma, coming from a big, built male body warmed and scented with yet another odor, that of hot, sweat-bedewed flesh, and he felt the other man's exploring fingers gently working their way inside his open fly, then up under Trent's shirt to caress his chest. Trent groaned and let the man play with his tits, sliding his own hand down to squeeze his partner's hard, round ass through those threadbare jeans.

Now Trent could feel a warm, moist hand pulling his swelling, heated prick out of his fly, and then another naked prick rubbing hotly against his, as he and the leather stud writhed slowly to the strong but subtle beat of the music. Trent glanced about a little nervously, but immediately felt foolish—it was so dark that nobody could get a really good look at his exposed meat, and nobody at this social gathering was likely to be surprised or shocked by the sight of two guys with their dicks out. Hell, at least half a dozen men were stark naked in the immediate vicinity of the dance floor, making out quite openly, in pairs or threesomes.

Trent's partner suddenly whispered, "Oh shit—have you got a big dick! I've never seen one so thick on a guy with your build, outside of a porno film! Let me suck on that mother!" And, with that, the big, dark-haired man sank to his knees on the floor in front of Trent, and grasping his buttocks to hold him in place against his body, he pulled Trent's cock out of his unzipped fly and began to go down on him. As he sank down the length of Trent's body, moaning, open-mouthed with hunger for that juicy young meat, the blond cop realized where he had seen this guy before—in a courtroom! On the bench, no less, when Trent had been in court to testify about an arrest. He felt the arms tighten around his ass, pulling him closer, and then his hot prick was engulfed by his admirer's warm, saliva-filled mouth, the wet lips immediately establishing a steady back-and-forth pumping rhythm as they sucked and slurped with undisguised greed.

I'm getting blown, in front of an audience. And I'm getting blown by none other than Jeremy Huntington, the judge! He sure looks sexy, without his robes on. And he's one hell of a good, hot-mouthed cocksucker!

His amazement at the discovery that the judge was not only gay, but hot for him, a mere rookie police officer, was so great that he did not notice at first that he not only had an audience, and an appreciative one, but that it was growing. He was now the focus of many men's attention. Many eyes were gazing at his body, and especially on what they could see of his thick, hard, mouth-loved prick as it pumped into Huntington's sucking mouth again and again and the kneeling judge took every inch of the throbbing tool into his mouth and throat with reckless abandon. Too turned on to care about the voyeurs surrounding them, Trent stood there quietly, groaning softly from time to time as, legs spread, he rocked gently on his heels to drive his shaft deep into the sensationally talented mouth that was working on him with such passion.

Soon—too soon—he felt his own passion building up inside his pelvis, making his sucked cock pulse hard, with almost painful excitement and eagerness to explode. The pressure quickly grew to intolerable levels and Trent knew that he had to blast his wad down Jeremy's throat. He gripped the man's head between his hands and shoved his prick all the way down that gulping maw. His taut thigh muscles quivered from the strain. Then, finally, unable to resist the urge to come any longer, Trent felt his body convulsing, doubling over that of the cocksucking judge. Bucking his hips to fuck the guy's handsome face even harder, pushing his cock deeper down that gaping throat to rape it with brutal satisfaction, pushing deeper and deeper still—Trent came in a rush of hot, foaming fluid that seemed to go on and on, spurt after wet spurt, with Jeremy choking and sputtering but still sucking furiously, even though the white semen ran from his busily milking lips and dribbled down his chin to drip onto the floor.

His ejaculation over, Trent jerked his cock, now super-sensitive, out of the judge's mouth. As he struggled without success to cram the still-hard rod back into his jeans, he realized that his performance had drawn quite an audience. Men were smiling at him, approvingly, almost in congratulation. Embarrassed, he walked brusquely away, staggering a little, and went through the first door he found.

It opened into another room full of half-naked men having sex with one another, but there was a bar set up against one wall. Trent mixed himself a stiff drink and sat down in a chair to watch the action taking place on the floor and the other pieces of furniture all around him. When his joint had cooled down enough to be flexible, he stuffed it back into his pants and zipped up, grunting a little at the effort it took to force the zipper closed over the bulge made by his bulky tool. He could feel that his cock and balls were slippery from Jeremy's drooled spit. Smiling, Trent wiped his spit-slick hands off on his thighs. He had another drink and allowed a couple of guys to kiss him and fondle him through his clothes.

He wasn't particularly interested in balling any of these new acquaintances, however, so, after finishing his drink, he ventured back into the big living room. He felt a hungry kind of horniness that manifested itself in a blind desire to fuck and fuck and fuck, like an animal—the result of the intense sexuality of his surroundings, the presence of so many willing bodies, and the atmosphere of total hedonism created by so much liquor, pot, and poppers.

Nobody was dancing now. The air was thick with the smell of warm bodies, of cum and sweat, of grass and amyl nitrite. The action seemed to be concentrated at opposite ends of the long rectangular space. Near the far wall, Trent stopped and watched, along with several other curious or amused men, as Jeremy, who'd sucked him off only a short while before, struggled in a mock effort to escape the strong grip of two hard-faced, tough-looking, well-built young numbers in leather jackets and boots—they were wearing nothing else, a costume which left their cocks and balls swinging free and their asses fully exposed. They were forcibly stripping Jeremy naked, actually tearing his clothes in places, and for the first time Trent saw what a fine, gym-toned body the judge had. He was wearing a cock harness, and his dick swelled larger within the leather-and-chrome restraint as the two punks holding him now pinned him down on a sofa. A third, older man, who looked extremely big and rough to Trent, moved behind Jeremy's body. He was naked except for a gleaming chrome cock ring around his huge, solid erection, and he was encasing that thick dick of his inside a condom. Then he lubed it from a tube which another guest handed him. The two leather men pressed Jeremy back against the third man, who maneuvered his big body carefully to get his cock between the judge's butch buttocks.

"Fuck him, man," one of the two leather men urged. "Fuck the bastard who made me pay all those goddamn parking tickets, and slapped that fine on top of it!"

"You got off easy, you stinking punk!" Jeremy retorted. But then he let out a scream as the guy behind him shoved his cock up his ass in a single fierce lunge. The big bastard clamped the agonized Jeremy against his hairy barrel chest, and the other two men let go. They weren't needed anymore. Jeremy was impaled upon the huge man's prick, being fucked with hard, fast strokes as the bruiser pinched his tits and reached down to jerk him off, rubbing his cock painfully within its sheath of leather harness.

"Yeah, fuck him good," the leather boy growled. "Who's paying now, Your Dishonor?"

"You're just jealous because his cock's in me, not you," the judge gasped. "Oh, fuck me, big man! Fuck me hard! Ream me out!"

"You asked for it, bitch." The big man walked forward, into the center of the room, actually using his dick to push Jeremy ahead of him as he screwed him with it savagely, grunting and gasping, his body banging into the judge's buttocks with each stroke.

At last he stopped, humped his haunches viciously into the dark-haired man's ass, coming in the condom, then pulled his dick out quickly and let Jeremy fall to the floor. Jeremy rolled over it, moaning, writhing in pain, and Trent could see why. Even after shooting, the cock that the big fucker had jammed up that brutalized butt was one of the longest and thickest Trent had ever seen. It was certainly bigger than anything he'd ever had the guts to take on himself!

Another man picked up the trembling Jeremy and flung him onto the sofa, jabbing his cock into his ass roughly and without any preliminaries, other than putting on a rubber. Jeremy moaned, but worked his ass cheeks to grind them against the cockshaft that was plowing in and out of him. From the expression on his face, it was obvious that getting screwed by the first guy's monster tool had only whetted his anal appetite, and that this new asshole assault was more pleasurable than painful.

After several hot minutes of heavy fucking, the guy shot off inside the judge's ass, and Jeremy was passed on to another stud, who used him in the same callous way—only this time in a different position, with Jeremy flat on his back on the floor with his legs thrown over his fucker's broad shoulders and his asshole opened up eagerly to accept yet another thick cock. As Trent watched, mesmerized, Jeremy Huntington, one of the most respected judges in the state's legal system, gave his butch ass to a fourth man—then to a fifth—and a sixth!

"Yeah!" an onlooker commented. "That's one hungry hole!"

Jeremy ended up thrown on the sofa cushions like a worn-out rag doll, alone, crumpled up, convulsively humping his cock against the cum-stained cushions, begging "Fuck me—fuck me again, anybody, somebody! Shove a cock up my ass! Shove something up my ass!" Nobody obliged at first. They'd all had their crack at him, and it was time to move on to fresh meat. Trent wondered whether Jeremy could survive another screwing in the freaked-out shape he seemed to be in, both mentally and physically, after having been used by so many guys, one after another—but the judge was clearly a masochist who'd do anything and love every painful minute of it. Somebody finally took mercy on him and handed him a big black rubber dildo, and

Jeremy eagerly shoved it between his ass cheeks and fucked himself with it as he gratefully took the donor's cock in his mouth to suck!

Trent moved away, toward the other end of the room, and discovered Zerk slumped in a chair. He was naked and breathing hard, his hair sweaty and disheveled, with cum stains drying into white flakes on his belly, and his limp cock still encased in an obviously used condom. He'd evidently been enjoying the party.

"Hey there, partner. Give me a kiss—a big wet one. I thought I'd lost you, man," Zerk said.

Trent gave him the kiss. "Are you having a good time?"

"Hell yeah. This is one wild orgy. I wasn't here five minutes before I was in a bedroom, getting it on with two of the best-looking numbers in the place. And it's been nothing but fucking and sucking and rimming ever since—in twos, in threes, in groups, you name it. This is the first chance I've had to sit down and catch my breath, let alone get a drink." Zerk raised a bottle of beer to his lips and drank from it, thirstily. "Some guys were in one of the bathrooms doing coke," he said. "If you happen to see them—well, you *didn't* see them, okay?"

"Okay."

"No reason to get our host in any trouble."

"I understand."

"Good. Why don't you circulate? I'm going to get myself another beer. Go on, have yourself some fun. I'll catch you later, Trent."

"Sure." Trent gave Zerk a hug and another kiss then moved on.

At the far end of the room, where some armchairs and a coffee table had been pushed back to create a free space on the floor, he saw a remarkable group scene in progress—a vast mound of naked bodies, all sliding over each other indiscriminately with the slick sound of oiled and sweaty flesh rubbing against flesh. Trent saw that a king-sized mattress was on the floor, and it was covered by a fitted "play sheet" of heavy-duty black rubber. Every mouth seemed to be sucking a cock, every asshole seemed to be plugged with a condom-protected cock or with probing fingers, and every hand seemed to be either grasping an erection or fondling hard, muscled nudity with greedy possessiveness. It was one large, interlocked, sex pileup. Trent saw a bottle of massage oil on the floor and noticed that several of the roaming hands were slippery with the oil and rubbing it onto the heaving flesh they caressed. Several of the bodies in the heap were generously coated with the oil, slithering over each other with the aid of the musky-scented lubricant.

Fascinated, growing hard as he watched, Trent stripped naked and threw his clothes, bundled up, into a corner. He oiled his own body, then stood beside the mound of writhing bodies, not sure what to do next. A hand grasped his ankle, a body slid toward his prick, a mouth closed over it and began to suck, hard. Other hands reached out and seized his legs and buttocks. Trent lost his balance and fell onto the heap, then slipped down into it and was surrounded by husky male nudity, all oiled and sweating and slippery against his own threshing limbs.

He relaxed, enjoying the way he was being drawn steadily deeper inside the pile. Hands ran all over him, caressing each limb, fondling his hard prick and oily balls and ass cheeks. A few exploring fingers probed inside his asshole, but, after enjoying the finger-fucking for a few minutes, he brushed the hands away, not feeling in the mood to get fucked at the moment. Otherwise, though, he surrendered himself completely to the sensual experience. The anonymity of being just another naked body excited him.

Lying half on his side, sucking a dark-brown nipple on somebody's chest pressed to his face, Trent felt a pair of buns rubbing against his thighs, flattening his cock against his belly. As he and whoever owned those luscious cheeks shifted with the general movement of the orgy heap, Trent managed to get his cock down into the crack of the hairy ass, and he let the oiled tip of it press against the guy's hole.

"Go ahead," the faceless owner of the asshole urged him. "Fuck me!"

"Somebody hand me a condom, will you?" Trent pleaded.

He was accommodated almost at once. He wiped the oil from his dick, put on the rubber, and pushed himself through the other man's yielding pucker. He closed his eyes and fucked the guy's responsive ass gently, letting himself float among the other naked bodies, surrounded as he and his partner of the moment were on all sides by bare skin, oiled and perspiring, hard and muscular, smooth sometimes to the touch, at other moments hairy and masculine-rough. After a few minutes, his prick slipped out of the asshole he'd been fucking and lost contact with its owner.

Opening his eyes, Trent found himself at the edge of the pile, and he made an effort to wriggle out from under it. He slipped free, stood up, and started to retrieve his clothes, but then he decided not to put them back on—nobody else in the house seemed to be keeping much on, except for the odd item of leather attire. Instead, nude, Trent wandered out through an open glass door onto a terrace and descended some steps to the pool that lay half under the house, half alongside it, next to a steaming hot tub. The pool lights were on, and a couple of guys were swimming naked. Trent dove in, swam a few laps to wash the oil and gunk from his body, then soaked and sweated in the hot tub. He flirted casually with the other men in the tub and made small talk with them.

Finally, though, he clambered out and returned to the interior of the house. Horny, but a little fatigued by his sexual experiences so far, he decided that his host wasn't likely to mind if he checked out one of the many bedrooms and maybe found one in which he could rest for a while—preferably with a stimulating bedmate who would help him get back into a party mood.

In the living room the orgying continued, and Trent walked over to see what a large crowd was watching with appreciative murmurs.

"What's going on?" he asked a man standing next to him.

"Master Lambert is giving us a demonstration of how to discipline a slave," the other guest replied. "This really needy bottom volunteered to be the subject of the demonstration—and it looks like he's getting more than he bargained for. The lucky bastard!"

A young man was spread-eagled face-down on the floor. A burly number held his ankles, and a second man knelt with a hand around each wrist. Over the willing subject of the demonstration another powerfully built man stood, naked except for his body harness and his boots, whip in hand. This, Trent remembered from having had him pointed out to him earlier in the evening, was the infamous Master Lambert, the co-host of Cornell's party. He raised the long, black lash and brought it down on the young guy's unprotected ass, connecting with it with a loud crack that brought a scream of raw pain from the prostrate victim.

The top man struck him again. And again. Until his buttocks were crisscrossed with dark marks that Trent knew would quickly develop into welts. With each stroke, the young man jerked up into an arch of pain, twisting his body in a useless effort to free it from his captors.

"No, no!" he screamed as the whip descended upon his ass again and again, impacting harder each time. "Don't hit me again, sir! Ahhh! Oh please no! I'm burning up, my ass—it's on fire! God, I'll do anything, anything you want, if only—! It's unbearable, I can't stand it—! Uh, no, it hurts too fucking much. Please stop! Stop! Please, stop!"

"I hear a lot of talk coming out of that hot cocksucking mouth of yours, boy," the top man jeered. "About the only thing I *don't* hear is your safe word. Now, either you spit it out right now, if you *really* want me to stop—or, if I *don't* hear it, then you'd better shut up and take your punishment like a man!"

The sub immediately fell silent, except for faint whimpers which escaped from his lips.

"I thought so," Master Lambert commented, with audible satisfaction, as he continued the whipping.

A stud standing next to Trent grabbed Trent's cock in one hand, his own cock in the other, and stroked them both. He whispered into Trent's ear, "Master Lambert gets all of the good-looking young ones to become his slaves, sooner or later. They line up, begging him to use them. He does this sort of thing so well. Notice how evenly he lays the cuts across the submissive's butt, and how he changes the angle of his strokes when he moves into that especially sensitive area just below the ass cheeks—so that the whip tip will flick right into it, almost touch the balls each time, but not quite. The bottom's fear, that his balls will be hit the next time, only heightens his excitement. Amazing expertise. No wonder that little bitch pretended he wanted Master Lambert to stop, which was just a bottom's ploy to get Master Lambert to whip him harder. You can smell it, can't you? That smell of fear and humiliation, mixed with the sweat. I can't wait to see Master Lambert fuck that pretty behind, once he's gotten it good and warmed up from the whip. You know, big man, you look like you could discipline a disobedient slave—how'd you like to recruit a couple of guys to hold *me* down like that, so you can use a whip on *me* like that, too—master?"

The dude's increasingly rapid fist action on his cock was getting Trent dangerously close to coming. "Maybe later," Trent whispered.

"I'll be waiting, sir. Any time you want. Any *thing* you want."

Trent pulled himself away from the man's overactive hand. Feeling strangely excited, he left the room, retreating down a long corridor. Through the open door of what was apparently a guest bedroom, he saw Brandon lying on the crumpled sheets of the bed, his naked body flushed red and streaked with still-fresh jism, panting lightly as he caressed himself with one hand.

"Brandon? Are you okay, buddy? What's happening?" Trent asked.

The dark-haired bodybuilder looked up and grinned. "Hi, Trent. I'm fine. Just resting, trying to get my second wind. I just took on a whole bunch of guys, and I must be still half spaced out from all the poppers they gave me. It was the real stuff, too, not that fake shit."

Trent laughed. "All right, I want you to 'fess up—how many of them were there, and how many of them fucked your ass?"

"I don't know. Who was counting? There must've been at least a dozen guys in here, total. Some of them came back for seconds, so I couldn't exactly keep score. I think I've had more guys' pricks in my mouth and up my ass already tonight than I usually get in a whole month of hustling! Man, it was great. Once they found out I wanted it rough, they ganged up on me and held me down on the bed, here, and just went at it, one right after the other, fucking the shit out of my ass and making me beg for it. I know we ran out of condoms halfway through, and somebody had to go find another box. Thank God there seem to be plenty around. Our host must buy 'em wholesale. There's nothing like being a slave every now and then, Trent, letting men use you—there's nothing at all like it in the whole fucking world!"

"Yeah, sure, I guess that's one way of looking at it," Trent faltered, unable to think of anything more pertinent to say. It was surprising how quickly and wholeheartedly Brandon, like Cornell, now seemed to be embracing the whole S and M scene.

"By the way, I'm calling myself Royce here tonight."

"Yeah, so I gathered. I forgot. Don't worry, I won't forget again."

"I've been handing out my business cards—my *other* business cards, the ones in which I'm listed as Royce—as party favors, right and left," Brandon added with a laugh. "When they ask, I tell them, oh sure, I'm a very experienced top man who can get into any kind of a scene they might be interested in—for the right fee. I'm going to have to have you and Zerk give me a couple of crash courses before anybody calls my bluff."

"We'd be glad to. You know that."

Trent gave his friend a reassuring kiss and hug and went on down the corridor to explore the rest of the house. The distant sound of a lash striking flesh seemed to follow, though. It seemed omnipresent in this place tonight, no matter how far away from the orgy room Trent wandered.

Farther down the hall, Trent turned a corner and was startled to find a young guy, good-looking and muscular, who was tied up by his outspread wrists to some rings screwed into the top jamb of an open doorway. He hung from the straps naked, looking exhausted, hollow-eyed, his quivering legs scarcely able to hold him up.

The young slave looked up, saw Trent, and addressed him in breathless gasps. "Please, sir—please help me—I can't take this anymore!"

Trent immediately freed the guy from his bonds, which were not easy to unknot, noting with a grimace how the rawhide thongs had gouged into his wrists, leaving angry-looking red marks and scoring the skin deeply. He had to hold the slumping body up as he helped the other young stud, who was about his own age, into a nearby bedroom that happened to be empty—although the sounds coming through the wall from the room next door suggested that at least two men, possibly three, were in *there*, going at it hot and heavy. Trent kicked the door shut behind them and deposited the guy he'd rescued from his bondage onto the well-used bed that had obviously seen some action of its own earlier in the evening. The sheets were mussed and stained with still-damp spots of semen, and an empty condom packet was lying next to one of the disarranged and dented pillows.

"You okay, now?" Trent asked.

"I guess so."

"Who did this to you? Was it consensual?" For a moment, the cop in Trent resurfaced.

"Sure it was. My master brought me here. He told me he was going to share me with the other guests, anybody who wanted me. That Master Lambert—he paddled my butt, and then he fucked me without putting any lube on the rubber in front of a bunch of the other top men. Then he turned me over to them and said that whoever wanted my ass should take it. And they all gangbanged me—one big cock up my rear end after another. Then they brought me here and tied me up and flogged me. And a couple of them fucked me again, while I was hanging there. They said they'd come back later and work me over some more. My ass is really sore. Not just my hole, my cheeks, too. It feels burning hot back there. Take a look, will you?"

With a sigh, Trent turned the lithe body over and checked out the guy's tempting but—at the moment—bruised and reddened butt, looking for any signs of serious damage. He saw that the puckered entrance to the man's anal passage was chafed and irritated, but otherwise he looked okay—for a bottom man who'd recently been flogged. He'd survive the experience to get fucked again—and maybe sooner than he'd planned on. Trent liked the dude's hard, smooth body. He had a nice face, although his long reddish-brown hair, wet with sweat, kept falling down over his forehead and getting into his eyes. He was too fucked out to so much as raise one hand to brush it back from his face. He was hung, too.

"Does it hurt bad?" Trent asked.

"Not as much, now. It was being suspended like that, for such a long time, that started to get to me. My arms were killing me." The young masochist seemed to get his first real look at Trent. "Hey, I saw you and that other guy come in together. Is he your boyfriend?"

"Sort of."

"I heard somebody say you're both cops. Is that true?"

"Yes."

"Wow. I've never had sex with a real cop. Guys wearing cop uniforms, sure, but that didn't really count."

"Too bad I'm not wearing my uniform tonight," Trent joked.

"It doesn't matter. Don't go. I like you," the bottom whispered. "I want you to do things to me. Dirty things!"

His tongue flicked out of his mouth and licked Trent's nipple. His hand slipped up between Trent's thighs to his crotch, searching, groping, grasping, and caressing, until Trent got hard again. He threw an arm around the other man and drew him close. The masochist's lush but battered body reeked of the sweat of innumerable men, of their spurted cum—it was an intoxicating aroma. Trent felt a burst of lust erupt inside him as the other guy continued to use his hand on his prick, rubbing his body restlessly against Trent's with unmistakable intent. He turned his head to look the bearded blond cop in the eyes.

"Let me suck you off, sir," he pleaded.

"I did you a favor, slave." Trent growled, trying his best to imitate the tough way some of the other masters talked. "I don't want just a lousy blow job! You're going to suck me, all right, and you'd better suck it good. But then I want a piece of ass. I'm going to get in there where all those other guys were, and finish the job they started. I'm going to ream you out, but good."

His bedmate moaned, but the expression on his sexy young face was one of pure lust and submission. And he said nothing but went right on fondling Trent's steely prick and lapping at his nipples and armpits with his tongue.

"Do it, pretty boy!" Trent said roughly. "Get down there and suck my cock!" He didn't wait for compliance but seized the other man's head between his hands and forced him down to his groin. "Start swinging on that cop dick!" Trent barked.

He lay back and exulted in being sucked for long, delightful minutes. The slave boy was good at it. Trent almost didn't want to interrupt the blow job. He was tempted to just keep fucking that face until he came in the guy's mouth. But he spotted a box of condoms and a tube of lube on the nightstand, and that decided the issue. He'd told this hot-mouthed little cock whore that he was going to fuck him, and fuck him he would!

"That's enough," Trent gasped, using a handful of the guy's hair to pull his mouth away from his cock—none too gently. "Get up and straddle me and sit on my cock." He reached for the box of rubbers.

"But—you're hung so fucking big, and I've already been screwed so many times tonight that my asshole's all sore and tight, and—!"

"Shut the fuck up." Trent gave the guy a smart slap on his cheek, making him moan with delight. "Stop your goddamn whining, or I swear to God I'll take you back out in that hallway and string your sorry ass up again. And then I'll go find as many horny, big-dicked motherfuckers as I can, and I'll line 'em up and watch them take your ass. And when they're all done with you, *then* I'll fuck you, myself. I'll probably be pretty frustrated by then, boy, from watching all those bastards fuck you, and I'll take it out on you. I've got a mean streak in me—you don't want to bring it out of me, trust me. Now you shut up and sit on my dick. And that's a fucking order. You sit on my dick, or you'll wish you had, when I'm done punishing you for disobeying me."

During this rather one-sided conversation, Trent had put a rubber on his cock. Now he reached for the tube of lubricant and flipped open its hinged cap.

"You can grease it up first," he conceded. "I'll go easy on you, as far as that goes. I won't fuck you without any lube. Put some of this on me. Quick."

The other youth quickly slicked up Trent's throbbing cock and his own chafed asshole, and then he straddled Trent and tried to impale himself on the cop's thick prick.

"Open your ass and take my cock," Trent snarled.

"Oh! Jesus! I can't!" his companion protested, his body convulsing with pain as he tried to comply with the demand. "You're too big, and I'm too tight!"

Impatient, Trent took the guy's big balls in his hand, making a snug ring around them with his thumb and forefinger, and began to pull downward on them, stretching the ball sac. The other young man resisted, reaching down to grab Trent's wrist.

"Let go," Trent warned, his blue eyes blazing as he looked the guy in the face. "You better get that ass of yours down on my cock, fast, unless you want me to give your nuts one hell of a yank."

He tugged harder on the scrotum. With a stifled cry, the other guy released Trent's wrist and shoved his ass down onto Trent's prick, letting the rest of the solid shaft stab up into him.

"Is this what you want?" Trent demanded. "You like having my big cop dick shoved up your ass?"

"Yes! Yes, sir! I want it! I want your cock up my ass!"

"Good! Now fuck yourself on my cock. Ride it! Move that hot ass of yours up and down on me," Trent commanded savagely. "Faster, you little slave whore!" he spat, threatening to crush the slave's balls within his fist unless he obeyed. "Faster, faster—take that cock of mine—take it, slave! Get fucked, punk—get fucked! *Fucked!*"

The whimpering young man did as he was told, pumping his ass wildly up and down on Trent's pistoning fuck tool, until he could really endure no more of the pain. Then, just as Trent was about to explode inside his ass, he fell back, almost fainting from the combination of pain and excitement. Trent laid the limp body flat on the bed and finished himself off inside it, fucking as hard as he could.

His spent cock was still hard, still planted deep inside the other guy's flesh, when the bedroom door was opened from the outside. Trent looked up, gasping for breath, and saw Zerk standing in the doorway—with Brandon beside him, his massive arm draped around Zerk's shoulders in a loose embrace. Both men were stark naked, and both grinned insolently at Trent and his exhausted victim.

"Oh, excuse me, partner," Zerk said. "We were just looking for an unoccupied bed so we could fuck some more, only in relative privacy, this time. It's hard to concentrate on what you're doing when you've got *too* many guys in the same room with you."

"Get your asses in here"—Trent growled—"and close the door. I've got a hot-assed bottom here who'll take you both on. I want to watch you guys fuck him—one right after the other. That ought to give me a chance to spring back, and be ready for another crack at him, myself."

"Your partner's starting to talk like a real top man, Zerk," Brandon said, admiringly, and he and Zerk complied with Trent's demand.

"Yeah," Zerk grunted. "But we'll see about that. We'll see who the real top is, before the night's over!"

Chapter Eighteen: Partners in Crime

There were three of them, the Dom and his two assistants. The Dom was older, in his forties, a brutally handsome man. His henchmen were both young and good-looking—one was blond and bearded, the other dark and clean-shaven. Both wore full leather bikers' outfits much like the master's. Their ruggedly handsome faces, bathed in the flickering candlelight, remained blank of emotion as they stood motionless, awaiting the top man's commands.

"This is my new slave boy," the Dom announced. "Prepare him." The order sounded so matter-of-fact that the sub jumped when the two assistants stepped up to him, grasped him firmly by the arms, and pulled him to a large, rectangular, steel-topped table in the center of the play room. Without a word, the two men shoved him face down on the table and spun him around roughly until he was in the position they wanted. Then, holding his naked body firmly in place on the cold metal slab, they reached under the table and pulled up a set of steel manacles attached to lengths of heavy chain.

The only sound in the room was the rattle of metal as the two men chained the sub's wrists and ankles to the legs of the table, drawing the restraints taut until he was spread-eagled on the steel, arms and legs parted in wide V's, his erection jammed against the cold metal he was lying bound on. He was naked except for his boots, his buttocks exposed and vulnerable. His entire body shivered, not from cold—the air was warm in this improvised dungeon—but with the eroticism of total helplessness. He closed his eyes and gratefully pressed his burning cheek against the cold steel table top.

"Lick it," one of the men said softly. Without opening his eyes, the

sub parted his lips and thrust out his dry tongue blindly. It rubbed over the leather-gloved fingers of the man's hand and tasted a bitter powder, which the unseen assistant had evidently dipped his fingertip into.

The drug seared the sub's tongue and taste buds—he had no idea what it was, and the fear of possibly tripping out on some unfamiliar substance inflamed his senses even more hotly, his cock pulsating madly against his belly, dribbling semen onto the table top under his groin. The manacles were beginning to chafe his wrists. At least the ones fastened around his ankles had been placed on top of his boots. The discomfort amplified the excitement pounding through his chest and brain.

He turned his head as far to one side as he could and opened his eyes, a low moan escaping his lips when he saw the Dom standing there, holding a dildo in his gloved hand, not looking at the sub or at the other two men in the room as he contemplated the business end of the implement. It was no ordinary dildo—it was obviously an expensive model, made out of some silicone material that imitated the color and texture of actual erectile flesh. The object was penis-shaped, with a pair of balls molded at its thick base, but it was enormous—much larger than any human cock could ever be. The sub's mind reeled as he wondered how long it would be before the man used that thing on him, as part of the scene which—his whole consciousness knew—could now be only moments away from beginning in earnest.

The Dom didn't look up but had heard him moan. "You made a sound without my permission, slave," he said, without anger. "You must be punished. Punish him."

Hot electric pulses of raw sexual energy surged through the sub's outstretched body when he saw the floggers flashing in the gloved hands of the two assistants. The two whips were identical—each consisted of several soft leather strips set into a braided handle.

The first blow exploded in a cloud of red pain across his

shoulders, the redness progressing across his line of vision, burning deep into his brain, into his guts—into his cock. His torso twisted up from the steel table top, but the manacles bit into his wrists and held him taut as the second lash seared into the meat of the backs of his thighs like a hot knife edge. Despite the top man's admonition to remain silent, and this all-too-tangible proof that any outcry would be punished, the sub did scream as both whips whistled shrilly through the air and burned into his buttocks simultaneously, fusing his mind and his flesh into one writhing, sweating, cringing mass of agony. The scream choked into silence in his throat as his cock throbbed with the most intense pleasure he had known in a long time and he almost came.

"He isn't a very submissive slave," the Dom observed. "He resists—he struggles. He needs to learn discipline. Punish him," he repeated coldly, unemotionally, as he continued to toy with the huge dildo in his gloved hands.

The whipping continued—unrelenting in its steady, monotonous impact on the sub's naked and vulnerable flesh—and his body began to shudder with slow convulsions of pleasure. His cries of pain were no longer involuntary. He emitted urgent grunts of encouragement, courting punishment deliberately, as each new blow across his shoulders or back or buttocks or thighs brought his blood to a boil in his veins, until his entire body matched the swelling excitement in his sex organs.

He felt himself developing an erection infinitely bigger and more sensitive than any hard-on he could remember having had recently, and he lifted his body as high as he could force it against the restraints to free his bursting prick as it erupted, a hot volcano blasting its lava in thick streaks across the table top he was lying on.

He'd shot his load, helplessly, prematurely. But his erection never faltered. His cock stayed hard, his balls turgid and aching, as agitated as though he hadn't lost a drop of semen, but was still quivering on the desperate verge of climax.

"You came, didn't you, slave?" the Dom asked, quietly.

"Yes, sir. I came, sir. I couldn't help myself, sir." The sub gasped.

"You are going to have to do better than this, boy. You are going to have to learn self-control. You do not shoot your wad without your master's permission—ever. Your cum belongs to your master, for him to do with as he pleases. Do you understand?"

"Yes, sir."

Several minutes must have passed in total silence, except for the sub's labored breathing as he slowly recovered from his orgasm. He had lost all track of time, and so he had no idea of how long it was before he finally opened his eyes again and tried to look about him. He realized with a fresh jolt of excitement that the two assistants had taken advantage of the pause in the action to get partially undressed. The sub watched them through half-closed eyelids, enjoying the display of their supple young bodies, muscles rippling and tensing under their skin, as they approached the table again, both men naked except for their boots, belts, and unzipped motorcycle jackets. Both sported thick metal cock rings. Both were well-hung and uncut. Both radiated eroticism and menace. They were indistinguishable from one another except by the difference in their coloring and facial features, the bearded blond just as hot-looking—and as sadistic-looking, at the moment—as his brown-haired counterpart, who took up a position opposite him on the sub's left, with their naked and helplessly restrained victim sprawled between them, his body wet with sweat and jism, his back criss-crossed with welts.

"Take him," the Dom barked after another long, ominous silence. "Take him and use him. Do anything you want to him. I don't have any use for a fresh, unmarked, unused slave," he added as his two henchmen sprang into action. "Break him in for me, and break him in good. Treat him like the dirty sex pig he is." There was no menace in his tone of voice, only a far more unnerving calm and detached patience.

His unemotional observation of the wild sexual melee that

followed was in stark contrast to the sudden lust exhibited by his two assistants, who seemed to revel in their opportunity to act out their master's instructions and defile their willing victim in every way possible, with a callous disregard for his discomfort or pain. There was nothing studied or deliberate about their actions as they helped themselves to the sub's body. The blond took a heavy C-clamp and screwed it down around the sub's right nipple, smiling to himself with cruel satisfaction as he watched his prisoner's lips curl back in agony. The sub's pain only spurred the blond on to torture his left tit with an identical piece of hardware, seizing both clamped nipples in his hands—squeezing and twisting and tugging on them until the sub almost fainted and opened his mouth to scream in protest.

As though this were a pre-arranged signal, the other stud leaped to that end of the table and pushed his turgid prick over its edge, toward the sub's panting lips. Half of his thick cock disappeared inside the sub's mouth before the recipient of this unexpected oral attack could actually cry out. Gurgling, choking, the sub accepted the dick, savoring this oral rape as the dark-haired man seized his head in both gloved hands, forcing the sub's lips to ride in a steady rhythm up and down the full length of his bloated shaft. The sub gagged and strangled, desperately trying to accommodate the bulky prick. His molester's muscular thighs banged into the edge of the table under his chin as his hands forced the sub's head to stay all the way down on his meat.

"Swallow it!" the man grunted savagely, pumping in and out of the sub's plugged throat. "All of it—take it all down your cocksucking throat, slave! You'll have to suck cock better than this if you expect to please our master!"

The sub realized that the blond, still tugging on his burning tits, had mounted him and was stretched out full length on his back—which seared from neck to knees with new pain at the contact of the other man's body against its welts and bruises. The sub, still sucking, twisted his head back, eyes rolling upward in their sockets, as the *blond got ready to fuck him.*

"I ought to shove my dick up your ass raw," the blond jeered. "But God knows how many guys have already bred that cum dump of a butt of yours. Better play it safe." He was already putting on a condom. But then he didn't bother to use any lube, but sank his huge cockshaft into the sub's unprepared asshole with rough violence. "Don't act coy with me, bitch," he advised as the sub writhed under him. "You're no virgin. Far from it. Now, you stop resisting, and you lie there and you take my cock. You get fucked!"

He waited only for a moment to catch his breath before he started the actual fucking, hammering deep into the sub's butt in a series of hard, deep-driving strokes. The tightly bound slave could only lie there, his throat and ass stuffed full of solid, throbbing cock, able to express his pain and fear only through his groaning, whimpering respiration around the prick that was ravaging his throat.

When the blond had climaxed, spurting his full hot load into the rubber deep inside the sub's unresisting guts, the two men immediately changed places, as though this, too, had been previously agreed upon between them. The dark-haired guy's prick was longer than the blond's, so it penetrated the sub's asshole to an even greater extent as he rammed his cock into that vulnerable, freshly fucked ass, like his predecessor, using a condom but no lube.

Meanwhile, the sub was forced to suck and deep-throat the blond's cock, which had scarcely lost any of its potency after coming. The sub sucked it eagerly, completely carried away, lost in the mindless, bestial craving for humiliation that rose within him—until he deliberately stopped sucking for a moment in order to goad the blond into getting rougher with him. The blond angrily held his dick in place all the way down the sub's throat until his face turned first red, then purple. Only then did the sub begin to suck again, struggling violently—not to escape from the thrusts of the cock into his mouth and throat, but to force even more of those virile, punishing inches between his lips, the dark warning signs of strangulation gradually draining from his face as the two men went on using him.

His wounded buttocks clamped tightly around the other man's impalement, and his entire asshole surrendered greedily to this unusually agonizing penetration. "Fuck me, fuck me!" he wanted to shout. But of course all that emerged from his cock-plugged throat was a guttural rasp of lustful acceptance. Groaning, he shoved his face hard against the blond's groin, sinking the torpedo-like length of the dick deep down his throat. It vibrated fiercely, and suddenly the man's jism spurted into him. The sub pulled back as far as he could within the tight clasp of the blond's gloved hands around his head, gripping his shaft around its middle with the firm seal of his lips so that the gushing stream of sperm could fly over his tongue and he could taste it. The discharge was sweet yet salty, shooting thickly from the guy's balls despite his previous orgasm and passing through the length of his prick with the force of pent-up sexual rage. The sub took it all—not that he had any choice in the matter!—and swung on the emptying tube of flesh until it gradually softened a bit and its throbbing turned into a smoldering, flaccid heat.

Meanwhile, the other man fucked him up the ass, gripping the sub's naked body with arms locked around his chest, his hot breath beating against the sub's ear and the side of his face as he twisted the tormenting tit clamps between his fingertips. The steady pounding of his cock in and out of his already battered rectum drove the sub into a helpless frenzy. His own seed bolted spontaneously out of his cock and wet the table top under him for a second time. And, as though he had deliberately held something in reserve until this moment, the guy fucking the sub sped up the tempo of his humping until he, too, was spurting—his thick, wet jism trapped inside the tip of the condom deep inside his victim's cringing, madly excited body as he pounded his way through his ejaculation.

Both men slowly pulled away from the sub, who lay limp on the table top, still spread-eagled, still bound, his body still their property to abuse in any way they saw fit. Saliva ran from his slack mouth as *he panted for breath and struggled to clear his sperm-clogged throat. He was high, he realized, numbed and disoriented by whatever drug he'd licked off the man's fingertip at the start of the session—but his body still responded to pain, and to sexual stimulation. He had no wish for his degradation to end, no desire to be set free. He wanted these men to use him again—and they did!*

"Suck my ass," the blond commanded hoarsely, turning his back to the sub, bending over, and reaching behind himself to spread open his ass cheeks and expose the blond-furred cleft between the muscular mounds with both black-gloved hands. He shoved his ass into the sub's face, and automatically the slave extended his tongue, found the hole, penetrated it as far as he could reach with his stiffened tongue, and began to lick and suck, laving the musky-tasting pit eagerly while the blond groaned with satisfaction at the expert rimming he was getting.

"That's enough," the Dom, who remained standing nearby, once again intoned quietly, without audible emotion.

As the blond reluctantly twisted his buttocks away from the sub's mouth and tongue, the sub wrenched his head around to look at the leather master. The top man's eyes were cold and unsympathetic, his lips compressed with mockery and contempt. He too had stripped off most of his clothing, except for his boots and torso harness, and his heavy, sleek muscles gleamed beneath their coating of sweat, turning him into a polished and oiled statue.

For the first time, the sub saw the Dom's cock. It was strapped into a leather-and-steel harness which lifted it, up and away from between his thighs, and also separated and hefted the man's balls—which were shaven as bare as his chest and thighs—and it was enormous, an uncut cylinder like a sawed-off length of baseball bat turned on a lathe and polished to the same glistening smoothness as the rest of his flesh.

"Your cock," the sub heard himself moaning. "Let me suck your cock!"

The dark-haired number gave the sub a smart slap on the face with his gloved palm. "You speak only when spoken to, slave! And you will address the master with proper respect!"

"Please, sir—please, master. Give me your cock. Let me have your cock. Put it in my mouth—and up my ass!" the sub begged.

"You haven't even started to earn this meat, slave. And you came again without permission, didn't you? Don't think I didn't notice. Punish him," the Dom said, at last with a flash of anger in his voice.

The other two men retrieved their whips and slashed away at the sub's buttocks and back again, making him jerk and hiss and shudder in raw, burning agony—but also making his cock spring back into full, throbbing erection again, painfully distended between his belly and the unyielding steel surface that was now warmed by his body and slippery wet with his sweat and cum.

"That's enough," the Dom told his two assistants, who immediately ceased their abuse of the prisoner. "Move aside. I think it's about time I stretched out that tight little asshole, so it will be able to take my cock!" He moved toward the table and began to insert the dildo between the sub's buttocks, forcing its blunt rounded tip through his sphincter. "Take it, slave," the Dom commanded. "And don't you dare make a sound!"

The artificial prick plunged roughly into the depths of the sub's asshole, and the top man began to fuck him with it, with fierce, steady thrusts powered by the full strength of his brawny arm.

The sub's asshole was one fiery tunnel of raw pain. His mind reeled with contradictory sensations—excitement, self-disgust, frustration—frustration, because it was a dildo in his ass, not the Dom's flesh-and-blood cock, which was what he so desperately wanted to feel inside him. His own cock was hard—and then, helplessly, he began to ejaculate, for a third time, as the thick, unyielding bulk of the silicone penis fucked him harder and harder.

"He's coming, sir," the bearded blond reported in a breathless gasp, thrusting one hand under the sub's threshing body to confirm his suspicion. "Without your permission, again! The fucking whore likes it—he likes taking that big dick up his ass!" As he spoke, the pressure of his leather-sheathed fingers around the knob of the sub's cock was all that was needed to send the sub over the edge. He spurted wildly, his aching nuts seeming to turn themselves inside out with the force of his climax, his asshole convulsing insanely around that agonizingly impaling fake prick.

"How dare you shoot your load without my permission, boy, after the warnings I've given you," the top man said, his voice not angry, but soft and insinuating—almost caressing in sound, but a caress behind which lurked menace. He stopped thrusting. The dildo was still jammed deep up the sub's asshole but was no longer pumping away. "Keep that toy in your ass while I decide what kind of punishment you deserve," the master said.

Still struggling to catch his breath and calm down after his orgasm, the sub swam in semi-consciousness. Then fingers plunged into his sweat-soaked, disheveled hair, pulled his head up from the table. He opened his eyes and stared blankly into the Dom's handsome, impassive face.

"Are you ready to take your punishment, slave?" the man asked, in the same calm, imperturbable voice he had used before. "Are you ready to serve and satisfy me, cop?"

The submissive police officer licked his lips then struggled to speak. "Yes—yes, sir. Anything you decide—anything you want to do to me."

"I think we'll start with a little cock and ball torture, boy. That ought to improve your attitude!"

As he spoke, the Dom groped for the cop's cock and began to stroke it, roughly, squeezing it...!

"Hey—watch it!" Zerk protested. "You know how sensitive my dick gets right after I've come!"

The sound of his partner's voice jolted Trent out of his erotic reverie and brought him back to reality.

"Sorry," Trent said, grinning, but he kept right on playing with Zerk's limp tool, stroking it back into erection. "I wasn't paying attention. My mind was wandering."

They'd slept together, naked, although Trent hadn't bothered to take off the dog collar he'd allowed Zerk to fasten around his neck at one point during their nocturnal sex play.

Zerk groaned and tried to push the masturbating hand away from his cock. "I want to go back to sleep," he protested, offering a yawn as proof of the fact.

* * * *

"It's almost noon. You can't sleep all fucking day, even if it is our day off," Trent said, his breath warm on Zerk's chest as he leaned over to lick at Zerk's tits.

"You haven't let me get any sleep. And shit! Now you're getting me horny all over again." Zerk moaned as Trent's warm, wet lips touched his pectoral muscle and that slithering tongue poked at his nipple, teasing it into agitated erection and sending the familiar thrill of response through Zerk's body.

Trent was sucking hard on his tit, and Zerk could feel his dick getting hard. Suddenly, he didn't give a damn about going back to sleep. Nothing mattered except making it—again!—with his big blond stud lover. He'd lost track of exactly how many sex acts the two of them had performed since they'd gone to bed the night before. Every time Zerk seemed to drift off to sleep during the night, he'd found himself awake again shortly thereafter, with a reinvigorated erection and a willing, eager bedmate.

"Oh, Trent—you bastard!" he groaned, helpless to resist the other cop's skilled advances.

Trent laughed. "Let's fuck." His hand seized and stroked Zerk's cock. "Oh, yeah, man! You're hard again already! How'd you like to put that big hard thing between my butt cheeks, partner—and fuck me?"

Zerk bit his lip to keep from coming just at the thought of taking his buddy that way. Trent was generous with his anal favors—especially when he was restrained, which he often was during their sessions together—but Zerk never got tired of plugging his butt with his cock. He had to admit it. Trent was the wildest, hottest fuck he'd ever had on a steady basis. Zerk could feel his prick trembling with anticipation and impatient need. God, did he want to fuck that butch ass!

"Yeah," he muttered. "Get it good and hard, first, though. Get it wet!"

Trent immediately went down on him and sucked on the head of his throbbing hard-on for a moment. He held Zerk's tool between his slurping lips and pulled on it from deep in his throat until Zerk had to reach down and tug at Trent's blond hair to warn him not to do it so hard, or he'd come before he wanted to.

"I guess you're ready, sir," Trent said, breathlessly.

"I was born ready, slave."

Trent, too, was as horny as hell again. "Which way do you want me, officer?" he asked. "On my back or on my belly?"

"It doesn't matter much how we start off, because I can take you any damn way I want you," Zerk boasted. "And if one position doesn't satisfy me, then we'll just have to try another, and then another, until you get it right!" As long as he could shove his cock up the other man's tight asshole, he didn't care if they tried it swinging upside down from the ceiling light fixture!

"Then let me sit on it, sir," Trent suggested wantonly. Zerk knew that Trent liked that position best, especially when his wrists were bound behind him, because then Zerk could jerk him off while he fucked him.

Zerk leered at him. "Beg for it, slave!"

"Please, sir, let me sit on your cock. Please let me take your cock up my ass!"

"I don't know, boy. What's in it for me?"

"I'll be a good fuck, sir. I'll let you shove it in and out of me just as hard as you can."

"I'll do that anyway, whether you like it or not," Zerk threatened. "Because your ass belongs to me, bitch, as long as you've got that dog collar on!" He reached out and fingered the leather collar, which was still buckled tightly around Trent's neck.

"Yes, sir," Trent whimpered. "My ass belongs to you, sir. I'll ride your cock good and hard, sir, if you'll let me sit on it and fuck myself on it. I'll get so hot for your cock—you'll see—I'll shoot all over you while you come in my ass!"

"You'll shoot when I damn well give you permission to shoot, boy," Zerk grumbled.

"Yes, sir."

"You'd better be a good, hot fuck. This had better live up to all the goddamn hype."

"Yes, sir."

Zerk went about the preliminaries with deliberate slowness, to remind the bottom man which of them was in charge and to increase the sexual suspense. First, he groped about on the mattress in the darkened bedroom, searching for the handcuffs they always kept nearby. He found them, and Trent, without needing to be prompted, turned his back to Zerk, holding his wrists together in the small of his back. He let out a little moan of pleasurable anticipation as Zerk snapped the cuffs on him. Next, Zerk rolled across the bed and fumbled in the drawer of the nightstand until he found the supply of condoms and lube they kept there—and which they had already made good use of earlier. Zerk put a rubber on his cock then unscrewed the cap of the tube of lubricant and squeezed out a small glob of the transparent, water-based jelly. He leaned over and slowly, painstakingly rubbed the gel all over Trent's cock until the other man was writhing with frustration.

"Hurry up, will you, please, sir?" he pleaded.

"Shut the fuck up," Zerk retorted. He punctuated the command with a light, open-palmed slap across Trent's bearded face. Trent moaned—with pleasure. "Oh, you like that, don't you, you horny little bitch? You like it when a man slaps you around a little, and you can't do anything about it because your hands are cuffed."

"I like it, sir." Trent panted. "I like it when *you* do it to me, sir!"

"You like being my bitch."

"I like being your bitch, sir."

"Let's see if that hole of yours is ready for my cock." Zerk took another blob of lubricant from the tube, massaged it deep between Trent's ass cheeks, and, grunting, pushed two of his slippery fingers partway up Trent's ass. "Oh, that feels good," he reported. "Still nice and tight—considering how many times it's been fucked." He reluctantly pulled his fingers out of the hole. "I'm going to ream you out good and hard this time, boy," he promised. "That ass of yours had better be ready to take some punishment!"

Sheathing his dick in a condom and slicking it up with some of the lube was only the work of a moment. So was shoving it up the bearded blond's ass!

"God—! Let me get used to it for a minute, before you start to fuck!" Trent begged.

"Shut the fuck up, and stop acting like some dumb little anal virgin who's never had a dick up his ass before," Zerk taunted him. "Ready or not, you're going to get fucked!"

"Yes, sir."

Although he'd been screwed many times by guys with cocks of every imaginable size, it hadn't—contrary to ignorant popular belief—loosened him up any back there. He did, in fact, feel as tight and as sensitive as any dumb little anal virgin as Zerk's bulky prick throbbed hotly inside him.

"How's that feel, slave?" Zerk asked.

"Good, sir. Oh, so good!"

At this point, though, Zerk didn't really care if Trent felt good or not. Zerk was thoroughly in his top-man mode. Incredible heat and friction had engulfed Zerk's dick, and the tingling, vibrant sensation was spreading rapidly, excitingly, through the rest of his body. There could be no turning back now. Zerk was in that ass, and he was going to have to fuck it until he ejaculated. Trent was just going to have to take it!

"Don't just sit there, boy," Zerk ordered. "Start fucking yourself on me. Get that ass of yours moving."

"Yes, sir," Trent gasped. He was squatting over Zerk's body. He pushed himself down to make sure that Zerk was inserted in him all the way and that the other cop's cock would not slip accidentally out of his butt. Trent began to work his hips and buttocks, grinding them to increase the pressure of Zerk's prick in his ass. "Fuck me, sir," he pleaded, his face beaded with sweat. "I'm your prisoner—I'm your whore. Please, really fuck my ass now! Give it to me! I want to feel you come in my ass, sir—but not yet, not for long a long while yet—I want you to fuck me for a long time before you shoot off in me, sir! I want you to fuck my asshole raw with your big, thick cock!"

Trent was doing all of the work, and Zerk had to admit that it felt great. Zerk hardly had to move, himself, but he clenched his buttocks and shoved upward in a quick, stabbing motion that drove his dick even deeper into Trent's fuckhole. The handcuffed blond cop let out a loud cry somewhere between a scream and an excited laugh and threw his ass into high gear, moving even faster and working his anal muscles in a way that made some of the other guys Zerk had fucked seem frigid by comparison.

Zerk had both of Trent's tits between his thumbs and forefingers now, and he was pinching them, hard, timing each pinch to coincide with one of his thrusts. Every time he pinched Trent's nipples, he was rewarded by a firm, milking squeeze of that tight, experienced ass around his dick.

Zerk was as excited as though his orgasm was only seconds away, but it was Trent, paradoxically, who was now in control of the fuck.

Trent knew just how to keep his partner continually aroused, but without bringing him off before Trent wanted him to come. Which man was the top, and which was the bottom, now? Trent was using Zerk's body for his own pleasure every bit as much as Zerk was using his.

They were both panting for breath and were covered with rivulets of sweat that drenched the sheets they were fucking on.

Trent was riding up and down on Zerk's prick like a kid on a merry-go-round's pony. He'd raise himself up until most of Zerk's fat dick had slid out of him and only the thick head was still trapped between his ass cheeks. Then, grunting, Trent would recklessly slam his body back down and thrill to the painful yet pleasurable sensation of driving that hard cock right up his ass again in one mighty lunge that had them both gasping.

Up and down, up and down, Trent rode his buddy's cock. It slammed in and out of his tight, flexing asshole, driving them both repeatedly to the verge of ejaculation but never quite pushing them over the edge. It was every bit as exciting a fuck as Zerk had anticipated it would be!

"Permission to speak, sir!" Trent whispered.

"Granted."

"Please—please do me a favor, sir."

"What makes you think you've done anything to deserve any special consideration, slave?"

"I've been a good boy, sir."

"I don't know about that. You're a good fuck, I'll grant you that. But you can still be an arrogant little prick, rookie."

"Yes, sir."

"You need some good, hard training, and some attitude adjustment."

"Yes, sir, that's exactly what I need."

"Well—since you're in such a compliant frame of mind." Zerk gasped. "Though I wonder if the handcuffs have anything to do with that? Anyway—what can I do for you, boy? What do you want?"

"Please, sir—jerk me off, with both hands, while you screw me," Trent begged.

"You like that, huh? That really turned you on, the last time I did that to you?"

"Yes! Yes, sir!"

"Horny little bitch." Zerk gave Trent's nipples a final, wrenching manipulation. Then he relinquished his grip on them, moving his hands to Trent's cock instead.

He wrapped one fist around the base of Trent's erection, the other around the shaft, higher up. Trent was so well hung that this left the head of his dick and an inch of the shaft still exposed. Zerk began to work both his fists roughly back and forth, massaging that immense hard-on and letting the heel of his upper hand rub continually against that super-responsive area just beneath where the cock knob swelled out.

He yanked Trent's foreskin back and forth to bare that sensitive spot and get the other cop hotter and hotter. Trent began to groan and squirm as he rocked back and forth over Zerk's groin. His long hair flew as he threw his head back and then tossed restlessly from side to side on his dog-collared neck, until the tendons stood out in high relief against his sweaty skin. Trent clenched his anal muscles rapidly and seemed determined to squeeze Zerk's cock right off as it leaped and twitched and stabbed inside his rectum, fucking him with brutal abandon now. Zerk was certain that he and his partner had reached the point where they could no longer control themselves, or try to delay their climaxes.

They both threw their heads back and howled as Zerk felt his orgasm build up deep in his body and explode through his ass-embedded cock. His balls tensed—and then they erupted, firing a geyser of hot, wet sperm right through the center of his dick and making the tip of the condom balloon out with its sudden load of fluid. Trent crushed his ass down against Zerk's body as though he was fiercely determined to keep that detonating cock lodged firmly all the way up his butt. His own ejaculation was set off by the anal eruption, and his cock jerked spasmodically within Zerk's fist. It shot a wad of jism with such force that the cum splattered onto the pillow beside Zerk's head.

The second blast hit Zerk square in the face, and the third and fourth smacked wetly onto his throat and chest. More cum followed, leaving a sticky trail of white scum all over Zerk's chest and belly. Still shuddering his way through his own ejaculation, he worked his fists to pump Trent's prick dry.

Every spurt from the blond's dick was echoed by a fierce flexing of his anal muscles that bit into the flesh of Zerk's embedded cock and made him shoot again and again. Zerk kept jerking Trent off until the blond's huge cock poured the last of its fluid over his knuckles. Then, just to remind Trent who was in charge, at least this time around, Zerk suddenly released Trent's cock—and attacked his tits again. Trent's nipples were already bruised and sore from the pressure of his partner's pinches. The sudden, unexpected new pressure on them made Trent gasp and sent a final dribble of semen oozing from the tip of his sagging prick.

The two cops let go of each other, and Trent slumped down on Zerk's hips. He kept working his ass to feel Zerk's cock in it, but the other stud was already going soft inside him. With a sigh, Trent reluctantly lifted his butt and allowed Zerk's limp meat to slip out of his anus.

"Fucking whore," Zerk gasped.

"Don't knock it, partner. After all, I'm *your* fucking whore. And you're mine. We could both do a lot worse."

"Speaking of doing other guys—and speaking of whores—we really ought to call our buddy Brandon and find out when he can join us for another threeway session. Provided, of course, he can work us into his busy schedule."

"Don't be such a bitch, Zerk. It doesn't go well with the ballsytop-man image. Neither you nor I is in any position to throw stones at Brandon. We're no better or worse than he is. Maybe that's why the three of us seem to get along so much better, now that you and he have had a chance to get to know each other a little better."

"I remember getting to know him a *lot* better the last time he invited us over to his place," Zerk said, with a smirk. "Man, that was one hot session! I wouldn't mind a repeat of some of that action."

"You try to be a good boy and behave, and maybe I'll arrange for you to get some more of it," Trent teased his partner.

"*You* make *me* behave. That's a laugh, coming from you."

"Um, let's not argue. Let's face it—you, me, and Brandon are three of a kind. Let's not fight it. Let's make love again."

"Your idea of lovemaking can be awfully rough at times, partner. Even downright painful."

"Now listen to who's talking. I don't recall hearing any complaints from you."

"Oh, no complaints," Zerk said airily. "Just a request, maybe."

"And that is—?"

"I want to be the bottom, this time. Put the handcuffs on me, officer—and then read me my rights."

Trent twisted around, so that Zerk could reach for the handcuffs and unlock them. "Okay. But remember—you *have* no rights, when I'm on top!"

"*Now* you're talking—sir."

THE END

ABOUT THE AUTHOR

Roland Graeme is one of several pseudonyms used by a prolific writer of erotic fiction. Graeme, a descendant of Swiss immigrants and a native of Pennsylvania, resides in Buffalo, New York. He earned a Ph.D. in English by writing his doctoral dissertation on the novels of Sir Walter Scott ("Roland Graeme" is the protagonist of Scott's novel *The Abbott*). His interests, in addition to literature, include classical music (especially opera), history, and world religions, as well as, not surprisingly, human sexuality, in all its variety and richness.

Graeme has been, at one time or another, a teacher, a factory worker, a civil servant, and a music critic. The one common denominator throughout his career(s) has been his passion for freelance writing. He continues to hold down his current full-time "day job" while writing in his spare time.

Readers of *Good Cop, Bad Cop* will not be surprised to learn that Graeme has extensive first-hand knowledge of the BDSM scene. He also has a great admiration for men in uniform, especially police officers.

Roland Graeme can be reached at www.couesnon1@aol.com.

Also by Roland Graeme

Ménage and More ManLove: *Algerian Nights*

Available at
BOOKSTRAND.COM

Siren Publishing, Inc.
www.SirenPublishing.com

CPSIA information can be obtained at www.ICGtesting.com
Printed in the USA
LVOW100306190112

264565LV00006B/194/P